DISORDER

DISORDER

Part One

Martha Adele

To order additional copies of this book, contact:
Xlibris
1-888-795-4274
www.Xlibris.com
Orders@Xlibris.com
790354

CONTENTS

CHAPTER ONE

Sam

The forest floor streams through my fingers as I run my hands through the thick turf to find the ground. The pressure on my hip slowly becomes more obvious as my eyes flutter open and my surroundings come into focus. I find my face scrunching in response to the weeds around me tickling my nose and puffing out air to get the dirt and bugs away.

I push myself to a sitting position, and what feels like sandbags in the back of my skull pull me down. Forcing myself to sit up is more difficult than I have ever recalled it being before. The shade provided by the towering trees surrounding me makes the cool weather cooler, causing it to feel as if it were later in the autumn season than it actually is. The patches of light breaking through the canopy of leaves above me causes there to be rays of sunshine streaming through the forest, illuminating the floating pollen.

An odd tingling erupts in my feet as I rise from the ground. The feeling of hard marbles migrates from my toes up my body the longer I stand. When it reaches the back of my head, most everything gets knocked back to its normal sensation. What is left of the metaphorical sandbags slowly dissipates and trickles down my neck, rolls off my shoulders, and streams down my arms to my fingertips. I look down to my fingers and wiggle them around slowly, feeling the imaginary sand sift through my skin, and fall to the forest floor as the rest of my body slowly receives the message from my brain to start walking.

I look down to my foot as I take my first step. The ground's soft and spongy feel soothes my joints, all except one. The pain feels as if a knife is being slowly stuck into my hip and twisted the higher I lift my knee. With my groan being the only audible noise I can hear at the moment, I kick the palm-sized rock on the ground beside me as I realize that my hip was resting on it the whole time that I was unconscious.

The hip pain lessens the longer I stand and the more I try to walk. The golden rays of the sun and pollen that surround me remind me of the rays that would shine into my house through our cinder block–sized windows. Even though Mom would spend all her days under the blazing sun, she always managed to point out how lucky our family was to have windows and how beautiful the sun could be. Mom would use that opportunity to teach me a corny lesson and tell me that the "light shines even brighter when it is surrounded by darkness."

All I can think about as I walk around is the last time I saw her and how that was the last time I would ever see her. I had been preparing to fight for my country since I was born, so when the day came, I would be prepared for the draft.

On the ninth hour of the day that a citizen of Bestellen turns eighteen years of age, the pledge in question will be fully admitted into their selected career.

The only reason that it was going to be the last time I ever got to see my mom is because when you are assigned to the Stellen military, it means that the day you turn eighteen, you would be drafted. Those who are drafted remain in the military as long as they are physically capable to fight. After a certain number of years in the military, those who are unable to successfully fight due to age or physical damage are assigned to be an official, a teacher, a trainer, or part of the wall's security.

I had always figured that after all of those years of brutal fighting, I would want to be part of the wall's security. It seems like the easiest job. All they really do is walk the top of the large concrete wall that surrounds Bestellen and make sure no one is trying to get in. It seems easy because no one would ever try to get out of Bestellen. Why would anyone want to? We, as a country, are taken care of very well. And no one would try to get in because of how hard it would be. We have security guards, cameras, weapons, and so much more according to Chancellor Lance Meir II.

Meir is our current ruler and is probably the best ruler anyone could ever ask for. Under his reign, Stellens have free health care, an amazing bartering system between states, and the best education system anyone could ask for. When we are born, babies get all of their shots and medication, along with a full checkup, and are assigned a future career. When the kids are assigned careers, they are educated for that career and that career only, which saves both time and resources.

With Mom's assigned career as a farmer, she got to stay in her home state, *our* home state. Though every state can have different careers for their citizens, Bouw is mainly an agricultural region. Its citizens are laughed at and called Koes, which translates to "cow." Even though we are responsible for most of Bestellen's wind power, our contribution to Stellen society is often overlooked due to the assumption that all we do is farm.

The state of Verwend is mainly associated with weapons and the Stellen military. We call its citizens a Vend. Metropolis, Bestellen's capital, lies inside of Verwend but is toward the outskirts of the province. Other than that, I still don't understand why Verwend is Metropolis's favorite state. There are rumors in Bouw that people in Verwend are spoiled by Metropolis. I have heard that every household has a show box and an air system that controls the temperature of their home. In Bouw, only the officials' quarters have air systems, and we have one show box per precinct. In Rose, my precinct, we only ever use the boxes for news purposes. When those boxes came on and the officials gathered us in the squares, we knew something was wrong.

Metropolis is where Meir and all of his government officials stay. They make all of the economic choices, all of the defense choices, and all of the laws for Bestellen. They also handle all of the scientific research for the medicines they provide in our health-care system and all of the future developments to come.

The state of Hout is directly above Bouw and beside Meer on a map. Hout is mainly a large forest filled with a bunch of lumber mills, lumberjacks, and hunters. We call its citizens a Timmy. Metropolis favors them no more and no less than Bouw, I would say. I never hear anything interesting about them, so I would guess that they are like us, people who just do their jobs.

The third-most-favored state of Bestellen is probably Meer. It is filled with a few large lakes that take up most of the area of the region, and its main career set and contribution to Bestellen is aquaculture and waterpower. Its citizens are nicknamed the Vis.

Bloot is less than one-third the size of Meer and is mainly a textile district. From what I have heard, Bloot gets most of their resources from my state, and they have to work with that. We call Bloot citizens a Bloot. These guys are definitely the least favorite. Why else would they be so small?

Minje is probably the second favorite. Though they have quite a few power plants to go along with their many wind fields, they are still associated with the mines over anything else. Minje citizens are called Merkers.

Bouw has shops and some power plants, but most of our citizens end up working on the farms, which earns us our name. My dad was in the small percentage of people that weren't chosen to work on a farm. He was a salesman in one of Bouw's marketplaces for clothes, yarn, and other things he made from the sheep's wool from one of the farms near our house. When Dad was a baby and the Raad (the counselor who assigns careers) told his parents he would be a spinner, they were happy he would get to live a new, different, and exciting life rather than the life of livestock and crops his family had become so well acquainted with.

My mother told me she felt the same way about me being chosen to serve the nation. So when the Stellen officials came to pick me up, I figured that they would be taking me to my post or to a training center for further evaluation. As they knocked on my front door today, Mom and I were in midhug. We both knew that this moment was the last time that we would ever get to see each other. Mom pulled back from our hug with tears streaming down from her face, causing her crystal blue eyes to be even brighter than usual. Our eyes locked for a moment as three sharp knocks against our door pierced our ears.

Mom wiped away her tears and smiled at me. "Ready, Samuel?" The whites of her eyes had settled into a light pink shade, which I rarely ever saw with her.

I nodded to Mom and marched over to the front door. As my fingers met the door handle, the officials pounded on the outside of the door and shouted in a deep and authoritative voice that obviously scared Mom. "Open up!"

Her shoulders jumped, and she put her hand over her chest as the man's voice boomed through the house. I scurried over and opened the door before they had the chance to shout again. My eyes met their dark and reflective masks. My reflection bounced back to where I was staring at a slightly distorted version of myself. My dark and flat hair seemed longer than it normally was, and my nose seemed more birdlike than usual. Even though I was distracted by my obviously contorted features, I noticed two sets of bright blue eyes in the mask—one being mine and the other belonging to my mother in the background. The officials both parted and made a pathway for me out of the doorway. I turned back to Mom, who was holding her chest and smiling as she sniffled back tears.

That moment was the second time I had ever seen her cry. The first had happened a few weeks before when the accident at the marketplace happened. Due to some sort of mistake made by one of the workers in the marketplace, there was an explosion at one of the stands, causing a domino effect and more explosions throughout the building. Some people made it out alive, but everyone near the first explosion was found dead on arrival, including my dad.

Mom's sad expression when the officials came to pick me up was not the same expression that she had when Dad died. This one was more of pride mixed with sorrow. The other tears were obviously of anger, sadness, and fear. All I wanted to do in both moments was run over to her and give her a hug.

But the officials waiting by the door wouldn't let me this time. One of their stern voices blurted out the command "Now" as the other grabbed my arm and started pulling. I didn't know what to do, and I didn't feel as if I could control my actions in that moment. It was like my brain stood still as my body shoved the officials off me, and I lunged for Mom. She backed away from my hug just as the men grabbed my arms and dragged my kicking and flailing body out of the house. The last look that my mother ever got to give me was one of pure horror, and I will never be able to change that.

I remember watching my house become smaller the farther the officials pulled me away and seeing the deep shadow that was cast over everything when they threw me into their carrier van. I remember nothing else before I woke up on the ground in the jungle.

As I slowly regain my sense of hearing, the sounds of what I can only assume are birds come into focus. Their light chirping noises bounce off the trees and meet my ears with their sweet song. I have never heard such chirping before, which leads to my first real question.

Where am I?

The cool breeze that is blowing through the hundreds of trees meets my face and chest as I walk through the woods, searching for answers. I notice as the breeze blows through my thin shirt that I am wearing the same clothes I was when I left with the officials.

I weave through the trees, and my hand slides onto the bark. I realize that I have never before felt any tree or plant quite like it, nor have I ever heard of bark feeling choppy and jagged. All of the trees inside of the Bouw were smooth fruit-producing trees, none of which was rough to the touch.

My heart, along with the rest of my body, jumps as a scream echoes through the woods. Without effort, my feet shoot off from their resting place and push me as far away from the screaming as I can go. The horrid and high-pitched sound is coming from what sounds like a mile away, but I don't care.

The longer I run, the thicker the foliage around me is getting. The leaves and branches slap me all over as I push through them.

Thicker, thicker, thicker. Stop.

The large and concrete barrier in front of me prevents me from going any farther.

My thoughts sort through themselves and shout to me, *The wall!*

My hands meet the vines and bushes that are growing up the wall as I raise my eyes upward to look for an official. The moment I look up, I realize that I am on the outside of Bestellen. The top of the wall is rounded outward toward my direction to prevent anyone from being able to see up at the security. The inside of the Stellen wall had always been perfectly vertical until the top section, which holds the security guards. Once their top strip, where the guards work, is reached, the wall bows outward, away from Bestellen.

I shout to my full capacity toward the top of the wall, "Hey!" hoping for the Stellen Wall Security to hear me. "Hey! I'm down here!"

No answer.

A low growling from behind me causes my whole body to jolt and spin around. I shoot my eyes back to the woods to look for the source but see nothing except for the very plants that I had to push through to get to this point.

"Hey!" I continue to scream. "I'm outside of the wall . . . Hey!"

But there is no answer.

My back is pressed against the concrete as the growling grows louder. I can feel whatever is about to end my life coming closer. Too many thoughts to count are running through my head. Too many to sort through. Too many to think. Only one thought shouts out above all the others as the growling beast approaches: *I am not going down without a fight.*

I launch myself off the wall and through the woods, trying to avoid the beast. The low-hanging branches coupled with the thickets and thorns are not my allies. I duck, weave, and climb over and through the obstacles until I am caught on a set of incredibly thick briars. They cling to my left arm as I turn back to the woods and look for the source of the growl.

My eyes scan my surroundings and find a pair of lopsided yellow eyes looking in two different directions as the animal slowly comes into one of the golden rays of light. First, its head with black, orange, and white stripes and its teeth the size of my hand come into sight, followed by its matching large and catlike body with no tail. The beast creeps toward me as the reality begins to set in. The briars are to be my downfall.

The beast inches its way toward me, growling its low growl as I notice the oddities of the catlike features. The animal's ears look a lot like the ears of my neighbor's cat, but it looks as if there was an extra small set attached to the top of the ear flaps. The odd-shaped ears lead me to notice how off the eyes of the animal were. One eye is focused on me while the other is a little farther down the animal's face and is looking to my left. The teeth of the beast are much larger in proportion than those of my neighbor's cat. They are about as long as the length from my shoulder to my elbow.

All I can think about as the huge animal approaches me is *What is wrong with this cat?*

I figure this thought will be my last, but no. The cat's posture straightens up as its eyes jerk up and back to where the wall is. Bullets ring through the air, causing it to rain leaves as the cat runs back through the forest. I take off running in the opposite direction, ignoring the fact that I was trapped by briars, which tear half of my arm's flesh to shreds. As I run, I look down to see the large cuts and gashes all over my arm, but I don't care. The pain only motivates me to run faster.

I listen to the bullets raining on the path behind me as I push through the woods. Every time I look back, I see the dirt behind me bouncing up, flying high, and raining around me, just like the bullets.

Who is shooting at me? Why are they shooting at me?

My flustered thoughts are interrupted as my foot gets caught on an aboveground tree root. My whole body is flung forward as I throw my arms out to catch myself, only the ground isn't there.

My plummeting body crashes against the grassy bowl of the large sinkhole, causing the pain in my arm to radiate to the rest of my body as I tumble. I lie for less than a moment on the soft basin before I hop up and continue to run. The adrenaline pumping through my body allows me to overlook the pain as I flee from the open fire. I run for at least a full ten minutes away from the wall before I realize the gunshots have stopped.

As my pace slows, I look back at my arm to find that its gashes have begun to scab over. My arm is cloaked in so much dried blood that it looks like I had someone cover my arm in maroon paint. I slide my right hand over to meet the torn skin, feeling as if the wounds are being retorn in the spot where my fingers make contact. I jerk my hand back and glance around the woods to find that I still have no idea where I am.

The towering trees look like the ones that surrounded me when I first awoke. The trees surrounding me now have thickets engulfing their bases. I know that I am not back where I started physically, but mentally, I am.

I am back to wondering where I am and what is going on.

I continue wandering around hopelessly in the woods for what feels like hours when I am interrupted by another menacing growl. The growl of hunger.

My first thought is *Food. I need food.*

My second thought is *Am I going to starve?*

All I can think about from this point on is food. I wander around, looking for berries or a squirrel or something that is familiar for me to eat. I am absolutely not going to eat something that I am not 100 percent familiar with. Dad used to always warn me about eating unknown foods. He forced the idea that "there is a good chance that it could be dangerous" in a way that I can't help but abide by it. He was very serious about following this rule because his baby brother died at a young age due to the natural curiosity of what birch berries taste like.

Birch berries are small poisonous bright-green berries that grow in bunches on vines. We often planted them in hanging planters and hung them up around gardens or places where we didn't want birds. Due to their poisonous nature, birch berries are a natural bird repellent. I guess when the birds realized that the berries were poisonous, they decided that it was best to stay away from them altogether, which can help those who know how to use them.

The whole time that I wander around the woods, I never once see any sign of game or fruit, which puts a damper on my hunter-gatherer spirit. As the sun begins to set, the temperature begins to fall, and any hope I have left begins to flee. I can't imagine how I am to survive the night without any food, water, fire, or shelter.

But I push myself to keep walking.

After hours of running and roaming, a glimmer of light catches my eye through the bunches of trees. For a moment, I feel another hint of fear, not knowing what the light is coming from. Could it be another animal? Another weapon?

The thoughts fly through my mind as I quickly duck behind a tree. The longer I listen, the more I hear the soft and smooth crackling noise that belongs to one of man's greatest utilized tools. The fear that originally strikes me when I see the fire quickly flees and is replaced by relief.

I connect the dots and speed off toward the light. I see, through the trees and bushes, a boy sitting on the ground with his legs crossed as he uses a stick to stoke the fire in front of him.

CHAPTER TWO

Sam

The leaves around me crunch as I spread the bushes apart. The dark-skinned boy quickly turns his head in my direction. He hops up from his grassy seat and aims a staff-like stick that he had been poking the fire with at me. His eyes narrow at me as the smoke rises from the orange-glowing tip of his staff.

His deep voice booms through the air, straight into my ears. "Who's there?"

With my hands raised in surrender, I emerge from my hiding place behind the bushes to what seems like the only open area in the whole forest. "Sam. My name's Sam." His defensive stance lessens none, and his staff remains pointed at me. I continue, "Samuel Beckman."

The boy continues to hold his weapon toward me. Our eyes meet as the fire beside him flickers light on and off his face. His eyes scan me up and down as he inches toward me. "What are you doing here?" Before I have the chance to respond, he shakes his weapon at me and screams, "Answer me!"

I flinch, but my hands stay in the air as I answer, "I . . . I don't know!" The boy cocks his head as if he is confused. He loosens and readjusts his grip on his weapon as I repeat, "I don't know."

The boy lowers the stick as he straightens his posture. He closes his eyes and twitches his head and neck as if he is fighting back an urge.

I stay in this one position and continue, "I was hoping you would know."

He squints at me. The silence between us seems to make the crackling of the fire grow louder. The tension slowly eases, and I lower my arms. He stares at me for a moment as we listen to the wood shift in the fire.

Feeling safer than I did just moments ago, I ask him, "What about you?"

He takes a deep breath and continues looking at me.

I step forward. "What are you doing out here?"

His grip on the stick tightens as I move closer, so I stop. Still holding my gaze, he sighs. "I don't know either." He slowly backs up to the fire, keeping his tight grip on the stick. I follow him to the fire as neither of us let up on our slightly standoffish position. He motions with the stick to my blood-covered arm. "What happened?"

I glance down to my wounds and then back at him.

"Briars," I answer.

He stays silent and raises one eyebrow to me.

I continue, "I was running from a . . . a thing. It was like a big cat . . ." I look around to see if I can find the wall, but the plants surrounding us cover it all. "And bullets." I pause and think back to the hailstorm of bullets. "I was running from bullets, hundreds of them. I just kept running until the firing stopped."

The boy's large and fit body seems even more muscular the closer he gets to the fire. He turns away from me and sits back in front of the flames, continuing to poke the fire with the stick. He squeezes his eyes closed and tilts his head, seemingly freezing in a state of pure will as he tries to speak. "Bullets and a cat, huh?" The boy chuckles as he pats the ground beside him. He continues, staring straight into the fire, "I guess I have been lucky enough to not have been spotted yet."

"What do you mean?"

"There was a boy here before me." He sniffles and wipes his nose with his knuckles. "His name was Carl. Carl Montey. He died two days ago after a bear-looking animal invaded his berry spot."

I raise one eyebrow to him, though he still doesn't look back at me. His eyes twitch as he twists the stick in the fire. I have so many questions I want to ask, but I have no idea where to start.

The boy blankly stares into the fire, forcing out the words, "Carl showed up here the same way I did." He pauses and looks at me as if I am supposed to understand what he means.

The first question that came to my mind pops out of my mouth. "How?"

"Draft day came. He told his family goodbye, got in the officials' car, and woke up in the woods."

I break a twig that had been lying beside me, and the boy flinches. After a few more moments of silence, I throw it into the fire and ask him, "What state are you from?"

My feet twitch. I look down to them as if they somehow decided to do that on their own. I tighten my legs and make sure my feet are still as the boy answers, "Bloot. Carl was from Hout."

I nod. "I'm from Bouw."

"Ah," he chuckles, "so you're a Koe."

I turn back to him and smirk. "Yeah. And you're a Bloot."

"Sure." He sighs. "But you can call me Charlie." He extends his hand to me, and I return the gesture. Our hands shake for a split moment before we break apart and continue to stare into the fire.

Bloot is the smallest state in Bestellen, but it happens to be next to my state. I had been to only one of Bouw's borders, and it is the one that separates us from Meer. The border wall is a thirty-foot electrified barbwire fence. It runs from as far as you can see from one side to the other. The fences are always on the very ends of the states. The buildings and houses, along with any other things that our citizens would need to go to or use, always lie at least a mile inland from the fence; so when you are standing by it, you cannot see anything from either state because of all of the hills around. I guess that the people who helped build Bestellen designed the floor plan for the states for security purposes.

I have always wanted to know more about the other states, but I figure that it is not the right time to ask. I continue snapping twigs from around me. "What do you think happened?" I throw one half of the stick into the fire and begin peeling the other. "Do you think this is a test? To, you know, train us for the military?"

Charlie leans back and puts all of his weight on his arms, finally releasing his grip on the staff. "I had this same conversation with Carl. He thinks that this is some sort of sick training regime."

I stop peeling the stick and toss what's left into the fire. "Well, what do you think?"

He sighs. "I don't know what I think. It could be training. It could be a way to reduce our population."

"Reduce..." I pause, allowing his guess to sink in. "The population? As in just throwing us away?"

Charlie nods his head and squeezes his eyes closed. "Yes. There were rumors in Bloot." He continues bobbing his head up and down. "There were a lot of rumors in Bloot. This population one was a far shot, but apparently, it could be true." Charlie turns to me and stares for a moment. He turns back to the fire and squeezes his eyes closed again. "They say that in order to keep Bestellen in a state of 'prosperity,' they get rid of extra people in order to have more to give to the rich."

I have never bought into any of the conspiracy theories about Meir, and I am not about to start now.

The only theories I ever indulged in were stories that my grandfather used to tell me. He used to speak of a people that called themselves the Diligent. Like Meir, they believed in low spending and that everyone is equal. The only real difference I could ever tell between Meir's reign and the Diligent's ideals was the Diligent believed in something called "druppelen."

Apparently, druppelen is the idea where if you work, you reap the benefits of that work without sharing with anyone else. Some people become rich, while other people become poor. Our teachers in school always taught us that if everybody works hard, then everybody will get paid equally so that nobody falls behind. That way, everybody is equally rich.

Grandpa used to have a small tattoo on his back of two hammers crossed over each other inside of a circle, which was the Diligent's seal. He was a huge sympathizer. For some reason, he always told me not to ever mention his beliefs to anyone. Grandma and Mom always backed him up in that command. Mom always told me that "tattlers have never prospered, and they never will, so mind your own." Meanwhile, Grandma would stick to the cliché "snitches get stitches."

I still don't know why Grandpa was so ashamed of his beliefs, but I always respected his request to not tell anyone about his fairy tales. I did ask my teacher about druppelen once, but she just pushed it off and told the class that it wasn't a real thing. That was one of the very few moments I had ever really questioned my teacher, but my curiosity didn't last. I couldn't ask her about it because I was afraid that she'd ask me where I got such ideas.

The last day that I saw Grandma and Grandpa was the day that some Stellen officials came by to take them to pensioen. Pensioen is the dream retirement plan that most people only hear rumors about, much less get taken to. Grandpa was the winner of the randomly chosen early retirement reward for Bouw, and Grandma got to go with him. Until then, I had never met anyone who had ever won. They were taken to his reward the same way those who are drafted are taken, by an official's van. The officials come to your house, give you a ride to your next location, and there you begin the rest of your life.

Or at least that is what I hope is happening. I hope that I am sitting by a fire in the middle of the woods with a Bloot named Charlie because this is all part of me serving my country, part of my training.

That is all I can hope for.

Charlie and I sit in front of the fire. After a few moments of silence, I ask him about his home. I ask him if his family worked in the textile mills and how life was in Bloot. Charlie continues to stare into the fire. I consider mentioning all of the rumors that I had heard about Bloot, about them being poor and neglected by Bestellen.

Instead, I stay quiet and wait for him to answer.

His grip tightens on the stick that he was threatening me with earlier. I can feel the tension between us thickening the longer the silence floats between us. Staring at the side of his face as the light of the fire flickers off it, I notice that his grip on the staff tightens. Very calmly and quietly, he asks me, never taking his eyes off the fire in front of him, "Why do you care?"

"Well, um . . . I was just curious. I figure that if we are going to be together through this training thing, we should know more than each other's names." I chuckle, trying to ease the tension.

It doesn't work.

Charlie twists the stick in the fire and shifts some of the embers. "Why would you need to know anything other than my name? I already told you where I am from."

The tension between us thickens even more, causing the air to feel more defensive than before. "I didn't mean to pry." The end of his stick breaks off into the fire and seems to make Charlie even more tense. I continue to try to ease our situation but stutter through the statement. "You don't have to answer anything if you don't want to. No worries."

Charlie stands, yanking out his staff from the fire. He swings it back at me, inches from hitting my face in the process. I feel the heat spread over my face as he holds his now-flaming weapon at me. I lean back and put all my weight on my hands as I sit at stickpoint, trying to distance myself from the flames.

His voice shakily makes its way to my ears as the brightly colored fire makes everything around me appear pitch-black. "Why, you were just trying to convince me . . ." Charlie shakes the stick in my face and starts scratching his head as he very obviously twitches. "You tried to convince me that this is *all* part of some Stellen training regimen!" He pulls back his stick and swings it around. "When obviously, it isn't! This . . . this is all some big way to . . . to control population!" He swings his stick back to me, burning the tip of my nose and causing me to scurry back to keep myself from getting seriously burned.

"Charlie." I put one of my hands up to try to show him that he has no reason to hurt me and that I won't hurt him. "I don't know what you are talking about!"

"Oh yeah? Of course!" Charlie raises his voice, producing a great echo through the woods. "The boy from Bouw doesn't know what I am talking about!" He turns around and screams to the trees like they are listening to him. "This rich boy from Bouw doesn't believe that his precious Bestellen would do such a thing!"

"Charlie, I—"

"Well, guess what, you privileged prick! Bestellen isn't the best place in the world. There are killings every day in Bloot. Officials would break into any house they deemed 'unfaithful' and kill anyone they believed was a threat to their delicate little society! I guess you never had that issue in *your* state."

I stand, avoiding his flaming weapon, and begin screaming back, "*My* state? Rich kid? I don't think so! We are the scrappy little farmers. I am sorry if you feel like you had such a bad life in Bloot, but look around. Where has whining gotten you? Here, abandoned in the woods. Left to—"

"Ah!" Charlie swings his stick back to me and points it back at my face. I take a step back and brace for a fight. "So you admit it! We are abandoned!" Charlie's eye twitches, along with his neck and head. "You! You are with them!"

"What? What are you talking about?"

"You! You are all part of their plan! You are helping the officials! You are helping them kill me! And Carl! You probably killed Carl too!"

"Carl? Charlie! I don't know what you are talking about!"

Our screams overlap each other as he accuses me of being the person who put him out here to die. I deny his accusations, causing him to only grow more infuriated. We stand by the fire yelling at each other for a good minute before I pull out a thick, long stick from the fire to defend myself. We both hold out our sticks and have them pointed at each other as our screams echo through the trees.

The darkness around us becomes more and more apparent to me as the creaking noises and the footsteps in the woods grow louder. Charlie takes notice just as I do. I shake my head, just as he does, and get back into my normal and rational state of mind. No more unnecessary screaming, but necessary preparation for the worst. The thudding footsteps of something smaller than the beast that chased me earlier in the day is growing louder, meaning the new animal is getting closer.

Charlie and I get back–to-back and aim our small and flaming sticks out to the woods surrounding us, only to be startled by a boy holding a stick just like ours, without the fire, running toward us while screaming what seemed to be a battle cry.

The new kid runs out of the group of trees from my right and swings his long stick around our open and treeless space. He grunts with every swing as he runs up to us. Charlie and I both point our sticks toward him and start screaming back. We both lunge forward and start going after the new boy but are interrupted when the kid starts shuffling backward and whining, "Hey! Hey! What are you doing?"

Confused by the boy's defensive response, both Charlie and I let up on our duel attack. The boy stops running and turns back to us. Charlie, still holding up his stick, shouts at him, "What are you doing?"

"What am *I* doing? What are *you* doing?" The boy pats off the ashy residue we left on his shirt and looks to Charlie and whispers, "I came here because you guys were screaming! I thought you were being attacked! I was just trying to help!"

"What do you mean?" I scoff in a quiet tone. "Did you not see that there were no animals around when you came running out of the woods?"

The kid drops his stick, still whispering, "Yeah, I did! But I had too much momentum to stop immediately, and the moment I started to stop, you both attacked me with your flaming weapons!"

I nod to him as he adjusts his shirt. There is a long pause between the three of us as we wait for Charlie to lower his weapon. I nod and ask the new boy, "What's your name?"

He breaks his gaze from Charlie and looks over to me, still breathing heavily. "Logan. Logan Forge." His breathing seems to have a slightly rhythmic state. It is almost as if he breathes in three times and then out three times.

Ignoring his breathing patterns, I plainly respond, "Sam Beckman." Logan and I fix our eyes on Charlie, who refuses to lower his weapon. "And this is Charlie," I interject.

Logan nods at me and then to Charlie. "Hey."

Charlie slowly lowers his flaming staff. "Hey." His head jerks into a tilted position. His eyes squeeze closed once again as he struggles to regain normalcy.

We have a short and small standoff to see who will move first.

I decide to make the first move and head over to the fire. Logan follows without breaking eye contact with Charlie until Logan takes a seat beside me, and Charlie takes one across from us. I break the silence by asking the question that I know two out of three of us had to be wondering. "Logan, how long have you been out here?"

Charlie shifts his gaze back to the fire in front of him and waits for the answer. Logan and I first watch Charlie to see if he is going to do anything, but we look back at each other after a moment. Logan answers, "Two days. I showed up yesterday afternoon and slept in a tree last night."

The crackling of the fire seems to be soothing Charlie, but not enough to keep his breathing steady. His nostrils flare the longer he listens to us talk, but I don't care. "Was it the draft?" I ask Logan.

He nods to me.

I continue, "Same with Charlie and I. What state are you from?"

Logan sighs. "Minje." The smooth crackling of the fire seems to grow louder in the quiet of the night with only the rustling of the leaves to keep it company. "What about you?"

"Bouw." We both look to Charlie, who seems to be scowling at the fire. "Charlie is from Bloot."

Logan smiles. "Ah, a Koe and a Bloot, huh?"

I smile back, but only for a moment. Logan's comment seems to have set Charlie off.

Charlie slowly stands up and pulls his stick back out of the fire. "A Bloot, huh?"

Logan and I glance at each other as we stand to even the playing field.

Logan holds his hands up and out in a similar way to Charlie that I did when I first met him. "Hey, you might want to lower your voice."

"Oh yeah?" Charlie shouts. "You want me to lower my voice? Am I embarrassing you?" He swings the stick around like he did earlier and is once again drawing in the air with the tip of the glowing stick. "Am I embarrassing you in front of your new friend, Sammy Boy? Or should I say, your *coworker*?"

Logan glances over to me, looking for an answer. I clench my fists and buck up to Charlie. "Man, I told you, we are in the exact same situation you are in. We didn't put you here!"

"Shh, guys!" Logan loudly whispers. His head jerks around sporadically as he checks the woods. "Last time I got really loud, a pack of small rat-looking things came out of the woods and chased me up a tree." Logan picks his staff up off the ground and continues looking around.

"You, you . . ." Charlie continues to shake the stick at us both. "You both are working with the officials." He backs away with his flaming weapon. "You are ganging up on me!" Charlie's voice echoes through the trees in what sounds like a giant ring. It starts on my right and flies around me to my left and back to Charlie. He swings his head around and starts twitching his head and neck as his eyes flick in every direction possible. "There are more! There are more of you!"

Logan steps forward with his hands still held up. "Shh! Charlie! Come on, man!"

"No! Get away!" Charlie launches his staff at us, almost hitting me in the process. Before either Logan or I can do or say anything, Charlie takes off running in the opposite direction of us. It doesn't take long for his dark-colored body, mixed with his brown scrubs, to get lost in the dark woods surrounding us.

"What was that?" Logan whispers to me, now squeezing his eyes shut with every blink.

I shake my head and look from him back to the direction that Charlie ran off in. "I don't know. I wish I could tell you."

Logan and I sit down by the fire. I ask him if he had eaten anything since he had been put out here and if he has ran into anybody or any animals other than the pack of rats he had just mentioned. Logan tells me that he found a few berries when he was walking earlier but didn't eat them because he didn't know if they were safe to eat or not. "They didn't look like birch berries, but I still didn't want to take a chance."

Logan goes on to explain that he found a water hole that someone had dug before him earlier that day and that he had drunk a few cups. He also says that he killed off one of the rats by accident when he kicked it, but he didn't eat it. Logan says that he "wasn't hungry enough to eat a rodent."

We chuckle at the thought of starving to death and make jokes about what we would eat if it came to that point.

"Rat kabobs, dirt stew, and so much more," Logan chuckles.

After discussing all of the wonderfully disgusting courses we could think of, I ask Logan what he thinks is happening. I explain that from the moment that I met Charlie, he seemed extremely paranoid and that he seemed to be dead set on believing that we were exiled because of "population control." I fill Logan in on everything that Charlie said about his theories and everything about Carl. I then ask Logan if he thinks that this is training or something else.

Logan shrugs. "I think that the whole 'population control' theory is plausible, but then again, so is the 'training' theory."

I scoff. "So in reality, you have nothing else to bring to the table."

He smirks. "Pretty much."

We sit by the fire and listen to the crackling for a while and think. I think about Mom. I think about Dad. I think about Grandpa, Meir, Charlie, Carl, and Logan. I glance over to him to see him lying back, propping his head up with his hands, and staring to the ceiling of leaves above us.

The fire makes his skin look reddish in tint and his hair even darker than the darkness around us. He has all the same major features that people would use to describe me. Dark hair, white skin, and tall body; and yet he doesn't seem as birdlike as I feel. His nose doesn't seem to protrude from his face like mine does, and his body looks a lot more fit than mine. I feel like I am with my twin, but one that stole all the nourishment in the womb and left the crappy parts for me.

My comparison between myself and Logan is interrupted by a shriek from far out into the woods that shakes me to my core.

I hop up and let out a whisper. "Charlie." It is undeniably his scream.

"They found him," Logan whispers. The shouting sounds like it is about half a mile away, which feeds both my flight response and Logan's. "Go!" Logan whispers as he picks up the staff Charlie had thrown at us.

Our feet launch us away from the fire and through the forest, in the opposite direction of the horrid sound of Charlie being torn apart by whatever beast found him.

CHAPTER THREE

Logan

The low-hanging branches are easy for me to duck under and dodge but seem to be a challenge for Sam. I can hear him grunting and stopping every time I pass another branch.

I slow down, only slightly, and turn to see him caught on a set of thorns.

Running back to free him of the branches, I shout a hushed "Come on!"

We pick up our pace, and I make sure to stay close to Sam to help him through the woods. The sound of Charlie's screams ceased minutes ago, and the screeching and bellowing of what sounds like animals fighting over his body lessen the farther away Sam and I get.

Other than the shrieks, the only sound I can hear is one I can feel in my head. My heavy heartbeat is quickening as it pounds in my ears and against the back of my head. The nearly blinding pain of the beat doesn't stop me. What does stop me is Sam.

He grunts behind me as he trips over an unearthed tree root and lands on his hands and knees.

The thudding sound of his impact to the ground is muffled by the spongy grass-covered floors of the woods. I shuffle back and extend my hand to help him up. "Are you okay?" I ask.

Remaining cautious, I continue to look around and make sure we are safe as he slowly rises to reveal dirt and grass on his pants. "Fine." He wipes off the debris from his hands onto his shirt while trying to catch his breath. "Do we have to keep running?" Sam squints and looks around as he brushes off his shirt and knees. "Can't we just hide?"

What he is saying makes sense. At this rate, we don't have very many calories to spare, but I still feel that waiting to be eaten by something bigger than us is not something that I want to do. I glance back to Sam, who is clearly in need of rest.

"How about the tree?" I ask. Sam follows my pointed gesture to the tall and large tree behind me with thick low-hanging branches that would be very easy to climb.

Sam finishes wiping the dirt off his hands and follows me over. "I guess so. As long as we can sit for a while."

Ducking under the leaves that are on the end of the branches, I make my way toward the trunk, which splits into two separate trunks at about ten feet up. The branches of this tree are arranged like some of the trees back in Minje, my state.

Minje is mainly a mining and power province and has very few forests. Most of them were cut down for resources and replaced with power plants and wind turbines. The few forests and trees we do have are very small and are mainly by the wall. A few of my friends and I would sneak off whenever we could and go racing through the trees. The fact that it was considered illegal by certain officials made the task all the more fun. I guess all that "training" came in handy.

I make it to the top of the tree in less than twenty seconds, while Sam struggles to climb behind.

"Do you need help?" I whisper.

Sam pulls himself up onto a branch like he weighs three tons. "No," he moans back, "I got it." After about two minutes, he makes it up to where I am and sits on an adjacent branch, out of breath.

I sigh and lean back against one of the trunks of the tree. "How long do you think we will be out here?" Sam turns back to me and raises one eyebrow. I continue, "You know, if this is training."

The sounds of crickets' night songs grow as I wait for his answer. Sam turns back and looks out to the walls of leaves that surround us. "I don't know."

"Do you think this is training?"

He continues to stare outward without responding.

"I don't." I think back to the sounds of Charlie being devoured and attacked by the unknown beasts. "At least not anymore."

When I first woke in the woods, I had no idea what was going on. I rose from the ground, feeling dizzy, and looked around to see that I was surrounded by trees. For a moment, I thought that I was out in the woods a few miles away from my house. I figured that I had fallen out of a tree or something and hit my head, but I slowly came to realize that none of the trees surrounding me looked like any of the trees I had ever seen before. They appeared to be much larger, much thicker, and had bark much rougher than the trees back home.

A fuzzy feeling in the back of my skull became more apparent the longer I stood in that one spot. I started walking to see if the pain would go away, and the memories of what had happened came back to me in flashes—a flash of my grandpa waving goodbye to me, a flash of the inside of the Stellen officials' van, and a flash of the small syringe one of the officers stuck into my arm. The more I tried to remember what happened, the more my head hurt. I decided to try to walk it off, just like Dad would have told me to.

As I sit here in the tree, I listen to the surrounding sounds of nature and the soft snoring coming out of Sam next to me. I try to fall asleep but am stumped by constant scenes of my past flying through my brain. I think about Dad and how hard he tried to give me a good life. I think about how he tried to make up for the "lost love" ever since Mom died, and about two months ago, I lost him too.

There was an incident in the mine where he was working, an explosion. I can still remember the sound of the large boom in the distance. Everyone shuffled out of their houses, classrooms, workshops, and any other indoor place they were at to find a large sum of smoke floating over the mountains on the horizon. Later that day, Governor Rome, my precinct's leader and head of security, came onto the block's show box and explained that due to a lack of focus and an incompetent worker that would not be named, mine number 1-9-4 had an explosion and crumbled. I can still hear his voice telling me that "there are no survivors" from the explosion.

After Dad died, an official assigned me to live with Gramps, my dad's dad. To me, Gramps looks just like my dad, just older. The top half of his back is always hunched over, causing the once-six-foot-three-inch man to be about five foot ten inches. He has the same head as my dad—just tanner, wrinklier, and balder. Gramps has hair only on the sides of his head, but he is in a constant state of denial. Instead of shaving it all off, like I tell him, he tries to grow out the sides and force an extreme comb-over.

Bald or hairy, I love him. He took me in and stepped up when he was needed. He sacrificed being the happy-go-lucky grandparent who gets to spoil their grandkids to being a dad who has to discipline and teach his child. It definitely isn't an easy transition, especially if your kid is me—Chump, as Gramps always calls me. He has always thought that I am too soft just because I have always taken the words of my mother to heart.

One of the most memorable things my mother ever said to me was "Remember to debate, never argue—for arguing is you versus the other person, while debating is you and the other person versus the problem." She lived by this motto.

According to Dad, Mom was the nicest person you could have ever met. She always told me all about how beautiful the world could be if everyone accepted everyone else in spite of their flaws. She would go on and on about how wonderful it would be if instead of yelling at people when things weren't going your way, you would hug them and spread the love and joy that should be filling humanity.

Gramps, on the other hand, considers this compulsion a weakness. "The only people you should be hugging is your family . . . And only on special occasions!" He has always been a tough person who shows his love in different ways from others.

His voice echoes through my head as I sit on this branch, staring out to the wall of leaves surrounding us. Sam's breathing begins to annoy me as I take notice of the lack of pattern.

Breathe in, breathe out.

In. Out.

In . . . out.

In, out . . .

No pattern. No rhythm. Only pure madness. His foot twitches against his breathing patterns, causing my unrest to exacerbate even more. I have never been bothered by this type of thing before, but at this moment, this is all I can think about.

Not long after I try to shift my focus from Sam to the rustling of the leaves all around, I notice that my hands have found their way to each other and have begun to rub each one of my fingernails. From the top knuckle, running to the tip of my finger.

First, I use my right thumb and rub my left thumbnail. One time, two times, three times. Then my left thumb does my right thumbnail. One time, two times, three times. The rest of my fingers follow. I loudly breathe in and out to try to drown out the sound of Sam's nose whistle and establish some sort of peace.

After sleeping a total of maybe two hours in the last two days, I drift into a painfully light sleep that seems to make me more tired than I was before. I wake for what feels like every five minutes and glance around to make sure nothing has found us, then drift back into my uncomfortable slumber.

A bloodcurdling high-pitched scream pierces my ears and jolts me awake from my first stream of continuous sleep since my exile and almost knocks Sam off his branch. He gasps as he grasps the branches beside him for balance and turns to me to whisper, "What was that?"

By the time that he finishes his question, I am already three branches below him.

I have to go help whoever is being attacked.

"Logan!" Sam scream-whispers as he hobbles down the tree. "What are you doing?"

My feet meet the hard and mulch-like ground underneath the tree as I fix my grip on the staff I managed to keep with me throughout all of this. "We have to go help!" My feet launch me out from underneath the guard of the tree's natural barrier and forward through the maze of trees around me. I hear Sam's thudding footsteps behind me as he tries to catch up.

The screaming continues in waves. Each time seems louder than the last, which leads me to believe that I am getting closer. Closer. Closer.

Here.

Through the bushes, I see a flash of something light colored run from my right to left. Before I can comprehend what is going on, I hop out from behind the foliage and run after the large pack of rodents that look just like the pack that chased me when I first arrived.

I shout, hoping to help scare them away but end up earning all of their attention. The large cat-sized rats turn to me and begin scurrying my direction. I swing my staff back and forth violently at the animals, swatting them away as if I was batting at a ball. Their drool splatters with every hit, leading me to hope that it isn't toxic. Their dirty brown fur flies through the air, falling off each rodent as they soar.

A battle cry comes shrieking out of the trees from the same direction that I just came from, and a body emerges with an even longer, thicker stick that resembles a long log. Sam takes one large, hard swing, taking out three of the largest rats closest to him. We bat, swing, and kick what feels like over twenty of these animals before they flee to the surrounding foliage. We watch them scurry away when I hear clawing and growling in the distance.

"Come on," I whisper to Sam.

As I track the rest of the rodents, Sam ignores me and runs off, swinging his log at what I am guessing is another rodent his eyes fix on. His battle cries shoot through the air as he runs off in one direction, and I run off in the other.

I sprint to the person's aid, and the rats' low growling and crazed scratching grow louder. Louder. Louder.

Here.

A few other rodents are jumping and clawing the base of a tree about fifty meters away from our batting point. The person's body is clinging to the tree about five feet above the ground. I look around to see a few stumpy bits protruding on the large and thick tree trunk, which was most likely what made it possible for her to escape the rats.

I run over and use my full upper-body strength to take one final swing, knocking three rodents away and launching them off into the air. They squeal as they fly and let out a small squeak when they hit the ground. The three thud noises come one after another as they meet the ground. *Thud. Thud. Thud.*

The blonde hair is the first thing I notice. It hangs over her face and runs down her shoulders but stops at the bottom of her shoulder blades. I hear her loud wheezes and try to follow her attempts to speak but fail to understand what she is saying.

I hesitantly ask her, not knowing how she will react, "Hey, are you okay?"

Her head jerks over to me, causing most of her long and wavy hair to flip aside and leaves a few strands in her face. With eyes as wide as they can be, she stares at me, seemingly pleading. Pleading for what, though? Does she want me to go away? Does she want help down? Is she hurt? Is she scared? I'm scared too, but I haven't gone into complete panic mode. Her wheezing seems to get quieter, and her grip on the tree loosens the longer our eyes are locked.

I extend my hand upward to her and wait for her to take it. "It's okay. They're gone," I say in a calm voice, hoping to coerce her into coming down.

She takes a few deep breaths, and we stand there for a few moments, me holding out my hand and her holding the tree. After what felt like a minute, she slowly makes her way down without my help and meets my eyes again. She pushes some of the hair out of her face, revealing her bright green eyes that matched the color of the trees back home. The same color eyes that my mom had. The color my dad would describe as "golden hazel" and that Gramps would describe as green. Right below her left eye lies a scar, hopefully one she didn't get here. It looks as if she had been grazed by something sharp.

There are so many questions to ask, but the first one that comes out is "Are you okay?"

Her breath, still shaky, squeaks as she tries to answer but is interrupted by Sam's pounding footsteps running up to us, causing the girl to begin wheezing like she was when I first came to her.

Sam runs up to us both with the log in his hand and growls at me, "Logan, I got them," causing the girl to fall back and grab my shirt as she leans against my chest. Sam looks from me to her and twitches his head while trying to contain his scowl. Before I know what I am doing, my arms are wrapped around her, holding her close. Sam drops the log and puts his hand up in surrender, not really knowing what to do. I stare at him for a moment, then look down to find her hands covering her face as her breathing steadies.

We all stand there for minutes. I feel her breathing slow as I watch Sam's face unscrunch slowly. His twitching eases slowly over the course of our wait for the girl to calm down. I watch as his breathing pattern slows and feel as hers follows.

"I-I'm sorry." Her voice, muffled by her hands, surprises Sam and me. She pulls away slowly and wipes away any and every tear on her face. She sniffles, "I have never been that . . . I've never had that . . ." She looks from me to Sam. "Never."

"It's okay." I nod to her. "I doubt you have ever been attacked by a pack of rats before."

She gives me a weak smile.

I return the smile. "I'm Logan." I find myself squeezing my eyes into a blink three times.

Squeeze. Blink.

Squeeze. Blink.

Squeeeeeeze.

Blink.

Each blink is harder than the other and satisfies me less than the one preceding it.

She turns her head to look at Sam as he wipes his forehead.

"Sam." He lifts his hand and gives a quick wave.

Her eyes follow his dried-blood-covered arm as it falls back to his side. "Mavis." She gulps as she turns and glances at me and then back to Sam. "Thanks for helping me out."

Sam nods.

I nod back. "Come on," I whisper to them. "We need to go ahead and find somewhere to stay for the night." I bend down to pick up my staff and begin walking into the woods.

Confused, Mavis hesitantly follows. "Huh?"

"Those rats aren't the only things that can get you down here," Sam whispers.

I turn to Mavis, walking backward now, and point upward. "The trees are the safest place to be. So far, we haven't met any animal that can climb them."

Mavis nods to us and looks around. She scratches her arm as she follows.

"How long have you been out here?" I ask.

"Me?" Her scratching ceases for a moment as she processes. "Oh, um . . . today." She looks around, and the scratching picks back up. "Or maybe yesterday, depending on the time."

Sam's head jerks back to her. "Today?"

Mavis's scratching slows, but not to a complete stop. I continue to stealthily move forward and stumble upon another tree like the last one Sam and I rested in. I reach out for one of the large flat shiny leaves and slide my hand across it. "I think this'll work."

Mavis gives Sam a shy smile, ignoring what I just said. "Yes, today. What about y—"

Sam interrupts her, saying, "Is today your birthday?"

She tilts her head and raises an eyebrow to him as her scratching becomes slowly more violent. "Yes? Why?"

"It's mine too." He smiles back to her. "Happy birthday."

I wave them over to the tree, hoping that they will listen this time. "Come on. Let's talk up here."

Sam makes his way over to the trunk and puts his hand on one of the lowest-hanging branches. "Where are you from?" Before she can answer, Sam bombards her with questions and information. "Were you assigned to the military too? We were. I'm from Bouw. Logan's from Minje. We met so—"

"Sam!" I shout in a hushed tone. He looks back to me, confused. "One thing at a time," I chuckle.

He turns back to Mavis and shrugs. "Sorry."

She stops scratching long enough to grab on to a branch and pull herself up. She chuckles, "It's fine."

We all make our way up the tree and stop about thirty feet up. After everyone finds a branch to settle into, Mavis fills us in. She is from Bloot, just like Charlie was. She lived with a single parent, just like Sam and I did. And she was drafted, just like we all were. We talk a bit about ourselves before we start discussing the theories of why and how we ended up out here.

Sam holds up one of his pointer fingers to us and taps it with his other. "Option 1," Sam lists, "this is all part of some sort of training. Only the strong are allowed into the Stellen military." Sam leans back into the tree's trunk and stares somewhat angrily at his finger. One of his eyes begins to twitch slightly, but he squeezes his eyes closed to try to get it to stop.

"Option 2," I add, thinking back to all of the times I went against the officials' orders and played in the woods, "we are now old enough to face a punishment for any and all crimes we have committed." I turn to Mavis, who is counting off these options on her fingers as well but is staring blankly at them as opposed to Sam, who has his eyes squeezed tight as he counts. I continue, "Meaning we are criminals, and this is our punishment."

We all sit in silence and think these options over. The heavy sound of the cricket songs around us seems to make this punishment seem a lot more soothing than it actually is. The light breeze blowing through the air ruffles the leafy dome around us, sending me into a bliss that I hadn't felt since I woke up here.

"Option 3." Her voice surprises me with its serious nature. I have never heard such a mix of deadpan and realization before. Mavis looks up from her fingers, which are now holding the number 3, and straight into my eyes. Through her knowing smile, she chuckles out the third theory. "Bloot was right."

CHAPTER FOUR

Mavis

Logan cocks his head. "What do you mean?"

"I mean what I said. Bloot was . . . *is* right." The boys continue to look confused, so I try to elaborate the best I know how. "What do you know about Bloot?"

"They are small!" Sam blurts. "And poor."

Logan gives a quiet gasp as if he thinks I am offended. "Sam!"

"No, no! It's fine," I tell them. "Is that all you both know about us?"

Sam takes a moment and shifts his weight on the branch he is using as a seat. "Sort of. Am I right?"

I confirm by nodding.

Sam continues, "My grandpa had always wanted to move there for some reason, so I guess it was a pretty cool state either way."

My mouth finds its way into a smile, and I let out a slight chuckle. "Thanks. I know we are hardworking, but cool?" I shrug as the thought passes through my mind. "I don't know." I have never once thought of Bloot being a "cool" state. It is definitely not considered cool in Harbaugh, my precinct.

Sam shrugs. "Well, Grandpa was a bit of a loon anyways, so what do I know?"

I take a deep breath and look around us to find the dome of leaves shedding as it releases a few old leaves to fall like rain over us. One in particular floated down beside me and brushed my arm on its way to the ground.

I give my arm a quick scratch and catch a glimpse of the boys, who are obviously still confused. I sort through my many thoughts and begin, "Where should I start?"

I look back to Logan, whose eyes seem to be staring at my hand as it scratches my arm. Feeling self-conscious, I stop scratching and continue as his eyes meet mine, "Let's start with what I know . . ." I hold up one of my fingers as I begin to count off the things I need to cover. "One, Bloot is absolutely hated by the Stellen government." We are forced to be poor so that the government can supply luxuries to the other states. "Fact." I hold up my second finger. "Two, we are only educated for things that the Stellen government considers helpful. Fact."

Logan's eyes dart toward Sam as they share a quick moment of realization.

I continue, "Three, there are rumors throughout Bloot that people were being exiled for no apparent reason other than population control." I look back and forth to and from each of the boys. Logan's thumbs rub each of his fingers rapidly, and Sam's feet twitch out of rhythm. Another leaf falls, and we all watch it slowly float to the ground between us.

I take a deep breath to finish and am interrupted by Logan, who says, "Fact."

I shrug. "That's what it looks like."

We sit in silence, watching a leaf fall once every few minutes before Sam scoots back on his branch and leans against the trunk of the tree. "Well, enough revelations for now. I'm going to sleep."

Logan and I exchange one final look. "Good night," he says.

I smile and nod back to him as I climb up a few more branches. With the boys below me, I find myself sitting toward the top of the tree trunk, with a thick branch in between my legs to help keep me stable. I lean forward and rest my head on the trunk and try to get some sleep but fail. I notice that the bark covering these trees is much rougher than the trees back home. If I had tried to lay my head on one of those trees, their smooth surface would have comforted me, reminding me that I am safe. But the rough, bumpy, and protruding bark of this tree is cutting into my skin the longer I sit.

I pull my head back and observe the bark for the first time since my arrival. My hands run across the surface of it slowly as I feel the uneven texture. The higher up into the tree you climb, the thinner the branches, trunk, and dome of leaves become. I glance by the trunk in front of me and take notice through the leaves surrounding us that in front of me, a long ways away, is a mountain range.

The very top of the mountains is covered by what appears to be low-hanging clouds, while their bottom is hidden by the jungle of which we are in the center. I turn around and try to look through the leaves on the other side to see if I can find the wall anywhere but fail. The leaves are too thick on this side to see, so I shift back to my original resting position and try to sleep. I lay my head back against the tree and lean in. Before long, I fall asleep to the sounds of crickets chirping and a sort of bird's song that I have never heard before.

It is a restless night. The cool breeze sends shivers through my body every time the wind picks up. I admit, I most likely would be warmer if I moved down the tree a bit more, but I don't care. In and out of sleep I go, only to be woken by a ray of light peeking through one of the patches of missing leaves around me.

I squint and look around and see that the sun rose directly across the mountains, which helps me slightly figure out where we are.

My eyes slowly flutter open as I wake and take notice of Sam's heavy breathing. It is not exactly snoring, but it is loud enough that I can categorize it as such. I wipe my eyes and look down to see Logan with his eyes closed, still rubbing his fingernails, one by one, three times each. I find his rubbing routine soothing. Watching it is mesmerizing and somehow makes this whole situation seem less horrid than it really is. I am reminded of the horrors when Logan looks up at me and rubs his eyes open.

"Hey," he whispers.

I smile to him and look back at Sam, who is fast asleep. I crawl down the branches to sit closer to Logan. Trying not to wake Sam, who appears to be the only one of us who can get some sleep, I whisper back as quietly as I can, "How'd you sleep?"

Logan shrugs. "Not important. How about you?"

Not important? I tilt my head at him and wait for him to answer my question.

He sighs. "In and out. Mostly just uncomfortable, waiting for the sun to rise."

I scoot back and lean against the tree trunk. "Me too."

"Same here," Sam moans. He turns his head back to us and takes a deep breath, still not opening his eyes. "What time is it?"

"The sun just came up, so maybe six?" I guess.

Sam moans.

Logan smiles and turns to me. His eyes are pools of tawny and caramel that blend together in a way so that you can distinguish each strand of color from the other. Not so much that it looks like stripes, but enough that you can tell the different colors radiating from his pupil to the cinnamon barrier on the outskirts of his iris. "What's the plan for today?" He looks to Sam but is ignored due to the fact that Sam's eyes are closed. Logan glances back to me and continues, "We need to secure food and water. I know that much."

I nod in agreement.

Sam gives a light grunt of what seems like approval.

I lick my chapped lips in hopes of bringing back a little moisture. "I saw that there are some mountains west." I point in their direction. "Doesn't that mean there should be a freshwater stream?"

Logan smiles back. "Sounds about right to me. Back in Minje, we have a few mines in the mountains. All of the construction happened to be close to a few of the streams, making them dirty and undrinkable." His dimples become more obvious as the sun rises, along with the temperature. He sighs. "Hopefully, we will have better luck over there."

Sam sits up and wipes his eyes. "Wait, which way is the wall?"

I yawn. "I tried looking earlier, but I couldn't see it."

"As long as the mountains are far away from the wall, we should be good." Sam yawns back.

Before I can ask why, Logan joins in and yawns with us. We chuckle as we try to finish yawning but get stuck in a state of openmouthed laughing that we cannot control.

I wait a bit and catch my breath from our quiet laughter before asking, "Why do we need to stay away from the wall? Can't they help?"

Sam leans forward, finishes his yawn, and stretches. "You would think so, but apparently not."

Logan, just as confused as me, asks, "What do you mean?"

"Well, while I was being chased by that cat beast that I told you about, I found the wall."

"What?" I scoff. "Cat beast?"

"Oh, there was this big cat thing that was chasing me earlier. It was a lot taller than me and a lot longer too. Anyways"—Sam shakes his head and changes the topic back to the wall—"I shouted and screamed for help, but there was no answer. The beast had me trapped, and somehow I got away—only to be trapped again, that time by briars. That's what caused this." Sam holds up his torn-apart arm, the same arm with the wounds I noticed last night.

He continues, "Just when I thought I was a goner, bullets came hailing out of the sky, scaring the cat away and forcing me to flee, even if it meant having my arm torn to bits. I wasn't that far away from the wall when the bullets were shot, so I assume that the wall security were the people responsible for the firing."

Logan stares wide-eyed at the leaves surrounding us, seemingly putting the pieces together.

I don't know what to say other than "I'm not surprised," which somehow finds its way out of my mouth.

I don't know exactly what I meant. Bloot had always been hated by Bestellen. If any of our citizens were found near the open wall, they would be shot on sight. Lucky for us, most of Bloot is overgrown by jungle—trees, weed, vines, and a lot of wildlife. The deeper you went into the woods, the stranger things seemed to get. The animal prints would grow larger the farther you went in; and the trees and foliage became larger, tougher, and rougher. I guess that's why these trees outside the wall are so rough; it's because of their placement. The closer the plants are to Metropolis, the smoother they are.

Due to Metropolis's neglect of Bloot, there are not many officials in the unpopulated provinces of Bloot. All of the officials are sent to keep an eye on the sweatshops and neighborhoods, none to really cover the woods.

No one I have ever met has made it to see the wall through the woods. I assume it is covered by vines and hidden by trees and other foliage. I have only ever been about ten miles into the woods, and I usually only ever went with one person—Derek Page, my best friend. Other than my uncle Randy, my mother's brother, Derek is the only person I have ever trusted enough to talk to about . . . things. Whenever we needed to escape everyday life in Bloot, we would manage to get past the officials and make our way into the woods.

We had a shared favorite spot. It was a large tree, just like the one I clung to last night during the rats' attack. We would go there and hide in the branches, listen to the sounds of nature, and talk about anything and everything.

As peaceful as it sounds, we often spent our time together hunting for food. Neither of our families made a lot of money, so we were the main providers. Derek started providing for his family by hunting at the age of thirteen. He is twenty now and a transporter. He gets "the privilege to take supplies from one sweatshop to another," or at least that's how he describes it. His job doesn't pay but maybe ten credits a week. At the most, that could buy a sack of potatoes and a loaf of bread, which isn't a lot.

Derek took me in when he was fifteen after he caught me following him one day. We crept into the woods, and I watched him fix a few snares along the way. Snares that I wouldn't have noticed if I hadn't seen him playing with them.

I followed him, making sure never to step onto a twig or leaf or anything that would crunch under pressure. Snare by snare, we went farther into the woods. About twenty traps in, Derek finally found a snare that had caught his next meal. I watched from behind a tree as the scrawny red-haired boy lifted up a small brown rabbit about half the size of those rats from last night.

I leaned forward a bit to try to get a better look, but my hair had gotten caught on one of the small twigs protruding from the trunk of the tree, which caused a large snapping noise as my hair yanked it from its base. Derek jerked his head back and looked around as I hid behind the tree trunk.

"I saw you!" he called out to me. "I hope you know that!"

I sighed and pulled the twig out of my hair. Walking out from behind the tree, I broke the twig in two and hesitantly made my way to him. "You wouldn't have if it wasn't for this stupid stick."

Our eyes met for the first time. Slightly squinted, his eye color was one I had never seen before. His irises had navy barriers while his pupils had almost a boysenberry color radiating from them, changing into a sapphire blue as they migrated out. His bright-colored eyes caused his pale skin to be even paler, and his freckles and acne too seemed to be the same color as his hair. I broke our gaze and looked back down to the rabbit.

I didn't know exactly what to say, so I said the first thing that popped into my head. I pointed down at the rabbit he was holding and stated the obvious. "You caught one."

Derek's smile grew just as his dimples did. Both Derek's and Logan's dimples are the type that run up their face, not just resting in one spot. Derek's seem a little smaller than Logan's, though.

"Yeah," Derek laughed at my statement. "I did. I was beginning to think I wouldn't get one today."

I smiled back at him.

He took the rabbit out of the noose and fixed the snare. "So is this the first time you've followed me out here?"

I nodded.

"Hmm . . . Okay." He grabbed the hare by the ears and started walking farther into the woods. "Were you planning on coming back out here and stealing my game?"

I followed. "No." I had seen him go into the woods for that last year and never followed. That day, I really needed to get out of the house, so

I went and hung out in the outer rims of the woods. I watched Derek sneak into the woods and finally decided to see what he was doing.

"Then what was your plan?" he asked me.

I shrugged. Derek couldn't see me shrug because he was in front of me, so I answered, "I don't know. I guess the plan was to finally see where you sneak off to."

He stopped in his tracks in front of me and slowly turned around to reveal his squinty smile. "You've been watching me?"

I shrugged again; this time, he took notice. I could feel my face getting hotter as I realized how embarrassing that sounded. "Not in a creepy way!" I claimed.

Derek nodded at me and chuckled, "Yeah, okay, Mavis."

Before that day, we had never officially met; so when he said my name, my skin crawled. We got to talking as we walked through the woods resetting his snares and grabbing the few rabbits he caught. He introduced himself and told me that he knew me because his mom knew my mom and that his mom used to talk about how sad it was when my mom and brother died. Derek said that he kept meaning to come over and ask if he could help with anything but was always too scared of my dad, for which I don't blame him.

That day, Derek gave me one of his rabbits and told me to meet him out here after school the next day. I did. Ever since then, we have been best friends. He knew that I was assigned to the military, so I doubt he is worried about where I am. He probably just thinks that I am in training or already on assignment or something. I don't really know, but right now, talking to him is one of the main things I want to do.

Sam, Logan, and I climb down from the tree and start walking. Logan, still holding his staff, and Sam, still somewhat twitchy. We walk and walk for hours, trying to stay quiet. We creep around without many words said. Every now and then, we sit to take a break and talk about how thirsty and hungry we are.

I crawl up a tree and peek my head out of the leaves. We seem to be slightly closer to the mountains, but they still feel too far away to reach by tonight. I climb down to tell the boys that according to the position of the sun, it is about 6:00 p.m. and that we should probably search for food.

"Wait," Sam says loudly, earning a finger to the lips from both Logan and me. Sam's shoulders rise, and he puts his hands up, mouthing "Sorry." He looks around and walks over to us. "You mean neither of you have been looking for food? That's what I've been doing this whole time!"

Logan and I chuckle. I reassure Sam that we have been looking for food as we walked, but that wasn't our main goal. Water was. "How about this?" I suggest. "I will go and make a box trap, and you guys can look around a bit for some berries or something to bait the trap or for something we can eat."

Sam shrugs and scratches the back of his head. He twitches and nods back to me. "Yeah, yeah, that sounds . . . fine." He squeezes his eyes closed and takes a deep breath.

Logan and I glance at each other and back to Sam. Logan steps forward. "You okay, man?"

Sam squeezes his lips together and opens his eyes. "Yeah, yeah. I'm fine." He looks back to me. "I'm just going to go look for some berries or something."

He turns around and storms off. I have no idea what just happened, and by the looks of it, neither does Logan. We both stare at each other for a second, not knowing what to do.

I work up a smile. "I . . . um . . . guess I will go ahead and get started on that box trap."

Logan nods and smiles back. "I will keep looking. Meet back here?"

I nod, and we part ways and search for what we need. I go straight for a tall and skinny tree with some long and extremely thin branches. I break one of the branches off and begin peeling it to see if I can use it as cordage. I can't.

The next idea that comes in my head is a set of briars. After breaking off decent-sized branches and forcing them to a size that fits my needs, I find a large patch of briars blocking off what looks like a path made by an animal much larger than me.

Very carefully, I break off multiple sets of briars by pinching and bending them between the thorns, earning myself a few accidental pricks. When all is said and done, I have built a decent-sized box trap that could catch something a little smaller than those rats that tried to kill me last night. I set it up a good distance away from where Logan, Sam, and I separated because I assume that spot is where we are to meet up again. I look around for something that I can use to set the box trap and find a species of berries I am unfamiliar with, just like everything else in these woods.

I set the trap and head back to where we all split up. I bring a few berries back with me to see if either of the boys knows if they are safe. When I make it back, the sun is almost fully hidden by the mountains, and the trees' natural roof causes the darkness to consume my surroundings.

A slight stir of anxiety rises in my stomach and makes its way into my head. The berries I am holding in my hands are the only things seemingly keeping me from scratching. I have noticed that ever since I have been dropped off out here that any time I am uncomfortable, nervous, or scared, I feel the need to scratch something. My arm, my leg, my head, my neck—anything that I can.

I look around to find that neither of the boys have made it back to the tree and begin to worry even more. Should I call out for them? That would definitely attract attention of any surrounding animals, but wouldn't it help us stay together?

No. All it would do is cause trouble.

I move all of the berries into one hand and climb up the tree. Once I get as high as I can, I push leaves aside and peek out of the top. I am blinded by the sun, which is now at my eye level and barely peeking over the mountains. The orange glow of the sun causes the leaves and trees surrounding me to look like an ocean of reflective surfaces that magnify the beauty of the sunset. I raise my hand with the berries, dropping a few, and try to block out some of the light that's blinding me. I squint toward the mountains and see a picture-perfect view that looks like a million-dollar painting, just like the ones that Derek's mother would tell me about.

Derek's mom was one of the people who transferred things like crops from one state to another. During her travels, she would make sure to go and peek at the paintings that decorated the head offices she had to visit. Art appreciation is something she and my mother had in common.

The sky behind me is black, and the twinkling stars are splattered across the sky. As you turn from the darkness back to the mountains, the colors change from black to a deep purple to a rosy pink to a smooth and heavy sunset orange. The stars become less and less obvious the closer they are to the sun, causing me to be conflicted. Both views are absolutely beautiful. The skies on one side remind me of a night at home, while on the other is a view I have never seen before.

My ogling is interrupted by a twig breaking underneath me. My heart jumps, along with the rest of my body, and causes me to drop a few more berries. My eyes follow the berries as they make their way down the tree and rain on top of Sam.

His arms rise up, and he covers his head as he lets go of the branch he was about to use to pull himself up. "Hey!"

I whisper back, "Sorry!"

Sam bends down and picks up a berry off the ground. He holds it up in front of his face as if he is a buyer trying to decide if this is the real deal or not. He crawls up a few branches as I crawl down. We meet halfway, and Sam holds up the smooshed berry and gives it a surprised look. "Whoops." He drops what was left of it and wipes his hands back and forth to erase the residue. "Do you know what kind of berries those are?"

I open up my hand with all of the berries in it to find most of them squished. "No, I was hoping you or Logan would."

Sam sighs. "Well, I don't." He looks up and meets my eyes. "I guess we are waiting on Logan now."

Though our surroundings are almost pitch-black, I can still make out the color of his eyes. Their bright blue color is almost frightening in how pure it is in contrast with the darkness of his hair and the light color of his skin. They are not as complex as Derek's, but still extremely unique.

I smile to him. "Did you find anything?"

He shakes his head. "I looked and looked and looked but found nothing. I did come across a bird, though. It was walking around on the ground and pecking at something that I couldn't see. I am guessing bugs." Sam's eye twitches. He obviously takes notice of it because his whole body tenses, and his hand shoots up, and he begins rubbing his eye with his palm as he continues with the story. "I ran for it to see if I could grab it, and I got really close too!"

I chuckle.

Sam drops his hand slowly and eases a bit. He chuckles too. His eye continues to twitch, but his aggravated persona lightens. "Now that I think about it, I probably looked pretty funny running after a bird."

"Maybe just a little," I confirm.

Before either of us get to ask about Logan, he appears at the base of the tree and zips up at twice the speed that Sam and I used. When he makes it up to us, he sits on the branch underneath us and gives a deep breath.

"Any luck?" Sam loudly whispers.

Logan takes another deep breath and answers, "Nope. Nothing."

"I might have something." I hold out the berries toward Logan, and his eyes grow two sizes.

Logan leans in and observes the berries closer. "Are they safe?"

His face shines with hope and somehow seems to brighten the darkness around us. I hate to be the one who tells him that we don't know if they are safe or not, but I do. His glow slowly dies out, but his light smile lingers, like he feels the need to keep our morale up.

I try to ease their worries by commenting, "We don't have to eat them. We aren't going to starve for at least a few more days." I know this fact all too well. "We can only go three days at the most without water, but we can go a lot longer without food."

We all exchange a few looks, but no words. It is an unspoken agreement. I continue, "I can show you where I got these tomorrow if you decide you want them." The dark-colored berries rain out of my hand and fall to the ground as I wipe my hands off. "We can go and check my box trap then too."

They both nod in agreement. We decide to go ahead and try to sleep for the night and try again in the morning. This time, we all sleep much better. One full day of walking can really tire a person out. That mixed with dehydration and a lack of sufficient nutrients could knock anyone out.

We wake because of a large gust of wind that shakes all of the leaves around us. My eyes flutter open and take notice that the sun appears to have been up for at least an hour. "Crap," I moan.

Sam sits up, whining, and wipes his eyes. "What?"

"Sun's up," Logan utters. "We're wasting time."

Sam groans and settles back into his sleeping position. "If you call a good night's sleep time wasted, I don't want to be your friend."

I couldn't help but smile at how much Sam was not a morning person. "Sam," I chuckle, "We have to go find water and food."

Sam doesn't move.

I continue, "There might be something in my trap."

"Okay, you've convinced me." Sam sits up and wipes his eyes again. "Sleep, bad. Food, good."

Logan and I chuckle as we make our way down the tree and wait for Sam to follow. Logan smiles at me and whispers, "Do you really think there might be something in your trap?"

"I hope so." I look back up at Sam, who was slowly but surely slinking down the branches. "Either way, it got him up, so it's a win."

We all get down from the tree and take a minute or two to stretch and pop every joint that will allow it. Soon after, we head back through the woods and find my trap broken. It is crushed, as if something or someone had stepped on it. The berries that were beneath it are gone, causing me to assume that something has eaten it.

The boys and I all come to the same conclusion that these berries must be safe to eat, so we grab a few. Hesitant to eat the still-unknown food, we put them in our pockets and keep going.

After hours and hours of walking, Logan takes notice of the altitude change. "We are definitely getting higher." He wheezes, trying not to seem affected.

Sam and I both agree.

We all keep walking and walking until we feel like we can walk no more. We decide to stop and take a break by sitting on some of the lowest-hanging branches we could find. Sam complains that his head is pounding and his stomach is turning. He claims that he can't walk any more unless he gets some water. I look around and see that the sun is getting closer and closer to being gone for the night, and that worries me. If we don't find water soon, I doubt any of us will make it any longer.

Sam's weakened stance quickly changes as the sound of tires crunching the leaves and twigs on the ground grows. We all quickly climb up a few branches and wait.

The sound of the car grows louder as it weaves through the trees, closer to us. We can see through the gaps of leaves the large dark gray van slowly driving past us. The windows are darkly tinted and works as a mirror. As it drives by us, we watch as our faces appear in the reflective window through the leaves. Each of our faces shows a different emotion. Fear is one, pain is another, and concentration the other.

As it slowly passes, the bronze ring comes into view. Two bronze hammers, crossed over each other, on top of a bronze ring. The shiny coloring of the seal in contrast to the dark gray van makes it even more dazzling.

Sam murmurs something under his breath, and Logan and I look over to him to find his eyes wide and his stamina seemingly back. Before we could do anything, Sam scurries down from the tree and runs out to the van. "Hey! Hey!" Sam shouts at the vehicle. "Hey!"

The vehicle stops.

Logan and I make our way down the tree to hear the side door of the van sliding open, and a man waving Sam inside. A large and muscular tan man with a dark buzz cut emerges wearing dark gray clothing, matching the van, and black armor, matching his gun. He sits on one side of the eight-seat van as Sam scoots into the corner seat on the opposite side and waves Logan and me in.

"Come on, we need to get going!" the man barks at us.

We hesitate. Logan steps up in front of me and questions the man like he needs no help. "Why should we?"

The man gives a gravelly chuckle. "Stay out here if you want, but the sun is setting. I figured you would rather come with us than be beast bait."

Logan looks pleadingly at me. I nod back to him, and we get into the van. Logan waits for me get in first, so I sit next to Sam, and Logan scoots in next to me.

The man slides the large metal door closed and introduces himself in an accent that is strikingly similar to that of Metropolis's citizens back in Bestellen. "I'm Major Cole Mason. You can call me Major Mason."

I nod to him and somehow find myself tucked behind both Sam and Logan. Sam has his arms crossed, one over one of my arms; and Logan has his hands folded in his lap, with one of his arms over my other arm.

I turn and look behind me to see another man in the front, driving the van. Major Mason nods to the other man. "And that there is Private Yate Groves. You can call him whatever, as long as it's decent." Mason smiles back at us. Though I'm sure his smile was meant to reassure us, it didn't.

Sam butts in, saying, "I came to the van because I recognized the seal on the side. Before now, I had never thought that this seal was a real thing or that it existed, but I was out of options." Sam clears his throat. "When I saw this van, something told me to go to it, to see if you could help us. I'm hoping I made the right choice because now I have dragged these two into it." Sam looks from Mason to us, then readjusts his posture and stance. Sam clears his throat again and asks the question that we are all wondering. "So what exactly is going on?"

Mason gives another slight smile as he pulls out bottles of water and passes them to us. We are hesitant at first but are too dehydrated and out of options. We need the water. Mason looks from Sam to me to Logan and then out the window as we chug the water. "Sit tight, bud. Everything will be explained as soon as we get back to Bergland."

CHAPTER FIVE

Logan

The ride to Bergland is slow, seemingly taking forever. Mavis, Sam, and I all sit quietly, watching the forest fly by as we drive through it. My hands rest folded in my lap, but my right arm remains slightly in front of Mavis—enough in front to help her feel secure, but not enough to make her feel trapped. This is how Gramps would stand by me during our attendance checks in the sector square. It's a form of protection without smothering. Mavis seems to feel comforted by this, just as I always did when Gramps did so.

I stare at Major Mason as we drive to see if I can read his face. But he wears an unreadable smug smile. The sun has fully set, leaving us in a state of almost total darkness, which is only illuminated by the glow of the taillights from behind the van and the headlights in the front. The ride comes to an end as we proceed through the mountains. The twists and turns at the extreme heights give me an odd feeling in my stomach that I usually don't get, so I ignore it.

"Make sure to yawn every now and then," Mason tells us. "You don't want your ears to pop."

None of us obey.

"You don't have to yawn. Chewing or swallowing works just as well," Mason chuckles.

The three of us exchange a few looks. Sam tries to fight it, but he lets out one large yawn, leading Mavis and me to do the same. I feel small bubbles in my ear shift and pressure being relieved. I focus on swallowing and yawning every now and then for the rest of the ride while questioning every twist and turn we make.

It feels like they are just as lost in these woods as we are and that they are driving us up the mountain with no particular direction.

The driver, the supposed Private Yate Groves, turns off the head- and taillights, leaving Sam, Mavis, and me in what I would describe as a breathless moment. We drive directly toward a steep and rocky point of the mountains when a piece of what I thought was rock lifts forward. A large door rises, and the van enters.

The darkness that has been consuming us for the long drive slowly gets darker as we enter something that could be classified as a tunnel. As the door behind us closes, a loud clank echoes throughout the room. The van continues to move forward, and the head- and taillights click on. The three of us position ourselves to look out of the front of the car to see where we are heading.

My eyes fall upon a long concrete tunnel that has orange-yellow lights hanging toward the end. The tunnel twists right as soon as we arrive under the lights. The van drives through, swerving, swerving, swerving what feels like once every quarter mile. It takes us a few minutes to get to the end of the tunnel, where we are met with a large steel door.

Mason taps on his wrist, and a blue light radiates from it. He raises his wrist to his mouth and speaks into his cuff. "We're back. We have three. Tell Hash to prep the IR." He lowers his wrist, and we hear another large clank, followed by the whirring of mechanics, which I assume are responsible for opening the doors in front of us.

As they slide open, a room filled with vehicles is revealed. From where we park, I can see a few more vans like the one we are in, along with a few larger vans that look strikingly similar to the ones the officials back home would use to bring in their servicemen.

"All right. We're here." Mason smiles to us and slides open the side door beside me. "Are you ready for your briefing?" I watch him as he scoots out and holds the door open for us.

Nobody moves.

Sniffling and wiping his nose with the back of his free hand, Mason nods us out. "Come on, I won't bite."

I look back to Sam and Mavis, who seem to be looking to me to move since I am the one closest to the door. I take the nonverbal cue and step out. The large concrete- and steel-lined room that surrounds us is filled with the scent of rubber and is dimly illuminated by the orange-yellow lights that we found in the tunnel.

After stepping out and taking a quick glance around the room, I follow Major Mason's gaze and find Mavis frozen in her seat. Sam, who sits behind her, stares past her and looks around.

I lean forward and put my hand on the side of the open door. Mavis, still frozen, looks past me. "Are you coming?" I ask.

Sam stands up as much as he can and waddles past Mavis and out of the van.

"I'm out," he grunts.

Mavis stays frozen in her seat. Major Mason sighs and looks from her back to me. "What's her name?"

Sam answers before I can as he stretches. "Mavis. Mavis Wamsley." He looks back to her. "Or at least that's what she told us."

Mason nods and slowly gets back into the van. He sits across from Mavis and tries to meet her eyes. Her breathing becomes more violent the longer we watch her.

"Hey, Mavis." Mason's voice softens from its original grittiness and becomes more comforting and seemingly more trustworthy.

Mavis keeps her eyes averted from his stare as she maintains focus on her knees.

Mason leans forward and says slowly, "Hey, it's okay. I have a friend here that's going to explain everything." Mavis's breathing steadies as Mason continues, "Her name is Emily. Will you come with us?"

Mavis raises her head and looks at Sam, me, and then back to Mason. She takes a few deep breaths and slowly nods.

Mason smiles. "Don't worry. I won't separate you and your friends. Come on." He holds out his hand for her as she comes out of the car, but she shakes her head and denies his help. Mason nods to her, retracts his hand, and allows Mavis to get out of the car herself.

She stands between Sam and me as Mason closes the van door and leads us out. Private Yate follows, I guess to make sure we stay in line.

We walk for a minute or two and approach another concrete wall with a set of glass sliding doors just a little taller than Mason.

"Bullet trains," Mason announces. A semiloud squealing noise comes barreling behind the wall and sounds like it is coming straight for us. A white light slowly becomes brighter behind the glass doors as the low rumbling and squealing sound grows louder. Mason looks over to us and takes notice of our frightened expressions. He chuckles and tries to calm us, saying, "Faster than walking and better than cars."

The large black "train" pulls up, and its brakes squeal as it comes to a halt. The glass doors slide open as the train's doors follow. Mason steps in and grabs on to a handle hanging from the ceiling of the train. "It's the best way to get around the mountains," Mason claims. "Come on in."

Each one of us hesitantly enters the train, followed by Yate.

Yate slides his hand onto one of the poles in the middle of the train running from the floor to the ceiling. He looks to us and smiles. "Grab on to something. When this train takes off, you will feel it." The doors close, and Yate wiggles his eyebrows at us.

Sam's eyes dart from Yate to me, then to the tall pole closest to him. Sam grabs it with both hands, and I reach for the side railing beside me. Mavis and I both grab the same railing, and our hands graze over each other. Neither of us makes a big deal of it; we just slide our hands away from each other's and grab the pole. I can't help but wonder if she noticed, but I move that thought to the back of my mind and focus on the reality that is unfolding.

The doors close beside us, and the train's engine whirs up. I watch as Sam tightens his grip on his pole. Mason chuckles at the sight of Sam being so nervous. "Just hold on. It isn't that bad."

Sam straightens up and rolls his shoulders back. The train takes off from its position and pushes us back only slightly. Mavis and I lean only slightly back due to the force while Sam leans none.

"That's nothing," Sam chuckles, loosening his grip on the pole.

Mason flicks his wrist, and the blue rectangular hologram pops up with some sort of map and a dot floating through it. The dot is originally a lighter blue than the rest of the map but begins flashing red as the brakes on the train begin to squeal once again.

Mavis and I slide forward a bit, still holding on to the railing, while Sam falls directly into his pole.

"Careful," Yate chuckles. "Landing is just as hard as takeoff."

The train comes to a complete stop, and the doors beside us open. Yate lets go of his pole and nods Mason out.

Mason puts his hand over the hologram and seems to push it back down into the cuff. He walks out of the train and finger-guns us out. "Follow me," he insists.

Sam rubs his chest and marches out behind Mason. Mavis and I follow him while Yate follows us. I can't help but wonder about how much Sam seems to trust these people and wonder why he does so.

The hallway from which we exit the train is completely different from the hallway from which we entered the train. The one we entered it from was a large concrete- and steel-lined room with vans in it. This one is a room no bigger than my house with stairs leading upward from both directions.

We follow Mason up one set of stairs and into a narrow hallway with doors on one side leading to a larger set of stairwells and on the other side, multiple sets of twin metal sliding doors. Mason makes his way over to one of the metal doors and presses a button beside them. A green light overhead of one of the frames comes on, and that one opens into a little room.

Mason waves us over. "Come on in." Again, Sam is the first to follow. When Mavis and I find our way in, the small room has a wall of buttons with numbers and letters on them. Mason taps one of them, and Yate piles in. The small room is big enough for us all to not be cramped, but small enough that we don't feel too free.

The doors close, and another whirring sound begins. I look to Sam and Mavis to see her clutching the railing on the side of the room and to see him jump the second the room starts moving. The room flies upward and sways back and forth slightly the farther it flies up.

Sam jerks over beside Mavis and grabs the railing. His eyes grow, and his breathing grows heavy as he turns to Mason and Yate. "What's going on?"

Within a few moments, the room stops flying, and the doors open into what looks like a lobby. Mason steps out and is followed by the three of us, almost leaping out of the room. Yate walks behind us and casually explains that the room we were just in lifted us to another level.

"Level of what?" I ask, only to receive the same answer we originally got.

"Everything will be explained shortly."

The ground we walk on is covered in a brown and white carpet, and the walls are the same color as wet sand. The few people that are walking past all give us a smile as we follow Mason. Though their smiles are supposed to be interpreted as a kind gesture, to me, they seem more disturbing than reassuring.

Mason leads us into a small dark gray room that has a large table and about nine chairs that all match the walls. Inside the room is a dark-caramel-skinned middle-aged woman who appears perfectly groomed like she has never seen a speck of dirt in her life.

She stands from her seated position at the head of the rectangular table and flashes a bright white smile at us. "Hello! Welcome to Bergland!" She scoots her chair on wheels backward and makes her way over to us. She too has the accent that sounds just like those from Metropolis.

"My name is Emily Hash. I am the newcomers' coordinator along with a few other things that will make more sense in a minute. Is there anything I can get you to help make you more comfortable before we start?"

Mason and Yate nod to her behind us and close the door, leaving us alone with this new woman. Sam looks behind us to the closed door, then back to her. "Start what?"

Emily smiles and waves us over to the table. "Please, take a seat."

Sam openly follows her request, leaving Mavis and me standing alone, still trying to figure things out. I look down to find Mavis had started scratching her arm once again, along with beginning her deep breath therapy she seems to do whenever she gets nervous.

Emily takes notice and picks up a small black panel off the table in front of her. The panel looks just like one of the tablets that the officials back home used when they took attendance checks.

"Here," Emily states as she swipes the tablet. The wall to our right lights up with an image of Chancellor Lance Meir I. "Do you know who this is?"

Mavis takes another deep breath and nods. Sam jumps in, saying, "Yeah, that's Lance Meir I."

Emily smiles. I put my hand on Mavis's back and nod her toward the table. Only after I sit down beside Sam does she take a seat.

"That's right. Today, I will be giving you a quick briefing of the things you don't know about Bestellen." Emily swipes her tablet, and the image on the wall in front of us changes from Meir to a picture of what looked like a meeting of men in suits gone wrong.

Two men were leaning over their desks, shouting and pointing at each other, while the people surrounding them were in chaos. They were screaming, fighting, pointing, and seemingly tearing their fellow men's suits apart.

"This is a picture that was taken over a century ago. It is of one of the last meetings between two groups of people."

Emily swipes, and a picture of two seals comes up: One, a bronze-colored seal with two hammers crossed over each other enclosed in a ring, just like the one on the side of the van. The other, Bestellen's seal, a gold ant, enclosed in a ring, just like the first seal.

Emily looks from the images on the wall, back to us. "Do any of you recognize either seal?"

"Yeah." Sam leans back into his chair and points to each picture. "The one on the left is the Diligent symbol. The one on the right is Bestellen's."

Emily smiles at Sam. "Great job, um . . ."

"Sam," he fills in.

"Great job, Sam." Emily nods. She then turns back to Mavis and me. "Do either of you know what these seals are? Or what they mean?"

The two of us shake our heads and shrug. I know what the Bergland seal is, but Sam just answered.

How does she expect us to know what these are? How does Sam know what the other seal is?

Emily pulls out her seat and slides in, sitting at the other end of the table. "Okay, then you are in for a history lesson." She swipes again and pulls up a picture of a town being built. People on the ground, on ladders, and on top of buildings are all working on a common goal.

Rebuilding.

Emily clears her throat and looks over to us. "A long time ago, our land was destroyed by a war between men. A squabble that could have easily been solved destroyed a countless number of lives and killed billions more. This is one of the first pictures taken of us attempting to rebuild our lives after the nuclear war was over."

She swipes her tablet once again and leads us back to the picture of the men in suits, fighting. "Sadly, the peace we fought so hard to try to keep was short-lived after our population segregated naturally. We split into two groups. One, we called the Diligent."

The screen changes to show the crossed-hammers seal. "The Diligent believe that you should get what you work for and that anyone who doesn't put in the effort shouldn't reap the benefits." Emily swipes the tablet, and the screen changes again, this time to the gold seal with the ant.

"The other group, we called the Amiables. The Amiables believe that no matter how hard you work, everyone should be given the same benefits." Emily sighs and turns back to us. "It is an idealistic mind-set. As good as the Amiables' beliefs sound, they aren't realistic. They claim that this method would keep everyone equally rich, but in reality, they are just keeping everyone at the same level of destitution."

The image in front of us changes from the picture of everyone arguing to a picture of a map—a blob, really, that had certain areas marked off and labeled. The northern portion is labeled "Diligent," and the southern portion is labeled "Amiable."

Emily clears her throat and folds her hands on the table. Her voice—quiet and calm, but authoritative enough to make an impact—floats through the room. "The two groups decided to split up to avoid conflict, but inside, trouble was still brewing. The survivors of the nuclear war continued on with life by starting families and making their own governments. Almost fifty years after their separation, a civil war broke out, and the two groups fought for thirteen years."

Images of the war flash before us. Gunfire, swordplay, cannon fire, bombs, and so much more. Buildings being blown to bits, along with forest fires burning nature, people, and animals alike. I see Sam beside me twitching as the images pass by, and I listen to Mavis's breathing. Her breaths have become longer and heavier, and her eyes have focused on the screen in front. Emily swipes slowly and watches our reactions.

My eyes lock with Emily's. She sends me a sympathetic head tilt and continues, "The war ended with an Amiable victory." A picture of their ant on a flag comes into focus. "During the war, the Amiables wasted no resources. They killed off anyone who refused to fight, even those who couldn't, just so that they wouldn't be supporting those who couldn't support them in return. The Diligent, on the other hand, did not. They supported those back home who couldn't fight, and they showed mercy to many Amiable soldiers whom they should have killed. The Amiables showed no mercy and ended the war by forcing the Diligent to surrender."

An image of Metropolis flashes onto the wall. Emily turns back to us. "This is where your homeland comes into play. After the civil war, a dictator rose from the ashes. This dictator's name was Lance Meir I. He and his council instituted a state of socialistic causes where everyone is assigned a different job in which they have to comply, or they will be arrested or killed. Nobody gets to have any input in their desired career—they just have to do what they are told. They are only educated for the specific jobs they are assigned when they are children, and nobody is ever taught history. Lance Meir was very determined to keep all of his citizens uneducated and have them blindly follow his rule." Emily pauses and looks back to us as if she is waiting for a comment or some sort of answer.

In this moment, my mind is running wild. Everything she is saying makes sense, but at the same time, they all seem so ridiculously unreal.

"Without a proper education, you never really learn to think for yourself. You just learn to blindly follow and listen to what you are told." Emily pauses and turns her head back to us. Mavis is scratching her arm but pauses the moment she sees me watching. She avoids eye contact with everybody while Sam looks from me to Mavis to Emily. His puzzled look is almost laughable, but definitely understandable.

Emily takes our silence as a cue to continue explaining. "Lance Meir I passed on his rule to his son, Lance Meir II. Both men share similar views. They both believe in assigning careers at birth and educating citizens for that one career in order to save resources. They both believe in free health care per se, and they both believe in geven."

Emily pauses again and explains to us that "geven" is the term they use to describe the economic system where everyone shares everything. For some reason, she seems to think that we completely understand everything she says.

She turns back to the screen and changes the image to a picture of Meir II. "Though he claims he is following his father, Lance Meir II's views on everything are much more radical than his father's. For example, when Lance Meir I came into power, what was one of the first things he did for the health-care system?"

Emily swipes her tablet and pulls up another picture, this time of Lance Meir I giving a speech on one of his podiums. "He and his team of scientists came up with a serum that prevents any and every sort of disorder in the human body. They began to administer it to every infant within hours of its birth so that it could grow up and live without any sort of restriction caused by a disorder. As wonderful as this sounds, the beautiful and amazing program was quickly trashed when Meir II came into power. As soon as he began calling the shots, he decided that they were spending too much money administering their miracle serum, so he cut the funding for the program."

Sam, Mavis, and I all exchange a baffled look. None of us have ever heard of any of this, and to be honest, I find this quite difficult to believe.

Emily looks to us for answers but soon picks up talking again. "As the generations continued to come, the effects of the serum slowly began to fade out of its people. What I mean by that is that the children born in the last twenty years have not been granted the same good fortune as those who had been born previously."

Too many thoughts are running through my mind. I don't know what I want to ask first, but Sam does. He slides his hands onto the table in front of us, cocks his head at Emily, and squints. "Why?"

Emily smiles at him. "I am happy you asked that, Sam. Meir II and his new team of scientists created a serum that delays the disorders rather than destroys it. This serum is cheaper to make and administer, and they only have to administer it to certain people. The serum will delay the disorders for eighteen years after it is injected."

I manage to force out a question in between the rubbing of my fingernails. "Which people?"

Emily smiles again. "Good question . . ." She tilts her head at me, waiting for my name.

"Logan," I say. "It's Logan."

"Good question, Logan. When Stellens are born, they go through a screening process that helps the nurses and doctors figure out what disorders they will have in the future and how severe they will be. Some disorders that aren't extreme they let go by, while others that are more unpredictable are considered too dangerous to ignore.

"So what they do is inject the infants that will grow up to have these disorders with the delaying serum and assign them to the 'military,' when really, they are being exiled for monetary purposes. Since those who enter the Stellen military are never seen again by their families, it isn't considered suspicious that these people go missing.

"An example of a disorder that isn't considered too dangerous when it is mild is germaphobia. It would have to be a severe case in order for them to determine you would be a threat to society. An example of a disorder that would be considered dangerous at any level is schizophrenia." Emily pauses. She looks to us and tries to read our expressions. I don't know what the others are thinking, but it is probably the same thing I'm thinking.

Monetary purposes?

Monetary purposes?

"You mean they threw us into the wild to fend for ourselves because we have some sort of mutation that we cannot control?" I fume. "One that they could have prevented for a few extra bucks?"

"Yeah!" Sam shoots up from out of his chair, throwing it backward in the process. "And who are you people anyway? Why should we trust you? All you are doing is telling us that we are unnatural and that everything we know is a lie?" His eyes begin twitching, along with his neck.

I get ready to start questioning again when I hear Mavis's shaky breath behind me. I turn to see her with her hands over her ears and her head down on her knees. She takes quick and loud gasps as her body bounces up and down with every breath she takes.

"Hey, guys." Emily walks around the back of the table. "Please stop shouting. I am jus—"

"Stop shouting?" Sam shouts. "Do we not have the right to shout? Just because you don't like our chancellor? Just because yo—"

Mavis gasps loudly, which scares both Sam and me, still keeping her head down and her hands over her ears. Emily reaches up and presses a button on her watch. Two men in white clothing rush in with a small metal rolling table. One of the men quickly grabs a small glass vial about five inches long with a needle on the end. The vial has a bright blue liquid inside of it, which quickly drains as it is stuck into the side of Mavis's thigh.

She shoots up from her seat and leaps forward. She lands against one of the walls and presses her back against it. Mavis's eyes grow three sizes. The green bits of her eyes are barely visible as her pupils grow to fill up the colored portions. Mavis darts her eyes from the men who stuck her with the needle over to me. Our eyes lock for a moment before she slowly slides down the wall into a sitting position.

Sam and I both are in shock at what has just happened. Sam is left gaping at the men with the needles while I look back to Emily. "What was that?" I demand.

The second the words leave my lips, I realize that I may be their next victim. Sam seems to have the same idea. He tenses up and backs away from the men and Emily as they fix their eyes on the two of us.

"What?" Sam shouts at them. "Are you going to sedate us too?"

Emily brings her hands up and approaches us the same way Sam and I approached Charlie. "This is what I was trying to explain," Emily answers. "Each one of you has a disorder that is considered extreme in one way or another. By the looks of it, this young lady has severe anxiety."

Emily walks over to Mavis, who is sitting against the wall with one knee to her chest and one leg stretched out. Mavis is looking around the room to each of us as her breathing steadies. Emily and Mavis stare at each other for a moment as Emily proceeds with an explanation. "Since none of you have ever had any experience with your disorders before, we want to help you learn what it is and how to handle it. Until you get a good grip on it, we have medicine that can help you."

Now Mavis is staring into Emily's eyes and ignoring the rest of us in the room.

Emily crouches down and gets to eye level with Mavis. "Are you okay?" Emily waits for a response, but Mavis remains silent. Emily whispers, "I am sorry we had to do that. I know how scary those attacks can be. We just want to help you."

Mavis takes a few more deep breaths.

Emily gives her a calm smile. "Did it help?"

Mavis returns her gesture with a slow and calm nod.

Looking over to Sam and me, she sighs. "We don't like to do that, and I am sorry it had come to this. She was in a lot of distress, so I thought we could help." Emily returns to her standing position. "Just like if either of you ever feel overwhelmed by your issues, you just let me or someone know, and we will not hesitate to help."

Mavis stays in her relaxed position and watches us as she takes her deep breaths. Sam turns to me, and we share a stare for a few moments before he turns back to Emily. "So Mavis has anxiety? That's a disorder?"

Emily nods.

Sam turns back to Emily. His body is stiff other than the twitching of his hands, neck, and cheeks. "I thought that was just a word to describe nervousness."

Emily shakes her head and smiles. "I wish. Sadly, there is a lot more to anxiety than anyone ever assumes. Attacks can come in many forms, ranging from unpredictable fits of rage or irritability to sitting in silence, being consumed by a lack of ability to think properly or really function."

Sam's voice, blank of any emotion, floats through the room. "What about me?"

"Excuse me?" Emily folds her hands in front of her as she glances from Mavis to Sam.

"What about me?" he repeats. "Can you tell me why I keep twitching? Why I have uncontrollable . . . anger inside of me? Why every little thing sets me off, and I have to fight myself to maintain composure?"

Emily gives another light smile, though this one seems painted on. As she forces a kind smile onto her face, her perfect features become more noticeable. How many times before has she had to use this fake smile? Her shoulder-length black hair looks about as soft and shiny as can be, and it makes her skin even more chocolate-like than I originally thought. Does she keep such a perfect appearance in order to assure others that it can get better? Or does she keep this appearance because she is conceited?

Emily turns to the men in white before answering Sam. "We can help you find out what your disorder is, Sam. We have a very similar screening process to the one you underwent when you were infants. It is easy and harmless and takes a few hours at the most."

Sam nods and looks back to the men in white. Before he can say anything, I butt in and ask Emily the same question. "What about me?"

She chuckles. "I think I already have yours figured out, but you can get checked out too if you want."

I cock my head at her answer.

"OCD," she states. "I can recognize the signs anywhere. The rubbing each finger three times, the way you aligned your rolling chair with certain lines of the screen and table in the room, the way you squeeze your eyes closed every time you blink, and the pattern when you do so."

I can't help but question her once again, "OCD?"

"Obsessive compulsive disorder. The short explanation is a disorder that creates the need to repeat certain things or engage in certain behavior that will drive you crazy if you aren't able to follow through with those desires." Emily smiles at me once again. "I have it too." Her smile fades as her eyes fall, and she fixes her focus on the ground. She pauses for a moment before looking back up at me. "I have a mild form. You seem to have a moderate form. That's interesting. We didn't know that they considered mild to moderate OCD a threat."

She turns back to Mavis and meets her eyes. "I have anxiety too, a severe form, really. But I have been able to overcome both of these with the help of the people and staff here at Bergland." Emily's fist clenches, and her fingers rub up against each other. She then brings her hands up and begins bending her fingers and gesturing with her hands as if speaking with them. "Mine usually results in severe attacks where my OCD suffocates me. I can't help but notice everything around me that needs to be changed or fixed, but I can never satisfy the need." She holds out her hand for Mavis and helps her up to a standing position. "These guys only gave you a small dose, so you should be back to normal in a matter of minutes. This dose was just to help you calm down for a moment so that we could explain some of this."

Mavis crosses her arms and nods back to Emily.

Both of them make their way toward us, and the two men in white open the meeting room doors. Emily walks over to the opening and nods us out. "Are you ready for your screenings?"

Sam and I exchange a look, one that we both understand. Are we ready to find out what was so wrong with us that we were kicked out of our homes? Are we ready to be tested by complete strangers? Are we really ready to blindly follow people who claim we were blindly following others?

We have only one real answer to all of these questions, one that I am not even 100 percent sure of.

Yes, we are ready.

CHAPTER SIX

Sam

BPD.

I have BPD, or borderline personality disorder.

Or at least that is what the doctors tell me. As I sit on one of the small beds in one of the observation rooms, a doctor and nurse come back with a clipboard and a small vial that is very similar to the one with which the nurses stuck Mavis just hours ago.

The doctor moves over to me with the vial while the nurse holds the clipboard. His name tag reads "Dr. James" while the nurse's scrubs remain nameless. Dr. James leans in, places one hand on my thigh, and holds out the vial in the palm of his hand so that I can take a look at it. He speaks to me in the same accent that the other Berglanders did. "Just a little prick, and it will be over."

I can't help but connect their accents to the privileged citizens of Bestellen and wonder if the original group of people that split into the Diligent and Amiable factions had these accents also.

I guess it makes sense. After separating into different states and being exposed to only those within their state, the citizens should end up with the same mannerisms as everyone else within their state.

I nod to him, and the needle goes into my thigh. My shoulders jump a bit as a feeling of relaxation floods over my body. I feel my shoulders, neck, cheeks, and legs finally find rest—a rest that they haven't felt since Bestellen.

"The form of BPD you have is extremely mild, but difficult to deal with nonetheless." The doctor pulls the vial back and scoots his chair away to give me some space. "This medicine is designed to hold you over and keep any and all symptoms you may have very mild and possibly unnoticeable. We will give you all of the instructions for the medicine later. But for right now, all you need to know is that unless something triggers a full-blown attack, this medicine should help you go back to your normal state once your body adapts to it. Now can I ask you a few questions?"

I nod. No words escape my mouth. It is all I can do not to lean back onto the small bed, close my eyes, and enjoy the sense of peace that I so desperately needed.

"Have you found yourself having to fight off any urges you haven't had before? Such as physical harm toward others, yourself, or anything you could get your hands on?"

I nod.

"Have you been having trouble with uncontrollable twitching or convulsions?"

I nod.

"Where?"

The relief I feel is something I want to take advantage of. I have no desire to talk and ruin it. I have no desire for it to go away or wear off.

I don't want to talk, but I don't want to point, so I stay quiet.

"Can you speak?"

I nod and realize I have to speak in order to help these people out, in order to help myself out.

"Eyes. Arms. Neck." I take a breath and work up enough energy to continue. "Legs. Feet. Hands."

"So everywhere?" the doctor responds.

I shake my head. "My back was fine."

The nurse with the clipboard chuckles and makes a few notes.

Dr. James goes on to ask me a few more questions about if I have lashed out recently and how I felt during the episodes. Toward the end of all of the questions, the medicine they gave me begins to wear off as he explains that BPD can be different for everyone. Some people find that they have trouble twitching. Some don't. Some people find they can't control themselves or their thoughts. Some don't. Some have a large variety of symptoms. Some don't. Dr. James continues to say that with the medicine, I can become the master of my disorder.

As he continues blabbing, I continue wishing for more of that medicine.

The nurse smiles at me and exits the room, leaving the doctor and me alone. Still sitting on the bed, I listen to Dr. James speak as he and his rolling chair squeak over to me. "All right, Mr. Beckman, before we let you go, we need to go over some things."

I nod to him and cross my arms.

"First, let me ask you, are you okay with the medicine we just gave you? Did it help you feel more relaxed or more tired?"

"Relaxed."

"Good!" He smiles. "Here in Bergland, for those who have certain disorders at certain levels, we have a prescription vial system."

I can't help but shoot him a perplexed look. As the medicine wears off, my ability to react seems less inhibited.

"What I mean by that is we provide portable vials like these"—he lifts the empty vial that he used on me earlier off the counter and wiggles it in the air—"to those who need it. What we will do for you is give you a certain amount of vials at a time. When you run out, you can come get more from us."

He stands up and sticks the empty vial in one of his pockets. "Whenever you feel like the BPD is getting out of hand, you can stick the flat side of these tubes onto your thigh, and a needle will come out and inject you with all of the medicine inside of it." The doctor opens the door and ushers me out. He hands me a set of folded light-blue and gray clothes and tells me that they are mine to keep.

Dr. James hands me a bag with another set of the same clothes, along with my old clothes that I wore through the woods. After I go to the restroom and change into the new clean clothes, we weave through the office and past other observation rooms.

We approach the front desk, and Dr. James smiles at the lady typing something into her holographic keyboard. "Good evening, Ms. Lansley."

"Good evening, Dr. James! Who might this be?" She pauses for a moment and turns to me. Her bright red lipstick and overuse of makeup begin to make me uncomfortable the longer I look at it. Her eyelash goop has clumped up and stuck to her eyelid, and her eyebrows look so painted on that all I think I need to do to get rid of them is wipe them with a rag.

The doctor smiles again and pats me on the back. "This is Samuel Beckman. I do believe that Alice brought out his chart."

Ms. Lansley pulls a clipboard out of a pile of clipboards and sings out, "Here it is!" She begins typing into her keyboard once again. I follow her gaze to a holographic screen that seems to be changing too quickly for me to understand.

There are so many holograms in this office that I begin to doubt that the desks and pictures on the wall are really there. I slide my hand onto the counter just to make sure.

It's real.

"All right," Ms. Lansley tells us. "I will go get you your prescriptions. One moment please." She gets up and leaves her desk, leaving me with the doctor.

For a moment, it's quiet. Other than the sound of pages flipping behind us in the waiting room and the sound of fingers hitting their desks, it's quiet.

Dr. James slides his hands into his jacket pockets once again. "I hope you find yourself at home here."

I turn back to him and give a half-life smile. "Thanks." The quiet resumes.

So many questions are running through my mind. I can't seem to sort through them. I can't even seem to fully understand half of them. My mind is scrambled.

I force out a question. "Is there anything I need to know? About Bergland?"

The doctor seems pleasantly surprised. He smiles at me and bobs his head. "Well, I guess the main thing is that we all want what's best."

I nod, and the desk lady returns with a small black metal briefcase. She slides it over the desk to me, along with a clipboard.

"I need you to sign here on this contract stating that whenever you come in for more vials, that you will bring your briefcase." She points with her pen to what seems like every other sentence and explains what the contract states, but I get stuck observing her face. Her skin seems to be covered in chalk, a sort of chalk that doesn't match the color of the rest of her body. The colored chalk stops at her jawline and makes the rest of her body seem much darker in comparison. "This also insures your briefcase if it is stolen, misplaced, or broken. Each briefcase has a serial number on it. Yours is right here." She points to the number on my case and then hands me a pen. "Please sign right here."

I sign.

She takes the clipboard and hands me my case. "Your code for the case is 7629. Go ahead and put one or two in your pockets for quick and easy access. Please use these responsibly, and if you ever need anything, just let us know!"

I nod to her and write down the number on my hand. The lady notices and hands me a sticky note with the code instead. I keep both, just in case.

"Thank you," I mutter.

Dr. James walks me out of the office and into the hallway that is open and as large as my town square. The roof above us is glass, and we can see the second floor. People walk over the glass, and beams hold them up like it is nothing new. For them, I am sure it isn't; but for me, it is wild.

I see Major Mason, Mavis, and Logan, all standing around an abstract statue of iron rods twisted and mangled around each other in the middle of the room. Mavis and Logan are both wearing the same sort of new clothes that I am as they all talk. Mason on one side and Mavis with Logan on the other. Logan stands slightly in front of Mavis with his arms crossed, mimicking Mason's stance, almost as if he was trying to be intimidating. Mavis is holding a briefcase, just like mine, and watching the boys talk. I can tell Mavis wants to say something but is holding back.

The doctor pats me on the back as I take a deep breath. "Do you know where you are going?"

I nod and point over to the gang. Dr. James nods back to me. "All right. Good luck. Come back and see me whenever you want."

I doubt I will be coming back, but I give a polite smile back to him anyway; then I make my way over to Mavis and Logan.

Mavis

Beside me, Logan continues questioning Mason. "So what about you?"

Smug. That's all I can see when I see Mason smile. They mimic each other's stance. Crossed arms, cold stare, and feet aimed at each other.

"What about me?" Mason chuckles.

"Do you have any disorders? Like us?"

Mason squeezes his lips together and focuses his eyes on Logan. Before he has the chance to answer, Sam approaches the group.

Sam mumbles out, "Hey."

I turn to him and can't help but smile. "Hey."

I hope he'd smile back, but Sam ignores me and makes his way over to Logan and me without another word.

Logan eases up and turns back to Sam. "What did they say?"

"BPD," Sam answers.

Logan and I exchange a confused look while Mason behind us sighs. "I'm sorry, Mr. Beckman."

Sam shrugs back. "It's fine. They gave me these." He lifts his case, the same case I have. "They said to take them whenever I needed." The group is silent for a moment before he glances down at my case. "I guess they gave you the same news."

I nod. Another moment of silence passes. Mason waits a moment before chiming in, "All right. Are you guys ready for a quick tour?"

I feel a small gurgling in the center of my stomach as Sam shrugs at Mason's question. The gurgling is followed by an eruption of a violent loud growl in the same area of my stomach.

Mason is taken aback by the magnitude of the outburst and chuckles. "Whoa, let's start with the cafeteria."

After the meeting with Emily Hash, we were all given more water. The water was refreshing and as wonderful as it could have been, but it wasn't enough. The pain I am dealing with from the hunger is excruciating, but I don't want to complain. I am just happy that someone finally heard one of my stomach's overbearingly loud growls.

Mason leads us to one of the small flying rooms, what he calls an "elevator," and we all pile in.

Logan, never making eye contact with Mason, continues with his earlier statement. "You never did answer my question."

Mason reaches up and rubs his chin.

"Do you have any disorders?" Logan repeats.

Mason lowers his hand, and the elevator doors opened, leading us into another hallway with stone walls and a few doors here and there.

"Not really, but that doesn't mean anything." Mason clears his throat and asks us to follow him out. He senses our confusion in the silence and continues, "Just because I am not medically diagnosed with a disorder doesn't mean that I am perfect. I feel that everyone, in some way, shape, or form, has some sort of mental disorder. Whether it be mild or major, we all have our own problems."

In this moment, I have two thoughts: one of them being that Mason is lying in order to gain our trust, and the other being that he is actually telling the truth.

We have no way of knowing what he is really thinking; so we follow him up some stairs, through some halls, and into a large and empty room with tables lined up throughout. There is a large square column in the middle of the room and the tables. It is about the size of the first elevator we got in and painted the same color as the rest of the room, a grayish blue. The tile floors in this room match the ceiling in its blandness, but not color. The floors are white tiles while the ceiling is made up of gray paneling.

Mason continues his marching and allows his voice to boom through the room. "Follow me, and I can get Sarah to get you guys some food." We follow him to the sound of pots and pans rattling. Mason calls out, "Sarah!" His voice echoes through the room and bounces off the walls. "Hey!"

We turn the corner to find another set of counters with a set of glass panels over empty silver buckets and a large lady bent over, storing pots underneath a counter in the back. She sings out "Dinner is over!" in a way that I have only heard from Bestellen officials. The accents are shockingly similar. Never before have I ever heard someone other than officials or Metropolis inhabitants speak with such an accent.

We stand and wait on her, looking around and observing our surroundings. Sam and I look over to each other and share a silent expression of "What are we waiting on?"

The woman pushes herself up to a standing position using the steel counter and turns to look at us with a surprised expression. "Cole! Who are these lovely young kids?"

She hobbles over to us, and Major Mason chuckles, replying, "These 'kids' just came from Bestellen, believe it or not." Sarah's eyes grow, and her jaw drops as Mason asks her for some food for us.

Sarah turns on her heel and makes her way over to the large steel refrigerator. "Of course! Anything for these poor brave souls." She pulls the doors open and disappears behind them. "How long have they been out there? They need some meat on those bones! But at the same time, I doubt that stuffing them would be the best thing . . . Maybe I could . . ."

She turns around with a large tub of some sort of purple fruit cut into little bits. Sarah pops off the lid and smiles down at the fruit. "Ah, you should enjoy these." She pulls out a few slices and hands one slice to each of us. "Go ahead and try some. I will go and get some plates."

The three of us are too hungry to question what we are eating. Sarah fixes each of us a plate full of slices, and we all sit down to eat. I feel my stomach start to reject the new food, but I don't care. I pile each piece in as fast as I can, producing an odd gurgling feeling that I have felt multiple times before. I have gone days and days without eating before, but I have never had to go that long without food and do that many acts of physical exertion. We walked for miles and miles, we climbed trees, and we ran for the last two days—and without food? That is a ridiculous amount of calories expended with no promise of their return.

After minutes of nonstop eating by the three of us, Mason speaks up. "Emily will be sending me your sleeping arrangements tonight. Until then, I can take you guys up when you are done eating and show you around the sleeping quarters." He goes on to explain that their sleeping quarters are arranged based on gender, marital status, superiority, and career. For example, families bunk together. As Mason tells us what our sleeping arrangements will be, I see Sam take a break from shoveling food to crack open his case and sneak one of his vials into his pocket. He closes his case immediately and turns back to his food like he hadn't ever stopped eating.

Sam sees me staring at him and gives me as much of a closed-mouth smile as he can without letting food spill out of his cheeks. I chuckle as Mason tells me that I will be bunking with a few girls from the age of eighteen to twenty-one. The maximum number of residents per room is seven people, but the average is five. There is a dorm head for each section, along with coordinators. Everyone, by this age, usually knows what they are to be doing every day; but Sam, Logan, and I are all an exception.

Cole, after thanking Sarah for the food, takes us all to one of the bunks' hallways. People around our age crowd the open way and mingle as if this is something they do every night. I look around to see women taller than me, shorter than me, stouter than me, but none skinnier than me. I feel like I stick out like a sore thumb. Yes, I come from a place where eating more than two meals a day is unheard of, but that doesn't mean I am any less than them.

At least that is what I have to keep telling myself.

My dad would say differently. He used to always criticize my weight. He thought that my being so skinny made him look bad, not that he ever helped bring home food. Compared with most of the other people in Bloot, I am a very healthy-looking individual. If it wasn't for Derek showing me how to hunt, I know for a fact that neither my dad nor I would be alive. The only sort of food my dad ever brought home was distilled grain mash. I brought home meals at least three times a week, whether it be squirrels, rabbits, or larger game like the occasional deer.

Considering hunting is illegal in Bloot, bringing home a deer is not an easy task. You have to carry it through the woods, sneak it past any and every official, make sure you go nowhere near any security camera, and ensure no one sees you with it. Word travels fast in Bloot; one blabbermouth will spread the word to all, and next thing you know, you will have twenty starving mill workers at your door begging for food.

Before Mom and Steven, my brother, passed away, we had at least one piece of food a day. Mom brought in enough labor for one meal for each of us a day, while Dad's labor brought in enough for a few meals a week. Usually, Dad used his credits to bring home alcohol against Mom's wishes. He claimed that his "juice" was the only way he could handle living in Bloot.

He would complain all day long about Bloot and how privileged all the other states were. "The constant state of destitute that Meir keeps us in is . . . *horrid*." Dad wouldn't say "horrid." He had a large reservoir of harsh words he would rather use. Mom used to beg him not to be so harsh with his words in front of Steven and me, but he wouldn't listen.

He wouldn't listen.

He never listened.

My train of thought is interrupted by Yate speed walking through a few people and over to Mason. He straightens up and murmurs something to Mason that I can't make out.

"Okay," Mason answers. "Kids, I have to go. I should be back shortly. Until then, go socialize. Make yourselves at home." They turn and make their way through the sea of people and out of sight.

The three of us stand awkwardly, watching the other Berglanders mingle.

"So," Sam chuckles, "um, how do you guys feel about all of this?"

Still in disbelief at what has happened in the last few days, I shrug. Sam continues staring into the crowd while Logan and I exchange a nervous look.

"Hey!" a male voice cries out in what sounds like joy. We turn to our left and see two guys around our age walking toward us. The same voice chuckles. "Are you guys new here, or have I just never seen you before?" He extends his hand toward Logan and smiles at us all. "My name is Caine." He nods over to the slightly taller boy beside him. "And this is Grayson."

We all shake hands and introduce ourselves. Grayson seems slightly on the quieter side, while Caine seems to be a social butterfly. Caine points around and names a bunch of people that I doubt will ever want to talk to us and acts like this is just one big welcoming party.

After a minute or two of Caine's sarcastic babbling and sneering, he realizes that he hadn't let us get a word in. "Oh man! Sorry, I should shut up." He smiles and lets his nose scrunch up as he tilts his head. "I just get really excited. So you guys are from Bestellen?"

His question feels like a jeer.

Logan nods in response. "Yeah."

Caine crosses his arms and smiles at us again. "Are you all from the same state?"

I shake my head, and Sam explains. "I'm from Bouw, Mavis is from Bloot, and Logan is from Minje."

Grayson and Caine both glance at each other. Grayson chimes in before Caine has the chance to blab off. "Were any of you affected by the bombings?"

The three of us jerk our heads back to him and mutter the same question in unison, "What?"

Sam raises his voice a bit to be heard over the hallway commotion. "What bombings?"

Both Grayson and Caine look to each other with wide eyes in disbelief. Caine turns back to us and tenses up a bit. "You don't know about the bombings?"

CHAPTER SEVEN

Logan

I scoff. "What are you talking about? What bombings?"

Grayson and Caine exchange another look. Caine's crossed arms tense up with the rest of his body, and Grayson looks at us with a certain sort of sympathy.

"You . . ." Grayson pauses and clears his throat. "You don't know about the bombings?"

All three of us shake our heads.

"No, we don't. Spit it out!" Sam growls.

Caine smirks. "Um, well, as you might know, Bergland and Bestellen have been at war for a while. Recently, a few of our bombs reached Minje and Bouw." He looks past us and scrunches his nose at Mavis. "None in Bloot, though."

Mavis, behind me, shifts her briefcase from one hand to another, muttering something under her breath.

I shift my focus from her back to the nonsense Caine is telling us. "What are you talking about?" I ask. "We haven't been bombed."

Caine squeezes his lips together and tilts his head. He squints at me, like I have just said something idiotic. "Um . . . yeah you have."

Grayson loosens up and smacks Caine in the chest with the back of his hand. "Hey, what if they didn't live near any of the bombings?" Grayson turns back to me. "You live in Minje, right?"

I nod. Unlike all of Caine's sneers, Grayson's words come off respectfully.

"Do you live near the middle or southern ends of the mountains?" Grayson asks.

My heartbeat grows louder in my head as I nod again. "Yes," I tell them. "At the southern tip."

Caine smiles and clears his throat nervously. "That sounds like the section that was bombed a couple months ago."

"Two months ago," Grayson corrects.

Two months ago?

The mountains?

Is that not . . . No, it couldn't be.

I shake my head and try to ignore the thoughts running through it. I take a deep breath and allow the question to escape my mouth. "Did you bomb one of our mines?"

They nod their heads and look to Sam. Caine uncrosses his arms and smirks over at Sam. "And you, you said you were from Bouw?" His smile grows even more smug as he folds his hands behind his back.

Sam nods.

"Do you live anywhere near the northeastern region?"

Sam nods again. His eyes grow bigger than I have ever seen them as he hesitantly answers Caine, "Yeah."

Caine opens his mouth to say something, but Grayson nudges him. Grayson shoots him a look saying something along the lines of "Be gentle."

Caine nods to Grayson, then looks back to Sam. "We bombed that whole region just a few weeks ago."

"Wait." Sam holds up one of his hands to Caine. "What did you bomb?"

Grayson and Caine turn to each other and mutter something.

Sam clutches his case with both hands. As his right eye begins to twitch, he stutters out, "A . . . a market?"

Mavis and I glance at each other, then back to Sam, Caine, and Grayson.

Caine nods his head, and Grayson gives Sam a nervous look. Grayson clears his throat again. "I think so. I thought you guys said that you didn't get bombed?"

Sam's eyes dart to the floor, then back and forth rapidly. He drops his briefcase to the floor and clenches his small and bony fists, though they are nowhere near as bony as Mavis's.

Mavis sets her briefcase on the floor also and touches Sam's back. She lets out a soft question, "Hey, are you—"

Sam's eyes dart up and over as he grits his teeth at the two boys. "You! You people killed my dad!" He rubs his eyes with the palms of his hands and groans. "I can't believe it! I thought it was a workplace accident!" He sucks in air and spits it out, seemingly unable to get his anger under control.

I watch as Grayson's eyes flick down to Sam's pocket. My eyes follow his gaze to the top part of a vial sticking out.

Grayson holds up his hands to show he isn't a threat to Sam, and he slowly speaks in a low and authoritative voice. "Hey, buddy, do you want to pull out one of your vials? One of the ones in your pocket?" Sam looks back to Grayson angrily, but concerned, as if he can't control himself. Grayson gives Sam a soft smile. "The medicine will help you feel better, and then we can talk."

Sam looks down to his pocket and pulls it out. He stares at the vial for a moment before sticking it into his leg. Sam's eyes close, and I watch the medicine drain from the clear glass tube. The vial empties itself completely and appears as if there was nothing there in the first place.

Sam pulls it out of his leg and walks over to one of the hallway walls. He lies up against it and slides down, just as Mavis did in the meeting room when she was injected.

Grayson looks around the hallway as he walks over to Sam. "It was a small dose. He should be able to talk and comprehend everything as he regularly would." Grayson brings Sam's briefcase over to him and sets it down beside him. "This sort of dose is just to help calm you, okay?"

Sam nods. He takes a deep breath. "It did." His eyes appear too heavy for him to hold up, but he keeps trying anyway. "This doesn't change the fact that . . ." Sam takes another deep breath and forces out the last few words, "You people killed my dad."

Grayson slides down the wall beside Sam and takes a seat. He sighs. "I'm sorry, Sam. This is war, and in war, deaths are almost inevitable. I am so sorry that your father was one of them." Grayson sighs again, this time looking to each one of us. "Truly, I am."

"Wait," Caine says, butting in. "How are you just now finding out about this? What did you think happened?"

Sam slowly raises his head and gives Caine a look that I can't describe. If I had to, I would use the phrase "Shut up, you idiot." But I don't think that phrase does this look justice.

Sam scoffs. "Nobody knew it was a bombing. We were told there was an incident in the marketplace due to someone not doing their job right. They said that because of that one person, we lost many loved ones." He weakly shakes his head and lets out a mixture of a sob and a growl. "It's not my fault no one told me the truth."

One, two, three.

One, two, three.

One, two, three.

I rub each of my fingernails over and over again as I try to keep myself from squeezing my eyes shut to blink. I consider using one of the few pocket-sized vials that the nurses gave me for my "moderate OCD," but I don't need them. I don't. The longer I rub my nails, the more I realize that I focus on doing this whenever I am nervous. But why would I be nervous?

Oh yeah . . .

I choke back the tears and force out the one thing I feel I need to say. "Your bombs killed my dad too."

Grayson, Caine, Mavis, and Sam all look to me at once. Mavis looks down to my hands and watches me rub my nails while Sam meets my eyes. Both he and I force our tears to stay in our eyes, but we can't help but let a few escape. Memories of my dad come flooding back—him telling me about my mom, him telling me about his childhood, his hugs, his stories of his times in the mines, even his corny jokes.

Mavis steps over to me and swallows. "What?"

I nod, keeping myself calm, and stand straight up, not falling under the weight of pain like I did the first time I found out Dad had died. "Yeah. My dad died in what I thought was a mining accident two months ago in the same place that you guys said you bombed." I chuckle, trying to ignore the feeling of a knife twisting and turning inside my heart. "I guess it wasn't an accident, huh?"

"Oh man." Grayson shakes his head in what looks like sorrow. "I am sorry. Again, we aren't aiming for innocent people. I am sorry that this happened."

"Oh yeah?" I scoff. "Then what were you aiming for? A marketplace?" I gesture to Sam. "Filled with people just trying to earn their way? A mine? Filled with people doing the same? What's next? Have you guys aimed for a hospital yet?" I clear my throat and swallow back what I can.

"Hey," Caine defensively stammers, "we . . . we weren't aiming for innocent people. We were aiming for—"

"Did any of you know your country was at war?" Grayson interrupts.

The three of us remain quite. The more I think about it, the more all of the signs point to a war. The way they were easing back on our rations, the abundance of officials, the early curfew . . .

"Why would the government hide a war from us?" I ask.

Sam and Mavis give each other a look of disbelief and confusion, just as another question comes flying out of Sam's mouth. "And how come you guys are bombing us? We haven't done anything!"

Caine squints at me and scoffs. "Really? Nothing? You guys don't know anything?"

Sam slowly stands up and gives Caine the awful glare that I can't describe. He crosses his arms and opens his mouth to say something; but before he can, a blaring alarm wails through the hallways, along with the white lights above us changing to a deep orange.

Everyone around speed walks through the hallways and past us.

Mavis tightens her grip on her case and shouts over the alarm, "What's going on?"

Grayson hands Sam's case to Sam, then yells something at Caine. Caine nods and stands in place even though the people rushing through the hallways make it hard for him.

Grayson turns to Sam, Mavis, and me. He barks orders over the sirens to follow him, so we do. Caine stays behind us the whole time to make sure none of us get stranded while Grayson leads us through the chaos. It feels like hundreds of people jog down the stairs beside us, trying to get through. Too many people to count.

Through the halls, down the stairs, into another set of stairs, down those stairs, and into a large room lined with bunk beds. The alarm is much softer in this room; and the orange lights have gotten gentler, warmer in tone, and more bearable. The room goes back as far as I can see and turns both ways at the end. We follow Grayson and walk through the lines and lines of beds and boxes, turn right, and walk through more lines of beds and boxes, then turn left and repeat the process.

As we walk through, I see a few men here and there who are wearing the same electronic wristbands that Emily Hash and Major Mason had, the hologram bands. Before I get the chance to ask about the men, Grayson looks over his shoulder at me and announces that we can stay with Caine and him for now.

We pull over to the right and stop on a few open beds. Caine passes Sam and walks over to one of the bottom bunks. "Here, Mavis, you can go ahead and have my bunk until you are assigned one." His smirk changes into a wink and makes everyone uncomfortable.

Mavis gives a shy smile and sets her case onto the ground. "Thank you, but I think I am okay right now."

Caine is taken aback by her "No, thank you," but he nods it off and turns back to the Sam and me. "The bed is open for either of you if you want."

"Thanks," I answer, not ever considering his sarcastic pity offer.

After a moment or two of watching people file into the bunker, Sam catches my attention. His twitching seems to be getting a little worse.

He brings the palm of his hand up to his eye and rubs as he squeaks out. "So is anyone going to tell us what is going on?"

Caine chuckles, earning a glare from Grayson. Caine raises his hands in playful surrender and backs off to go sit on his bed.

Grayson shakes his head and turns back to Sam. He points to the overhead speakers above us. "That siren? That's our 'bomb threat' alarm. Whenever that alarm goes off, everyone immediately comes down to these bunkers and prepares for the worst. Nine times out of ten, when that siren goes off, we are bombed."

Caine, lying back in his bed with his hands behind his head, retorts, "You know how you said Bestellen hadn't done anything? Well, guess who forces us down here at least three times a week?"

"Shut up, Jacobs!" Grayson growls at Caine. "It's not like it's their fault. For goodness' sake, they didn't even know about the war!"

Caine lies in his bed, silent, but unaffected. His smirk remains resting on his face.

"I'm sorry about him." Grayson scratches the back of his head and stares at the ground. He takes a deep breath and looks back up, past me, and then to Mavis. "I know you must have some questions. Are there any you want to ask me?" He moves his focus from Mavis to Sam to me.

When our eyes meet, Caine sits up on his squeaky bed and points around. "Those guys standing around the room will take attendance once the doors close and help keep everyone organized." He turns to us. "Just in case you were wondering."

The three of us ignore Caine and turn back to Grayson. Before anyone gets to ask a question, an announcement by a woman's voice comes from the overhead speakers. "The doors will be closing in five minutes."

Grayson glances around to the people flooding in and takes a seat on the bunk above Caine's. "Once those doors close, they don't open until the threat is clear." He gestures forward to the empty set of bunks in front of him. "You guys can take a seat if you want. No one uses those."

Sam and Mavis take a seat on the bottom while I take a seat on the top. The view from this height is better than the view from the floor, but not by much. I can see that there is a lot more people than I originally had thought and that this system is actually really organized. Everyone seems to have their own set of beds and know where they are to be going, which is really impressive for such a large number of people.

The woman's voice echoes through the halls once again. "The doors will be closing in four minutes."

I watch as many of the people settling into their assigned quarters talk, just as they did back upstairs by their sleeping quarters, as if nothing is wrong. I have to wonder if what they are telling us is really true. Who is in the wrong? Bestellen? Or Bergland?

"The doors will be closing in three minutes."

The first bomb drops seconds after the announcement finishes. I feel the sound of the explosion in my stomach and chest. Everyone on the top bunks hops down and sits with the person on the bottom bunk. I follow their lead.

"The doors will be closing in two minutes."

The second, third, and fourth bombs drop. Each explosion is louder than the other. I feel the ground shake and hear the walls of the bunker crumble. I look around to see Sam holding Mavis in his arms; both of them have their eyes squeezed shut in terror. I see Grayson and Caine sitting in the bottom bunk and staring at us. I look around and see that no one else in this room besides us three seems to be nervous.

More bombs drop. More terror enters.

"The doors are closing. The doors are closing."

The doors close.

More bombs drop, and a low murmuring floats through the room as we wait for the threat to end.

"Hey," Grayson whispers, "guys, you don't need to worry. This bunker, along with the rest of Bergland, was made to shake and sway with any sort of attack or natural disaster."

Mavis is quiet. She remains still, with her head in Sam's lap. Sam's head rests on Mavis's back as he takes large, loud, and deep breaths. Both of them hold their hands over their ears, trying to block out reality.

"What about escape routes? Just in case something does happen?" I ask Grayson. Caine raises one eyebrow at me and smiles, and I can't figure out why.

Grayson nods. "There are exits—"

He is interrupted by another bomb but continues as if nothing happened. "There are several exits in each branch of the bunker, as well as several for every branch on every floor. If you can imagine a way out, we have it. We even have one running underneath one of our mountain's rivers."

Another bomb drops. Sam's breathing is heavy, but steady. Mavis's is short, quick, and shaky. "How did you make all of these tunnels? All of these rooms? Floors? How have you powered all of this?"

This time, Grayson chuckles. "The tunnels are just old mines that we have added on to and perfected, just like most of the rooms and floors we have. We get our power from a few devices that we have placed in our mountains' rivers and waterfalls and a few of our windmills that are hidden throughout the mountain ranges."

Caine adds, "We have them placed to where the wind tunnels itself through, directly to the mills. It's more efficient that way."

"Do the bombs not affect your . . . things?"

Grayson shakes his head. "No, they don't affect our . . . things. Not usually anyways, and if they do, we go up and fix them when the time is right."

"What would you do if they all got destroyed at once?"

"Well," Caine answers, "if that ever did happen, which it won't, we have backup power stored for cases like that."

A few more bombs drop, earning a jolt of fear from Sam and Mavis.

"Oh yeah," Caine adds. "Grayson forgot to mention our solar panels on the sides of the mountains and how we have machines that filter oxygen through the mountains to the floors and bunker."

Grayson shoots Caine another look but shoves his comment off.

"What about the medicine?" Sam moans, still in his defense position with his hands over his ears and his eyes squeezed shut. He lifts up his head a bit but keeps himself sealed off. "What about the medicine they gave us?"

"What about it?" Caine snorts.

"Where . . ." Sam takes a deep breath and forces out his words as fast as he can. "Where did you get it? How did you make it?"

A few of the men with the wrist cuffs begin walking our way with their hologram screens pulled up. They walk by bunks and pull people's names up to check them off. Grayson ignores their approaching presence and answers, "We have a team of scientists that help engineer these sorts of things. They came up with the formula a long time ago with the help of their genetically modified plants and natural plants found in the woods."

One of the men walking around taking attendance stops by our bunk. Without even giving us a second look, he types something into his hologram. "Names?"

"Grayson Andrews."

"Caine Jacobs."

I follow their lead and answer, "Logan Forge."

We wait for Sam and Mavis to answer, but they don't. I turn to the man and tell him their names, but he takes a moment to stare at them before listening to me. "I need to see their faces," he says.

I nudge Sam in the arm and whisper to him that he needs to look up for a moment.

He does, but for only one moment. Sam swings his head up from Mavis's back, and with his eyes closed, he smiles. I tap Mavis on the shoulder, and she sits up straight. Her hands remain over her ears, but her eyes open, unlike Sam's.

The man nods his head and walks off to check the other bunks, leaving Mavis and Sam to go back to their "crippled in fear" position. We wait in silence, listening to each bomb drop one after another, each shaking the mountains. I lose track of time as I think about everything and wait for the walls to cave in.

Why do I feel the need to squeeze my eyes closed when I blink?

Another bomb drops.

Why do I feel the need to rub my fingernails?

The lights in the bunker flicker, and one of the men who took attendance walks by.

What am I going to do? Just start a new life in a mountain? What are these two going to do? Stick a needle into their leg every time they get upset? What about me? When do I know when to use the medicine?

Another bomb drops, earning a smug chuckle from Caine. Grayson shoots him a puzzled look, but it does nothing. A shuffling beside me grabs my attention, and I watch as Mavis pulls a vial out of her pocket and sticks herself in the leg. Still tense, she sets the vial down on the bed between Sam and me, then lies back down in his lap. Mavis puts her hands back over her ears and lies in that same position that she has been in this whole time, but her breathing becomes much more steady, as if her holding her ears is just a precaution. Sam puts his hand on her back and rubs up and down, just as my mother used to do for me when I had trouble sleeping at night.

I watch as Sam keeps his eyes closed and takes deep breaths, trying to calm himself. I wonder why he isn't taking the medicine or if he still feels the effects from his earlier dose. I wonder if his BPD is really as mild, as the nurses say it is. I wonder if my OCD is really as moderate as they say it is. The nurses and doctors said that Bestellen kicks out people with disorders that aren't manageable without medicine. What do they use to determine what is severe and what isn't?

Another bomb drops.

How do they choose who they throw out?

The lights flicker.

Why do they kick people out?

Another man walks by.

"Why don't they want us?"

Grayson looks back up from the floor to me, surprised at my question.

Caine shakes his head and loses his smirk. For one moment, he answers seriously, "They think that people with disorders are . . . 'hindrances' for any advancements in their society. That, and they are too cheap to help people who need it."

Taken aback by Caine's sincere, yet slightly cocky answer, I nod.

Shaking his head and maintaining focus on his shoes on the floor, Grayson sighs. "Their twisted ideas seem logical to them." He lifts his head and meets my eyes. "And that is one of the reasons their reign has got to come to an end."

CHAPTER EIGHT

Sam

I lie restlessly on the bunk above Mavis, trying to keep my eyes closed and sleep. The bombings stopped hours ago, but when the announcement came on the overhead speakers that the threat was cleared, they also announced that we would be staying down here for the rest of the night until the structure has been checked for security and stabilization.

"Don't worry," Grayson tells us. "They always check after bombings. Everything will be back to normal in the morning."

The morning . . .

I can usually tell what time it is by looking out of my window at my house, but here? Where there are no windows? Where there is no sunlight? No moonlight? It's just a dark gray ceiling with an extremely dim orange light lining the edges of the room. As I look around, I can see the bunks all around me enough that I wouldn't run into them if I got up to walk around, but not enough that I could make out any details of the bed or the person sleeping in it.

I lie here, on the mattress with a spring digging into my back, with my eyes squeezed closed, listening to Mavis's rapid and short breaths and the light squeaking noises of the rest of people shifting in their beds. Logan is on the bottom bunk to our right while Caine and Grayson are sleeping in the bunks to our left. The front branch of the bunker is packed. Every bunk bed is occupied. The branch we are in has a lot more room than the first and second branches, which means we have beds to spare.

I listen to Mavis's small and slight murmurs beneath me. She murmurs something I cannot make out. It is probably something about how crazy this all is. Probably something about her family she may never see again. Probably about something that is making her nervous or scared. Probably something about Bestellen or Bergland. Maybe something about Bestellen *and* Bergland.

Beneath me, Mavis's bloodcurdling scream screeches through the room, spooking everyone in its path. I feel her jump up in her bed, causing the whole bunk to shake. She gasps for air and begins to wheeze once again. Before either Logan or I have the chance to do anything, two girls hop down from the bunks in front of us and come rushing over.

Peeking over the side of my top bunk, I see one of the girls rummaging through her greenish-brown bag and the other leaning inward to Mavis. The girl who is rummaging through her bag looks up at me and smiles while the other one, the older-looking one, continues trying to calm Mavis.

"Hey, hey, shh . . . It's okay."

Mavis, no longer screaming, slows her breathing a small bit. Her hands find their way through her hair as her fists clench, seemingly pulling some of her hair out of her scalp. She holds this position as the girl who is going through her bag pulls out one of the vials and hands it to the other woman, who sits down on the bunk with Mavis. The woman waves off the girl holding the vial and continues to whisper to Mavis. "Hey, listen, if you want some medicine, we can give it to you. But only if you want it."

I watch the girl holding the vial out toward them, and I watch Mavis and the woman's heads underneath me. Mavis shakes her head and slowly releases her tight grip on her hair. "No. It-it's fine. I'm fine." She takes another deep breath and rubs her eyes with the palms of her hands.

The woman beside her nods and places her hand on Mavis's leg. "Okay, okay. I want you to know that this will get better."

Mavis continues to rub her eyes. She takes a deep breath and scrunches her face. "What?"

"Your anxiety," the woman answers. Two men in white clothing come rushing over with a bag but get waved off by the woman sitting with Mavis. The men nod to her and walk off as the woman continues, "It will get better once you know how to handle it."

Mavis lowers her hands and sniffles. She looks down to the woman's hand on her leg. "What do you mean 'handle it'?" Mavis looks up and points to the vial in the other girl's hand. "Take more medicine? Stick a needle in my leg every time I get upset?"

"No, no, honey," the woman answers. "One of the reasons it is so bad right now is because you have never experienced it before. This is all new to you. Once you find what soothes you and what helps you, you can get past the worrying . . ." The woman slowly reaches for Mavis's hand but hesitates. She and Mavis make eye contact before the woman takes her hand. When she does, Mavis doesn't seem to mind. "And the nightmares. They won't be perfect, but they won't be nearly as bad."

Mavis looks down to the woman's hand and stays quiet.

The other girl slips the vial back into her bag and joins in, adding, "She's right." Mavis looks back up to the girl, earning an easy smile from her. "Trust me."

They wait for a moment before leaving our bunk to make sure Mavis is okay. When they leave, Mavis lies right back down. Though she lies down, I can tell that she never fully goes back to sleep.

Sometime in the night, I managed to doze off. I only realize when my eyes flutter open, and I find myself in the fully lit bunker, along with everyone else who is rising with me. I wipe my eyes as Caine and Grayson both hop out of their beds and stretch beside us. I look over to Logan, who is holding his pillow over his face, and over to the girls from last night. The woman who sat with Mavis is gone, but the girl with the bag is rising just like Caine and Grayson. After a few minutes, I sit up and look around to see most of the people filing out of the room. Everyone who has already left piled their bedsheets at the end of the bed in a ball, leaving their mattress and pillows stripped.

"Look who's up!" Caine groans as he pulls his arms behind his back. "Are you ready for your first day?" I glance over to him, then to Grayson.

Grayson nods. "Good morning."

The bed below me creaks as Mavis sits up.

Grayson smiles down to her. "Good morning."

I crawl down the ladder and stretch a bit with Caine and Grayson, earning a chuckle from Caine. "These mattresses are *super*comfy, right?" He groans, "Every time I sleep down here, I end up with a crick in my neck. And my back. And everything else."

After Caine finishes complaining and trying to be funny, I head over to Logan.

"Hey." I knee his mattress and shake his bed. "Get up."

Logan grumbles something and slowly pulls the pillow off his face. He turns his head to me and stares at me with large purple bags under his eyes.

I take a step back. "Are you okay?"

"Yeah," he moans. "No sleep."

I nod my head. Logan rises and follows me over to where Caine, Mavis, and Grayson are. The room has almost completely cleared of people, and every bed has been stripped, and every sheet has been balled up and put at the end of the bed.

I point to the sheets at the end of Grayson's bed. "Do we need to do that?"

"Yes," Grayson answers. "We have workers that come through after we leave to take the dirty sheets and change them out for clean ones."

Logan turns around and heads back to his bed to take off his sheets, as the rest of us do likewise. As I finish rolling my sheets into a ball, a few men and one woman with those hologram bands walk by us, checking each bunk. At first, one of the men stops and looks us up and down, but Grayson nods him off. When they all leave, Grayson turns back to us. "Are you all ready for breakfast? We can take you up when you are ready and show you the restrooms on the way."

"No, that's okay," Yate Groves interrupts as he walks up from behind us and closes his holographic screen. Groves turns back to Caine and Grayson. "You two can go ahead to breakfast. I will take care of them."

Caine shrugs. "Okay." He walks off immediately.

"Are you sure?" Grayson looks from Groves to us, as if asking permission to leave.

Yate nods, and Grayson leaves.

"Okay, I don't know if you guys remember me, but I am Private Yate Groves." He extends his hand to Logan, shakes it rapidly, then does the same to Mavis and me. "But you can call me Yate. Or Groves. Or Yate Groves. Just don't call me Private. I don't like that. Major Mason does, but I don't. He calls me Private sometimes just to get on my nerves, but whatever." Yate shakes his head and places his hands on his hips in a proud manner. "Anyways, welcome to Bestellen!"

Logan lets out an unsure chuckle. "Thanks?"

"You're welcome! All right, before we get started, I need to ask you guys a few questions. Well, 'need'? No. More like 'want to.'" Yate sits down on one of the stripped beds and pats it. "Come! Sit! Or go over to the one right there and sit. Or stand. Do whatever makes you most comfortable."

We scramble and end up all sitting on the one bed across from Yate. Once we get "comfortable," Yate picks back up. "Okay! So my first question, how did you sleep last night?"

A pause. No one answers, so I shrug.

"Ah," Yate chuckles. "Would that be a good shrug or a bad shrug?"

Logan meets Yate's eyes and stares at him for a moment. Not glaringly, nor in a loving way, but more in a blank and mindless way.

"Oh. No sleep? I understand. These beds can be pretty difficult to rest in."

Mavis shoots him a look as if he was crazy.

Yate's eyes grow wide, and he jolts with what seems to be surprise. "Oh yeah! And those dreadful bombings. I forgot for a split second that you all are not used to the attacks. I am so sorry about that. I was going to ask about the bombings next! Well, not about the bombings, more about how you guys handled them. Are you okay? Do you have any questions?"

Yes. We do.

Or I do.

I want to know if we will be subjected to such fear every night.

I want to know how safe we really are, not how safe everyone hopes or thinks we are.

I want to know when the war will be over . . .

War . . .

Up until last night, I didn't even know we were at war. I want to know what caused the war! I want to know how many innocent people have died! I want to know . . . "Who dropped the first bomb?"

Those words jump out of my mouth before I get the chance to stop them—not that it is a bad question; it just isn't the first one I wanted to ask.

Groves takes a deep breath and looks to each of us on this bed, as if it was time for a long and hard explanation. But with the few minutes I have just spent with Yate alone without Major Mason, I can guess that he will turn this answer into a very long one.

"Bestellen did," he answers.

I guess I was wrong in assuming he would elaborate. Why did he elaborate on something as trivial as his name? I don't know. Why isn't he elaborating on the things I need him to? I still don't know.

Logan croaks, "Why?"

"Before we lived in the mountains, we had multiple aboveground bunkers, cities, and towns—all of which were hidden very well, though not well enough. When the Amiables took over, they captured most of the Diligent and stole all of our land. Some of the Diligent, however, managed to escape and created some of their own hidden cities."

I look from Groves to Mavis to Logan. Each of us has a mixture of confusion and suspense written on our faces.

Not taking time to breathe between words, Groves continues, "The Amiables, oblivious to the Diligent's cities being built, then built themselves a huge wall, which took ten years to complete, around their country that spans about two million square miles. They built up their cities, their population, their military, and their weapons. Years passed, and somehow, the Amiables found a few of our small cities and bunkers. They bombed them all. To this day, there is nothing left."

"What?" I protest. "Then how did any of you survive?"

"Lucky for us, we had already started building Bergland from old mines, and Bestellen had no idea. There were over one hundred workers in those mines during the bombings and even more people outside of the cities, hunting, harvesting, and planning where to put the next hidden cities. After the bombings, everyone salvaged everything they could and made their way to the mountains."

I shake my head, trying to prevent the twitching I feel rising in my eye. "That was years ago. Why are the bombings still happening?"

"Yeah," Logan adds. "And how did they even find out about the mountains?"

"One day, we sent one of our rescue teams out to look for people that Bestellen had exiled, and I guess we got way too close to the wall. An official saw our van and had someone track us. They watched us enter one of our tunnels. After that, they began bombing us again. We destroyed that tunnel, but they still knew we had ways in and out. Within a week, they had sensor bombs placed throughout those woods that would blow up our vans if we drove past a certain point. These bombs don't harm any wildlife, just large and steel vehicles."

"Wait." Logan holds up his hand, trying to get Groves to slow down. "How did . . . when did they start throwing 'us' out?"

"Well, let's see." Groves holds up his fingers and starts counting them off. "It was after Meir II, but it wasn't immediately after . . . They started using people as bait to draw us out of hiding a few years after Meir II came into power."

"Bait?" Mavis queries. Though she sits in between Logan and me on the bed, her silence makes her appear invisible. "What do you mean 'bait'? I thought they threw us out because we were too 'expensive' to take care of?"

Groves nods. "That was originally the plan, but they decided to use you guys as bait to draw us out so that they could get the upper hand. I am sorry. I want to remind you all that here at Bergland, no one agrees with Bestellen's ideals and morals. Just because you have something that others have deemed undesirable doesn't mean that it is. I hope you all realize that. I also hope you all realize that in one way or another, everyone has some sort of disorder. For example, Grayson Andrews, the trainer you bunked next to last night, he has a slight case of OCD." Groves chuckles. "Every now and then, I will catch him fixing the weights to all face the same way."

"Wait, a trainer?" Mavis asks. "How old is he? I was under the impression that he was eighteen or so."

Groves stands, pulling his pants up and cracking his knuckles. "Yes, he is twenty. We needed a new trainer, and he was the best person for the job. Here, once you finish basic schooling, you get to choose your career path. Once you choose your path, depending on your choice, you either go directly into training for the career, jump directly into the career, or go to further schooling for your career. Grayson finished schooling when he was eighteen and was ready to start being a trainer by then. He works with the younger people as of right now. Ages ten to fifteen."

Everyone follows Yate and stands. We all stretch a bit, and Yate picks up talking again. "Okay, onto my next question. Are you guys ready to come upstairs and eat?"

"Yes," I blurt, earning a chuckle from them all.

Groves leads us through the maze of beds and tells us a little about how our day is going to go. After taking us to the restrooms to wash up, he takes us to a large set of stairs that we climb for what seems like ten minutes. After we finish hiking, Groves leads us to an elevator. Never before have I been so relieved to climb into one of these flying boxes.

Groves explains that everyone in Bergland, even the newcomers, have to go through schooling. He says, "Even though you guys just got here, you are going to have to go to classes, but don't worry! Today, you can hang out wherever you feel most comfortable, and then tonight, I can give you guys a schedule."

First, we will have to learn some basic history. Then move onto other subjects. According to Yate, every age level goes to one of the training rooms at least twice a week to exercise. After an original assessment of the children when they are younger, they are put with a group of people that are similar in skills as themselves if they choose so, or they could request to be put in with their friends.

Either way, everyone in Bergland has the opportunity to run, play, exercise, or do whatever they want in there. Every citizen is taught basic self-defense from a young age, when to use it, and when not to. After they finish schooling and basic training, they get to choose whether they want to fight or do something else because Bergland has never gotten to the point where they had to force their people to fight, unlike Bestellen apparently.

After we make it to the cafeteria, Groves leads us through the tables packed with people to a long line of even more people. The line leads up to the glass casing where Sarah, the food lady, works, scooping each person a scoop of what I can only hope is food. We grab a tray at the beginning of the line and carry it up to her. As soon as she sees Mavis, who is in front of both Logan and me, she lights up with a large and toothy smile. Her dark hair manages to stay in its netted covering and its tied-up position as she jumps. "Oh, honey! Hi! How are you? Mavis, is it?" She looks down the line to Logan and me. "And the boys! Oh, hello! What would you all like today?"

Groves leans forward to look at the food as he is in front of Mavis in the line. "They will want some beans and mash. A good bit of it too." Groves gives her a kind smile and scoots forward, away from us. He doesn't grab a tray, which makes me think he must have already eaten.

Sarah returns Groves's smile and chuckles, "Oh, okay!" She takes Mavis's tray and plops down a large scoop of a thick yellow fluff and a side of what looks just like parsle beans, the same type of beans that we ate at my house for dinner at least three times a week. "Here you go! Thank you, kiddies! Come back and visit me when you can!"

We all give her a smile and a thank-you as we walk away with our trays of heavy food over to another woman sitting in front of a computer.

"Names?" she asks us.

Groves speaks up. "Mavis Wamsley, Logan Forge, and Samuel Beckman."

The woman nods to us. "Got it. Have a good day."

We follow Groves past the woman and to the middle of the room. "Every time you get your food, you'll check in with whoever is at that computer and tell her your names so that she can mark you down. You will receive free food until you finish your schooling, which none of you have to worry about yet. Okay?" He stops and looks down at his little computer watch. "Oh. Okay, guys, I have to go. Before I do, would you like me to help you find a table? By yourselves or with someone you know?"

We all look around to find that every table appears to be full, and many of the people are staring at us. Out of the corner of my eye, I notice a hand shooting up out of the crowd and a woman waving at us. Groves turns around and points at the woman. "Hey, I think you guys would like it over there with them."

Mavis gives a slight smile as she adjusts her grip on her tray. "Those are the girls from last night."

The woman at the table hops up and walks over to us as casually and yet giddily if possible. "Hello, do you remember me?" the woman asks Mavis.

Mavis nods. "Yes, ma'am. I do." She pauses a moment before nodding to the woman. "Hi."

"Hello." The woman smiles to each of us before gesturing over her shoulder. "Do you guys want to come sit with me? It is just the other girl from last night and myself sitting there right now."

Logan and I glance at each other and give a shrug. Mavis looks to us, then back to Groves. "Can we?"

"Of course! You will be in good hands." Groves pats the woman on the shoulder and thanks her for coming over. He bids us adieu and marches off, typing something into his hologram.

We follow the woman, and the three of us sit on one side of the rectangular table while the other two sit on the other side.

The girl who was rummaging through her bag last night is small. Shorter than Mavis and skinny, but not as skinny as Mavis. Her hair is cut short up above her shoulders and has more of a dark purplish tint than I am used to seeing. The shininess and sheen of her hair seems almost unreal in its silkiness and perfection. The woman has longer and lighter brown hair, which looks more like a natural color than that of the girl beside her.

Logan takes a seat on one side of Mavis while I sit on the other, like we have been doing since we met. We all set our trays down and examine our food for a moment before taking the brave step to try it.

"Don't worry, it tastes a lot better than it looks," the deep violet-haired girl garbles with her mouth half-full of yellow fluff.

The woman beside her shoots her a jokingly baffled look. "Mandy, you do realize that this is their first impression of you, right?"

The girl nods and swallows her food quickly. "Yeah, sorry. Hi." She extends her hand across the table and gives a big smile, even bigger than Sarah's. "I'm Mandy Horrace."

The woman beside her pulls back Mandy's arm. "Put your hand down. It isn't clean."

"Well, my bad," Mandy grumbles. "I was just trying to be nice." She looks back to us and smiles again and swings her arms into an open and grandiose position. "Welcome to Bergland!"

The woman chuckles. "Welcome to Bergland indeed. My name is Janice Ludley. I am one of the teachers and coordinators here. It's so nice to meet you all." She looks to each of us and gives a slight nod, but once she gets to me, she looks back down at our trays. "Oh my! You guys must be starving! Go ahead! Eat up!"

I look down at my food and unwrap the silverware, trying to figure out whether or not this is real food. I don't hesitate for long because at this point, I am hungry enough that I will eat my napkin if I have to. Within seconds, the three of us have our mouths full of the yellow fluff and are loving every bit of it. The parsle beans that we eat after the fluff are just as good, maybe even better because of how familiar they are.

"So," Janice says in between bites of food, "it must have been pretty difficult getting through the woods to the mountains. I can't imagine what you all had to go through."

I try to swallow the food so I can comment on what Janice says, but every time I swallow, I take another bite without any thought. My mouth is staying full, and so is my stomach. After just a few bites of food, I feel sick. I feel like I have just stuffed myself.

"Yeah," Mandy forces out, still holding food in her mouth. "What kind of animals did you guys run into? Or did you run into any at all?" Janice narrows her eyes at Mandy, who quickly swallows her food and smiles back to Janice. "Sorry."

"We did." Logan finishes chewing. "We ran into a few things. Even a pack of something we didn't get to see."

Mavis nods her head in agreement with Logan's statement as she keeps her mouth full.

Mandy swallows her food loudly and looks back to Logan. "Wait, what do you mean a pack of something? How do you know if you didn't see them?"

Logan and I look to each other. Suddenly, the sounds of Charlie's horrid screams echo through my head. Logan and I look back to our food, waiting for the other to explain so we wouldn't have to. I guess Logan gets that I won't be the one who says it, so he does.

"We heard the animals rip apart another kid."

Janice's jaw lowers as well as her whole expression.

Logan, avoiding eye contact, swallows another bite and continues, "His name was Charlie. He ran off to get away from us and found the beasts lurking less than half a mile away from our camp."

"I'm . . ." Janice stumbles to find the right words. "I'm so sorry."

We nod. I answer, "So are we."

After a few seconds of silence, Mandy finishes her food and clears her throat. "Did you run into anything else?"

Logan nods, still shoveling food into his mouth. He, unlike myself, is taking time in between bites to answer their questions and hold a conversation. "Mainly a pack of giant rats. I ran into them once by myself, and then we all ran into them again." He chuckles and gestures to Mavis. "That is actually how we met."

I manage to stop inhaling my food for a moment and laugh with Logan. "Yeah, Mavis found the pack of rats, and then we found her." I watch as Mavis scratches her arm for a split second and squeeze her fist closed the next, as if she is trying to keep herself from scratching.

"Before the rats, Sam said that he had a run-in with a huge cat." Logan looks to me and nods back to the girls. "Go ahead."

"I did." I set my fork down as all eyes fall upon me. "When I first woke up, I was wandering around, and then I felt something stalking me. Next thing you know, I am being chased through the woods by a giant orange-and-black-striped cat with teeth as long as my arms." I hold up my arm that was torn apart by the briars and take a look at it.

I hadn't yet noticed how much scabbing was going on. I lower my arm and scoop up another fork full of beans. "I ended up getting caught on briars and having the cat slowly approach me. Man, I don't know why it just didn't eat me immediately, but it didn't. The only reason I got away was because someone started shooting at me right before the cat took his chance. After the gunfire started, I ran one way, and the cat ran another."

I force the food into my mouth and look up to Mandy, who watches me with awe. Janice, beside her, smiles at me. "Wow. That is crazy. Were you close to the wall? Is that where the bullets came from?"

I nod, swallowing the last bit of my food as Mandy covers her mouth and chuckles. Mandy looks from me to Logan, earning confused stares from us all. She looks back to me, still covering her mouth as Janice's eyes follow hers. Janice chuckles as I shake my head and slide my tray forward. "What?"

Mandy removes her hand from her mouth and points behind us. Logan, Mavis, and I all turn around to see a group of about eight girls piled up at one table, all looking, smiling, giggling, and waving at us. They can't be more than fifteen years old.

Baffled, I turn back to the others at our table. Logan and Mavis look just as confused as I do. "What are they looking at?" I ask.

Mandy lets out one big laugh. "What do you mean 'what are they looking at'? Obviously you!"

Janice nods in agreement, but with less enthusiasm.

"Oh my!" Mandy throws up one of her hands and starts dramatically fanning herself. She mockingly moans, "Look at those cute newbies!"

Janice elbows Mandy and playfully hisses through her teeth, "Hey, cut it out."

Mandy rubs her arm and laughs. "We both know that's what they are saying. I'm just the only one who would point it out."

Janice rolls her eyes. "Sorry about her. She is a little . . . I don't know how I would describe it."

"Fabulous?" Mandy suggests. "Peerless? Perceptive? Extraordinary?"

"Crazy?" She looks past us, then to the girls at the table behind us. "And those girls? Don't worry about them."

A semiloud anthem from the overhead speakers interrupts Janice. Everyone in the cafeteria stands and turns to the center of the room, where hologram screens pop up on every side of the large boxlike post. Beside the post hangs a large dark gray flag with their golden two-hammered seal on it.

The song halts, and a man comes onto the hologram screen. "Good morning, Bergland. I hope you are all doing well. I am General Luke Wilson with your morning announcements. We are all happy to announce that we survived another bombing from Bestellen with no damage to any of our major structures. We do have two windmills down between a few valleys, but other than those two easily repairable machines, we are perfectly fine."

The only part of the man that is visible is his torso and his extremely thick head. From the fine and fancy suit he is wearing, with armored shoulders and elbows, he looks to be about two hundred pounds of pure muscle. He has a mean face. Plain and simple. The more he talks, the more he looks like a traditional bad guy. General Wilson goes on to thank the workers who check and make our structures and so many other workers that I lost track. General Wilson looks mean but sounds decent. "Remember to check in with your teachers, trainers, and/or supervisors for any new scheduling or announcements. Thank you for your attention. Now time for the minute of reverence."

Everyone raises their right hand and places it onto their hearts. The room grows silent. The three of us follow and place our hands on our hearts while remaining silent.

We stay quiet for what feels like minutes. I look around to see everyone either with their eyes closed or focused on the flag. The silence is interrupted by General Wilson. "Thank you. Good day and good morrow, Bergland. Work hard and achieve more."

The holograms disappear, and everyone goes back to their seats and their chatter. Janice sits across from us and folds her hands. "That minute of silence we just had is what we call 'the minute of reverence.' Instead of a mindless pledge to our flag, we look to it as a reminder of what we fight for and all those who have given their lives in the process."

"You do that every day?" Logan asks, returning to his seat.

Mandy and Janice nod. Mandy smiles and folds her hands too, mimicking Janice. "Yep. We have those little morning greetings from our officials every morning, with the occasional news story." Mandy elbows Janice excitedly. "Janice here gets to do them sometimes!"

We all look back to her. Mavis beats me to ask, "You're an official?"

"Well," Janice corrects, "a coordinator. I am the assistant secretary of education to Emily Hash, just like General Wilson is the secretary of defense. But I told them when I accepted the job that I wanted to teach, so they let me."

Logan pokes at what's left of the food on his plate and looks back to Janice. "What do you teach?"

"History." Logan and Mavis exchange a look, then shift their focus back to Janice as she continues, "First of all, I absolutely adore history. Second of all, I believe that if you don't know about past mistakes, you are doomed to repeat them. Third of all . . ." Janice looks down at the table, then back up at us. She waves her hands. "Nope, I need to stop there. I can list reasons I teach history for hours."

The thought of someone listing reasons why they are passionate about their love makes me happy. I can't help but smile. "Yate told us that we would need to learn history tomorrow. Are you going to be our teacher?"

Janice returns my smile. "I can request that you guys are put in my History Basics class if you want. It is filled with kids about twelve, thirteen, and fourteen. But I would love to have you guys with me!"

We all nod and exchange looks of "Sure, why not?"

"Okay, I will let Yate know when I get to my class. A bell is going to ring in a minute, and everybody is going to leave the cafeteria. This is the last breakfast shift of the day, and it ends in . . ." Janice checks her watch, the same sort of watch that seems to project holograms, and she looks back to us. "About three minutes." She stands up and looks around the room. "Okay, guys, I don't see Yate anywhere. Do you guys know where you are to be going next?"

I shake my head.

Logan answers, "No. Yate said that we would get to just hang around wherever today since it is our first day here."

"He said that?" Janice smiles at us as if she has a plan in mind.

We nod.

"Okay, so I guess that means you guys can come with me if you want. My History Basics class starts in about an hour, and I can go over some of the things we have already learned in there with you guys to help catch you up. After a while, we go to the training room, and I can show you guys the ropes."

"Hah!" Mandy lets out a loud and unnecessary chuckle. "You said 'ropes.' For the training room." Mandy turns to Janice and nudges her mumbling. "Get it? That was a pun."

The girls at the table behind us all giggle at once. Their voices echo in the room, spooking everyone at our table. I shake it off and ignore Mandy's laughter at Janice's unintentional pun. "Will we have to train today or what?" I ask.

Janice shakes her head. "No. You can if you want to, but we won't force you."

"So . . ." Logan pauses, seemingly thinking long and hard before he asks a question. We all wait in silence for him to continue. But before he gets the chance, the bell rings overhead, and everyone in the cafeteria scrambles. Janice tells Logan to go ahead, so he clears his throat and speaks up above the chaos around us. "Will this training room help us learn how to fight?"

Janice leans forward a bit to make it easier to hear. "What do you mean?"

"Fight," Logan answers. Our table gets bumped by a passerby, shaking everyone who sits here. Logan slides back onto his seat and looks back to Janice. "How do you figure out who goes to fight and who stays here?"

Janice glances back to Mandy and tells her to go ahead and head to class. Mandy waves us goodbye and heads off. Janice turns back to us and stands. "Well, before we get that far, you guys definitely need to take some history. And I need to fill you in on everything." Janice looks from Logan to Mavis to me. "I strongly believe that before you decide to fight for something, you need to know what you are fighting for and why."

I know why. The words fall out of my mouth as I rise to my feet. "I need to make sure my mom is safe."

Logan and Mavis rise beside me.

Logan nods in agreement. "And my grandfather."

Reaching up to scratch her arm, Mavis stays quiet.

"All right." Janice smiles at us. She waves us over to her side of the table, and we follow her out of the cafeteria. "Then I guess we better get started."

CHAPTER NINE

Mavis

"And here we have Chancellor Meir's most recent announcement to Bestellen about the series of bombings that happened last night. As you all know, last night's attacks were the heaviest and strongest attacks we have ever taken on."

Janice takes a seat and activates Meir's last video. Her hologram screen is tinted blue but has other colors, like Meir's signature wooden desk from where he makes every video. You can see its brown coloring, Meir's white facial hair and his greased-back equally white hair on the top of his head. Meir wears a brown suit jacket, a light purple vest underneath it, a dark-purple tie that's almost black tucked into his vest, and a purple scarf that hangs from his neck, serving no real purpose.

"Good afternoon, Bestellen." His voice sends a shiver down my spine. Never before have I ever favored him, but everything that has been revealed to me in the last few days hasn't helped my opinions of him at all. "I am sure you have all been wondering what exactly happened last night that caused all of the noise from outside the wall, and that is why I am here today. Last night, there was an earthquake beyond magnitudes we have ever seen before. Though due to the brilliance of our engineers and workmen, we, the Bestellen government, were able to keep you, our citizens, safe. Our masterfully built walls and protection systems have triumphed once again and kept us all safe from the horrors beyond our borders. Remember, if you don't fully dedicate yourself to us and your work, your safety will not be possible. Thank you for your dedication, Bestellen. Keep up the good work."

The screen freezes on his face, his undeniably smug face. Logan, who sits in front of me, looks back; and Sam, who sits behind me, looks forward. I look to them both as Janice rises again to address the class. She walks over in front of her screen and looks to all of her students, including us. The thirteen others in the room glance over to us every now and then to see how we respond, and every now and then, I glance back at them. They look to be about twelve or thirteen years old and very judgmental. One girl glared at me when she first walked in, as if I had somehow offended her with my presence.

Janice goes over a few questions with the kids and elaborates on everything extensively. She explains that Meir and his regime keep its citizens uneducated in order to keep them from thinking for themselves. She explains that this doesn't mean they are stupid; it just means that they have been tricked, all of this time, into believing in a system that is flawed.

"Sure, every system has its flaws," she drones. "And yes, no system will please everyone, but this is obviously absurd. If they aren't being honest with their citizens about something as important as a war, their system is too far gone to revive, not even taking into account all of the other horrendous aspects of their government."

The more she explains how Bestellen has been lying to us, the more I want to go and get Derek and his mother. Everything Janice says makes sense. Everything she says she backs up with facts, time lines, and examples. Never before have I had someone actually explain things instead of just forcing me to accept that they were right. By the looks of it, neither has Logan or Sam.

The three of us are quiet the whole way to the training room. We follow Janice, who follows her thirteen students. The kids are laughing, bumping into one another, skipping, and chatting all the way to our next destination. When we get there, a few of them swing the doors open and go rushing inside while the others casually walk in like they have no real interest in it.

When we make our way inside, I look around to see a set of what looks like ladders in the air, held up by more ladders to my left and weights, machines, and a few other things that I don't know how to describe to my right. The kids that came running in run directly to my right toward this line of different obstacles. They separate into two lines and wait behind a bar that comes down to their waist. Whenever two of them finish the course, two more start it. They have to weave through swinging obstacles, jump and duck under still obstacles, climb over walls, jump through things, swing on ropes, climb up more things, jump from ledges to ledges, and try to beat each other to the end without falling.

To my left, a few of the kids who walked in nonchalantly climb up one set of the ladders and then dangle from the set on top. They swing their arms out and climb horizontally on the ladders and make their way to the other end. The ladder breaks off into two separate paths in the middle. One way, it leads directly to another ladder, while the other leads to a ledge. From that ledge, you can climb down another ladder or swing from a rope to a few other obstacles. This whole room is filled with weights, obstacles, and competition. Though there are a few girls racing through the large obstacle course on the right, the boys seem to be the ones who participate the most.

A few men and women wearing light-blue collared T-shirts appear from one of the side doors and supervise the kids as they run through the obstacles.

"Look over there," Janice chuckles as she watches one of her students dangle from the hanging ladder. The girl giggles as she tries to pull herself up and make it one more bar but drops to the ground trying. All of her friends giggle with her as she falls into the pit below. At first, I expected it to hurt or for someone to show concern, but when the girl hit the ground, the blue floor seemed to engulf her, then spit her back out. The girl stands up and walks off, laughing.

"What?" Logan sputters. "What was that?" He points to the girl who just fell twenty feet. "Janice, what happened to the floor?"

"We came up with a special type of foam flooring that, when hit with a certain amount of pressure, turns into an extremely soft and flexible foam that won't hurt when you land on it. Then it hardens up the longer you are on it so that you can walk off." Janice walks over to where the blue flooring starts and walks across it. She turns back to us and holds her arms out. "See?" Janice jumps, and the floor caves in slightly underneath her feet. It hardens and goes back to its flat position almost as quickly as it had become soft.

Logan walks over and steps onto the blue. Sam and I follow. We all push our feet into it, but it seems just as hard as wood flooring. I jump slightly, but it doesn't do anything.

I turn back to Janice and shoot her a confused look, earning a chuckle from her. "Mavis, I think you would need to jump a little higher to get it to do anything."

I do. I jump up a little higher and get a very slight softness underneath my feet, but nothing much. Janice gives me a little smile. "It's because you weigh so little. If you fall from any of our equipment, the force will be enough so that the floor will cushion your fall. So don't worry. For half of these kids, if they jumped, the floor wouldn't react either."

Logan looks down and jumps, and the floor gives way immediately. Not much, but a lot more than I got. Logan chuckles and looks to Sam.

"Nope." Sam shakes his head. "I'm good." As Sam steps off the foam, I assume he doesn't want to jump now that Logan has proved it can be dented.

My attention is caught when I hear a loud thud and a shout. I look back around the room to see a kid dangling from the elevated race obstacle course. The kid catches himself on the bottom of the ledge and tries to pull himself back up after a few seconds of dangling. The kid he was racing runs right by him and finishes the course first, earning cheers from some of his classmates, while the kid who tripped and fell gets laughed at.

"Do you guys see anything you would like to do?" Janice looks from the kids cheering and jeering back to us. "Anything you would like to try? I don't know how interested you all would be, but behind that corner, there is a sparring mat for anyone who is interested."

Logan shrugs and takes a few steps forward to peek around the corner. Sam and I stay still, looking around the room and observing our surroundings. I quickly find myself looking at a small boy in the corner, behind the air ladders. He looks considerably younger than the rest of the kids and very lonely.

"Hey." I nudge Sam and point to the kid in the corner. "Janice, who's that?"

Janice glances over to the boy; and before she can answer, she is interrupted by Logan, who walks over to the ladders, where there are no more kids.

He calls out, "Hey, can I use these?"

"The monkey bars?" Janice nods. "Sure."

Logan wipes his hands on his pants and looks the bars up and down. He places his hands on the first set of bars in front of his face and begins climbing up to the part where there were no more bars except for the ones above him that he would have to climb horizontally. The kids in the room all stop what they are doing to watch Logan. He waits at the top of the bars before grabbing them.

Logan takes a deep breath, then places his hands on the first bar. Within seconds, he whips across the set and takes a right to the harder path of the monkey bars. He flies through, swinging his arms quickly and powerfully, until he makes it to the ledge. Once he gets to the ledge, he pauses, and stares at the next set of obstacles. The next part is a rope that he is to swing on, straight to a set of metal rings, dangling from chains that lead from one point, to another ledge. Logan takes one more deep breath before launching himself forward. He grabs the rope and swings forward once, backward once, then forward once more. Logan jumps off the rope and grabs on to one of the rings. Almost as fast as he did the regular monkey bars, he swings through the rings.

From the rings to another ledge. From that ledge to a beam that runs from one ledge to another. Logan crouches and holds out his arms as he quickly skids across the beam to the final ledge, where another ladder leading to the ground waits for him.

Every kid and adult in the room cheers and claps for Logan as he tries to catch his breath. Every kid except for the kid in the corner, who just smiles at him. Sam and I slow our clapping and watch Logan come down the ladder.

"Logan!" Janice exclaims. "That was awesome! Have you ever used one of these before?"

Logan shakes his head and wipes his hands on his pants. "No. Back home, I hung out in the woods a lot. I climbed trees a lot, and I have some friends who tied ropes in the trees to make it easier to get around."

Janice nods to him with a smug look on her face. "Ah! Say, how fast do you think you can run?"

Logan looks to Sam and me as if he is waiting for us to answer. He shrugs back to Janice. "I used to race people back home, but I don't know the exact speed."

"Huh." Janice smiles and ushers us over to the large and difficult-looking obstacle course. "Would you be interested in trying this out for me?"

Logan shrugs. "If you want."

Janice shakes her head, almost violently. "No, only if you want to."

Logan smiles at her and shrugs again. Janice clears the other kids out of the way easily, and we all wait to watch Logan run this next course. I look back to the kid in the corner of the room and see him watching Logan with the rest of us. Unlike everyone else who has gathered around the large course, he remains far away.

Logan rolls his shoulders back and steps up to the bar, which comes about to his waist. He slowly looks over the whole course and observes it carefully. I can almost hear him counting down in his head as he taps each of his fingers to his thumbs.

Pointer finger, thumb. Middle finger, thumb. Ring finger, thumb. Pinky, thumb.

Repeat.

Logan reaches up to grab the bar in front of him, and he rubs it on the palm of his hands.

One time.

Two times.

Three . . .

He swings himself under the pole and through the course. He dodges the swinging obstacles without any thought, ducks under and jumps over the poles and rods he needs to, jumps through hoops, swings on ropes onto ledges, jumps from ledge to ledge, and so much more. He does the whole course seemingly effortlessly and finishes strong.

All the kids fawn over him. Some cheer, some clap, and others rush over to the course's start to try to do what Logan just did.

Janice walks over to Logan with her arms crossed and her smile so overly smug. "Logan, that was very impressive! You know what I think?" She looks around to the kids trying to do what he did. "I think that you are a natural-born Taai."

Logan keeps his hands on his hips and takes a few deep breaths, trying to regain his normal breathing pattern. "Taai?"

Janice nods. "They are our special forces group and are extremely exclusive. They handle special missions that our regular militia is unable to handle."

"Missions including swinging from ropes and jumping through hoops?" Logan surmises.

"Maybe," Janice chuckles. As Janice and Logan continue to talk about the Taai, Sam elbows me and points over to the kid in the corner. He is just standing there, looking around the room with glasses too big for his face and his arms crossed in a way that makes him look like he owns the place.

Sam and I make our way over to him, but as soon as the boy realizes that, he averts his eyes from us and keeps them pointed at his feet. Sam and I approach the little blond boy and try to get him to look back to us, but he ignores us.

"Hey," I say to him.

An awkward silence fills the air between the three of us.

I look to Sam, who has the phrase "I don't know" painted all over his face as he shrugs to me.

"Um . . . I'm Mavis, and um . . . this is Sam."

The boy nods but keeps his eyes averted from ours.

I continue, "We're new here."

The boy nods again. "I know. You guys stick out like a sore thumb."

"We stick out like a sore thumb?" Sam scoffs. "What about you? You are like half the age of the other students in here."

The boy looks around to the others and pauses for a moment. "Yeah, I'd rather be younger than everyone in my class than older." He looks up to Sam with a worried look in his eyes. "Oh, I'm sorry! I didn't mean to be rude. It just came out that way. I'm Henry." He extends his hand to Sam and me, and we give it a shake. "Henry Smalls. And I'm older than half their age. Most people in our class are twelve or thirteen. I am eight."

I chuckle. "Okay, Henry. Why aren't you over there with them on the bars or on the course?"

Henry pauses and resumes his gaze outward, "The other kids call me weird. I don't like that, so I don't train with them."

"Why?" I ask. "You don't seem so weird to me."

"I think it's because I answer most of the questions Ms. Ludley asks." Henry pushes his glasses back up onto his face using the sides of the frames. "The other kids think I am weird because they aren't as smart as me."

I chuckle again. "Well, that doesn't sound weird to me. It sounds pretty cool actually."

I think back to how we in Bestellen never had any classes to help us prepare for the military; we only had training. The more I think about it, the more I realize that I only went to light training once a week while many others who were assigned to the military went almost every day. I think back to how much I envied the kids in the stories about the other states. How those kids got to go study to be engineers, farmers, lumberjacks, and so many other things.

Oh, how I envied those who got to go to school.

Henry nods in acceptance of my compliment. "Thanks. I skipped a few grades in order to be put in classes with those of my same mental status." Henry narrows his eyes behind us as a large boom of laughter explodes throughout the training room. Sam and I turn around to see one boy hanging from another's legs as he dangles from the monkey bars.

"I may need to skip another grade or two," Henry continues.

Sam and I stand by Henry against the wall and watch everyone as they laugh and cheer for the boys on the bars. I cross my arms and add, "Back home, we were never allowed to jump ahead of our level of training, even if we were ready."

Henry shakes his head. "I know. That's another thing I don't like about Bergland. If you aren't encouraged to do your best and rewarded for doing so, then how will you ever improve?"

A long pause filled the air between us. Sam breaks the tension by forcing out a fake chuckle. "You are a very smart little boy, you know that?"

Henry smiles.

"Hey, Henry." The longer I think about it, the more the questions force themselves out of my mouth. "I haven't seen very many other kids your age around." I pause, thinking back to my entire experience here at Bergland. "Actually, I don't think I have seen any your age. Do they stay in a separate section of Bergland or what?"

Henry's smile fades. His silence seems to grow louder the longer he remains quiet. Though he is only quiet for a few seconds, it feels like much longer. When he finally speaks up, the kids drop from the monkey bars and land on each other. The foam flooring consumes them for a moment, then pushes them back up to the top effortlessly.

Henry shakes his head. "Last year, we had a mass epidemic of a virus we call resporite. The virus killed off thousands of people, mainly those under the age of ten and over the age of fifty-five. I am one of the few lucky children that made it through without getting extremely sick."

Our eyes follow Henry's back over to some of the boys who are trying to hang from one another under the monkey bars. Henry shakes his head and glances over to Janice, who is watching the boys with her arms crossed, as if she is just waiting for them to fall. "Mrs. Ludley wasn't so lucky. Sure, she lived, but she lost something she valued much more than her own life." Henry sighs. "She lost her husband, her two-year-old son, and her unborn child to the virus. She lost her whole family, and there was nothing she could do about it but watch them get worse every day."

Janice makes her way over to Logan, who is watching the kids try to complete the obstacle course as well as he could. A kid falls off the balance beam while racing her friend and gets swallowed by the floor, then spat out once again. Henry slides down the wall and takes a seat on the floor. Sam stays standing while I slide down beside Henry. I watch as Janice puts her hand on Logan's shoulder and as she smiles to him, pointing at the kids as they fail the course.

"Henry," I ask, "what can you tell us about the Taai?"

He smiles and pauses for a moment. Henry pushes his glasses by their frames back up his face once again and chuckles. "The Taai . . . Where should I start? They are the most prestigious of all our top career groups." He holds up one finger and begins counting. "The Taai is our special forces group. You don't ask to be put in it. You have to be chosen or suggested by an official. You have to be fast, fit, and so much more. I assume you are asking because Mrs. Ludley looks to be interested in signing Logan up for the group. His mental state and responses will later be determined through further testing and analysis if he is to join the Taai."

Henry holds up his second finger. "Our second special forces group is known for its brain power. We call them the Slim. They are the Berglanders who test well above average levels. If they desire to join the Slim, they have to go through multiple different tests, officials, and training courses. They design all of the weapons, energy systems, electronics, communication devices, and pretty much everything that takes electricity to power. They have even genetically engineered a few of our fruits and vegetables to be superfoods with all of the nutrients and proteins you need to survive. They even modified the produce's growth times and sun needs to fit our desires."

One kid runs as fast as he can through the monkey bars onto the ledge to the rope and to the hanging rings. He runs through the whole easy course quickly without any flaws, but not as quickly as Logan. A bunch of his classmates ignore his success and try to do it themselves.

Henry holds up his third finger as Sam slides down the wall and takes a seat beside us. "That leaves the generals and government officials, which includes the secretaries of any given subject or career and head officers. Secretary of education, secretary of health, head of Department of Sanitation, head of security, general of defense, or our military, and so much more."

Henry brings up his pinky. "With those all listed, we have one more unofficial group. The group made up of our farm overseers, our chefs, and our energy suppliers. By 'energy suppliers,' I mean the people who go outside the mountains to fix our solar panels, windmills, waterwheels, et cetera."

Janice glances over her shoulder and leaves Logan to watch the kids. She smiles at us as she makes her way over. Sam cracks his knuckles and turns to Henry, who continues to stare off into the distance. "Do you want to be part of the . . . um . . ." Sam squeezes his lips closed and cocks his head as he tries to come up with the name.

"The Slim?" Henry fills in. "Well, I would like to, but I don't know if I'm smart enough."

"What? You are totally smart enough!" I chuckle. "And if you aren't ready by the time you finish schooling, you will probably be, like, eleven. Which means you will have more than enough time to study for whatever you have to study for to be a part of the Slim."

Janice approaches us, and Henry shoots up to his feet. She smiles at him, then at Sam and me. "Hey, guys. I see you've met Henry."

Henry nods sporadically at Janice as Sam and I rise. "Yes, ma'am! I was just telling them about the Taai and the Slim."

"Ah." Janice's smile grows as she turns to Sam and me. "The Taai and the Slim. Did you guys ask him about the groups? Or did he just start showing off his big brain without any warning?"

"We asked him about the Taai," Sam confirms, "since you were telling Logan about them."

Janice nods and smiles again. "Yes. I think that Logan would be a perfect addition to the Taai. Just like I think Henry here would be a perfect addition to the Slim."

Henry blushes and looks away. He folds his hands and mumbles, "Thank you, Mrs. Ludley, but I don't know about that."

"Oh yeah?" Janice rolls her eyes. "You are several grades ahead of your fellow eight-year-olds, and you can answer nearly every question I ask in my class. Not to mention your ability to comprehend material as fast as you can."

Henry blushes even more to the point that his whole face is red. It is clear to me that he has a big crush on Janice.

I chuckle at the thought, but my giggles are interrupted by an idea.

"Hey," I snicker, "Janice. I . . . I mean Ms. Ludley. May I use the monkey bars?"

Janice nods happily. "Yeah, sure! Go ahead."

"Henry, can you come with me?" I ask.

Henry does a double take, almost causing me to snicker even harder. "Me? Why?"

"Please?"

Henry sighs at my plea, then agrees. He follows me over to the ladder, and we stop at the bottom. "Hey, Henry?" He looks to me as I try to hide the smile on my face. "Could you show me how to do this first?"

"Whoa, me? Out of everybody, you chose me?" Henry pushes up his glasses and looks up to the bars.

"Well, I figured that since you are the smartest kid in here, you could show me the . . . um . . . most efficient way of doing this."

Henry takes a moment to consider. He looks back to Janice, who holds up two thumbs to him. "Um . . . I guess so. I do come in here sometimes when I am not with my class, so I can show you what I do when I am without them. I am pretty slow at it, though."

"That's perfect!" I exclaim, trying not to sound too enthusiastic. "Everyone knows that in order to show someone how to do something, the teacher needs to go slow."

Henry nods in agreement. Lucky for us, everyone has migrated over to Logan and the hard obstacle course. They are all trying to impress him, so Henry shouldn't feel too much pressure.

Henry makes his way up the ladder, then pauses at the top. He looks down to me and takes a deep breath.

"Go ahead, Henry," I say loud enough that Janice can hear me, but not loud enough to attract attention from the rest of the class. "Show me what to do."

Henry nods and, very quickly, slower than Logan, but still quickly, swings through the monkey bars and makes it to the other end. He climbs back down the ladder on the other end and hits the floor with pride. A kid from across the room hollers out, "Woo-hoo! Go, Henry!" This makes Henry blush even more.

Janice careens over to Henry with her mouth hanging open in surprise. "Henry! I have never seen you do any of these before other than the weights! That was wonderful!"

Henry's face reaches a red that I had never expected it to hit, though I can't tell if it is from exhaustion or embarrassment. He smiles and nods to Janice. "Thank you. I practice in my free time."

"Well, good job, Henry!" Janice says.

"No!" a boy's voice booms from across the room. "I would've won if you wouldn't have pushed me!"

The four of us glance over to see two boys shoving each other by the end of the course.

"I didn't push you!" the other boy shouts. "You were in my way!"

Janice shakes her head and rolls her eyes. "I have to go take care of this." She quickly rushes off to the aid of the blue-shirted workers and helps separate the boys.

Sam chuckles and saunters behind her.

"I know what you did," Henry jests to me. I turn back to him to see his glasses in his hands, using his shirt to wipe the lenses.

I am sure he does know what I did. I am sure he knows that I only did that to help his mini ego. I am sure that he got what I was doing from the moment he reached the top of the first ladder, but I am not going to admit to anything.

"I don't know what you're talking about."

Henry places his glasses back onto his face and pushes them up his nose by the center of the frames. He looks up to me and squints with a smile. "Yes you do."

I roll my eyes and turn away. "I'm going over there with Sam."

I walk for a moment before Henry's small voice floats over to me. "Thank you." His comment forces me to smile as I continue over to Sam. It's the same comment that Derek got when he did that same trick with his little brother and me.

I had always known that Derek's little brother liked me. One day, when Derek decided to help out Sander, his brother, he chose to pretend that he couldn't climb one of the trees in our woods. Sander gladly decided to "show" Derek how to climb it once I was there to watch, and after he made it to the top, Derek elbowed me and gave me nonverbal hints to praise him. I did.

Not too long after that, Sander passed away from an unknown parasite. He got it from an unsafe piece of fruit he bought from someone in town. I guess Sander reached the point where he felt that he really needed to get his own food in order to help his family out.

I don't really know for sure why he decided to buy the fruit without his mother or Derek. All I know is that unless you are mentally equipped with the knowledge of what good and bad fruits look like, you would never last more than a week shopping in our marketplaces. Vendors sell whatever they can without worrying about the good of their customers. All they worry about is making enough money to survive the next few days.

I see a lot of Sander in Henry. I see a lot of the things I loved about Sander in Henry.

Would Sander and Henry have been good friends? Definitely.

Would Sander have grown to be an amazing kid? Probably.

Would my dad drink less if he didn't have the guilt of selling Sander the bad fruit? Maybe.

Would my mother and brother still be alive if Sander hadn't gotten sick from the fruit? I don't know.

CHAPTER TEN

Logan

Dreary. That's all it is. Dreary.

And bright. Dreary and bright.

I wake up on my new bed in the same room as Sam, Grayson, Caine, along with a few other guys. As I force my eyes open, I take a breath and enjoy the fact that I just got a full night's sleep for the first time in days and in a bed that doesn't have a spring in the middle that wants to penetrate my spine.

The light above is brighter than I originally expected it to be. Sam, in the bunk beneath me, takes notice much more verbally than I do.

I look around to find Grayson making his bed, along with one other guy. Caine and the rest of our roommates have already made their beds and left the room.

Sam beneath me groans. "Why is it so bright in here?"

I slide out of bed and rub the crust off my eyes, trying to figure out that same question.

Sam continues to hold his pillow over his face. "Can we turn the lights off?"

Still making his bed, Grayson chuckles, "No, we can't. Not until everyone has left the room."

I sniffle and stretch my arms out. "Did the lights just come on?"

"No." Grayson finishes making his bed and turns back to us. "The lights start coming on at seven thirty. They gradually grow brighter as time goes on. Once it reaches about 8:00 a.m., they are up all the way."

The other guy in the room finishes his bed and heads out. Sam shoves the pillow off his face and narrows his eyes at the other roommate as he leaves. "Okay. Why would they do that?"

Grayson crosses his arms and looks around to check everyone's beds. "Because in this dorm, our breakfast shift is from eight fifteen to nine. We are the last shift of the morning. Everyone usually gets up at around seven forty to go to the restrooms to shower, brush their teeth, whatever before breakfast." He pauses at the end of the row of beds and nods. "Before you leave, you guys are going to need to make your beds."

I nod. As I make my bed, Sam slowly gets up and asks Grayson a million questions. Grayson explains that he is his room's advisor; and he is responsible for making sure everyone gets up on time, makes their beds, and makes it out of the room okay.

After Sam and I finish with our beds, we head out to the restrooms and do what we need to do. Grayson leaves us and heads up to breakfast after Sam and I meet up with Mavis in the stairwell between our dorms.

I ask Mavis how she slept last night, but I already know the answer. The bags under her eyes are as dark and purple as mine and Sam's. All of our brains were too distracted to be able to sleep well, but the exhaustion we felt overpowered our brains and knocked us out within minutes of lying down. Though we slept for a good nine hours, we still feel dreary.

On our way up the stairs, a bell rings, and people scatter. The cafeteria is packed with people by the time we make it up there. People who are leaving and people who are coming in. Most of the tables are already filled up, but there are a lot with just a few people sitting here and there.

"Over there." I point over to the table we sat at for every meal yesterday. Mandy and Janice are both over there talking with a man that I have never seen before. He looks to be a bit older than Janice. If I have to guess, I would say he is about thirty.

As we make our way over to the table, the ladies catch a glimpse of us.

"Hey!" Mandy perks up and excitedly waves us over, so excitedly that for a moment, she shakes the table. "We were waiting on you to eat."

The man gets up out of his seat adjacent to Janice and moves to sit beside her. He nods to the three of us and gestures for us to take his seat on the opposite side of the table.

As Janice scoots over a bit to make room for the man, she looks to each of us and gives a large and warm smile. "Good morning, I trust you slept well?"

Sam looks to the new man beside Janice. The man smiles and nods to him, then to me, then to Mavis. He holds Mavis's gaze a bit longer than he did for us, but Mavis averts her eyes after a few seconds. The man continues to subtly smile at Mavis even though she has looked back to Janice.

Sam shrugs in response to the question. "If 'well' means passing out from exhaustion, just to be wakened by a bright light, then yes, very well."

Mandy chuckles. She quickly looks over her shoulder at the lines of people waiting to get their food at one of the five different service bars. "That's good. Are you guys hungry?"

Before anyone can answer, Janice interrupts. "Before you all go and get something to eat, I want to introduce you to John Young, the leading Taai recruiter and trainer."

John nods his head. His dark facial stubble matches his hair in its color but seems to get even darker when he flashes his obviously bleached teeth at us. "Morning." John extends his hand to Sam. "Mr. Beckman, right?"

Sam nods and takes his hand. After a brief shake, John moves on to Mavis. "Ms. Wamsley." Mavis nods quickly, then retracts her hand. Their eyes lock for a moment, only because John refuses to move his eyes over to me as he reaches out his hand.

I quickly take his hand and give it a firm shake. John gives Mavis a final smile, then looks back to me. "And Mr. Forge." John looks into my eyes and smiles. Not the same kind and cocky smile he gave to Mavis, but more of a cocky and overconfident smile. After a moment, John begins to return my tight-gripped handshake. His hand clenches with mine inside and crunches my knuckles together. "Nice to meet you. I have heard nothing but good things."

He releases my hand and returns to his upright position. He folds his hands and sets them into his lap in a way that makes his arm muscles look bigger than they really are. Obviously flexing, he smirks at me.

Janice rises to her feet. "Okay. Sam, Mavis, Mandy, let's go get breakfast and let these two chat." The others rise and follow her, leaving John and me at the table, sizing each other up.

"So." John takes a breath and crosses his arms. "Mrs. Ludley tells me you would make a great addition to the Taai. What do you think?"

I shrug. "I don't know. I don't know what your standards are. I guess I could do it if I trained a bit."

"What's 'it'?" John puts his crossed arms onto the table in front of him and stares me down. "What do you mean you 'could do it'? Do what?"

For a moment, I have trouble coming up with an answer. I don't really know a lot about the Taai. I stammer, "I mean I . . . I can help. I want to help fight."

"So you want to be part of the Taai so that you can fight?"

I shrug.

John looks unconvinced and rises to his feet. "Come on." I follow him over to one of the service lines, and we stand. John sighs. "What's the real reason you want to be a part of the Taai?"

I take a moment to think. I recall everything that Janice has told me about the Taai, about how important they are to the cause, about how the whole defense division would be nothing without them, and about the real reason I want to join. "It is a great honor to be a part of the Taai, right? And I have been selected for a trial, and isn't that a great honor?"

John shakes his head as we move farther up the line. "No."

"No?"

"No," John confirms, "that isn't the reason." He freezes and holds up the line. "Tell me the real reason."

Our eyes lock. Someone bumps into me from behind, and I scoot past John to keep the line moving.

"Well?"

I hesitate at first. Why should I tell John? I don't know him. I don't know if I can trust him. Then again, it's not like telling him what happened can hurt me or anyone else. If I just tell him, it will be fine, right?

"Well?" John repeats.

I take a breath and a moment to gather my story but am rushed to spit it out by John's expression.

"When I was younger, I loved playing in the trees about half a mile out from my house. My friends and I would race through them and hang out there all day to try to escape our daily lives. Before we could get to the woods, we would have to dodge any and all officials to make sure that we remained unseen. If we ever got caught in the woods, we would get a public lashing for 'trespassing.'" I pause. John and I grab a tray, and he nods for me to continue.

"One day, I decided to go off on my own and play in the trees. I was nine." John and I step forward in line, and the man serving the food takes our trays and plops two patties and one scoop of some sort of mash onto our trays. John looks to me to continue. "I guess I didn't take all the precautions I should have. An official caught me." I think back to that day, back to the fear I felt when I was climbing one of my favorite trees, only to have my leg grabbed by something . . . by *someone*. The official yanked me off one of the low-hanging branches I had just started to climb, and I fell right to the ground. The thin grass did little to soothe my fall. I landed on some sort of hard mulch, which cut up my back and arms.

Before I could do anything, the official started screaming at me about how I was disobeying the law and how I should be killed for such a thing. I felt in that moment that he would be the death of me. I crawled backward as he followed me, screaming his lungs out. Tears began to stream down my face as I saw my life flash before my eyes.

Right as the official grabbed my arm and yanked me to a standing position, my mother swooped in. I guess my mother had followed me that day when she realized I had gone outside without any of my friends. Mom pleaded for the man to show mercy. She told him that I would never go back out there again and that I had learned my lesson, but the official refused to listen.

"My mom was killed after an official pistol-whipped her for defending me." I pause, thinking back to her grunt as the metal made contact with her head in one sweeping motion. Mom fell backward with blood dripping out of the side of her head. Her eyes stared out with an empty expression that I have seen in my nightmares many nights since.

"All she did was ask for mercy." My voice cracks. "And the guard killed her." After Mom died, the official told me to go home and to never return to the woods. We never even got to give her a funeral. After that day, she just disappeared, and the officials acted like it had never happened.

John nods to me as we walk back to our table with our full trays. After a few moments of silence, John speaks up. "Logan Forge." We stop and face each other. John extends one of his hands out to me while balancing his tray in one hand. "I have a few tests for you to take. Some physical. Some mental. After that, you can be admitted into the Taai."

"Thank you, sir."

We walk over to the woman at the computer, tell her our names, and bid her adieu. After checking in with her, we head to our table in silence to find Sam and the ladies all eating happily. Mandy is blabbing something excitedly to the others while Sam stares at her with some sort of annoyance. The closer we get to the group, the more I realize that John has his eyes fixed on something specific at the table.

As I sit back by Mavis, Janice smiles. She swallows the clump of food in her mouth and looks from John to me with wide eyes filled with hope. "So have you guys talked about it?"

John nods. "Training can start today."

"Perfect," Janice confirms. "Speaking of schedules, I have yours." The three white laminated pieces of paper she pulls out blind me with a flash reflected from the lights on the ceiling. After she finishes passing them out, she retracts mine almost as quickly as she administered it. "Wait! I printed off another one for you just in case John said yes."

The new schedule she hands me is the same as the one she handed Sam and Mavis. The only difference is that where their schedule says "Culinary Aid," mine says "Taai Training."

"So between breakfast and your first class of the day, you guys get to come with me, and we can catch you all up. You guys have the rest of your classes with me and your physical education with me. But after that, Sam and Mavis, you guys come in here and help prepare the food for dinner for the night and breakfast and lunch for the next day. Logan, you will go to the gym, and a worker will take you back to the Taai's training rooms."

Sam shovels a large chunk of food into his mouth just as Janice finishes her statement. "Okay . . ." He throws up one finger to let everyone know he wants to say something and then chews violently, trying to get the food down as quickly as possible. "Classes? As in multiple?"

Janice chuckles. "Yes. I teach a class on politics and a class on history, both of which you three will be needing to learn first. After you have the basics down, we can move onto more advanced courses and different subjects, like math and science."

Sam lowers his spoon. "Those are courses?"

The three of us shoot Janice a baffled look. Never before have I ever thought that we would need to know math. Yes, two plus two equals four. That seems necessary. How much money will I need to buy three pieces of fruit? That seems necessary. But a whole class on it?

This should be easy.

I shift my focus from Janice as she explains the classes and what we will learn in them to John. He eats his food slowly and watches Mavis beside me in a way that makes me uncomfortable.

The group of girls behind us all giggle at once and spook Mavis. She jumps a little, then looks back to Janice, trying to pretend she wasn't affected by the girls' joy. Mavis's eyes flicker over to John and Mandy before they fall back on Janice. When Mavis realizes John is watching her, she does a subtle double take and meets his eyes.

John gives her a small smile. Mavis returns with a shy smile, then averts her eyes back to Janice. I watch as she tries her best to keep her focus on Janice while John continues to stare at her with a smug smile on his face and fiddles with the food in front of him. Why he stares at Mavis, I don't know.

Why should he stop staring at her? I can think of a few reasons.

Sam

The screen changes to show us pictures of men and women in different uniforms matching their given positions. Janice walks to one side of the screen and points to the woman on the top-right corner, the same woman whom we met when we first came in.

"Who can tell me who this is?" Janice asks the class.

Many of the kids' hands shoot up, but a girl in the back of the classroom calls out, "Emily Hash!"

Janice shakes her head and lowers her finger. "Sarah, you have to wait to be called on, but that's correct. James . . ." She points to one of the boys who didn't raise his hand in the very front of the room. "What is her official position?"

Everyone lowers their hands as the boy answers, "She runs the . . . um . . . uh . . . I don't know."

"Ah." Janice smiles. "You would have known if you were paying attention instead of dozing off." The rest of the class giggle as she calls on Henry.

He pushes his glasses back up his face and corrects his posture. "Executive Emily Hash is the leading official who coordinates education and assists in the coordination of newcomers."

As the rest of the class moans at his extremely detailed answer, Janice nods to Henry. "Thank you for your clarity. That is correct, though I would have settled for 'education.'"

I catch a glimpse of a few of the kids in the back of the classroom whispering to one another and looking back and forth at Henry. Though Henry doesn't seem to mind, I do. These kids need to mind their own business and quit talking badly about a little boy just because he is smarter than they are.

Janice continues and points at another person on the board. We go through a whole list of officials in hopes to clarify who runs what and why it works.

Executive Emily Hash runs education with the assistance of her secretary, Janice Ludley. Major Cole Mason handles rescue with Private Yate Groves. General Luke Wilson runs the military with the help of many different majors and officials. Kaitlyn Arms runs the section of Bergland that utilizes natural resources such as the wind power, waterpower, agricultural needs, etc. Half of the class zones out as Janice continues to run through the different aspects and sectors that Bergland has under the rule of certain officials.

As half zones out, a few of the others get on my nerves. I sit behind Mavis, who sits behind Logan. Logan sits beside Henry, who is completely oblivious to the kids behind him, talking trash.

"Yeah, it's like every time he speaks, he has to adjust his glasses. What a poser."

"Why would he spike his hair up like that? It's not like it will change our opinion of him."

"Dude, I bet he isn't even that smart. He probably just got put into our class because everyone else his age died."

I can't stand listening to them. It irritates me beyond my own understanding, but I take deep breaths and try to tune them out.

"All right." Janice grabs my attention, along with everyone else's in the room. "Next question. Very easy. What kind of economic system does Bestellen have?"

"Geven," Henry answers.

Janice smiles and nods. "Does it work?" She clicks a button on a controller she holds in her hand and changes the screen to pictures of Metropolis. The fancy gardens, water fountains, buildings, parties, and people and their absurd fashion all consisting of different shades of gray, purple, and gold.

"No," the whole class, other than us three, answers in unison.

Janice nods in agreement and changes the screen to a picture of Bloot. Mavis in front of me tenses up a bit as the picture appears. Almost everyone in the picture looks like they are being starved even though, in the picture, there are food stands lining the street. I can even see a kid in the background walking a sheep that looks as if it has never even seen food before.

"Listen guys, the definition of 'geven' is where the government owns everything and redistributes it evenly to all. The idea behind geven is to keep everyone equally rich, but that sadly doesn't work." Janice changes the screen to another picture of Bloot. "It sounds like a great system, but in reality, it is flawed. Every system has a flaw, and geven's flaw happens to be the fact that not everyone will work. This system works well for small groups mostly, but with large crowds, people can fall through the cracks. And no one will do anything about it, leaving other people having to do more work."

Janice changes the screen to a picture of Metropolis side by side with Bloot. "If you look at this picture of Bestellen's capital compared with Bestellen's least favorite state, you can see how much favoritism affects Bestellen's citizen." She changes it to a picture of Metropolis, followed by Verwend, which was the first state made after the war between the Amiables and Diligent. The Vends are walking around their brick buildings, perfectly paved roads, and colorful markets in their perfect clothing like nothing is wrong with the world. Janice explains that Verwend is the state that manufactures Bestellen's weapons and trains their troops and that it is Metropolis's favorite state.

She changes the screen to the next picture, a picture of Hout, which was the second state added to Bestellen and the state that is responsible for our main supply of lumber. The picture is of one of their major cities. The only reason I recognize it is because at least once a month, on my town's show box, we would get updates about how much each state was flourishing. Hout always used this town to show how well they were doing. It isn't as nice of a town as Verwend's town of choice, but it is a bit better looking than Meer, our aquaculture state.

When Meer's picture comes up on the screen, we see a bunch of pastel-painted lake buildings, docks, water mills, power plants, and fishermen. The docks, houses, and buildings shown in the news every month look beautiful and perfect; but the ones in the photograph that Janice is showing are slightly broken-down and need repairs.

The next state shown is Bouw, my home state. Janice shows a picture of a large plot of farmland being worked by a few people in torn and ratty clothing. The picture the news shows is one of my precinct's town hall and the large mansion that our governor and his family lives in. The large light-pink building with white-lined roofs and columns down the road from an even larger columned white building is shown in our news at home to make our state look better than it really is. Our precinct is the most cared-for precinct of Bouw, but overall, that doesn't change what it is.

It's the fanciest part of a poor state.

Bouw is the second-most-hated state of Bestellen, right behind Bloot. Whenever the news comes on for all of the state updates, Bloot always sends one representative over to Bouw, and our representatives present together in the best parts of Bouw. I guess there is no picture-worthy bit of Bloot.

After Bouw was added to Bestellen, Minje followed. Minje is much bigger than Bouw and better treated, but only slightly. The picture of Minje that Janice shows is one of people going in and out of the mines, covered in soot, which is nothing like the picture that our news showed us. We always got the impression that it was nice and clean in the mines, and all of their neighborhoods were decent. The pictures Janice clicks through prove us wrong.

Bloot is the last state shown by Janice. Every image that flashes before us is of people that look to be starving or one of the well-fed and muscular officials. There are people in the pictures begging at street corners, like back in Bouw, but worse because there is a beggar on every street corner.

Every house has some sort of hole or crack in it. Every building is made of stone, with a chunk or two broken off it and replaced with a tarp or blanket. Half of the buildings aren't even buildings, but tents made out of ratty cloth that looks like they will tear any second.

"This is not the form of geven that Bestellen claims it uses. True geven provides for everyone evenly so that they wouldn't have certain states suffer in destitute, while letting others thrive without a worry or care." Janice changes the screen to a picture of Meir giving a speech at his famous steel and golden podium, which happens to be the only place he gives speeches aside from his signature desk. "Meir tries to make sure the citizens are completely convinced that everything is distributed according to the amount each state works and that if you or your neighbor are in any sort of state of destitute, it is your fault for not working hard enough."

Janice explains that Meir and his regime want to keep his people dependent on the government as much as they can so that there is no threat of rebellion. That is another reason that Bestellen doesn't have a good education system; they are afraid that if they encouraged people to think for themselves to solve issues or to be more observant, we would have rebelled a long time ago.

"Man, I can't wait for us to take over," a kid a few seats over from me yawns out. "Then we'll be able to get out of this mountain and institute druppelen." All the kids in the room nod and murmur in agreement.

"Well," Janice interrupts the murmuring and tries to get everyone's attention again, "that sounds great and all, but you do realize that in one way or another, we too will have a flawed system."

I raise my hand and attract attention from everyone in the room. Half of the kids look at me in shock, while the other half freeze in surprise. Janice acknowledges my raised hand, and I ask her what "druppelen" is.

Almost every kid in the room rolls their eyes at me. Every kid but Henry, who turns back to Janice to hear her answer. She smiles down at me and folds her hands. "'Druppelen' is what we describe as you earn what you work for. Meaning the harder you work, the more you succeed. In order to earn wages with druppelen, you have to work, while geven rewards those who work as well as those who don't."

"Well, that makes sense," I answer. "So what flaw would druppelen have?"

Janice takes a moment to consider her answer. The expression on her face isn't exactly a smile, but more of a mixture of amusement and disappointment. She lets out a small chuckle. "There's always a flaw." Janice unfolds her hands and walks back over to her desk and types something on her computer. "Whether it's small or large. No system is perfect. Geven is supposed to keep everyone equally rich, while in reality, it keeps everyone equally poor. Druppelen is supposed to reward those who work hard, but it may only reward those who get lucky or who work hard at certain jobs. For example . . ." Janice pulls up a picture on the screen of a woman in a white doctor's coat, very similar to Dr. James's, and a woman wearing a gray jumpsuit with gloves and a trash can. Janice stands back up and holds up her little remote toward the screen. "These two women work equal hours, and both of their positions are important to life in Bergland. The difference that I am trying to point out is that our doctors and our cleaning services are on much different pay grades."

Janice sits back down in her desk chair and turns the screen off. The light-blue hologram flickers away, revealing the white marker board behind it covered in writing about geven and druppelen. "In Bergland, we provide food, housing, careers, hobbies, entertainment, and retirement for every citizen. But then again, we have a very involved system that makes sure everyone is following their schedules. We give people free time to do things they enjoy, and we have offices that you can go to if you want your schedule changed or adjusted. We don't try to control your whole life. We just try to organize it."

The girl from earlier that answered the question without raising her hand butts in, saying, "But when we all move out of the mountain, we won't have schedules like these, right?"

Henry nods. "That is what we have been told, but wouldn't continuing the schedule system help maintain order?"

A few of the kids that were talking about Henry groan loudly at his question, but he ignores their arrogance and waits for Janice's answer.

Janice nods back to Henry and leans back into her chair. "Well, yes. The schedule system would help us stay organized, and we will administer schedules just as we do here. But there will be more options when we leave the mountains. We will have more career opportunities out there than we do in here. The space in Bergland is limited, meaning we have to restrict where you can go and what you can do. But outside, you will have more room to explore different places, ideas, and hobbies."

"Like what?" James, the boy from earlier who dozed off, sits up straight in his chair and stretches, obviously barely staying awake. "What can we do out there that we can't do in here?"

The obnoxious kids beside me all murmur something under their breaths to one another. I can't make out what it is, but Janice takes notice of their disruptions. She stares them down until they stop talking. It takes them a few moments to notice, but when they do, they all face forward and wait for her to continue.

"In the mountain," Janice answers after everyone stops talking, "we control all of the farming space. Out there, you can own your own farms and do what you want with them and sell what you want from them. That's just one example. Another would be reporting. We don't have any reporters in Bergland other than the ones who do the news every now and then, and even then, they are just reading a script."

"Why did you guys choose the mountains if you don't have much room?" I ask. Again, every kid in the room other than Henry looks to me with surprise, as if it was a miracle that I spoke, as if it was amazing that I could even come up with a question like that.

"Bergland has always been a temporary idea. Never have we planned on staying here forever." Janice rises from her chair and walks to the other side of the room. She points to a picture she has framed of people working on an old elevator in a stone-covered shaft. This elevator isn't one that is covered all the way with metal doors like the ones now, but only little gates that come up to the man's waist.

"His name was Jackson Renner," Janice tells us, "the man who helped save what was left of the Diligent. He was a miner before all of the Diligent's hidden bunkers were bombed. When the bombing started, he gathered his mining team, and they managed to help a little under three thousand people get to safety from many different Diligent bunkers and cities. Though they saved many, we lost hundreds of thousands. Renner and his team joined forces with all of the builders and engineers they saved to build Bergland. We have never stopped their task of adding on to Bergland and improving upon the structures. Their determination to work with what they could turned this mountain into what it is today."

"What happened to the hundreds of thousands?" Logan asks. The girls sitting behind me and to my right all seem shocked that he asked, but more pleasantly surprised than they did when I asked. "Did they all die?"

"No," Janice plainly states as she moves away from the picture and leans against the marker board. "Many of them, yes, but a good portion of them were taken hostage into Bestellen. Those who refused to conform and never speak of Diligent ways again were executed or tortured for answers. Others conformed to save their own skin, for which I don't blame them. I believe they are the ones responsible for spreading the word of the Diligent in a land where your speech is greatly restricted. I have always wondered if they chose to conform in order to tell others about their beliefs or if they actually complied with the commands of their new government."

One of the rude boys in the middle of the room snorts and leans back into his chair. "I bet they only did that so that they wouldn't be forced to stay in a mountain for the rest of their lives." His theory earns chuckles from all of his obnoxious followers.

Janice rolls her eyes at his comment. "I won't stop you from making assumptions, especially when you already know they aren't true." She looks back to Logan, Mavis, and me with an expression that says "Don't listen to him. His arrogance will be his downfall."

The class mutters to one another, giving Mavis an in to say something without feeling the pressure of everyone listening. She meets Janice's eyes and quietly asks, "Will we ever get to go outside again?"

Janice looks around the class to all the people talking among themselves. She moves past them to her desk chair and scoots it over beside Mavis, Logan, and me. "We have very few people who are allowed to go outside right now, and those people are really only our pilots and our engineers that fix things like wind turbines. We can only let those people go outside for very small amounts of time to protect them as well as us."

Logan shakes his head and looks from Henry, who is listening intently, to Janice. "Are we ever going to be able to go outside again?"

Janice takes a moment to think before she answers. "Hmm . . . 100 percent honestly? The best chance we have to be able to go outside again as we please rests in us winning this war." She leans in toward us three and Henry. "And between us, Bergland will be launching full attack very soon."

Henry, beside Logan, sniffles and pushes his glasses back up his face. "Are we finally getting sick of playing this game of back and forth?"

Janice nods to him and smiles. "It's time for a revolution."

CHAPTER ELEVEN

Logan

The sound of one of the hand weights clanking against the others snaps me back into listening to John drone. "After those, we do sprints until I say stop. Some days are longer than others." John turns from the track back to me. "Any questions?"

"No, sir." I look around to see around fifteen to twenty men. Every man looks to be built of pure muscle. Some are lean, while some are large. But there is one thing I know for a fact: I am the weakest one in the room.

"Good. John nods to me with a serious expression on his face. "Follow me." Though John's expression is serious and I should be focusing on my current surroundings, I can't. All I can see is John looking at Mavis the way he did earlier. All I can see is his smug face as he fiddles with his food and looks Mavis up and down.

I try to forget it as we walk around the corner of the room to a large obstacle course, similar to the one that was in the first training room Janice showed us. This course is larger, faster, and longer than the original course I was shown.

I watch as one of the leaner men soars through the course with ease. He dodges the swinging posts, jumps over and ducks under the balls being launched at him from afar, and jumps from ledge to ledge. The lean man is followed by a slightly taller and thicker one. The larger man goes through the course a bit slower. He gets bumped by one of the swinging posts but stays on his feet. He trips over one of the rolling bars but manages to get back up on his feet. The large man goes running, trying to make it through the ball portion, but gets hit twice and goes flying off the risen course. The man lands on the blue foam ground and gets spit out just like the kids from the other course.

The lean man walks off the end of the course and grabs a water bottle and a rag. He wipes his hands off and glances over to me. His short brown buzz cut matches John's, but his stance doesn't. His stance is somehow much less offensive than John's. The man sees that I'm watching him. He nods to me and takes a few gulps of water.

I nod back.

John walks past the course with his hands folded behind his back. "These courses are here to help you with your stamina, speed, and reflexes. These are not here to show you what it will be like to fight. They are only here to help you get stronger." The lean man in the corner stares at me for a moment before disappearing into the rest of the room. John continues to walk as I follow. We make it down the open room to a set of double doors.

John swings the doors open and reveals another room, which is much smaller. It has a wall of guns, suits, and helmets with face covers on one side and a man sitting at a steel desk in front of a wall of screens on the other side. Each screen shows a different area of what looks like video footage of a flat arena with a few walls here and there. Everything in the arena is the same bland brown color other than the people. In the footage, there are a bunch of men in black suits running around. A few of them are leaning against the walls, rolling, ducking, covering, and so much more. They are all shooting at things that aren't even there and acting as if they are in a real war, a real battle.

I point at the screens and turn to John. "What are they doing?"

The man at the desk turns around to look at John, who gives him a subtle nod. The man scoots his chair forward and presses a button on the desk that lights the whole desk up with holographic buttons that he begins pressing rapidly with no real pattern. Within seconds, every screen changes into the same image, but there is no more brown. The brown walls are now buildings, rubble, and trees. The ground's plain and flat appearance has changed into grass, broken roads, and water. The atmosphere in each screen is that of a real battle.

"This is what they see when they put those helmets on." John steps forward. One of the men in the top-right screen gets shot by an official and flies backward. He lands on the ground, holding his right shoulder. "This is our simulation room where we train our soldiers for battle. We change the room into what our actual targets look like so they are prepared for what is coming. We also change it into random maps to keep them prepared for any unexpected changes."

Two of the other men in the top-right screen run out to grab the man who had been shot. They each grab his underarms and drag him back behind a building. The injured man holds his shoulder and scoots up against the building.

The man at the desk in front of us clicks a few buttons. "The suit they put on simulates the pain of a real bullet wound or whatever hits them. The pain will fade within a minute, so he will be fine. No real damage is done."

"So the Taai train in this as well as the other soldiers?" I ask.

John nods. "You won't be doing this today. Don't worry."

We watch the men on the screens throw grenades, duck and cover, run into and up buildings, try to get citizens out of certain areas, and do hand-to-hand combat at certain points. They do everything imaginable in this simulation, which leads me to ask John, "What exactly is the difference between the Taai and the other soldiers?"

John ushers me over to the set of double doors, and we begin walking back out to the main area by the track course. "The Taai is our elite military group that we send to get citizens away from certain areas, to sabotage defense buildings, to lure large groups of officials to one area and take care of them, and many other special assignments that our regular soldiers can't do."

I look around to see a few men running around the track and a few men lifting weights, all looking at John and me. "Have any of the Taai gone on any actual missions yet?"

John shakes his head, and we continue to walk. "Not yet. We are holding off until we have our plan perfected. Right now, it looks like it won't be much longer before we unleash full-on ground and air warfare." He looks out to the obstacle course as another man runs through it, getting clobbered by the shooting balls. "And once we do that, there is no going back."

"Well"—I feel the words fall out of my mouth without any effort—"obviously."

As soon as the words fall out, I lower my head. I know that I shouldn't have said that, but it just slipped out.

John cocks his head at me and scoffs. "Well then." John turns to the rest of the room and barks out, "Attention!"

All of the men in the room come marching over and line up side by side. I look around, then back to John, who is staring past me to the lined-up men.

"Soldiers." John folds his hands behind his back. "It seems Forge, our new recruit, wants to show us how to do the course." He turns back to me and looks me in the eye, challenging me. Challenging me to speak up or to challenge him back, but I don't. John makes my blood boil just by looking at him, but I won't have him know that. I won't let him know he gets under my skin.

I walk past him, keeping a straight face, right up to the beginning of the course. I step onto the red plate and wait for the course to begin. The silence of the other soldiers, mixed with the snickering from a few of them, makes the pressure rise. I look over my shoulder to see the guys on the end of the line snickering and muttering things between each other. Beside the snickering boys, toward the center of the line, is the lean boy who had run through the course flawlessly. This boy stares at me for a moment before giving me a nod.

A whirring noise begins as the red plate I stand on lifts me into the air. After rising about ten feet, I hop onto the platform with the large swinging poles. I dodge left, right, right, left, lunge forward, and pause. I make it through the first set of obstacles with no impact from the poles. The adrenaline pumps through me as I know I have to finish this course to earn their respect. I can hear and feel my heartbeat in my head as I approach the swinging rings that are just like the monkey bars back in the other course. I wipe the sweat off my hands and jump up to catch one of the rings above me before I swing away from the ledge, only to have the chain holding it up give out.

As you grab each ring, the chain it is attached to gives out a random amount, meaning you have to get across the rings quickly before they lower you too much to the point you can't get back up.

I roll my neck and my shoulders back and jump into action. I swing from ring to ring to ring, only allowing each one to give out a few inches. I make it to the end of the rings within seconds and am faced with the next set of obstacles. The firing balls.

I look at the wall that the balls come out of to find a few small cylinders all aimed at me. I look down to see a yellow line marking where this obstacle begins. As soon as I step across the line, the balls start firing rapidly. Over and over. I step back behind the line to see if I can get them to stop firing, but they don't.

Realizing that there is no way out of this other than to run across and get to the other side, I take off. I duck, I jump, I freeze, I dodge. I make it halfway across the ledge, almost to the end, when one of the balls shoots out and hits me in the head full force.

The dense ball catches me at an angle that throws me off the ledge, and I land on the foam floor that swallows me up as I hit the ground. When the floor resumes its hard state, I sit up and look back to the line of Taai. The boys on the end of the line chuckle at my failure, while the lean boy that nodded to me earlier does nothing but looks to me with disappointment.

I rise to my feet and touch my temple, where the ball had hit. I am definitely going to have a bruise there tomorrow, but the pain I feel is nowhere near as irritating as the fact that John made me do that in front of everyone. I begin walking back toward John when one of the larger boys on the end chuckle a little too loud.

"Hey!" John roars. "What's so funny?"

The large kid with the zigzag pattern shaved into the side of his head and his pals on the end stop chuckling, but they have trouble wiping off the smirks on their faces. I can't help but clench my fist while I try to keep from forcibly blinking. I clench once. Twice. Three times.

"Oh, you must think it's funny that Forge here made it farther in this course on his first try than any of you did on your first ten tries." John lets out a little sarcastic chuckle as the smirks on the boys faces fall. "Yeah, that is pretty funny."

My head throbs along with the clenching of my fists. Once. Twice. Three times.

John marches to the end of the line to the boys who are no longer smirking and begins walking down the line. "I want you boys to keep in mind that Forge here is one of the only people that have ever made it to Bergland from Bestellen. One of the only people that have survived in those woods dealing with the flora and fauna without any sort of training. You show him just as much respect as you show your fellow soldiers. You treat him no differently than you treat any Taai newbie. Got it?"

All of the men in the line answer in unison, "Yes, sir."

I clench once, twice, three times. John makes his way over to me, and I straighten up. I make sure that I appear 100 percent fine, as if nothing has happened. I appreciate John's defense, but he still shouldn't have sent me up there in the first place.

He asks me in a hushed tone, "Are you okay?" as if he actually cares.

I nod.

John points me over to the end of the line, on the opposite side of the obnoxious boys. I go over and stand by a man almost a foot taller and definitely a good hundred pounds heavier than I am. We all face forward to John as he turns back to the group. "All right. I assume everyone has warmed up. Time to begin."

Mavis

The large white metal pot sits in front of us on the floor. It is the tallest pot I have ever seen. Even with it sitting on the floor, the top of it, with the lid on, comes up to my belly button.

Sarah, the food lady, comes over to Sam and me, who have just set the pot full of water on one of the metal plates in the corner of the room. Sarah reaches up and wipes the sweat off her forehead with her wrist. "Okay, so since it's sitting on a burner, you want to be careful and maintain a safe distance because you *will* get burned if you touch it."

Sam answers for both of us, "Got it."

As I look around in the kitchen behind the cafeteria, I see a room much larger than I imagined. There are at least twenty different coolers, multiple sets of floor and stove-top burners, and many worktables. Sarah is the woman who was assigned to show us the ropes while everyone else in the kitchen goes about their business. Overall, Sam and I have received a lot of attention. Not in a bad way per se, but a lot of attention. In the kitchen, people have been congratulating us nonstop about making it through the woods and welcoming us to Bergland. Not that I have a problem with all the kindness—it's just . . . I have never been a big fan of talking to people. Don't get me wrong. I will be nice to you all day long and humor you and talk with you, but I won't enjoy it.

Sarah scoots past us and twists the pot with its handles until it clicks into place. "Now we wait for the water to boil, just like we did with the pasta." She looks back and forth from Sam to me. "Any questions for that?"

Sam and I shake our heads.

The three of us have just made three pots full of what Sarah calls "spaghetti" as our first lesson. Never before have I ever heard of spaghetti, seen any sort of pasta, nor made anything like that—hard food made soft by the hot water, made flavorful by the pasta sauce, and made ready to eat by the workers. The amazing scent that radiated from every end of the kitchen was one I had never experienced before nor an experience I wanted to stop enjoying.

The other members of the kitchen team continue to work on preparing the rest of the spaghetti for lunch while Sarah ushers us through the kitchen. "While we wait for the water to boil, I'm going to show you two how to shuck corn."

Sam looks to me with an expression of surprise. "You guys have corn here?" he asks.

"Of course!" She rolls out a double-level cart stacked with boxes of corn. "We have a lot of foods you guys have, if that's what you mean."

Still confused, Sam crosses his arms. "What about the thing we ate the night we got here?" He quickly uncrosses his arms and waves his hands around to try to help him find the right words. "That . . . um, purple thing?"

"Oh, those were rollburries." Sarah lifts up one of the boxes of corn and plops it onto the steel countertop. "They are one of our original fruits."

"Original fruits?" Sam steps forward and grabs another box off the cart. He sets it onto the counter beside Sarah. "I am going to need further explanation."

Sarah chuckles and rolls the cart beside the counter. She steps onto a little brake to keep the cart in place. "When I say 'original fruits,' I mean specially designed fruits. Our team of scientists were able to breed superfruits that have a high content of everything we need to live. All of the vitamins necessary, all of the calories necessary, and a whole lot of protein. Rollburries are one of those fruits."

Sarah waddles over beside us, opens a drawer, and pulls out a knife. She reaches into one of the boxes and grabs one corn. "The best way to do this is to cut off the ends, then to peel off the husk. Like so." She does exactly what she describes, very slowly to show us what to do. Sarah slides out two pots on a wheeled platform from underneath the counter and drops the shucked corn into one and the shuck and ends into the other. "One more time." Sarah goes through, strips the whole corn within a few seconds, then hands the knife to Sam. "I think you guys are ready."

Sarah pulls out another knife and hands it to me. "I am going to go and add another few pots of water to the burners. Come get me after you have shucked all these, and I will show you what to do."

She waddles off, leaving Sam and me holding knives beside eight boxes of corn. Sam turns to me, holding the knife up in one hand and a piece of corn in the other. He chuckles at me and gets to work cutting and shucking.

"So . . ." I pull out a cob and start cutting. "How are you liking Bergland?"

Sam sets down his knife and tries to pull off the husk. He does it so quickly and efficiently compared with me. I try to do the same, but I have trouble getting off all of the little stringy bits that lie underneath the husk.

"It's okay. I like Janice. Grayson seems cool too. I just . . ." Sam tosses the cob into one pot and the trash bits into the other. "I miss my mom. I am worried about her."

I nod. "I'm sorry." I don't know what to say to him. I can't say I miss my dad. I miss Derek and his family. I miss my uncle. But my dad?

Sam looks over to me, still cutting up the edges of the corn. "I'm happy I met you and Logan, though."

I can't help but smile. "Thanks. I'm happy I met you guys too." The image of those giant rats from the woods comes into focus. I remember that feeling of walking in the woods all alone when, all of a sudden, I heard a gnarly gurgling noise behind me. I remember turning around to find one giant rat after another slowly approaching me. "I'm not too happy about the *way* we met, but I'm still happy we did," I chuckle.

"Yeah." Sam finishes two more cobs. "Sorry about that."

"Don't be. It's not your fault." I finish one cob and accidently toss the trash bits into the wrong pot.

As I fish the bits out, Sam continues with his cobs. "Can I ask you a question?"

"Sure. First, let me ask you a question." Bit by bit, I manage to get them out just before Sam throws in another cob. I toss the trash bits into the right pot and turn to Sam. "How are you so good at this? Shucking corn?"

He chuckles, "My mother is a farmer. We eat corn a lot."

"Oh." That sounds nice. Eating corn a lot. The only time corn ever makes its way into my house is when it has been distilled and bottled.

"My turn." Sam finishes another cob and tosses it. "Um . . . did you . . . um . . . notice John Young yesterday?"

"Notice him?" I pull off what I can of the shuck on one cob and toss it into the trash pot. I start picking at the little stringy bits of the cob and turn back to Sam, who is trying his best to avoid eye contact. "What do you mean? I noticed he was at the table."

He throws another cob into its pot. "I mean he was . . . um . . . staring. At you. I noticed he was looking at you a lot."

I noticed it too, but I don't want to admit it. "What do you mean? He was staring at you and Logan too. Not just me." I haven't really thought about John since breakfast. Sort of.

Okay, a little bit.

Why was he staring at me?

Sam pulls out a few cobs and cuts all of the corners off first. He sets down the knife and starts shucking each one. "Are you sure he wasn't staring? Because it looked like he was." Sam tosses the cobs into their pots. "I used to be really good at picking up on these sorts of things. I was always able to tell if someone liked someone else." He brushes off the counter and swipes all of the shuck trash into the pot beside him. "I guess I'm losing my mind."

"No, Sam. Don't worry." I grab another cob. "I did notice him staring at me a bit."

Sam pulls out a few more cobs, and a smirk rises up on his face. As he begins cutting, I realize that he pulled the guilt card on me and tricked me into admitting. Well played, Sam.

"I thought so," he affirms.

Neither of us say anything for a moment. The only sound between us is the chopping and shucking. The people on the other side of the kitchen are all busy with their chores. They are sweeping, cutting, cooking, talking . . . glancing. Glancing at us.

I avert my attention from our surroundings and go back to the conversation at hand. I slide the shuck and trash off the table and into my hand. I toss them into the pot behind Sam.

"So . . ." I grab another cob and cut off the ends. "Why do you think John was staring at me?"

Sam shrugs. "I don't know." Another moment or two of silence pass Sam finishes off one of the boxes and switches it out for a full one. "I mean, he is a little old for you. But who am I to judge?"

I chuckle and scoff. "What? What are you talking about?"

Sam picks up a single piece of corn that had fallen on the table and pops it in his mouth. He smirks. "Well, why else would he be staring at you like that?" He swipes off some of the trash. "He thinks you're good-looking."

I toss some of the corn strings left over from the table at him. "Shut up."

Sam pulls off some of the strings that stuck to his shirt and tosses it back at me. "Well, I mean, you asked!"

"Yeah yeah yeah. Whatever. John may have been staring at me, but at least I didn't have a whole table of preteen girls fawn over me at breakfast."

"What?" Sam is taken aback by my claim. He picks up the flung-around strings and puts them in the appropriate pot. "What are you talking about? Those girls like Logan."

I scoff again. "They may like Logan, but they definitely like you too. I mean, can you blame them?" I grab a piece of corn that separated itself from the cob and pop the piece in my mouth. "You are adorable."

Sam sputters. He tries to get some sort of defense out, but all he can spit out is "No! Uh-uh."

"Yes you are!" I grab another cob and start cutting. "You may not know it, but you are."

He looks down at the corn and tries his hardest not to make any eye contact with me.

I chuckle and continue with the corn.

After a few more moments of silence, Sam looks over to me, scratching the back of his head. "You think?"

I snort, "Yeah. I do."

His face grows red as he goes back to shucking. I turn back and try to catch up with his pace but can't. For every cob I do, Sam does three. The part that takes me so long is the picking of the strings. I can't seem to get them all as quickly as Sam does.

Time flies by, and Sarah returns to us as Sam and I finish the last few cobs of the first three boxes. "Oh good! You guys have almost filled the pot." She hobbles past us and to the pots in the corner of the room. Sarah peeps over and into the pot and gives a giddy chuckle. "Perfect timing too. The water has come to a boil." She makes her way over to us and rolls the filled pot of cobs over to the pots that are boiling.

Sarah reaches back and tilts one of the lids backward so that the steam rises away from her face. Once the large puffs of steam leave, she sets the lid on the counter beside her. "Now you are to take half of the cobs and put them in this pot and half in the other. Can you do that for me?"

Sam and I nod. Sarah smiles at us and pulls out a small gray plastic rectangle with buttons. She punches something into it and hands it to Sam. "When you get all the corn in, press the 'start' button. When it beeps"—Sarah waddles over to the wall beside the pots and points to a set of buttons on the wall—"press the blue button, and it will drain all of the water. Once you do that, come get me."

"Yes, ma'am," we answer.

Sarah walks off one way, and Sam another. I watch as he makes his way back to the table from where Sarah pulled the knife. He shifts through the utensils in the many drawers, leaving me alone with the corn.

I assume he knows what he is doing and begin with the corn. I grab five cobs at once and hold them over the pot. The steam rises up and burns my arms the longer I hold the cobs over, so I drop them.

"Wait!" Sam shouts at me as the water from the pot jumps up and scalds every bit of my arm it touches.

I groan and pull my arms back, holding them against my stomach.

Sam closes the drawer and scurries over to me. "Sorry, I was trying to keep you from doing that." I look up from the ground to him, who is holding up two long pairs of tongs, which he clicks twice when he sees that I have noticed them.

I chuckle, trying to forget the new burns I have on my forearms. Sam hands me one pair. "Watch." He uses his pair to grab one cob from the pot and sets it into the boiling water without making the slightest splash. "See? No mess."

I wipe off the rest of the water that is left on my arms and follow his example. One cob after another, Culinary Aid passes by much quicker than it had arrived.

I wonder how Logan's training is going . . .

CHAPTER TWELVE

Sam

Day 3 of following a schedule has been much easier than days 1 and 2. Now I know where I am going or where to meet up with Logan and Mavis at least. According to my schedule, today is the only day of the week that our class, including Mavis, Logan, and me, are to go to the "orange room."

Mavis and I have just finished our Culinary Aid session and are meeting up with Logan in the elevator room on the physical floor after he finishes his training. The physical floor is only part of the PL, or the "physical level," which holds not only all the training rooms but also the top section of the hospital.

Coincidence?

I think not.

Bergland is separated and built in levels. Each level has different floors with different things on it. That's the reason there are so many elevator rooms. There are elevators that take you horizontally and vertically, along with stairs that can take you every which way.

Mavis and I break off from our conversation about Sarah's guffaw when we see Logan come around the corner of the hallway. He holds one hand on the back of his neck, rubbing it as if he has a crick, and the other fist clenched by his side.

"Hey, guys." He makes his way over to us, moving his hands from their original position to the straps of his backpack. Logan shifts the straps and gives Mavis and me a smile. "Ready to go?"

Mavis returns the smile and presses the elevator button. A flat bulb above one of the elevators lights up green, and the doors slide open. The three of us pile in and go through an awkward pause as we realize just how many buttons and levels there are in this mountain. Almost a full wall of the elevator is taken up by these buttons. Lucky for us, there is an encased list of where everything is on the wall adjacent to the buttons.

After making it to the correct floor, we follow the sounds of rowdy kids to find Janice bent over, unlocking a door with the keys hooked on her lanyard, and our classmates hovering around her. Her keys clink against the door as she pulls them away and swings it open. She holds the door for us as we file in behind all of the other students.

As soon as I enter the room, the first thing I notice are the lights, then the bins, and then the smell.

Janice closes the door behind her and shuffles out from behind the three of us. "Welcome to the orange room!"

I look past her to the long orange bulbs lining the ceiling, the risen garden beds spaced throughout the room, and all of the plants seemingly growing perfectly fine without any real sunlight.

Janice pardons herself as she scoots past Logan, Mavis, and me to the large bins on the wall of the room. She hands us each a pair of gloves and turns to the rest of the students. "All right, everybody, go get a pair of gloves, a hand shovel, and a bucket."

The kids all rush past us to the bins, knocking into Mavis and me on the way. We scoot back to join Janice by a framed picture of the layout of the room and listen to the kids as they fight to get the best equipment.

"Come on! I need the gloves to match!"

"Yeah, so do I. So give it to me!"

"Um . . . no, I had this one first. You stole that one from me!"

"No I didn't! I had this first."

"Hey, come on. I literally had my hand on the end of the shovel."

"Oh yeah? Then how come the shovel is in my hand?"

"Mrs. Ludley! Marcus stole my gloves!"

Janice rolls her eyes at the commotion she obviously deals with every week. "I'm sorry about them. You'd think that they would have learned to share by now."

"Why don't they have their own gloves?" I ask, shocked at how quickly these so called "friends" are turning on each other.

"The only ones who have spent their credits on gloves are Henry, Rea, and Jackson." Janice points over to Henry, a boy twice his size in height, and a long-haired brunette girl who is about a foot taller than him, standing side by side, awkwardly awaiting instructions. They each have on a fairly decent pastel-colored pair of gardening gloves compared with the torn-up, ratty brown pairs of gloves the other kids have pulled out of the bins. "The others usually spend the few credits they earn on food or entertainment."

"Credits?" Mavis asks. "What credits?"

Janice pulls a pair of teal gloves out of her back pocket and fits her hands into them. "During the free time you have on your schedules, you can choose to sign up for different jobs here and earn credits that you can spend on whatever you want, like clothes." She wiggles her fingers into one of the gloves and points over to Henry. "Usually, we only get a few kids smart enough to invest in a decent pair of gloves even though we come here every week." She fits on her other glove and chuckles. "And then we have other kids, like Rea and Jackson, that have their parents buy their gloves."

I wiggle my hands into my gloves. "How do you sign up for the jobs?"

"It really depends on what you want to do. One of the easiest jobs that you can do without much training is join the cleaning crew. You don't make much, but you still make enough to treat yourself to a few desires. Such as . . ." Janice raises her hands to eye level and shakes them. "Gloves!"

Mavis cracks a smile, still sliding on her gloves. They look about a size or two too big for her, but she doesn't seem to mind.

"All right, class!" Janice shouts out, getting everyone's attention except for the few obnoxious kids. "Hey, listen up!" The kids grow quiet. Janice nods and scoots away. She raises her arm and points to the framed layout of the room. "Okay, today, we will be doing pod A3. Harvesting bugels and planting rollburries. Everybody, go ahead and start harvesting. Once we get all of the bugels harvested, let me know, and I will pass out the seeds."

I watch the class's reaction as all of their faces change into different expressions. Some seem excited to garden, while others seem like they absolutely hate it. Henry is one of the kids in the middle. He looks as if he would rather be doing something else, but he doesn't abhor it.

Janice turns back to us, and her eyes meet mine. She flicks her gaze over to Mavis and Logan to get their attention, then points to the mapped-out orange room. "These boxes right here are the tool bins. This little silver line on the wall is where we are by the map of the room, and this box back here that is labeled A3 is where the kids are over there."

She backs away from us and pulls out a few buckets. As she hands one to each of us, Janice explains that the lights they use in the orange room that make it orange are light bulbs that emit the same sort of energy that the sun does without the harmful UV rays.

The lights they use in the orange room are also the same sort of lights they use in the rest of Bergland, only much stronger.

Janice explains, "We use these bulbs throughout Bergland so that everyone gets some sun exposure. That way, when we leave Bergland, we won't be completely blindsided by the sun. We also use them to prepare our skin so that we won't burn too easily."

She points over to the kids covered in dirt. "They aren't replanting bugels in the same place from where they were just harvested because it is better for the soil if you rotate the produce you plant in it. It has a lot to do with the chemical compounds and the minerals in the soil. I can explain it all if you want."

"No. No, it's okay," I answer. "Thank you, though."

Janice chuckles and passes out small hand shovels to each of us. "No problem." She looks to us all and lifts her bucket and shovel. "Ready?"

Mavis and Logan nod, but I am distracted by a sudden movement. I shake my head to Janice and set my bucket down.

"May I use the restroom?" I plead, pulling off my gloves and setting them in the bucket. Janice sighs at me as if she is disappointed that my kidneys are doing their job. "Please?"

She chuckles, "Yes. Go ahead. It is right down the hallway to the left."

I nod and skid past them. As I open the door, I notice that its metal handle is cold to the touch compared with the rest of the room. The fact that its temperature is the polar opposite of the room strikes me as odd, but as soon as I make my way out into the hall, I realize why the handle was so cold in comparison.

The temperature shift from the orange room to the hallway sends a shiver down my spine the moment I step out. The cold temperature falls on me so quickly and so fully that I immediately want to go back into the orange room. The walls in this rounded hallway look just like most of the other walls in this country. They look just like the inside of a mountain.

My hand meets the rocky surface of the wall directly beside me as I adjust to the temperature. I begin walking down the hallway, running my hand across the cold and bumpy brown surface as I go. The air ducts are always in the same place in all of their hallways—in the top corner of the ceiling between the rounded edges of the ceiling and the wall.

The light fixtures are also pretty much in the same position and have the same design in every hallway in Bergland. They are always one long and large beam of light, attached to the center of the ceiling by its metal fixture. If I hadn't spent my free time with Mavis and Logan exploring Bergland the last few days, I would be totally and completely lost.

"Yeah right."

"You literally could not be more wrong."

Deep voices from around the bend of the hallway bounce off the walls right over to me. Their chattering and laughter grow louder much quicker than I expect as we both round the bend and meet. The boys look to be around my age, just much taller and more muscular. Four of the five boys are shoving one another and participating in horseplay while one thin boy stays a few feet behind them, shaking his head and smirking as he watches his friends be Neanderthals.

The boys quickly approach, and one shoves the other right in front of me without even realizing it. The largest boy that stumbles toward me catches himself and belly-laughs at the one who shoves him. "You're an idiot."

"You're the idiot!" The smaller boy laughs, pointing back at me, only a few inches behind the larger boy who had stumbled upon me.

The large boy turns around and looks over my head, then slowly adjusts his gaze down at me and meets my eyes. The top of my head comes to his chin, which doesn't help me feel any better about this situation.

I clear my throat and stammer out the words, "Excuse me."

The large boy in front of me scoffs. "Well, yeah. Excuse you." He turns around to the others, and I notice the zigzag markings shaved into the side of his head. All of the boys around him, except for one, all hoot and holler in agreement with his statement and shout something sarcastic at me. The large boy with the zigzag hair leans down to get in my face, backing me into the wall. "Are you stupid or something?"

"No. No." I stutter, "I-I'm just going to the restroom." The boys look at me, unconvinced and amused.

"Then why are you on the orange room level?" the zigzag-haired boy demands.

"I'm coming from the orange room. My . . . my class is in there." The boys look from one to another. I try to explain again. "I'm with that class."

"Really?" the boy with the zigzag hair asks, still looking down at me as I'm pressed up against the wall. "Are you an idiot or something? You're like seventeen. Why are you in that class? Don't the junior highers have the orange room today and tomorrow?"

"Yeah, they do." A guy struts up from behind Zigzag and slaps him in the back. "This guy has got to be stupid if he was held back that many years."

"Obviously!"

"Why else would he have been held back? Because the teacher likes him so much, she couldn't let him leave her class?"

"Those are some of the easiest years to pass."

I shake my head at the sound of all of their voices piling up together. The slight twitching underneath my right eye returns lightly every few seconds—so lightly that it is barely noticeable to others, but not light enough that I can ignore it. The medicine I took my first day here has held me over, and I haven't had many symptoms since. I had my first vial in the doctor's office and my second administered by Caine and Grayson. But these voices and these criticisms are piling up, and I can feel the relief I have felt in my days here slipping away.

"No! No!" I shout to them, trying to get them to stop and listen. "I'm new here. New to Bergland. I . . ." I clench my fist and come off the wall to speak to Zigzag and the others like an adult. "I'm from Bestellen. You may have heard about us. I came with two others. They are in the orange . . ." I turn to point back to the room and get shoved back into the rocky wall by Zigzag. My head hits first, and my shoulders follow.

"Oh! So you're one of them!" Zigzag growls at me, smirking. With one of his arms pinning me against the wall, he turns back to his friends and chuckles. "Hey, guys, did you hear that? This guy is from Bestellen! Can you believe it?"

I nod and try to get out from behind his forearm, but he jerks his head back to me and shoves me back against the wall harder than the time before.

"Hey? Where are you going? Trying to escape again?" Zigzag's face drops into a sarcastic expression meant to mimic pity. "Oh, wait. You didn't escape the first time, did you?" He pauses, waiting for me to answer. Not knowing what to say, I don't say anything at all.

My lack of response seems to further irritate him.

"No." Zigzag forces his arm against me once again. "No, you didn't. You didn't escape Bestellen. You were kicked out."

I shake my body, trying to force him off me, but my attempt to escape seems to make Zigzag stronger.

"Oh, I'm right, right?" he chuckles. "There was a reason they kicked you out, wasn't there? What was the reason, retty?"

All of his friends behind him join in and jeer.

"Yeah, retty?"

"What's wrong, rett?"

"What? Retty can't speak?"

Zigzag laughs, pulls his arm off me, and shoves me into the crowd of other guys. "Get a load. This guy is so much of a rett that he can't even explain himself."

One boy takes the back of my shirt and throws me forward. Zigzag catches me by my arm with a grip so tight that his fingers dig into my skin. They toss me back into the ring of boys, and all jeer at me, repeating the term "retty" in one way or another. I try to force myself through the circle and make my way back to the orange room or even to the restroom but fail. The boys have me trapped in a constant state of shoving and taunting. As I feel the anger rise in me like a large sum of compressed air, forcing my face and torso to get hot, I notice the one thin boy standing behind all the others shaking his head.

"Hey." The thinner kid approaches the others and shoves them off. Zigzag grabs hold of my arm and throws me once again into the wall. The cold and rocky surface does little to cool the rage that burns my skin like fire.

Zigzag pins me down with his forearm against my chest as I thrash, trying to get away. I let out a sort of grunt-scream that makes all of the boys laugh as I try to kick and hit my way out. My legs flail upward, and my fists swing forward as Zigzag slides his arm up into my throat.

The skinny one shoves past all of Zigzag's laughing accomplices and grabs his shoulder. "Come on, man. This kid is obviously defenseless."

"Yeah," Zigzag answers, pressing his arm into my throat so forcefully that I stop breathing for a moment. All I can feel are his arm hairs and his warm skin against mine. His forearm is so thick that it covers the whole surface area of the bottom of my chin, my neck, and part of my chest. Zigzag chuckles, "That's what makes it fun."

The thin kid growls, trying to avoid eye contact with me. "Picking on someone smaller than you proves nothing." Zigzag stays in his same spot, choking me until I start to see dark spots. I begin to feel a hard pounding in my head, matching the beat of my heart but amplified through the numbness my head starts to feel. The thin kid grabs Zigzag's shoulder and yanks him off me, leaving me limp and falling to the floor. I can hear a slight shuffling beside me as I gasp and try to catch my breath.

"Come on, man! What's your problem?"

"Me? What's *your* problem? All I was doing was giving the new kid a proper welcome!"

Their voices overlap as I rise to my feet with the pounding in my head even louder and more overwhelming. Not only is there a strong force, like a hammer beating in the back of my head, but the sound has almost tuned out all other noises around me. Their voices are muffled as if they are speaking into a pillow, but the volume is still at full capacity.

Before I know what I am doing or have any time to come up with a plan, I find myself launching forward and taking down Zigzag from behind. His body, almost twice my size, tumbles down, squishing me. In seconds, he has me pinned to the floor with his knees on my shoulders. I shout out in pain as his two-hundred-pound body bears down on my shoulders and crushes my bones against the floor. Zigzag raises one fist to punch me, causing me to flinch.

"Ha!" Zigzag lowers his fist without hitting me, surprising myself and all of his accomplices. I thrash underneath him but am unable to actually do any real damage or get him off me. The tingling I felt when I first awoke in the woods a few days ago slowly returns through my fingertips. The sandy feeling moves from my fingers at a leisurely pace to my elbows, making it much harder to make a fist and bend my arm at all. The boys around us laugh and point, jeering at me and calling me a retty. The imminent defeat begins to sink in, fueling my rage further, and the pounding in the back of my head has become almost unbearable. The pounding has gotten so severe that Zigzag sitting on me doesn't even hurt in comparison.

"Hey! Look!"

I glance over to one of the bullies as they walk out of my view behind Zigzag, who is blocking almost everything in front of me.

"Oh yeah!" Zigzag exclaims, reaching back to his friend. "Perks of being a rett." He slides off me and swings the vial in his hand down into my thigh. The medicine injects and drains out of the glass in seconds, sending me from a serious sense of rage and urgency to a mixture of irritation and relaxation.

"Ha! Look at that!" one of the boys shouts out as they all stand over me. "Look at how tired he got. This must have been a pretty strong dose."

"Yeah," another kid cackles. "He must be a pretty strong retty."

Zigzag crosses his arm and snorts, "Or a really weak one."

"He *is* pretty tiny."

"Yeah, maybe the medicine just has a stronger effect on weaker people."

"Obviously."

"Either way, he was too easy."

"Man, what a freak."

The boys walk off, leaving me on the floor, taking deep breaths by myself, trying to work up the energy to get to my feet. The sense of calm I feel is even more overwhelming than the pounding I had felt earlier.

I mean, I'm not even really angry anymore.

It's more of an irritation and annoyance with the boys rather than anger. I am too busy enjoying the feeling of sinking into the floor and at the same time floating above it.

"Hey."

I open my eyes to see the skinny boy of the group standing over me. Unable to move or *unwilling* to move, I just stare. Our eyes meet for no more than a second before the boy squats down and helps my limp body to a standing position. He holds my right arm over his shoulders and slips one of his hands around my waist.

"Hey, are you okay?" he asks me as if he actually cares.

I look back to him as he stares at me, waiting for an answer. I nod to him. "Better than . . ." I take a breath and brush off my desire to make a sarcastic comment. Speaking after taking medicine is one of the most difficult things I have ever had to do. All I want to do is just sit and enjoy the calm.

Just sit . . . and enjoy . . .

"Hey, it's fine. You don't have to talk. I'm sorry about them."

I take another deep breath as I dangle from the skinny dude's side. "Do you want to go back to your class?"

I take another breath and shake my head with what energy I do have. "No." *Deep breath.* "I have to pee."

The skinny dude looks surprised by my answer at first, but after a moment, he nods and helps me get to the restroom. He helps me get into the stall, and I handle my business.

After it's all said and done, I sit down on the toilet seat. The sound of the seat meeting the bowl clinks and echoes through the room.

"Hey, um . . . are you okay?" Skinny Dude asks through the stall door.

I nod. After a moment, I remember that he can't see me and answer, "Yeah, fine."

"Okay, um . . . so—"

"You can go now," I say, interrupting him.

"Yeah, I don't know." Skinny Dude sighs, "Are you sure you're okay?"

"Fine. You can leave now."

"Okay." Skinny Dude makes his way to the door and pauses for a moment. I can almost feel him contemplating asking me if I am okay again. Which I am. I don't need someone to help me only after his friends are gone but wouldn't help me when his friends were here.

Skinny Dude leaves the bathroom as the door squeaks closed. I lay my head back against the stall wall and close my eyes for a moment. I think back to Zigzag as I leaped from my spot and took him out. I bet I am one of the only people here who have actually knocked him off his feet. Except for maybe . . . well, I don't know.

I loved that feeling. The feeling of knocking him down. I didn't mean to get that feeling. I never meant to attack him. I didn't even try. I wasn't in control of my actions or my emotions. I just watched myself attack. Just like those other guys watched me attack. Just like those other guys watched my emergency vial fall out of my pocket and hit the ground. They didn't have any control over it. They just watched.

I have to wonder if I would have stabbed Zigzag with the vial, if he would have reacted like I did—like I am. I'm glad I didn't, though.

Honestly, I like the relief. I like the relief I feel when the medicine kicks in. It is the only sort of calm I feel. It has been the only sort of calm I have felt since Dad died.

Since Dad . . .

The door handle back to the orange room is cold. Cold and metal, just like it was forty minutes ago when I left the room. Just like it was before I was attacked. Just like it was before I blacked out.

The first thing I notice when I enter the room is Janice, Mavis, and Logan all being given the buckets of bugels to stack in the harvest bin in the corner of the room. All of the kids are bringing over their full buckets of fruit one by one. Mavis and Logan look to be having a fun time stacking and talking with Janice. Henry stands by the bin with a clipboard and a pen, writing down numbers that are meaningless to me.

"Sam!" Janice calls out joyfully, turning the heads of Logan, Mavis, and Henry, who all shoot me a welcoming smile.

I nod to her and try to return the smile. Janice immediately takes off her gloves and heads over my direction. "Hey, are you okay?" Logan and Mavis quickly follow, leaving the kids to talk among themselves.

Shocked at how quickly Janice jumps to the conclusion that something is wrong, I take a step back. "What? I'm fine. Why?"

Janice's face changes from an expression of concern to one of disbelief. "Because you were gone a lot longer than you should have been."

Mavis looks to me for an answer. "Sam, what's wrong?"

I shake my head and glance down at my feet, avoiding all eye contact I can. "Nothing's wrong."

"Are you sure?" Logan asks me.

"Yes," I spit back. "I'm fine."

Mavis and Logan continue to look at me. I can tell they are worried and want to keep asking, but they can tell that their curiosity is really irritating me.

Janice turns back to Mavis and Logan. She clears her throat and waves them off. "Kids, go ahead and go help plant the rollburries. I will be there in a minute." Mavis and Logan nod in compliance and make their way back over to the harvest bin with Henry.

Janice swiftly turns back around to me. She lowers her head, still keeping her gaze on my eyes. "Honey, I would have believed you if you wouldn't have reacted so defensively. I would have believed that you got lost or something," I lower my head to try to avoid further eye contact, but she crosses her arms and continues anyways, "But now I know something is wrong."

"I'm fine," I try to answer normally.

"Honey." Janice takes my hand and looks at my eyes—not *in* my eyes, but *at*. "Your eyes. The whites have a slight pink tone." She changes her gaze from the whites of my eyes back to my pupils. "Have you taken some medicine?"

I pull my hand away from her slowly. Janice is one of the only people in this mountain that I trust, but is it really any of her business?

"Sam?" She looks me in the eyes and holds my gaze. She stares at me for moments upon moments, waiting for me to explain.

"What . . ." I look over to Mavis and Logan, who glance from their spots by the planters back to me. I shake off their attention and turn back to Janice. "What's a 'retty'?"

Janice's eyes grow. "What? Where did you hear that?"

I look away from her back to my feet.

"Did someone call you that?" She pauses, waiting for my answer. When I don't speak, she steps closer to me and whispers, "Sam?"

I shrug, not wanting to answer. "What does it mean?"

She takes a deep breath and folds her hands in front of her. "'Retty' is an awful term that bullies have begun to use to describe people with mental disabilities. Even the slightest issues." I glance back up to her to see her shaking her head and clenching her jaw. Her hair, up in a ponytail, has begun to come so loose that the layers in her hair are falling out every which way. "Sam, did someone call you that? Do you know who it was?"

I shake my head and look back down.

"I can go and check the security cameras in the—"

"No!" I shout. Everyone in the room turns back to look at me due to my accidental scream. "I mean no. Please. It's fine." If Janice were to see the video, she would see the whole thing that happened. She would see me getting beat up. She would see me being sat on, being forced against the wall, being abused with my own medicine. "It's fine."

"Are you sure? We have no tolerance for bullying in Bergland. Anyone who messed with you can and will have serious punishments if I find out the names."

"No. Please, Janice." I learned from a very, very early age that snitches get stitches. "Please. I'm okay."

Janice sighs. She narrows her eyes at me and shakes her head. "Fine. Just this time, though, and only because you asked. If you ever have any trouble—and I mean *any* trouble—with anything at all, please know you can come talk to me."

I nod. "Yes, ma'am. Thank you."

She smiles and hands me a bag of seeds from the seed bin beside her. Janice sends me off to go plant with Mavis and Logan while she and Henry keep counting the bugels.

I notice when I approach Mavis and Logan as they make the mounds side by side that Mavis has already made her mound of dirt and planted her seeds. She is just standing by Logan and watching him. Logan's mound is a perfect square with rounded-off edges. Inside of the mound, he has drawn out a perfect circle, where the rollburry stand will go; and he is laying out the seeds one by one from what seems like a perfect distance apart from one another.

Sure, watching him achieve his obsessive idea of perfection can be calming, but it also makes me wonder. What if what the guys said in the hallway is true? What if we really are undesirable? Just for having mental quirks that others don't? From my point of view, Logan's quirk doesn't seem so bad. It doesn't seem like a big deal, but it was.

It was a big-enough deal that he was kicked out into the woods to survive on his own. Why was it, though? Are the guys right?

To those who don't have mental illnesses, are we freaks?

CHAPTER THIRTEEN

Mavis

As Logan, Sam, and I walk out of the classroom down the hallway, the lights above us flicker. We pause for a moment and look at the bulbs to see the only one flickering is the one directly above us.

I turn around, planning on going back to the classroom to tell Janice about the light, when it stops flickering and goes back to normal.

"Come on, let's go." Logan places his hand on my shoulder. His fingernails have obviously been chewed on and the tips of them bit off, leaving not a lot of the pink part left.

Slowly, I turn back. Logan's hand is still resting on my shoulder, and Sam is a foot or two away, standing with his hands in his pockets. Sam nods us over as he falters forward. Logan lowers his hand from my shoulder and walks by my side as we follow Sam.

I notice the top of one of Sam's vials sticking out of one of his pants pockets and another vial doing the same thing in one of the other pockets. The longer I watch him walk, the more I realize that he has his pockets full of the vials, and they seem to be weighing him down.

I try to say something but find that I can't get the words out. I turn my head and look to Logan, who continues to walk beside me. I try to get him to look at me, but he continues to stare and march forward.

A light fixture flickers above Sam, who freezes in surprise. He raises one hand and uses it as a shield for his eyes against the irritating lights.

Before he can say anything at all, the mountain shakes. A large rumble and boom take place, sending shock and terror through us all.

Another tremor hits. The walls begin to crumble, releasing a few pebbles at a time. All of the lights flicker and sway on the small wires holding them up.

The third tremor hits, and one of the strings on the light fixture above Sam snaps. The large metal box swings down, hitting him. The other wire holding it up snaps, dropping the full weight of the fixture onto his body.

A puddle of blood slowly begins to spread underneath the fixture as the fourth tremor hits, and all of the walls crumble over us.

My legs jerk, along with the rest of my body, as I wake from the nightmare. The bed above me shakes as I jolt, and the girls around me jump up as my gasping wakes them. My heart beats rapidly through my chest to my head and feet. Mandy hops down from the bunk above me.

"Hey, hey, shh . . ." Mandy kneels down and waves everybody off so that they can go lie back down. "Are you okay?"

I nod my head, trying to play off the fact that I just watched someone I love get killed, followed by another person I love and myself getting buried alive.

Mandy rises and pulls off a bag hanging from the top bunk. "Come with me." She backs up a bit and waits for me to get out of the bed. I stare at her for a moment, then look around the room to see a few of the other girls staring at me.

"Come on," she reiterates. I finally get to my feet and follow her out of the room to the dimly lit hallways, and she closes the door behind us. "Are you okay?" she asks me, her soft voice somehow echoing through the hall.

I sniffle and bring my hands up to my eyes. I rub until I see spots swirling around the room. "Yeah, fine." My hands lower to find Mandy staring at me, waiting for further explanation. "It was just a nightmare," I tell her.

Mandy leans against the wall beside the door. "What happened this time?"

"A bomb." I think back to the other nightmares, the ones where I was back home. I push those thoughts aside and answer Mandy. I sniffle again and lean on the wall beside her. "Bestellen had dropped another bomb. The walls caved in."

Mandy nods. She slowly slides down the wall and takes a seat on the ground. "I'm sorry." She pats the ground beside her, convincing me to sit. I slide down beside her as she looks into my eyes and becomes more serious than I have ever seen her before. "I get those too. In mine, the walls don't cave in. The floors break, and we all fall through."

I take a breath and force the words out, "I'm sorry." Why would she pull me outside if she has her own problems to deal with?

Mandy shrugs. "It's fine. It's not your fault." After a moment or two of silence, she pulls out a purple notebook. The shiny coating of the notebook's cover makes it hard to read the words written on it due to the glare. She sets the notebook in her lap and pauses.

"Here." She sighs, handing me the notebook.

It's thicker than I originally imagined. Mandy sets the book into my lap and opens it up, revealing an amazing rendering of the training room.

"This is my midnight madness." She turns the page, revealing a drawing of the room caving into itself. "Whenever I have a nightmare, I find that drawing helps me relax and later be able to go back to sleep."

She turns the page again, revealing a gorgeous drawing of a man who looks strikingly similar to Mandy.

I stop her hand before she flips the page over. "Who's this?"

She pauses.

"Is he in Bergland?" I ask.

"He . . . um . . ." Mandy clears her throat. "That's my dad." She turns the page. "Yes. He's in Bergland. Like everyone else you will see drawn in here, they're all in Bergland."

"These are amazing, Mandy." I continue turning the pages to see drawings of all sorts of different things. All perfect renderings of images I have seen in Bergland, but I keep thinking back to the picture of her dad. "Why is your dad in your nightmare drawings?"

"I don't just draw my nightmares." She points to a picture of an odd-looking tree. The branches are very short at the base of its trunk, but they get longer toward the top of the tree. "I draw my dreams too."

"A tree?"

"I've never seen one before." She shrugs. "It's just one of those things I have always wanted to do. You know, 'climb a tree.'"

I chuckle. Never before have I thought about how sheltered these people have been. "Have you ever seen an animal?" I ask.

Mandy nods. "Yeah, we have a floor especially set aside for dogs. But dogs are the only type of animal I have seen."

"A floor for dogs?"

"Yeah. We train them to, you know, fight. They're war animals."

"They're companions," I correct her. There were always a lot of stray dogs running around in Bloot, most of which would die of starvation. I always made sure to give any sort of scraps left over from my hunts, like intestines, to the nice dogs that lived near me. Though I never fed any dog more than once, mainly because of the officials' dog population control, there are a few dogs that I feel I will always remember. Their kindness and willingness to be my friend always warmed my heart.

Mandy shoots me a puzzled look when my claim meets her ears. I can tell she wants to debate but is too tired for it. She pulls a pencil out of her bag and holds it up. "Here."

I stare at the pencil for a moment, then look back to her. "What?"

"Take it." Mandy shakes the pencil at me. When it meets my hand, its smooth surface takes me back to when I was younger and would draw with my mother. We would set aside time to spend together and sketch each other or common things around the house while Dad and Steven would be out working.

"For what?" I ask, still holding her journal in my lap.

"For this." Mandy leans over and flips through her book to a blank page. "This is the same book that Janice gave to me when she was my room advisor. She told me about the therapeutic benefits of drawing and whatnot."

I look down at the pencil and twirl it in my hand.

"Listen, one thing may work for me, and another may work for you. But will you give this a try?" Mandy looks at me, waiting for an answer. After a moment of silence, she continues, "If you don't like it, you don't have to do it."

I set the tip of the pencil down on the paper and look back to her. "I will."

She nods and rises to her feet with her backpack. "Come back to bed when you are done."

As Mandy places her hand on the door handle to open it, I blurt, "Why didn't you give me the medicine?"

Her hand falls from the handle. "What?"

"The medicine," I repeat, "like you did the first night I was here. You tried to give me medicine then. Why not now?"

Her soft smile grows. "Because you didn't need it." I look to her, confused. She places her hands onto the straps of her backpack and pushes them forward. "You are learning about anxiety, and you are learning to control it. That first night, I offered because you had never had a panic attack before, right?"

I nod.

"So I was just trying to help. Now I think the best way to help you is to help you find out how to control it. Or at least manage without the medicine."

I look back down to the blank page before me, wondering how she would know what's best for me or how to help. "How often do you get them? The nightmares?"

"Often enough."

"That first night, when you told me to trust you about what Janice said . . . what did you mean?"

Mandy places her hand back onto the door handle and gives me a shy smile. "You aren't the first person with anxiety Janice has dealt with."

I nod and raise the pencil. Mandy smiles to me and accepts my silent thank-you as she heads back inside our room. When the door closes behind her, the click of the lock echoes throughout the hallway. I am suddenly much more aware of the empty presence surrounding me. The hallway floors are lined with luminescent paint to help guide the way in case of a blackout, but since the lights are still barely on, the green glow of the lines are only noticeable to me because of how close I am to the floor.

I look from each end of the empty hallways down to the pencil and paper Mandy gave me. What should I draw? Should I draw Sam and the fixture crushing him? Should I draw myself and Logan, with the walls crumbling down? Or should I go another way and draw the absolutely gorgeous view I got to see from the treetops in the woods? The view of the hundreds of trees and the gorgeous mountains against the beautiful backdrop of millions of stars twinkling away in the sky was one of the best sights I've seen in a long time.

No.

Mandy started out in this journal by drawing her nightmares.

So will I.

Logan

After almost a week of training, the aching of my sore muscles has finally began to lessen in intensity. Though they are still sore, I can now walk without looking as stiff as a wooden marionette doll. Mornings are the hardest but have been getting much easier the longer and harder I train. I guess my body is getting used to the daily beating I receive.

Sam has left the room this morning a few minutes before me. I guess he has gotten tired of my morning moaning and groaning. When I finally make it up to the cafeteria, I see the normal morning rush of people scurrying around the room to go sit with their friends or associates.

I see Mavis, John, Sam, Janice, and Mandy all sitting at the same breakfast table that we have been going to since I got here. John continues to smile at Sam and Mavis as he talks to them, telling them something that he must think is extremely clever.

As I enter the cafeteria and make my way over to the table, John leads Mavis and Sam up to the food line. He offers an invitation to

Janice and Mandy, but Mandy grabs hold of Janice's hand and tells John and the others to go ahead. Mandy watches the three walk toward the line as she continues to hold on to Janice's wrist. After the three are out of sight, Mandy pulls out a notebook from her bag.

Janice takes the notebook from Mandy and asks her something I can't make out. Mandy sporadically opens the notebook and points at something on one of the pages with a look of slight terror. Janice's eyes focus on the page as she listens to Mandy jabber on about something. Just as I approach the table, Janice nods to Mandy and says, "I think you may be right."

"Hey," I say as I sit across from them.

"Hey! Hi, Logan!" Mandy swipes the notebook out of Janice's grasp and plops it into her own lap. "Hey, man! How's it going?"

Janice raises one eyebrow and looks to Mandy. "That wasn't suspicious at all." Mandy darts her eyes back at Janice.

"So . . ." I fold my hands and lean forward to peek over the table. "What's that?"

Mandy's fake smile fades as she eases up and places the book back onto the table. "Logan." She looks to Janice, then back to me with an unsure look on her face. "Do you know anything about Mavis's background?"

"Background?"

"Yes," Mandy confirms, "like her homelife."

"Um . . . yeah. She lives with her dad. Her mom and brother died a while back. Why?"

Janice folds her hands on the table and leans forward. "How did they die?"

"I don't know exactly." I look past Janice and Mandy to the large groups of people shuffling across the room. I can't see Mavis or the others. "She just told us that there was an accident."

Mandy and Janice look at each other with a look that I am unfamiliar with.

"Did Mavis ever show any signs of anxiety when she talked about her dad?" Janice asks. "Did she ever scratch herself or try to avoid eye contact when the topic of family came up?"

I think back to every time I mentioned Gramps or Sam mentioned his mom. I think back to the times we talked about our family, and she would change the subject or ignore it completely and remain silent. I think back to when Sam and I talked about how we want to help save our family from Bestellen, and Mavis just stayed quiet. Every time the topic of family came up, she scratched her arm, averted eye contact, and ignored the subject.

"She doesn't like to talk about her family." I look from Janice to Mandy and ask once again, "Why?"

The two look to each other for a moment before Mandy opens up the notebook and slides it over to me. On the open page is a sketch of a small wooden shack. In the background, there are other out-of-focus houses that are about the same size as this shack but aren't nearly as well drawn. There are trees growing around, over, and through the houses and one large one right beside the main shack that takes up most of the page. The front of the house has a small overhanging roof over an even smaller patio, all wooden. Beside the open doorway lies a broken and dirty window, which I barely notice because I am too focused on the black figure standing in the doorway.

"What's this?" I look from the sketch to Mandy, who is picking at her nails. "What does this have to do with—"

Mandy swipes the book from out in front of me and shoves it back into her bag. "Mavis is coming."

I look over to the line of people as they walk back to us and see John smiling and talking with Mavis. He walks her over to the table and nods to me just before he walks off and sits with a few of his associates.

Mavis comes around the corner of the table and sits beside me with a kind smile as large as can be. "Good morning, Logan."

I smile back to her, trying not to seem too obviously distracted by Mandy and Janice's sketch. "Good morning, Mavis." John sits a few tables over from us, but I can still see him eating his food and glancing over to our table every now and then. "So why isn't Commander Young sitting with us? He was here earlier."

"Oh . . . um . . ." Janice clears her throat and straightens her posture. "He can't sit with us when you're here due to him being your commander. He is required to keep a professional distance."

Professional? What's professional about flirting with and making eyes at an eighteen-year-old girl when you are almost twice her age? Nothing at all.

Sam careens out of the large crowd, looking slightly irritated. He holds his tray close to his body as he makes his way over and plants himself beside Mavis. "Thanks for waiting for me, Mave."

She holds one finger up to cover her mouth as she chews. Then she swallows the food and chuckles, "I'm sorry! John told me to 'come on,' so I did."

"Yeah, yeah"—Sam rolls up his sleeves—"no big deal." He looks from his food to Mavis with a joking expression. "This time."

Mavis nods. "Got it. Last time."

The two chuckle as they dig into their food, leading the rest of us to become hungry just by looking at it. I see my chance to get Janice and Mandy alone and take it. "Do you guys want to go get food?"

Mandy and Janice nod as the three of us rise. We make it about twenty feet from our table when that group of girls a few years younger than me ambush Janice. It's the same group of girls that were staring at Sam and me the first day.

"I'll catch back up in a bit." Janice waves us off while she immerses herself into the group of girls. "Go ahead."

Mandy takes no time and marches forward.

"Hey!" I scurry after Mandy, who is refusing to look at me. "Mandy, Hey!" I grab her arm and turn her to face me. "What was that a drawing of?"

She looks away from me and down to my free hand. "Do you always pop your fingers when you're anxious?"

"What?" I loosen my hand, which has been popping its own knuckles. "Why?"

"I've noticed that everyone has a sort of . . . tick." She pulls free of my loose grip on her arm. "Yours is to fiddle with your fingers." She turns around and heads to the end of the line. "And to sometimes blink funny."

"Mandy, what did that drawing have to do with Mavis?"

Taking a deep breath, Mandy turns back to me. "That picture was drawn by Mavis last night." She crosses her arms. "I told her that drawing could help soothe her and help her recoup from nightmares."

"Okay. And?"

"Well, that black figure you saw?" Mandy pulls the journal out of her bag and flips through the pages to Mavis's sketch. "Here, look."

I glance over it, then back to Mandy.

"What do you see?" she asks me.

I look back to the picture. The black figure is a perfect silhouette of a man standing in the doorway. His head is tilted down, looking at something he holds in one of his hands. From the shape of it, it looks to be a bottle.

"A man with a bottle," I answer.

She closes the notebook and slides it back into her backpack. "Logan, what do you think that it means? The man with a bottle?"

I shrug, getting slightly annoyed with Mandy for not spitting it out already. "I don't know."

"Well, I have a pretty good guess."

"How?" I step aside and pull Mandy with me. "How do you know any more than me?"

"The class I am majoring in is psychology. Long story short, my best guess by looking at this picture is that Mavis's dad is a drinker."

A few people pass us by and make the breakfast line even longer. I set aside my stomach's growling and focus on her words. "How do you know? How do you know it isn't just a drawing?"

"Janice agrees. She had to study psychology in order to be a teacher, and she agrees." Mandy looks around and jumps in the back of the line. "One of the things we learn is how to analyze handwriting, art, and words. This fits right into what I have learned."

"What . . ." I take a moment. Everything Mandy says sinks in. All of the signs that Mavis has been having trouble at home have been obvious, but I never asked. I never cared enough to ask. "What else did you get from that picture?"

Mandy shakes her head. Never before have I seen her this serious. "Mavis may . . . um . . . have been abused." She turns back to me. "Don't hold me to that! I said 'may have.' I don't know for sure. But from what I have learned, it is very likely, according to her picture."

"Logan." Mandy meets my eyes. She glares at me and holds up the line of people behind us. "You have to promise me that you won't say anything. The only reason I told you is because you, Sam, and Mavis are all best friends."

I look back behind us to our table, where Mavis and Sam talk with each other. Mavis looks about as happy as I have ever seen her. Is it because this is the longest she has ever been away from her dad? Is it because she is finally free from an unsafe home?

"Can I at least tell Sam?" I ask her.

"No. Not yet." Mandy pulls me forward in the line. "I just want you to be aware and look for signs if you can. Don't bug her about it, though."

I nod.

"Promise? You won't say anything unless she says something about it?"

I nod again. "Yes, I promise."

Janice comes over to Mandy and me, laughing her head off. When she finally catches her breath, her face is red as a tomato. "Sorry about that." She straightens her posture, and we all move forward in the line. "Those girls crack me up. I miss having them in my class."

Mandy loosens her face and allows it to go back to its normal overly joyed expression. "What'd they want?"

"They—" Janice bursts into laughter once again. "They wanted to know . . ." She composes herself and looks over to me. "They wanted to know how old you and Sam are."

"What?" I ask.

"Yeah, they were wondering why they had never seen you or him before. When I told them that you guys had come from Bestellen, they got so excited." She chuckles again, adding, "One girl actually said, 'Oh my goodness! They must be so strong to have made it through those woods!' The others all agreed and began ogling over you guys."

I look over my shoulder to three of the girls who are standing by their table. Two of them see me looking at them and give me little waves.

Mandy laughs. "Logan, you're blushing."

"No I'm not!"

"Yeah you are!" We all step forward in the line and grab trays. Mandy continues, "You are totally blushing! Do you fancy one of those young ladies?"

"No, I don't." Not one of the ones from that table.

Mandy scoots over to me and playfully pokes me in the arm. "Then why are you blushing?"

"Maybe because you are embarrassing me?" I look Mandy in the face. "Ever think of that?"

Janice's mouth gapes as she laughs at the two of us.

Mandy turns from me, blushing. She hands hers tray to the lady who was to serve our breakfast and smirks. "Touché, Logan . . ."

CHAPTER FOURTEEN

Sam

The kids sitting behind me have just stopped talking about Henry . . .

And started talking about me.

I can feel the whispers and stares without even looking at them. I try to ignore them and focus on Janice, who has just changed the screen to our next assignment.

"Everyone, get into groups of four. I want each group to make two columns and list true Amiable beliefs versus Diligent beliefs. I don't mean what Bestellen does. I mean the true beliefs that Bestellen claims to follow. The group with the most factual beliefs listed by the time the timer goes off wins. Go ahead and start."

Everyone in the room scrambles together to get into their groups. Henry hops up from his seat and runs over to us, slamming down a piece of paper on Mavis's desk. "Do you guys want to be in my group?"

We all look to one another and send a mixture of shrugs and nods. Henry gives us a large smile and gets to work. He draws a line down the middle of the page and writes in large letters "Amiable" on one side and "Diligent" on the other. He starts scribbling down lists of beliefs on each side as the three of us watch.

Mavis looks over to me with an amused smile, then back to Henry. "Do you want us to help?"

Without looking up from the paper, Henry continues to scribble. "Well, with all due respect, I think I know more on this subject than any of you." He looks up and slides it over to Mavis. "But if you want to help, feel free."

Mavis's eyes grow as she takes the pencil from Henry. "No pressure there," she chuckles as she looks down to the list and jots something under the "Amiable" section. "They supposedly belief in free health care."

"Right." Logan leans over the back of his chair and points at that same column. "And they believe everyone should make the same amount of money."

"And that everyone should be treated equally," I add.

Mavis continues to scribble things under the "Amiable" column as I look around to see the rest of the students huddled over one desk per group. They loudly shout things that need to go on the lists, not even considering the fact that we could steal their answers.

"Wow!" Henry watches Mavis quickly fill up the "Amiable" side with different facts. "You guys are doing great. Much better than I thought you would." Logan and I shoot Henry a look. He throws up his hands and waves them at us. "No no no! I didn't mean it like that. I think you guys are very smart. I just meant that you haven't been in schooling as long as I have."

"We know," Logan chuckles. "It's fine, Henry."

Mavis slides the list back to Henry, who skims over everything she had just written. "This is great." He takes the pencil back from Mavis and continues scribbling down facts much faster than expected. Henry fills up the whole front page with facts and starts writing more on the back page in the "Diligent" column.

"You know, it's impressive enough that you are in this class as young as you are, but combine that with your writing speed?" Shaking my head, I lean back into my chair. "Henry, you are very impressive."

"Thank you." Henry, without looking up from the paper or ceasing to write, clears his throat. "I have been told that a lot."

We sit there in silence for a moment, listening to the other kids in the class shout answers at one another. The really obnoxious kids all grouped together, forming the alpha bully. I can see a few of them looking over their shoulders back at our group as if they have something they want to say.

"So how are you guys adjusting to life in Bergland?" Henry asks us, never shifting his focus from the paper.

I look to Logan and Mavis. Logan looks down to his hands and continues to rub his fingernails. "It's nice." He looks up from his fingers and over to the screaming kids on the other side of the room. "I miss my family, though."

I nod in agreement. "Me too. I miss my mom."

Logan and I look to Mavis for an answer. She takes a moment and keeps her focus on Henry's spasming hand as it scribbles. "I like it," she says. "Sure, I miss the fresh air, the sun, and going outside. But this is the first time in a long time that I get to have three meals a day and more than two sets of clothes."

We sit there for a moment, listening to the sounds of the shouting kids. Mavis breaks our silence with a question that has been on all of our minds. "When do you think is the next time we will get to go outside?"

Henry, still scribbling, answers, "When Bergland launches ground attacks." He sits up straight and looks his list over. "Which, at this point, I doubt will ever come."

My heart drops. Just thinking about being trapped in this mountain for the rest of my life while Mom is stuck in Bestellen makes my stomach turn.

Henry adds one more thing to the Diligent side of the list and shrugs. "The war has been going on for such a long time now that the bombings don't even faze me anymore. The only real reason I try to hold on to hope is because of the view."

"The view?" Logan asks.

"Yes. The outside of the mountains. I hear they are beautiful from the outside."

As the timer goes off, Janice rises to her feet. "Pencils down! Pass them up!" Henry immediately slaps his pencil down onto the desk. He hands his paper up to Janice and sits back into his seat right next to Logan.

Janice takes the paper from him and gives him a smile and a nod. "Thank you, Henry."

Henry's face blushes slightly as he sings back to her, "You're welcome, Mrs. Ludley!" She walks past him to the other groups. The three of us all look to one another, smiling. It is about as obvious as could be that Henry has a crush on Mrs. Ludley.

Janice takes up all of the papers as the rest of her students scurry to their seats. "Okay, talk among yourselves while I check these."

The kids erupt in chatter. Henry turns back and flashes us with a large and goofy smile. "Usually, those who win Mrs. Ludley's little competitions like this get homemade tarts!"

"A tart?" Logan chuckles.

"Absolutely positively the all-time best food I have ever eaten in my life." Henry flails his arms in excitement. "And you know what? Mrs. Ludley has mastered the art of tart baking!"

At her desk, Janice pulls out a red pen and writes something on the papers she has just collected. Still confused by the lack of explanation Henry gave us, I shift my focus back to him. "What exactly *is* a tart?"

"A combination of a multitude of things. Ranging from some of our genetically modified plants to things as simple as cane sugar. Nonetheless, it is amazing." Henry pushes his glasses back up onto his face. "And pretty rare too. You have to have access to a kitchen to make them or have a lot of credits to buy them."

I think back to Bouw, where almost everyone had a kitchen of some sort. Almost everyone was able to cook and make their own food, but here in Bergland, only a select few can. With the credits you earn after you join their workforce, you can buy your own room and whatever you want to have in it. You can even buy multiple rooms and make your own little house, but people here have no need to buy their own kitchen supplies. They are provided free food until they finish schooling and are forced to join the workforce. By then, they are used to being fed, so they will probably keep going to the kitchens and buy food.

"All right!" Janice rises from her seat with a sheet of paper in her hands. She marches to the front of the class and snaps for everyone's attention. "Okay, all right! Guys!" Everyone quiets down and looks back to her.

She smiles. "Thank you. We have our winners." Janice pulls up the paper and wiggles it. "Drumroll please!" Everyone in the class pats on their legs in unison, including Henry. Janice looks down to the paper and calls out my name, Logan's, Mavis', and Henry's.

The four of us can't help but smile. I look over to the other kids in the room and watch as they scoff. The obnoxious kids continue to whisper and give Henry dirty looks, now extending to me. Before I get the chance to say or do anything, Janice interrupts. "All right, you four, stay for a bit and come get your treats. Everyone else, class is dismissed!"

The kids all get up and sling their bags over their shoulders. One boy makes sure to stomp out and shove a desk out of his way. He scowls at me just as his body exits the room. Henry seems unfazed by all of the whispering and dirty looks he gets from his classmates as he jumps up from his seat and rushes over to Janice's desk, but it doesn't help me feel any better about the situation.

Janice grabs a green plastic container off her desk and pops off its lid. She leans it forward for Henry to pick his tart and chuckles. "Go ahead."

"Thank you!" Henry grabs his piece and scurries backward, out of our way.

Janice leans the bucket toward Logan. "I heard Henry tell you about tarts. I don't know that I 'mastered the craft' of making these, but I have had a lot of practice."

Logan looks over the end of the bucket and glances over all of the pieces and picks one out of the corner. He pulls out a small powdery ball and walks over by Henry, who has already eaten his entire piece.

Mavis picks her piece out quickly and heads over by the others. I follow her example and grab a piece at random. The small ball is squishy, like dough, and very pleasing to the touch. I look over to Logan and Mavis, who hold the tarts in front of them, hesitantly observing them.

"Well, what are you waiting for?" Janice pulls a ball out of the bucket and holds it up. "Cheers!" She takes a small bite out of the side of her tart and moans with joy.

Logan, Mavis, and I all sniff and/or squeeze the ball. We look at one another and chuckle. Mavis is the first one to take a bite. When she does, her eyes close, and her mouth curls up into a petite smile. Logan follows her lead and takes a bite. He doesn't react in the same way she does, but he seems to enjoy it just as much.

The moment the powder hits my tongue, I know everything Henry says about tarts is true. The soft dough is sweet and light. It leaves me satisfied, but not stuffed. I lick what's left of it off my fingers and watch Henry thank Janice, say goodbye to us, and leave the room.

Logan swallows the last few bits of his tart and chuckles to Janice, "Can we have more?"

She chuckles and wipes the powder off her hands. "If you win another mini challenge." Janice pulls out a pump of hand cleanser from behind her desk and takes a few squirts. "You guys are going to need to go ahead and get going. You don't need to be late for your next post."

Each one of us nods to her and takes a squirt of the hand cleanser.

Janice closes up her container of tarts as we all grab our things and begin heading out of the door.

She chuckles just before Logan crosses the threshold. "Hey, Logan, tell Commander Young I said hi."

Clenching his fist, Logan answers, "Yes, ma'am," and heads out of the room.

Mavis and I leave Janice to her empty classroom and head out into the hallway. We have quite a few minutes before we have to be in our cafeteria. There are two public cafeterias in Bergland, and the one we are to go to for Culinary Aid is only about two miles away by foot.

We make our way through the hall, chatting about what we've learned, about Henry, and about anything else that comes to mind. I slide off my jacket and tie it around my waist as a noise pierces my ears.

As we round a bend, the familiar sound of chattering and horseplay echo through the hall. Their deep and obnoxious laughs make my stomach curl as the group of guys that roughed me up the other day come into sight. Zigzag leads his pack of idiots down the hall straight for Mavis and me while the nice and lean dude who helped me to the restroom is nowhere to be seen.

"Ooh!" Zigzag looks Mavis up and down as he and his goons strut by. "Look at you, girl. How come we haven't seen you before?"

Some of the boys whistle at her. Another snorts, "Yeah, and what are you doing with the retty?"

I can feel my face get hot as they continue to catcall her. The boys walk past us and continue making comments about "the retty." I rush forward, leaving Mavis a few feet behind me.

"Hey!" she calls out, running after me. "Sam!"

The embarrassment rises in me as I stumble forward, ignoring her pleads.

"Sam!" She grabs my arm, which I jerk away from her, and continue forward. "Sam, what's wrong?" I feel her eyes watching as my cheeks grow red from anger and embarrassment. Mavis continues to walk beside me, keeping up with my pace. "Did you know those guys?"

I stop in the middle of the hallway. Mavis passes for a moment, then stands in front of me with her arms crossed.

"Sam?" she repeats.

"No," I answer, "I don't know them."

Mavis tilts her head and narrows her eyes at me. I lower my head and look to my feet. The embarrassment on my face is obviously showing.

"Then why are you upset?"

"Because they called me a retty." I storm past Mavis and march down the hallway.

She scurries beside me, trying to get my attention. "A 'retty'? What? What's that?"

I can't help but stop and turn to her. Before I know it, I am looking down at Mavis and shouting in her face. "It's one of us! A 'retty' is what they call people with mental disorders!" I pull myself back and look at the horror on Mavis's face. Her eyes have faded. The optimistic sparkle that found itself at home in her eyes when we arrived in Bergland has been swallowed up by a dark and fearful look that shakes me to my core.

"I . . ." I back away and take a few deep breaths. "I'm sorry."

"How . . ." Mavis chokes back the tears slowly rising in her eyes. "How do you know those guys?" She watches as I struggle keeping my anger and embarrassment in. "How do you know what 'retty' means?"

I stay silent. I don't want to share what happened. I don't want to relive the embarrassment.

"Sam." Mavis takes a step forward. She gets closer to me than she needs. She tries to look me in the eyes, but I keep my focus averted from her. I know if I see one tear fall from her cheek that I caused, I will lose it. "What did they do to you?"

I look up to see her focus on my elbow. The large and swollen black-and-blue bruise throbs as I realize how observant she is. I straighten my arm and get the bruise out of her sight, but it is too late.

"Did they do that?" She points to the bruise on my arm, formed from Zigzag's tight grip.

I throw my jacket back on to cover the bruising.

"Sam." Mavis reaches out, like she is going to hold my hand, but she retracts. "Please, just tell me."

I take another breath, trying to cool my cheeks. Nothing works. Maybe getting it off my chest will. I tell Mavis what happened with those guys. I tell her about how I was just trying to go to the restroom when Zigzag and his goons started throwing me around and calling me a retty.

She reaches out. This time, she takes my hand. "Sam . . ."

Pity.

That's all she has for me.

That's all she feels for me. I don't need her pity. I have enough on my own. I am embarrassed enough without Mavis making a scene and treating me like a child. I yank my hand out from her grasp.

She slowly retracts her hand. "Are you going to tell someone?" Mavis stammers out the words, "I . . . I mean, you have to!" She says it like it is an obvious decision that would be stupid to ignore.

"No!" I bark. "And you can't tell anyone either!"

"What? And let them get away with it?"

I square up and get in Mavis's face once more. Before I begin shouting like I did earlier, I calm myself and work the words into a growl. "My mother always taught me that snitches get stitches, and there hasn't been a single instance that has proven her wrong."

"But, Sam . . ." Mavis steps back from me. "I'm sure Janice would make sure that—"

"No!" I shout.

Her body jolts as my scream echoes off the walls, getting attention from a few passersby.

"No," I utter. "Don't tell anyone, Mavis. Just don't."

"But, Sam . . ." She looks to me, wanting to convince me to turn in the goons. Before she gets the chance, I storm off. I march away as quickly as I can and escape from Mavis's sight.

The bathroom I break into is a single. As soon as I get into the room, I slam the door closed and lock it. My heart spazzes as I struggle to get the overwhelming mixture of wet and dry anger under control.

Dry anger is the type of anger where your nostrils flare and your whole upper body clenches to try to get yourself under control. It is completely different from wet anger, which is even more uncontrollable. Wet anger is where you sniffle, your eyes flood, and you choke on your emotions.

I look into the bathroom mirror, panting. I slide off my jacket and try to sling it off, but one of the sleeves gets caught on my right wrist. I fling and flail my arm around, trying to get it off. When it finally comes off, I find myself picking it back up and trying to tear it to pieces.

Why did those guys treat me like garbage? There was absolutely no reason for it and no logic behind their actions. I throw my jacket back down after failing to tear it and stare at my reflection as it stares back at me. I pull down the collar of my shirt to reveal the long strip of bruising on my chest from Zigzag's arm.

Why did I let them do that to me?

Why did the nice dude let them do that to me?

Why didn't the nice dude jump in to help?

Why am I so useless? Pitiful? Unnecessary?

All I want to do is break the mirror. All I want to do is fracture the reflection that is me. I want the reflection to look just as awful as I feel. I want the reflection to cease to exist. I want to cease to exist.

Wait.

The vials. Last time, they made me feel so much better.

Better. That's what I need.

Better.

I reach down and open up one of my pants pockets. I pull out the smooth glass vial. Its blue medicinal contents drain into my leg the moment I inject it. Within seconds, I feel the calm warmth radiate from the injection sight. Slowly, it moves down to my feet, then circulates back up my legs to my torso. I slide down the wall and take my seat on the cold tile floor.

The wall supporting me seems to give in, just like the blue foam floors in the training rooms. I lie here consumed with the odd feeling of relaxation that I am not acquainted with. It's a feeling that I would like to have more often. A feeling that is so much more enjoyable than anger.

The gray grooves in between each white tile on the floor seem to collect dust much more than any tile. I wonder why they use tiling in the bathrooms, while the hallways have hard and flat flooring. Why would they have concrete floors on some levels, while carpet on others?

My head seems to sink further into the wall behind me, and my shoulders relax even more. I feel myself fall back into the wall as my breathing steadies.

Better.

That's what this is.

Better.

Mavis

With its hard and thin blue skin and its even harder solid yellow pit, bugels top my list of the strangest food I have ever come into contact with. The moment I enter the kitchen, Sarah asks me where Sam is. She puts me to work immediately after I told her I had no idea.

Sarah leaves me alone with all of the bugels to peel and pit. Hundreds, maybe thousands, all by myself.

That's not what I am concerned about, though. I'm worried about Sam.

Why did he storm off like that? Why did he get so angry? And why won't he turn those thugs in? What they did was assault, and they should be punished accordingly.

Forgetting the bullies, I can't stop thinking about their victim, Sam. I am worried. Where did he go? Why didn't he tell me sooner? Does he not trust me? I think of him as a brother, and I would hate it if he felt like he couldn't trust me.

At this point, I don't know if I can trust *him* anymore. I wonder if he even knows how loud he was shouting, how loud he was shouting at *me*. Never before has Sam scared me in such a way. He is one of the sweetest people I have ever met. I would absolutely hate to think of him as anything but.

I peel and pit for an hour before Sam comes into the kitchen.

I turn to him, not sure what to do. "Hey," I softly say, hoping to not scare him away, "Sam."

He ambles over toward me. Slowly, he lifts his head and looks to me. The whites of his eyes are glazed over with a subtle pink. He stares at me as if he has no feelings or thoughts at all.

Empty. He looks empty.

"Are you okay?" I set the bugel and the knife in my hand down on the table. "Where did you go?"

Sam shrugs. "Nowhere." He makes his way over to me and points at the bins full of bugels beside the table. "Are we doing these?"

I nod.

He turns from me and heads to the sink. He washes his hands, puts on a pair of gloves, and returns to the pit and peel station. We work together silently for a moment before Sam clears his throat. "I'm sorry I was shouting at you." He continues to peel.

I shrug it off. "It's okay." He was obviously dealing with something. "I'm just happy you're okay."

"I am. Thanks."

We continue to work with the bugels for the next thirty minutes. The process goes a lot faster with Sam helping. I watch him peel the fruits as the pink in his eyes fade. By the end of the period, he looks like his normal self, but my mind is still soaring.

Where did he go?

What was he doing?

I push my thoughts aside and try to do my job.

Sam and I work and work. We go back to our normal little side chatter and joking. We joke about Logan joining the Taai, about those girls who ogled him and Logan, and about how weird Bergland is.

Sarah comes by and takes the freshly peeled and pitted bugels away so that she can deal with them further. Another two workers in the kitchen come by and take all of the peels and pits away to an unknown location.

Everything finally seems like it is back to normal when the siren goes off.

CHAPTER FIFTEEN

Mavis

"Follow me!" Sarah hobbles through the crowd, rushing out of the kitchen. She pulls off her hairnet and waves us to follow. "We go to tunnel 48C."

Sam and I exchange a terrified look. Neither of us has heard this alarm before. The bomb alarm sounds like a buzzer. This is more of an overwhelming wailing.

"What's going on?" Sam shouts over the siren.

Sarah doesn't seem to hear him, so I repeat the question. "Sarah! What's happening?"

She looks over her shoulder but ceases to stop forcing her way through the masses. "Fire alarm. We didn't have a drill scheduled for today."

Sam and I look to each other again, still worried.

People flood down the stairs and exit through side doors I didn't even know were there. We follow Sarah past the side exits, down to a lower level. "Forty-eight C!" she shouts at us as we go farther down the stairwell.

After treading down what feels like thousands of stairs, Sarah finally pulls us over to one of the side doors.

"Where are we going?" I ask, still shouting over the alarm.

"When there's a fire, we go to an escape tunnel just in case we have to get out." Sarah grabs hold of each of our wrists and pulls us through the sea of people in an open and dark tunnel lined with luminescent floors and railings. "Each section of Bergland has a different tunnel assigned to it. They are all equally safe and are connected to each other, just in case."

Sam puts his hand on my back and pulls me closer to him to help us weave through the crowd. He shouts over the madness, "Just in case what?"

"Against the walls!"

Sarah releases our wrists. She separates from Sam and me as Bergland officers filter through the crowd, shouting at us to get against the walls. It takes a minute; but we all line up, side by side, against the two sides of the tunnel. The officers with their hologram wristbands walk up and down the lines, taking attendance.

With an officer only a few people away from us, Sam pulls my hand off my arm, preventing me from scratching any further. He cradles my hand in his and nods to me, mouthing the words "It's okay."

After a long wait, the officer gets closer to Sam and me.

"Name?" he asks the woman beside Sam.

"Lynds—"

The walls shake, and a loud boom echoes through the tunnel so ferociously that I can feel it in my chest. Everyone jolts into a hunched or squatted position. Many of us scream. We all fall silent a moment later as the officers raise their hands and touch their earpieces.

The sounds of people's horrific screams echo from their headsets.

Logan

Noise.
Ringing. High-pitched.
That's all I can hear.
So high-pitched that moving hurts.
Wait, why does moving hurt?

My eyes flutter open. My vision, blurry as my sight slowly comes into focus. I force myself off the ground only to find I'm not the only one down. When I get to a standing position, the room sways around me. Everyone in front of me runs in the opposite direction, away from me and back to the door from which we came into the tunnel.

The ringing slowly fades out as I turn around to see rubble. The stone tunnel, once open and sturdy, is now crumbled and piled up as if no such thing had ever existed.

I see bodies.

Dead bodies.

Some bloody, some crushed. Some, only legs or arms are showing. In what feels like slow motion, I run toward them.

They can't be dead.

No.

They can't.

The first person I run to is a man with a large gash oozing blood on his temple. He looks to be about forty. His dark hair and his perfectly shaved face make him look well-groomed. It makes me think this man had somewhere to be.

He has somewhere to be.

I feel his neck for a pulse but find nothing but lifeless flesh.

To his right, about three meters away, is a young lady. She looks to be about the age of everyone in my history class. Just a young girl, fifteen at most. Her arm is missing. It has been blown off. Behind her are many victims that suffered the same fate. Limbs, blood, guts, and gore cover what little I can see at the end of the tunnel.

I feel a slight rumbling underneath me. I look up to the roof and the walls around me to see them shaking. They won't hold much longer.

A hand grabs my arm from behind and pulls me away from the young girl's body. The lean man from Taai pulls me back from the rubble and drags me out of the tunnel. I shout out to him, asking, "What's happening? What happened?" I can barely hear my voice over the ringing in my ears. The small amount I can hear is muffled. I repeat the question over and over as my teammate pulls me out of the tunnel and into the hallway.

John and the other officers herd all of the citizens into the bombing bunker while the other Taai help. I sit in the hallway as one of the nurses patches up the skin on my bicep, which was hit with shrapnel in the tunnels.

My hearing comes back enough that I can hear everyone around me speaking, but barely enough to allow me to make out what they are saying.

As the final ringing fades out, John rounds up the lean man, three other Taai members, and me after all of the citizens are in the bunker. "All right," he barks at us, "listen up! You five will be clearing level 9." A man brings John a black duffle bag, from which John then pulls out guns for each of us, along with a hologram cuff. He distributes the guns while unlocking the cuff, typing in a clearance code and handing it over to me. I clip it on and wait for further orders. "You guys need to make sure that there is nobody out of place. If there is, do not engage until you report back to me. Got it?"

"Yes, sir," we answer in unison.

"Forge." John points to me and the cuff. "All you have to do to work that right now is press the red button and talk into it. That will go directly to me. Got it?"

"Yes, sir," I answer.

The lean dude looks from me back to John. "What happened with the fire?"

"There was none," John answers, loading in a new clip of ammunition. "No flames, whatsoever. Nothing was sensed, and there was no evidence of fire on any of our security cameras. It was part of the bomber's plan." He cocks the gun and turns back to us. "That's one of the reasons why we will be bringing these to clear the level. Move out."

While the officers go through the bunkers to take attendance and see who we are missing, the six of us split up. I go with the lean man, John goes with one of the other three, and the two left go together.

The lean man leads the two of us down the hallway, looking through his heat-sensing sight the whole time. We make it to one of the sharp corners, and he lowers his gun. "Hey, Young," he says into his cuff. "We have a body."

I come up and turn the corner to find a bald man lying on the ground, lifeless.

"On my way."

John tracks our location and is with us within five minutes. He quickly makes his way over to the body and scans his face with his cuff. The blue hologram screen on his cuff changes to red, with words scribbled on it.

"No matches," John mutters. He stands and types something into the hologram, which makes it disappear as he brings the cuff up and speaks into it. "We need a forensics team on 9 beta 3."

His cuff waits a moment before responding, "Copy."

"What does it mean, 'no matches'?" I ask, regretting my question almost instantly when I see the looks of disgust from the others.

John rises to his feet. "It means he wasn't a member of Bergland."

"Then how did he get in?" I stupidly ask again.

"My best guess?" John slides his gun to his waist and crosses his arms, looking down to the corpse. "The tunnel we were in. The one with the bombs in it."

The obvious answer burns my cheeks as I realize that I should have thought of this first. John waves us off, saying that he will wait for the forensics team. The other Taai members head one way while I follow the lean one.

"Hey," I say to him, trying to catch up with his long and continuous stride. "Um . . . what do we do now? Where do we go?"

"First off, it's Barnes. Eric Barnes. Now we will go down to the bunker and help take attendance."

"Oh." His statement came out as a mixture of kindness and sternness. I can't tell exactly how to feel about it. "Okay. My name's Logan. Forge." I cringe as my name escapes my mouth once again. "Logan Forge."

He looks over his shoulder and chuckles at me. "Yeah, I know who you are." Barnes stops and extends his hand to me. Though he is only a few inches taller than me and a lot more muscular than me, he is still one of the smallest in the Taai that I have seen. There are a few that are shorter than both of us and are amazing on the training courses, but most of the members are taller than 5'9". I take his hand and give it a good, firm shake.

Barnes nods. "It's a pleasure to finally have a proper introduction."

I nod to him, and we head back to the bunker.

Once we return, Barnes shows me how to take roll on the hologram cuff and leads me to the back corner of one of the branches. "Go down this side of the hallway. I will go down the other."

I pull up the software for the attendance and start with a woman about Janice's age. I hold the blue hologram square in front of her face as a line makes its way up and down the screen. "Name?" I ask.

"Walayla Hendrix."

The girl's name pops up beside a picture of her face. Twenty buttons pop up underneath her name for me to choose from, and I click on the one labeled "AF," which stands for "accounted for."

I move down the line just like that.

Girl. Woman. Woman. Man. Man. Woman. Boy. Man. They are all lined up in no apparent order. As I continue to go through the masses—much slower than Barnes, I might add—I watch the pop-up alerts on the bottom of the screen.

"Xander Holley. Dead at the scene."

"Tristan Smith. Dead at the scene."

"Jamie Fowler. Dead at the scene."

A name pops up every minute, and all I can do is hope that neither Sam nor Mavis was in that tunnel.

"Lucas Troy. Dead at the scene."

They weren't supposed to be! They were supposed to be in a different one. Everyone goes to the tunnel that is assigned to the floor they are on. It makes it safer.

Safer.

"Yasmine Quincy. Dead at the scene."

Bergland was supposed to be safe. The tunnels were supposed to be safer.

"Ronald Hucks. Dead at the scene."

What do we do if even our safest places are contaminated? How are we supposed to feel safe at all?

A soft wheezing meets my ears. Over all of the static and noise around me, I hear the heavy breathing clearly. It's a familiar soft wheezing. I can hear it over all of the noise in the branch. Soft wheezing.

Mavis.

I continue to scan everyone's faces while simultaneously looking around for her. I get about forty people down the line when I see Sam. He sits on one side of the bottom bunk, with his arms around Mavis. Her head is buried in her hands, and she is breathing slowly and heavily, trying to self-soothe.

Ignoring my job, I rush over to their side. Sam looks up at me, and his eyes grow. He loosens his grip on Mavis and gives me a very slight smile. "Hey, are you okay?"

"Yeah, no, I'm good! What . . ." I feel myself getting overly excited and compose myself. "What about you guys? What tunnel were you in?"

"Forty-eight C," Sam answers, releasing Mavis as she pulls her face out of her hands. Her eyes meet mine. I feel my mouth curl up into a subtle smile, just as hers does. I step forward and sit beside her on the bed.

"Hey," I whisper, not knowing what to say. Mavis smiles back to me, and I lean in. We wrap our arms around each other and hold for a moment. I feel myself melt into her, and I don't want it to stop.

But I know it has to. I have a job to do.

"Hey," Mavis whispers back.

We pull away from each other. My hand slides down her arm and finds its way into hers. "I have to go finish taking attendance."

She and Sam nod.

"I'm happy you guys are okay." I rise to my feet and release Mavis's hand. "I will be back after I finish." I head off and get the groups of people I skipped over.

"Wendy Louis. Dead at the scene."

It feels like for every other person I scan for attendance, another death alert arrives.

"Kate Greenwood. Dead at the scene."

I was in that tunnel. Why was I spared? Why was I spared and not them?

"Samuel Jenkins. Dead at the scene."

We have to do something. We have to retaliate. No more deaths. We have to end this war.

As I scan another man into the system and mark him down as accounted for, another death alert pops up. This name shakes me to my core.

CHAPTER SIXTEEN

Mavis

I pull my head up out of my hands and look around the room. Sam sits to my left and has his hand on my shoulder. A few bunks away from us, there is a family. One mom, one dad, one girl about thirteen, and what I have gathered is the mom's sister. They all huddle around the one bunk and wonder what's going on. Surprisingly, the young girl is the calmest out of all of them.

I look around and see people all chattering. Some calm like the girl. Some sitting and nervous like me. And some flustered and panicked.

Sam rubs my shoulder and sighs. "You okay?"

I nod. There's nothing I really need to say. I'm fine. I was even able to keep myself from a panic attack.

Well . . . sort of.

I'm getting better, though. I'm learning how to deal with it.

"How about you?" I ask Sam as I pat his leg. "How are you holding up?"

He looks to me and gives me the same comforting smile I have grown to love.

A silence falls over the crowds of people as the officers walk back up and through the aisles, telling people to be quiet. Multiple hologram screens pop up across each wall, all showing the same thing. General Wilson, sitting behind his perfect desk, with his hands folded.

His face rests into a mixture of pity and seriousness. "Hello, Bergland." His voice, deep and filled with concern, echoes through the halls. No other noise is being produced other than his voice. "I am grieved to have to address you with this news. About an hour ago, the Taai found the body of a man who was confirmed to be from Bestellen. He committed suicide after setting off the fire alarm and sending everyone into the tunnels. The reason that there were bombs found in only one tunnel was because this man only knew about that one tunnel.

"At the moment, we assume that the targeted tunnel was the one he came through. By blowing it up, he sealed up the only entrance that Bestellen knew about. Though this act puts us at an advantage because they don't know about any other entrances, they took many lives in the process. We cannot, and will not, let them get away with this."

General Wilson takes a moment. He looks away from the camera down to his folded hands. He takes a deep breath, then looks back to the camera. His face is more serious than before. "We begin launching ground attacks tonight. Effective immediately! The full war has begun and at the cost of a total of eighty-seven Bergland lives." The instrumental Bergland anthem that we listen to every morning begins to softly play. "Please take a moment to remember those whom we have lost in this horrid attack by Bestellen."

The victims' ID photos fade in and out on the screens. Each labeled with their name, age, and family members. They all slowly pass by. A woman that looks strikingly similar to Sarah pops onto the screen. Her name is . . . *was* Lucy. Lucy Cardillo. Her dark brunette hair makes her pale skin seem paler and her blue eyes bluer.

The familiar anthem continues to play; and the pictures continue to fade in and out when, suddenly, a man's voice comes through the speakers. His smooth voice floats through the room as he sings the bits of their anthem I have never heard.

> *Men and women alike,*
> *We all joined the fight.*
> *We fought, we fought,*
> *Until we dropped*
> *Because we knew it was right.*

A man, only twenty-two years old, pops up next. He was a member of the Taai. His picture shows his portrait and his profile. The sides of his head has a zigzag pattern shaved into it, making his haircut unique compared with most of the other Taai.

Sam's grip on my shoulder loosens, and his hand slides down my back. I grab his hand and hold it as I realize that this was one of the guys that hurt Sam. This was one of the thugs that should have been punished. I can't help but wonder if Sam would have turned him in, would the boy with the zigzag hair have been in a different tunnel? Would he still be alive?

> *We follow the babbling brook,*
> *Look through every cranny and nook,*
> *And meet the others down the way*
> *To avoid the evil crook.*

The person that comes up next is a man. He was thirty-six. He had kids, two kids. I can hear them sobbing. They burst into tears one hallway over as "Tony" comes onto the screen. One of them is shouting. He is crying out, "Daddy . . ."

> *No matter our race or state,*
> *We all want to stop the hate.*
> *We'll fight, we'll fight*
> *Every night*
> *Until we reach our fate.*

The next picture that appears is of a little boy. Eight years old. Short spiked-up blond hair. He wore black glasses that were too big for his face. He had no living family. His name was Henry. Henry Smalls.

> *We follow the babbling brook,*
> *Look under every cranny and nook,*
> *And meet the others down the way*
> *To take back what he took.*

Sam and I freeze. I'm paralyzed with shock and overwhelmed by so many different emotions. Too many to handle. I feel like I'm going to throw up. *Henry is dead.*

We watch as the rest of the victims fade in and out. The music comes to a halt as General Wilson comes back onto the screen. "Thank you for your attention." The only other noises in the room are the sounds of sobs and silence. "I know a lot has happened, and many of you will need time to mourn. But we have to act now. If you would like to help Bergland win this war, get with a recruiter. They will be available in the cafeteria today during all meal shifts. They can help you find the most appropriate position for your specific skill set. Again, thank you so much for listening. Good day and good morrow, Bergland. Work hard and achieve more." The screens flicker off, leaving the rooms and branches as silent as could be with the light sobbing.

"All right!" The officers walk up and down the aisles and clear us all out. "Head to the last post you were at. Follow up with your post leaders about the lunch schedule for today."

Sam and I are forced to head out of the bunker immediately without getting to speak to Logan. We then follow the masses to go back to the cafeteria and meet up with Sarah. The moment she lays her eyes on us, she rushes over and gives us both a hug. All of our arms wrap around one another, and we hold that position for a few long moments. Her hugs are much warmer and more comforting than I expected.

I rest my head on her soft and thick shoulder as her shaky breath warms my neck. "Are you guys okay?"

"We were in the same tunnel as you," Sam answers, pulling back from her.

"I know." Sarah sniffles and wipes a few tears from her cheeks. "That doesn't mean you didn't get hurt."

A moment of silence passes as I realize that Sarah knows most everybody by name. She got to watch them grow up, and she got to feed almost everyone in Bergland at one time or another.

I lean back in and wrap my arms around her once more. "I'm sorry," I say softly into her ear. She pulls away and brings us over to the sink. We all wash our hands and get back to work preparing the food.

Sarah explains that we will go about our schedule as we normally do, just with a two-hour delay. The only difference will be that the last post of the day is cancelled for most everybody so that we can go to bed on time.

During our Culinary Aid shift, a few recruiters with their hologram cuffs come into the kitchen. After talking to Sarah, one of the officers comes over to Sam and me. He asks for Sam's name and scans his face. The officer nods and presses a few buttons on his hologram. "It looks like the best thing that you would be suited for is continuing Culinary Aid throughout the war. By performing culinary aid, you will help provide food for all refugees, soldiers, and citizens." He turns to me. "Name?"

He scans my face as I answer, "Mavis Wamsley."

"Ah, Ms. Wamsley. The same applies to you. Your specific skill set would best be suited to a continuous post in the kitchen. I will go ahead and assign you both new schedules." He presses some buttons and gives Sam and me a smile. "Check in with your post leader for your new schedules. Thank you in advance for your services." The officer nods and heads out of our sight.

"Is that what you wanted?" I ask Sam. "To work in the kitchen?"

He shrugs. "I don't know exactly." We walk back over toward Sarah, our post leader, as Sam continues, "I really wanted to help get my mom, but working in here *is* helping, right?"

"Yes, it is!" Sarah exclaims, butting in. "We are a huge part of the war effort!" She puts down whatever strange food she is working on and hobbles past us to grab a few utensils. "I see you guys were put in here too, huh?"

We nod.

"Yeah, well, don't worry about it. Don't take it personally."

"What?" Sam asks. "What do you mean?"

Sarah's face falls as she realizes something. "What?"

"You said, 'Don't take it personally,'" I repeat. "Take what personally?"

Sarah shrugs, avoiding eye contact with either of us. "I mean, it's nothing really. It's just I was assigned here because of my disorder. They told me that I'm better suited for the kitchen than the battlefield."

"Your disorder?" I ask.

She nods and pulls up her sleeve to reveal a vial system attached as an IV. "See?"

Sam takes a step forward and observes the vial more closely. "What's wrong with you?"

"Sam!" I whisper.

"I mean . . ." He shakes his head and retracts his statement. "I meant what do you have?"

"Schizophrenia. Not a mild form either." Sarah pulls back down her sleeve and hobbles off. Sam and I follow.

"Yeah," she continues. "The only way I can really be a functioning member of society is to make sure I get my medicine. With this attachment, medicine is injected into my body whenever it senses I need it. It has something to do with the way it reads my blood."

"Really? Why don't they give one of those to everyone with a disorder?" Sam asks. "Wouldn't it be easier?"

"You'd think, wouldn't you?" Sarah chuckles at the thought. "These things are not cheap to keep up. They are pretty pricey. I spend almost all of the money I make here to keep this contraption working."

"Why do you use that? Why don't you just use the vials whenever you need them?" I ask.

"Every disorder is different, just like how everybody handles their disorder differently. It's just easier for me this way." She shrugs. "Like I said, I wouldn't be a functioning member of society without this."

"You know . . ." I head over beside her and help her dice whatever the strange fruit is. "That sounds a lot like what Chancellor Meir thought."

"How so, dearie?" she chuckles.

I look over to Sam, who is shooting me a puzzled look, then back to Sarah. "Well, he thinks that people with disorders have no place in society. That kind of sounds like what you were saying."

"Well, that's not exactly what I was saying," Sarah tells me. "I just feel like I am more useful when I'm medicated."

I nudge her arm and smile back to her as I cut through the yellow fruit. "I think you'd be great either way."

"Thank you, Mavis. Though I may not have agreed with your statement about me agreeing with Meir, I am definitely happy that you seem to be learning a lot."

I chuckle and look to Sam, who seems to be fuming. His face has become red, his fists are clenched, and his stature has changed completely. I turn my head back to Sarah and try to focus on her. "Yeah, thank you. I didn't think you agreed with Meir any more than I did."

"Oh yeah?" Sam snaps at me. "Well, maybe he was right!" Sam growls. "If . . . if we have medicine that can help us be more normal, why wouldn't we take it? Huh, Mavis?" His eye twitches, and he clenches his fist. "What's wrong with getting a little help?"

Sam storms out of the kitchen, just as the clock strikes time for the first lunch shift to begin. Right about now is the time that he and I would be heading to Janice's classroom to work, but I am guessing with our new schedules that the plan has been changed.

People come rushing into the cafeteria and over to the server's bar, where workers are waiting to help them out. I turn back to Sarah, and neither of us knows exactly what to say. I don't know why Sam got so upset. I don't know where he went. I don't know what to do.

After a few moments of silence, Sarah croaks out, "Let's go check and see what your new schedule is." She hobbles over to one of the hologram computers and pulls it up. Sam and I have the same schedule. We go to our morning class with Janice and then to the kitchen for the rest of the day. We do have two hours of free time in between, but other than that, we stay in the kitchen.

"Thank you," I say. "I'm sorry if I offended you by saying that about Meir."

"It's fine, dearie. I wasn't offended at all." She gives me a kind smile and chuckles, "Always feel free to speak your mind with me."

"Thank you," I say again. My arm begins to grow raw from my scratching. When I realize the extent of my harmful habit, I force my arm to my side. I know when I am scratching, but most of the time, I don't ever register that I am doing it because I am nervous. My arm just breaks out with the desire to be scratched, so I scratch.

I take a breath and try to let my skin heal. "Sarah?"

She turns around immediately and looks to me with a concerned smile. "Yes?"

"Can I . . . May I be excused for a few minutes?"

She smiles at me. "Yes, ma'am. Go ahead. I will get to see you the rest of the day anyway." She winks at me, and I head off through the cafeteria.

There are multiple recruitment officers walking around, assigning posts and new schedules to everyone. "Get your new schedule from your room leader," they tell everyone.

Doing my best to avoid people on the way, I quickly make my way to one of the libraries a few floors over. A few days ago, Mandy showed me her favorite spot to go sit and draw. It's in the corner of the room, behind all of the columns and rows of books. There's a single table with one chair resting on the wall behind it.

The moment I enter the room, I ask the librarian for a sheet of paper and a pencil. Never looking up, she hands me a clipboard with what I asked for. Before long, I am sitting at Mandy's table in the corner of the uncomfortably cold library, staring at a blank page. A blank page that is soon to be more.

Soon to be whatever I want it to be.

I have so many things to draw. I can draw the escape tunnel with all of the people in it and their faces when the explosion went off. I can draw Sam and myself walking down the hallway right before he yelled at me, when everything was fine and perfect. I can draw Sarah and her vial IV.

I can draw Henry. Little Henry Smalls.

The only boy who showed us any kindness as newcomers.

I can draw Henry.

No.

I can draw Henry's hopes. I can draw what he never got to see.

I can draw the mountains.

Logan

The Taai all meet up in the training room after an early lunch. Eric and John take the job and pass out armor to go under our clothes, along with our assigned weapons.

John heads to the front of the group as we all put our armor on and our clothes over top. "Today is your first ground mission. We have trained long and hard for this, and I expect nothing but success." He holds up his wrist cuff and pulls up a large diagram of Bloot, Mavis's state. "We will be entering Bloot over the wall and evacuating the people. Our sources have confirmed that the word has gotten out, and their people will join us with little to no resistance." John goes on to explain the plan in great detail to the group. He splits up the large number of the Taai and gives us all a specific assignment for each sector of Bloot. At the end of preparations, we all head down to the first place that I saw when I came to Bergland, the large concrete room filled with different sorts of armored vehicles.

All Taai members who share a certain assigned sector also share a vehicle. Once we get into our assigned cars, we take off. Eric and I sit beside each other in our car, and we listen to everyone else chat about their position and go over the plan as we strap ourselves into the seats.

I look past everyone and out the front of the van to see us exiting through the same tunnel Mavis, Sam, and I entered in. As we drive though, watching the circular lights overhead pass us, an odd feeling rises in my stomach, only to leave once we exit the tunnel. For the first time in a long time, I can see outside. The view from the top part of the mountain is gorgeous. The treetops run for miles and miles, blocking out where I thought the wall was. All of the beautiful scenery quickly speeds out of focus as we round a corner of the path just before we drive off the edge of the mountain. The slight feeling of safety I once knew returns after we make it back onto the ground.

I watch John as he rides in the passenger's seat of the car, scanning the paths for mines. Whenever he sees one, he is to shoot and detonate it, leaving the path safe for us to use. The path has been clear so far, and the ride has been smooth.

After a good portion of time, I lean over to Eric and ask, "Is this your first time on a mission?"

"Yes." Eric leans past me and follows my gaze to John. "This is the first mission that Young has been on too."

"Really?"

"Yup." Eric nods and rests back against his seat. "It's a first for all of us."

I turn away from John and look back to all of the other soldiers in the car. "So how did Young get his position as commander?"

"Favoritism. General Wilson trained Young, so when time came to pick a new commander, he chose his favorite student." Eric chuckles, "You might find that favoritism plays a big role in Bergland."

"There were no tests or anything that he had to go through?" I ask, thinking back to the lack of testing I went through to join the Taai. All I really did was answer some verbal questioning by John my first day of training. Was the only reason I was allowed to join the Taai because Janice recommended me?

"Nope. Not that I know of."

The vehicle slows down, and John aims the car's front gun. "Everybody buckled up?"

"Yes, sir," we all say in unison.

"Good. None of you have seen any of these bombs detonate." John fires his gun, causing a large explosion about a quarter mile out. The smokey and fire-filled explosion takes out two trees and every living thing within twenty meters of the center of the explosion.

"Now you have," John tells us. The fiery sparks that were spit out of the bomb are swallowed up by the smoke that followed it. When the smoke dissipates, what's left of the lumpy dirt road with fallen trees all around us becomes visible, and we drive forward.

CHAPTER SEVENTEEN

Sam

Breathe in.

Breathe out.

The blue irises that used to be as bright and light as could be now stare back to me with dark barriers. The ugly wrinkled nose, uneven furrowed brows, and weakly clenched jaw all aggravate me more the longer I stare at them.

Why are these my features? Why do I have to look like this? Not only do I fail to be a functioning member of society without the medicine, but I can't even make an angered face the right way.

A "functioning member of society."

Is Sarah right? Was Meir right?

Of course they were. If you have a cure, why wouldn't you use it? And if you have something that makes you feel better and that makes you feel calmer and more relaxed, why wouldn't you use it?

I listen to the commotion in the cafeteria as hundreds of people walk in and out, getting food. The bathroom walls echo with the sounds of their chatter. Their carefree lunchroom chatter.

I look down to the edge of the sink counter to see my two empty vials rolling off the edge. My hands immediately swing under it just as they fall off. One tube lands in my hand while the other falls to the floor. It tinks on impact but doesn't break due to its unnaturally strong shell.

The tube in my hand is much lighter now that it is empty. It's much colder too. I toss them both into the trash can beside the counter and look back into the mirror. Usually, when I take the medicine, the effects last at least forty minutes. Or they did the last few times I took the medicine.

Let's see . . . There was the one I took the day Zigzag and his crew got to me. There was the one I took that night to sleep. There was the one I took the next day. There was the one I took the day after . . . Wait, how many did I take that day?

I don't know. I've lost count. All I know is that I still have vials left in the case they gave me, which is a good thing.

I have more to spare.

I pull out the last vial I have in my pants pocket and roll it in my palm. The thick blue medicine in it now looks more like solid jelly with little patches of air bubbles. The warm tube calms me as I wrap my fingers around it. The effects from the last vial are wearing off much quicker than the medicine usually does. One more injection won't hurt anything.

Just as I lower the tube to inject, the bathroom door swings open, and a slightly chubby young man about my age enters. I shove the vial back into my pocket and turn to face him. I straighten up and wipe my eyes. After staring at me for a moment, the boy walks past me and into one of the stalls.

What am I doing?

I look back into the mirror and realize how pink the whites of my eyes are. I wonder if he noticed.

I splash water on my face and rub it all around, trying to get the haziness off my face. It's cold and quickly heats up when my hands rub it. I pull my shirt up and wipe the excess water off just as the young man comes out of the stall.

Avoiding eye contact, I head out of the bathroom as quickly as I can and make my way through the crowd toward the kitchen. The sounds of pots and pans clashing against each other is audible from the middle of the cafeteria and only grow louder the closer I get. The source of the clashing comes from one of the sinks in the back area.

"Need help?" I ask Mavis, who is dropping dirty pans into a larger-than-life dishwasher.

She turns her head to me and narrows her eyes. The bright green coloration that used to take over her irises is now a darker green, more of a deep emerald. I can tell she is conflicted. She wants to say something, but she doesn't know what to choose.

So she nods.

Her voice—soft, but stern—makes its way into my ears as she points over to the large pile of dirty dishes. "Grab all of the empty pans from the front and bring them back. I will set them up on the trays."

I follow her instructions and pass by the other workers in the kitchen, trying to avert from any unnecessary eye contact. I can't help but feel self-conscious. I don't know how long it takes for the pink to wear down, but it can't come soon enough.

Trying to carry multiple pans at once, I drop one on my way back to Mavis, causing a loud crash. I apologize to everyone who looks my way, pick up the pan, and scurry away. Once I get them back to Mavis, I set them on one of the steel tables beside the dishwasher. "Would you like help putting them in?" I ask, hoping to mend the bond I hope I haven't broken.

She shrugs. "I guess." I follow her guide and stack the pans according to her example. After a few moments of silence, Mavis speaks up, never looking away from the dishes. "I'm sorry if I upset you earlier."

"It's fine. It's not your fault. I just needed to go cool off."

Mavis looks over to me and gives me that beautiful and comforting slight smile. "By the way, you and I both had the same schedule changes. We are to work in here for the rest of the day. We get two hours of free time whenever we want, according to Sarah."

"Got it," I answer.

I wonder what Logan's new schedule is. If Mavis and I are to be in the kitchen all day because this is where we are best suited, where will Logan be all day?

Mavis places one last pan into the washer and heads off to do something. Just before I pick up another pan, I realize how quiet it has gotten. I realize that the only noises I hear are of Mavis and me with the pots and the other kitchen workers walking and talking. There is nobody in the cafeteria other than the people who are cleaning the tables and the floors.

I look around to have my eyes fall upon the large digital clock on the column in the center of the room.

I was gone for three hours?

"Here." Mavis taps me on the shoulder with a tray of food in her hands. She extends the tray to me and nods me off. "You haven't eaten lunch. Go ahead. I can do these."

"Are, are you sure?"

"Yeah." She gives a halfhearted chuckle. "It's not like you or I have any other place to be today."

"Thank you." I look her in the eyes and can tell something is off. She is trying to put on a happy face, but she is obviously upset. "Are you okay?"

She nods, this time with a more serious expression. "I am. Are you okay?"

I nod back. We have a brief moment where our eyes lock, and we say nothing.

"If you ever want to talk, you know I'm here for you." Mavis steps forward. Her voice now even softer. "Right?"

"I know." Our eyes are still locked, and our bodies are as close as can be with the tray in between us. "And you know that if you ever need or want to talk, that I'm here for you. Right?"

She nods. "Right."

Though she claims she knows, I don't think she believes.

Logan

Bloot, being the least cared for state in Bestellen, has allowed the outside jungle to overflow into their walls. This is the part that we are venturing through.

Usually, the inside of the wall is towns, buildings, and farms; but with this edge of Bloot, it is jungle. The top of the wall, where the guards usually walk, is overgrown with the top of the trees, which allow only a few Bestellen wall guards to walk through. Even though they have enough room to walk around, they can't see much because of how thick the trees are.

Our van pulls up to the point by the wall that the foliage is so thick you can't see anything below from the guards' position. We park about three hundred meters back from the wall and exit the van. Up the trees we go, one at a time.

Eric heads up just before me. I follow him, and John follows me. We all make it up in less than a minute except for the man who stayed behind in the van.

"Ready? Move out." John leads us forward through the intertwining branches of the trees. We jump, swing, crawl, and lunge to new branches and to new trees. After getting close enough to the wall to see a few of the guards pacing on the top, we halt.

Eric and John pull out small tranquilizer bullets that look like the medicine vials back in Bergland, only much smaller and filled with yellow liquid. They load the tranks into the guns and fire at the guards. The silent whistle of the tranks zooms through the air, and the tranks hit the guards in the spots where their armor is the weakest. Each guard that gets hit falls unconscious within seconds in whatever position they are in. A lot of the men stay standing, but there are a few that fall to the ground due to a lack of balance. None of them know what hit them.

"Move!" John calls out.

We head forward and get over the wall as quickly as we can into the trees on the other side. On the inside.

We're in Bloot.

The trees in this section are just as thick and odd as the ones outside of the wall, but I immediately notice a change. The farther we go into Bloot, the smoother and more recognizable the trees are. They remind me more of the ones back home in Minje.

We climb down just before we hit the edge of the woods and walk out. Everyone is wearing armor and has their pockets filled with everything they need for their specific assignment, but we wear ratty clothes over top to blend in. Bloot's evening air is growing cold, and the cool breeze isn't helping. The farther we get from the tree line, the more houses we see. The broken-down cabins are scattered, just like the people. Everyone here wears torn fabrics of some kind just to cover their skin, but there is no way that any of their clothes actually keeps them warm.

The sound of a baby crying echoes from the cabin to my right. Its horrible screams shoot through the house's broken windows and streams through the crowds. Eric and I seem to be the only people who have noticed. John and the others have already split off and gone to do their assignments, leaving the two of us to go do ours. None of the other Bloot citizens seem to care about the wailing child. They act as if it is nothing new. Barnes and I walk and watch as many rub their hands together to generate some sort of warmth while others beg on the corners of the small dirty streets and lie on the ground, awaiting their fate.

I have only seen one official on the ground among the commoners. He sticks out like a sore thumb with his dark uniform and the luminescent orange lines down the sides of his arms, legs, and torso. His dark helmet with the black face mask makes him appear even more ominous than he already is.

Eric and I walk through the scattered town and into the commons area. The first thing I see is a large tented area. Some sections of the wall have brick and stone supports, but there is more tent than stone. From what I can tell, this used to be an old building that got destroyed somehow. It appears to just be ruins with cloth on the broken bits so that they can use the area.

Eric stiffly states, "This is the marketplace," as we begin our walk over. The sun is setting right behind the officials' headquarters for this sector, making the shaded marketplace even colder. Every Taai member was supplied with long-sleeved shirts and long pants to help cover the armor and weaponry. In order to remain undercover, the clothes we were given had to be ratty, just as everyone else's. The thin layers give the chilly weather a slight advantage. Considering I'm cold and I have on armor and long clothing, I have to wonder how these people feel. I'm sure the officials' clothes are thick enough to keep them warm, but all of these poor people have got to be uncomfortably cold.

As we head to the marketplace, the gravel crunches underneath my feet. The whole commons area ground is covered in rocks, mud, and poop from livestock. Though the marketplace is the largest structure in the town, the other buildings are in much better condition. Not to my surprise, the officials' quarters is the best-kept building I have seen so far.

The floor of the marketplace is the same as outside, made up of gravel and poop. The large room has hundreds of tables and stands with people selling and buying goods. The air smells like old wood, dust, copper, and livestock; and the people smell just the same. Eric immediately splits from me and takes a right while I go left.

The first table I stop at is covered with balls of yarn. Not nice and soft yarn, but hard and dirty strands of wool. I lean over the table and look around, trying to make sure that the man selling the yarn doesn't become suspicious.

I bump into the table and slip the radio bomb to the bottom of it. "Oof! Sorry, sir."

The man gives me a slight glare at first but quickly lightens back up and shoots me with a toothless smile. He picks up a few balls of his product and holds them out, mumbling something about buying them.

I shake my head and return his smile. Though I repeatedly and kindly turn them down, he won't stop talking. I have to turn my head away and continue the mission.

The next few tables I do are easier. All I do is walk by, wait for the salesperson to get distracted, and stick the radio bomb to the bottom of their table. I have to make sure to stick it far enough under that it isn't seen from the aisles or from behind the table.

Just as I slip the bomb under my sixteenth table, someone grabs my wrist. Thinking that I have just been caught, I jerk my head back to look at the culprit, a little old lady. Her fluffy silver hair, adding at least four inches to her height, comes up to my chin. I look down to her to see a scowl.

The woman's bony fingers squeeze my wrist with one hand. Her eyes grow as she brings up her other hand to feel my arm. She gives my wrist a quick pat down and pulls up my sleeve slightly. She sees my hologram cuff.

Before I can do or say anything, the woman gives me a huge wrinkly smile. I lower my arm as she lets go and looks around as if to check to make sure the coast is clear. The woman pulls back her thick wool scarf and pulls down her shirt collar to reveal the Diligent's symbol tattooed on her collarbone. She excitedly points at it and looks to me as if she is pleading.

I nod and bring my finger up to my lips and gesture for her not to say anything.

The woman giddily covers herself back up and hops behind her table. The commotion in the room continues at the same pace, but it seems to get a little louder as the woman packs her things up. She slams down an old brown suitcase onto her table and throws in a bunch of her things, ranging from buttons to pieces of cloth.

I turn to leave and move on to the next table when a lady knocks something off her desk. I pick up the gray stone to hand it back to the woman when I see a beautiful painting of a little river, maybe a creek, painted on one side of it. The bright blue babbling brook runs beside a thick meadow of grass. There isn't much room for the rest of the picture on the stone, but what is on there is beautiful.

"Here." I hand the lady the stone, but she closes her briefcase without taking it.

The woman walks out from behind her table and closes my fingers around the stone. Holding her hands around my fist, which encases the painting, she points to my chest and gives me a big and bright smile. She wants me to keep it.

"Thank you," I answer, knowing I have to get going. The woman nods, and I move on. I slide the stone into my pocket and head on to the other tables. Eric and I meet in the middle of the marketplace after we have arranged all of our given bombs.

We look around to make sure there are no officials. "Ready?" Eric asks me.

I nod, and he brings his cuff up to his mouth. "Marketplace is set."

We hold our cuffs to our ears, and the voice of one of our teammates comes out. "Speakers are a go. Commander?"

John's voice pops out after a moment of waiting. "Good to go."

Eric and I wait. We stand in the marketplace and look around to all of the people. There's a kid walking around, trying to sell his scrawny goat. We watch his failed attempts and wait for the plan to commence.

The speakers outside of the marketplace by the officials' quarters squeal to life, grabbing everyone's attention. Something too muffled to understand comes out at first but quickly turns into the same message. "Everyone head to the commons for inspection." The voice of Johnson, one of our group members, echoes through the town over the speakers. "Repeat. Everyone head to the commons for inspection."

Everyone in the marketplace scrambles to get their things together. The boy with the goat pulls the animal out, followed by the old lady who gave me the stone. She prances out of the building with her suitcase swinging by her side, along with a goofy smile on her face.

Eric and I follow the crowds as they all flood into the commons and line up for "inspection," which is usually what the officials do when they suspect there to be drug or weaponry deals going down. This part of the plan is to evacuate every citizen from the officials by gathering them all together. And so far, it's working.

The officials come running out of every nook and cranny over to the hundreds of people who are lining up. They are running around, radioing to one another, trying to figure out who made the order for an inspection. As far as they know, there wasn't an inspection scheduled.

Eric and I, side by side, look to each other after all of the officials emerge from the crowd. They huddle together, trying to figure out what's going on while the large crowd of people continue to line up into three rows. Without any official order, the officials follow the speaker's instructions and begin searching everyone in the lines. Eric and I are toward the center of the line closest to the marketplace so we have a better view of the situation. We wait until the officials have all calmed down before proceeding with the next part of the plan.

Eric nods to me once the officials are about twenty people away from us and pulls up his sleeve to get to his cuff. Within seconds, the marketplace is booming with Bergland's anthem, which is the forbidden song throughout all of Bestellen.

> *Men and women alike,*
> *We all joined the fight.*
> *We fought, we fought,*
> *Until we dropped,*
> *Men and women alike.*

Once the first words come out of the speakers, all officials flee from the crowd toward the marketplace. They all aim their guns into the building and go crouching in. The crowd murmurs as it backs away from the guards and the marketplace, but they are quickly silenced by four officials who stay behind to watch the crowd.

The four officials swing up their weapons and hold the crowd at gunpoint but are paying too much attention to their fellow officials in the marketplace to actually be a threat.

> *We follow the babbling brook,*
> *Look through every cranny and nook,*
> *And meet the others down the way*
> *To avoid the evil crook.*

I look around in the crowd to make sure all of the kids are in the back, farthest away from the marketplace. My focus falls on an old man who holds an old lady's hand, the same old lady who gave me the painted stone. He looks down to the lady and gives her a sweet smile as he starts singing along to the song, slowly getting louder.

> *No matter our race or state,*
> *We all want to stop the hate.*
> *We'll fight, we'll fight*
> *Every night*
> *Until we reach our fate.*

The officials standing in front of the crowd shout at him to shut up and stop singing, but he doesn't. The old man gets louder quickly and projects the song but is shot in the head immediately. The blood splatter covers the woman beside him, along with a few others who stand near him. The old man's death is followed by other citizens, scattered across the crowds, singing along. The officials shout out and flail their guns, trying to get them to stop; but soon, everyone joins in singing.

The officials open fire on the crowd and are attacked by the masses. The people at the front of the crowd that live through the spray of gunfire kick, jump on, spit on, and tear apart the officials outside of the marketplace. Eric and I shout to everybody, telling them to get back as the song comes to a close.

> *We follow the babbling brook,*
> *Look under every cranny and nook,*
> *And meet the others down the way*
> *To take back what he took.*

We manage to get everyone as far away from the marketplace as we can as the bombs in the marketplace go off. Stone flies everywhere, along with shrapnel from what was left inside of the ruins from today's sales.

Everyone yells something different as they run through the town, attacking any and every piece of property that belonged to an official. From vans to buildings. They destroy everything. Eric and I check all of the citizens' bodies that we can to make sure anyone who isn't dead is getting help. I check dozens of bodies and stop when I find the kind gray-haired old woman who gave me the rock. She lies dead next to the old man who was the first to be shot.

As the rest of the citizens raid the officials' headquarters, John radios in. "Meet in front of the officials' quarters. I repeat, meet in front of the officials' quarters."

Eric answers back, "Got it."

Eric and I meet back up with the other members of our group in front of the officials' headquarters and get as many people out of the building and gathered around us as we can. John gets everyone's attention by standing on one of the officials' cars and using his cuff as a speaker.

"Attention! Attention!" Very few people stop talking. John pulls out his pistol and shoots into the air three times, getting everyone's attention and shutting them up. The gunfire echoes through the air and slowly fades as everyone shifts their focus onto John. "I am Commander Young of Bergland's elite force. We don't have any time for questions. Once we blow a hole in that wall, everyone needs to follow me. We will have vehicles waiting to take you guys out of here to safety."

The crowd cheers for John as he gets down from the car. He comes over to the rest of our Taai group and holds his hand to his earpiece. "Okay. Got it." John lowers his hand and turns to us. "You guys stay back to make sure everyone gets out. I will lead them out and then meet you guys at the vehicle we came in."

"Yes, sir," we all affirm.

"The jet should be coming any second." John turns around to the wall's general direction. We can't see it from where we stand due to all of the cabins, woods, and the fact that it's two to three miles away.

Everyone becomes silent as the deep sound of a roaring thunder comes barreling overhead. We look to the sky as a Bergland jet flies over top of us, and a large explosion shakes the ground, blowing a section of the wall to bits. All of the citizens remain quiet, in shock that this is actually happening.

John turns to everyone and shouts into his cuff's speaker, "Everyone! Follow me!"

Like cattle, they all go storming after him. Weaving through the buildings and running through the woods, the citizens cheer for freedom as they escape this desolate land of oppression. The Taai, including myself, help go through the town and make sure everyone is out. When Johnson called for everyone to meet in the commons for inspection, everyone in the town obeyed. They must have been really frightened of what would have happened if they disobeyed.

Bloot is overall a small state, but the sector my group is assigned is the smallest sector. Its population was a little over eight hundred people. Looking at the sea of dead citizens lying in the commons area, I know it's at least two hundred people less.

Once we finish checking the area, the rest of the guys and I head out toward the point of the explosion. After jogging about three miles, we make it to the giant section of land that is completely destroyed. All of the trees within a hundred-meter radius of the wall have been knocked over, and the wall itself is just crumbles of stone scattered around the woodland floor. We make it through and head back to our van, where John stands waiting for us. The sun has already set, and it is almost pitch-black within the woods other than the headlights from our vehicles.

"About time," John jeers. "I guess you guys were scanning the area pretty thoroughly, huh?"

CHAPTER EIGHTEEN

Mavis

Everyone has been assigned their new posts for tomorrow, which is causing all to be a bit more chatty than usual. It's either that or the fact that it is the first night of us raging a full war on Bestellen.

I lie on my bed, listening to the silence floating through the room. All of the other girls, including Mandy, are still in the showers, performing their nightly hygiene chores. I left the kitchen early today, which allowed me to get all of my rituals done before everyone else. It's a rare occasion to have some peace and quiet like this in this room, usually because there are so many other people in here. I've noticed that this particular group of girls hasn't become as close as many of the girls in the other rooms. There are some in here that hang out together, but not many.

The two girls who are the closest in this room enter, interrupting my thoughts. One of the girls is muttering something that sounds like an equation to the other girl. Not a normal equation like I've seen with Janice, more like one that sounds like a different language.

The other girl answers the first girl's question with an even longer and more drawn-out math problem with words that I have never even heard before. They continue to chat about an algorithm when I hear the word "weapon" slide into the conversation. I sit up straight in my bed to see which of the girls have come in and scare the two as they stand by the bunks near me.

"Oh!" the brunette with the ponytail exclaims in shock. "Sorry! We didn't know you were in here."

Her blonde friend clenches her teeth. She turns from the brunette to me. "Did we wake you up? Sorry!"

"No, no." I shake my head to put them at ease. "You're fine." The girls stand there awkwardly, not knowing exactly what to do. I slide my legs over to the ladder and let them hang off the bed. Sitting on the top bunk, I look down to the girls. "Out of curiosity, what were you two talking about?"

The blonde jerks her head upward. "What?"

"Sorry, I'm not trying to pry." I scoot backward on the bed a smidge. "It just sounded important."

"It's fine." The brunette shrugs it off and takes a seat in the bottom bunk across from me. "It's something you wouldn't understand."

The blonde follows the brunette over and takes a seat beside her. "Tara!" She slaps the brunette's arm. "That was rude," she whispers.

The brunette rubs her arm and smacks the blonde's. "It wasn't meant to be!"

"Hey," I say, interrupting them, "it's fine." It sounded pretty rude, but I need information. I smile and ask as politely as possible, "But I still want to know. What were you guys talking about?"

The blonde looks up to me, holds her hands up, and starts speaking with them. "We work in one of our technician labs, and we have just gotten intel that Bestellen is working on a new weapon." Her fingers twitch as she explains the intricacies. "A sort of drone involving tungsten, titanium, steel, and a magnetic field. It—"

The brunette elbows the blonde in the ribs. "We aren't supposed to say anything yet."

The blonde holds her stomach and looks to the brunette with a glare. The tension between them is undeniable. I guess that's what happens when you work together all day and then have to come home to a shared room.

"Oh." I scoot back onto the bed as more of the girls enter the room. "Okay, I'm sorry I asked." What I really wanted to say was "Thank you for telling me." But I didn't want to stir up anything else between the two.

The overhead speakers come on just as I get back to my pillow. A man's voice is projected. "Good evening, Bergland. This is General Wilson. I am pleased to announce that Bloot, Bestellen's smallest and most Diligent state, has been successfully freed." I unintentionally jump back up in anticipation.

Bloot has been freed.

Where are they? Where is Derek? Where is Uncle Randy? Where is Dad?"

Wilson continues overhead. "All of the freed citizens are getting all of the food and any medical care they need. They will be spending tonight in the bunkers. Bloot citizens, tomorrow morning, you will all need to go to the cafeteria at 7:00 a.m. to get your next meal. You will be given new instructions then. After that, you will have your skill sets assessed, and you will be placed in the position where you can help the most."

I hop off the bed and stream past the girls entering the room. I rush out into the hallway and past all of the girls and boys that live in this hallway, who seem to be surprised to see me running. Once I weave through the crowds and make it through the maze of hallways, I see two guards at the end of the hall by the elevator.

As I try to get past the guards to the stairwell, Wilson's voice slows down, and he says one of his ritual speech endings: "That will be all for now. Good night and good morrow. May our hard work pay off."

The guards see me as I turn the corner. "Hey!" one of them calls out to me.

I ignore his shout and head for the stairwell, but the hall I turn to has even more guards patrolling.

"Hey!" the guard calls out again. After I ignore him for the second time, he shouts to the others, "Stop her!"

I can't get my words together to explain. I am from Bloot. My family may or may not be alive. I just want to know.

Two of the guards grab me, one on each arm. They shove me against the wall and scream in my face. "What are you doing?"

I am trying to explain, but all that is coming out is "I . . . my family . . . I have to speak to . . . Bloot . . ." I continue to try to explain, but nonsense comes out as I wheeze, unable to steady my breath.

I thrash and jerk, trying to get away from the guards. I have to know if Derek is okay. I have to know if Uncle Randy is okay. I have to know if Dad is here.

One of the guards pulls out a vial from his vest pocket and stabs me in the leg. I look down to see what looks like the same medicine, but a different color, draining into my leg. The green jelly leaves its vial within seconds. I look up to the guards, now trying to ask what medicine they just gave me, but I become much too tired to open my mouth. Soon, too tired to fight the guards.

Sam

Early.

It's too early.

Why do we have to get up at seven thirty in the morning every morning? According to Caine and Grayson, they got to sleep in according to their work schedule; but since we are at war, we have to all "work harder than ever." The only time Logan ever complained about it being too early was the first morning we were here, and that's only because he didn't get any sleep.

Grayson, being our room's supervisor, wakes us all up and makes sure we are ready to go. Without the squeaking of Logan's bed above me, I find it much harder to get up. I spent half the night hoping Logan returned to Bergland safely and the other half drooling on my pillow.

"Well, good morning, sunshine." Caine walks by my bed and chuckles at me as my eyes flutter open, and their morning crust falls to the pillow. "Ready for breaky?" He snorts.

I wipe off my eyes and the dried drool from my mouth and watch him head out of the room, leaving Grayson and me alone.

He sits on his bottom bunk a few feet away from me. "Are you ready?"

"No," I whine. "But that doesn't matter, does it?"

Grayson chuckles and shakes his head. I get up and make my bed, and we all head up the stairs to the cafeteria after completing our normal morning routines. The whole way up the stairs, I listen to Caine and Grayson talk about where they are assigned to help.

"Yeah, they assigned me to Meer, the aquaculture state," Caine brags. "Besides Metropolis and Verwend, Meer is the hardest state to penetrate." He chuckles and starts walking backward up the stairs so that he can face Grayson and me. "Since Meer is one of the first states we have to capture, I'm not surprised they chose the *best* soldiers."

"Of course that's why they chose you," Grayson says, chuckling, "not because they need a body to throw at the opposition or anything."

Caine pauses on the stairs. "What's that supposed to mean?"

"Oh, nothing." Grayson smiles as we pass him. They continue jeering at each other as we make it up the hundreds of stairs. Caine seems to be proud that he was drafted. He keeps bragging about how he is being sent off to his death.

I only catch bits and pieces of their conversation. My mind is preoccupied with other things. Too many other things. I can't stop wondering if Logan is okay and how Mavis is handling all of this. And what about Henry? Did he feel any pain from the blast?

Did he die immediately or from bleeding after being injured?

If they got to him soon enough, would he have been able to be saved?

Would the vials have helped him?

The vials.

I need to head by the hospital and get more vials. I am running low.

We make it up to the cafeteria just as the shift change occurs. It's madness. I have never seen so many people in here. Half of the people are wearing the newcomers' clothes that Logan, Mavis, and I wore our first day here. I watch as they shuffle through the groups of people coming in for the official first breakfast shift. Half of the Berglanders in this room are stopping the Bloot citizens to talk to them. It's obvious the Bloot have places to go. The Berglanders need to leave them . . .

"Hey, sunshine." Caine nudges me in the arm as I find myself staring into the group of girls that have been asking about Logan and me. This time, all of the girls are focused on something in the center of their group instead of me. "Do you have a little crush?"

"What? No," I answer, not pulling my gaze away from the group. One of the girls on the end catches me looking at them and tells the group. They immediately become giddy and start squirming within their group. They part so that the whole group can see me and reveal a newcomer within the circle. Tall, fit, and gorgeous. This girl has obviously been pulled aside by these girls to be interrogated about Bloot. The newcomer's hair is cut short to her head. It's just a little bit longer than mine, but it looks so much better. It's a dark and silky brown that matches her eyes and tan skin.

"Are you certain?" Grayson nudges me in the other arm. "You sure seem to fancy someone over there."

The girl's eyes meet mine, and for a split second, I swear she blushes.

In response to her blush, I blush. I stupidly blush. What purpose does that have? Why do we blush? What's the point? To embarrass us and make us blush more?

Caine grabs my shoulders and squeezes them tight. "Dude! You totally like someone over there."

Say it a little louder, would you?

Our eyes break apart as the girl gets swept away with another crowd of newcomers. As I look to see if I can find her in the crowd, I see Mavis weaving through. Her eyes are large, and her expression is one of madness as she looks crazily through the crowd. Caine and Grayson follow my gaze to see Mavis spinning around, looking for someone.

Caine points over to her and chuckles, "What's wrong with blondie?"

Ignoring his question, I leave Grayson with Caine and shove through the crowd to get to Mavis. She looks through me as she spins around, still focusing on her goal.

"Mavis!" I grab her shoulders and look to her face. Her green eyes seem even greener with how small her pupils have become. "Mavis, what are you doing?"

She stutters out something that doesn't make sense, still looking around the room frantically.

I shake her shoulders and get her to look me in the eyes. "Mavis, what is wrong?"

"Bloot . . ." She pauses a moment to gather her words. "I am looking for my uncle Randy and my dad."

"Okay. Easy enough." I release her shoulders and cuff my hands around my mouth and shout, "Uncle Randy!" Mavis quickly punches me in the arm. Her bony knuckles combined with her being unnaturally strong makes her punch very effective. "Ow!"

"Shut up!"

"What?" My hands drop, and I rub my new bruise. "Why?"

Mavis scratches at one of her arms and looks around the room nervously. "I want to find Uncle Randy first. Calling his name out like you did will attract not only him, but my dad too."

"Why don't you want to see your dad?"

She stops scratching as her fist clenches. The only word I can use to describe her face as she looks away from me is "terrified."

"Mave, are you okay?"

"It-it's not that I don't want to see him. It . . . it . . ."

"Hey." I take her hand to get her to stop tearing at her arm. "It's okay. You don't have to explain. I'll help look for Uncle Randy."

She turns back to me and sniffles, somehow sucking the tears back into her eyes. "Thank you."

"What does Uncle Randy look like?"

"Um . . . tall. Taller than you. Um . . ." She looks around in the crowd. "Curly red hair. He's pretty muscular too."

After a pause, I ask Mavis what her dad looks like. She describes him to be about as tall as me, but with a large beer belly. "The little hair he has left is blond and on the sides of his head." She goes on to describe the greasiest-looking person I can imagine.

Mavis and I split up into the crowd and look around through all of the newcomers. I see redheads, but the few I see are too short to be Uncle Randy. I see blonds, but none that meet the description of her dad.

I continue scurrying through the crowd when I see a tall muscular curly-haired redhead talking to a recruiter. It has to be him.

"Hey, I'm sorry." I run over to them and interrupt their conversation. "You." I pull the redhead back a bit to see his face. The freckles splattered across his face are something that most redheads have, but his eyes are not. His eyes are blue, like mine, but have a hint of purple in the center. Distracted by this odd mutation of his, I pause.

When he turns his body to me, I see one of his forearms bandaged up with a small amount of blood coming through. He looks over to the recruiter, then back to me. "Yes?"

"Sorry." I shake my head, trying to get back my focus. "Is your name Randy?"

Before he can answer, Mavis comes out of the crowd behind him. Her face lights up with a smile as she scurries over. The redhead in front of me notices I'm looking past him and turns around. Mavis's smile fades of brightness but remains a smile still. They both pause where they are and stare at each other for a moment.

She says something under her breath, and they both leap into each other's arms. "Mavis!" the redhead croaks.

They stay embraced as they talk into each other's neck and shoulders. "Derek," Mavis mutters into his shoulder, "you're okay!"

He nods and moves one of his hands onto the back of her head. "Yeah. I'm fine. I'm fine. You . . . you're okay too." Derek clears his throat and squeezes her tighter. "We thought you were dead."

"I'm fine." Mavis asks him, "Randy? Dad? Are they here?"

Derek shakes his head as she sets hers directly underneath his chin. He takes a deep breath. "Randy went back for your dad during the riots. Neither of them came back."

She nods, placing her head against his chest as tears stream down her face.

"I tried . . ." Derek whimpers to her, closing his eyes and trying to keep his tears in. "I tried to get your dad out, but . . ." He sniffles and chokes back whatever he was planning to say. "And then I tried to keep Randy from going back."

Mavis rubs her thumb on his bandaged forearm, where her hand had been resting. She pulls her head back and looks to his wound. "What happened here?" She looks up to him. "Was it from the riots?"

He freezes. Not saying anything at all, he brings one hand up to her cheek and strokes the scar below her left eye with his thumb. Mavis takes his silent answer and nods quickly, squeezing her eyes closed to try to keep in the tears.

She takes a deep and shaky breathe. "What about your mom?"

"I don't know." Mavis sets her head into his chest, and he rests his chin on top of her head once again. "She was transporting something to Minje during the revolt." They freeze in each other's arms, trying to get a grip on reality.

"Excuse me." The recruiter taps Derek on the shoulder. "You guys need to go ahead and wrap this up."

They pull apart slowly. Mavis nods to the man and tells him it's okay and to go ahead with the recruiter. He obeys and pulls away.

I make my way over to her and stand by her side as a few tears escape her eyes. I want to comfort her, but I can tell she doesn't want to be comforted. At least not by me.

The recruiter says something about the Taai to the redhead and pulls him away. The two get lost in the crowd, and Mavis turns on her heel. I follow as she dashes into the kitchen. With silent tears running down her face, she slides down the empty wall in the far corner, away from all the morning madness. She wheezes as she sobs into her hands. I want to help her, but this may be something she wants to handle on her own.

I handled my dad's death on my own, and I'm fine.

One of the workers takes notice of Mavis's condition and rushes over. Before I can say anything, she pulls a vial out of her pocket and stabs Mavis in the thigh. The worker tosses the empty vial in a trash can and moans as she straightens back up into a standing position.

The rush of watching all of this happen within seconds stirs me.

Mavis looks up to the worker with pink eyes. I can't tell if the pink is from the medicine or from the tears. "Why did you do that?" she whines to the worker. "I was fine!" She sniffles and calms down.

She leans into the wall behind her as the worker chuckles. "Fine? Tell that to the tears streaming down your face."

Somehow, she manages to curl her legs up and scoot away from the worker. Mavis mumbles something under her breath about not being able to feel, but I miss what she says because I am off thinking about something else. I am thinking about the vials.

I am running really low. My case is almost empty.

I scoot away from Mavis to let her enjoy her newfound sense of relaxation, and I go up to Sarah, who is working at one of the service lines. "Am I allowed to go to the hospital right now?"

Sarah shoots me a puzzled look over her shoulder. "Now?" She plops some of the food onto a young man's tray. "Yes, but you'll miss breakfast!"

I thank her and head out. I'm not really hungry anyway.

After retrieving my case from my room, I make it through Bergland with the help of several different elevators going both horizontally and diagonally and get to the hospital in under ten minutes. The glass doors of their lobby slide open for me as I make my way in. Lucky for me, I come to the smallest section of the hospital that deals only with prescriptions. If I had gone to any other section, I assume it would be flooded due to all of the Bloot.

"Excuse me." I stand behind one of the front desks and try to get the lady's attention. Her blonde hair is twisted upward and pinned behind her head in a way that I've never seen before. It makes her hair look larger and thicker than I bet it really is. "I am here for a prescription refill."

She turns to me and lowers her glasses to look me up and down. The lady, whose name tag reads "Lucille Ian," turns back to her computer and begins typing something in. In between her obnoxious and cowlike chewing of gum, she sighs and then asks, "Name?"

"Um, Samuel Beckman."

She continues typing into the holographic computer for a moment, leaving me standing awkwardly behind the desk with my case. I turn to look around the waiting room to see one man sitting smugly in his chair. The first thing about this man that catches my eye is part of a tattoo that is visible on his neck. It appears to be a black original version of the Diligent's two-hammer logo, but more abstract.

"Here." The lady pokes me in the arm with a clipboard. "I need you to fill this out." I take the board from her and begin filling out the first few blanks. She rolls her eyes and continues smacking her gums. "You can take a seat, sir."

Trying not to take it personally, I scrape up the board and head to the waiting room.

The man who sits across from me snickers. "Prescriptions, huh?"

I nod.

"Yeah, me too."

"I can tell." I point with the pen to the case sitting in the seat beside him.

He smiles and bobs his head. "Aren't we lucky?"

I shoot him a puzzled look. How are we lucky having to get refills of drugs just to help us be "a functioning member of society"?

"My favorite time of day is when I get to use one of these." He leans back in his chair even more and crosses his legs. "These things are the greatest."

I shrug. "I guess so." We sit quietly for the next minute or so as I finish filling out the paperwork, and I think about how nice it is that I don't have to worry about a vial limit. I turn to the tattooed man and ask, "Do you get an unlimited prescription too?"

"What?" He gapes at me and looks down to my case. "No, do you?"

I shrug. "Yes. I thought everyone did."

"No." He shakes his head and chuckles. "Only the lucky ones. You must have a pretty bad case of something."

I shrug again and look down to finish the paperwork. The guy chuckles again as I bring the clipboard up to the desk lady, who holds out her hand to me. I hand her the paperwork, but she sets it down on the counter and shakes her free hand at me.

"Your hand. I need your hand."

Puzzled, I hold out my hand. She grabs my finger and squeezes the tip. "I am going to give you a little prick, okay, hon?"

Before I can answer, she pulls up a little plastic rectangle with a button. She presses the button, and a needle stabs me on the tip of my finger. My whole arm flinches, but the act is over before I can process it. She squeezes my finger again and presses the blood onto a little square in the bottom-right corner of the forms I have just filled out.

The woman pulls back the paper, places it into a machine scanner, and hands me a Band-Aid. I place it on my finger as the computer bings.

"Okay." She continues typing into her hologram. "Your prescription will be ready in a few hours."

"Hours?" I blurt, earning a chuckle from the dude in the waiting room.

The woman rolls her eyes at me and blows a bubble. "Yes. Hours. Come back at one."

I nod to her and leave the desk.

I pass the waiting room on my way out, and the man lifts his case to me, as if proposing a toast. "See you later, newbie."

I pause by the door and look back to him, surprised that he knows I'm new. As I realize that he means new to getting medicine, he sets his case back down. "The name is Bram."

"Bram?"

"Bram Nazk," he answers. Bram looks to me as if waiting for my name.

"Sam," I say to him. He nods to me, and I head out.

I wonder if he is in there waiting for his vials. That may be why he is waiting with his suitcase.

Why is the wait time almost five hours? That seems like a ridiculous amount of time. All they have to do is put them in my case, right?

I have a few vials left. I have four of them in my pockets now. I should probably go ahead and use one before I get too upset. Last time I waited until after I got upset, I shouted at Mavis, who was just trying to help.

I take my empty case back to my room, and I realize that taking the vial here would be better than taking it in the restroom. When I take them in the restroom, I am in other people's way. When I am in here, I am in my own space.

Alone.

Not bothering anyone.

I am staying out of the way.

I am being a functioning member of society.

CHAPTER NINETEEN

Logan

Walking back through Bergland after freeing Bloot is odd. Not bad per se, but odd. Each of the Taai got to sleep in their own room last night, so we all received a good night's rest. Each room was really just a tad larger than our beds, but still, having my own room for the first time in a long time was nice.

After hitting the showers, John calls us all out into the training room to meet the new recruits. We all walk in and line up like we usually do, side by side, with me on the end, Eric beside me, and the rest of the Taai beside him. We stand behind John, who is addressing three new men: The one on the end is about the same build as the Taai member we lost in the explosion, the one with the pattern shaved into the side of his head. The one in the middle is a little bit shorter than me and a lot skinnier than me but is obviously fit enough to be part of Taai. And the one on the other end is a little taller than me and a little more muscular than me and wears a crown of red curly locks.

"Each of you was recommended to join the Taai for the skill set you showed during the battle in Bloot." John marches down the line of the official Taai members as he addresses the newbies. "If you wish to be a member of our elite force, you will first have to prove yourselves to me before these guys come back from breakfast." John nods for us to leave, and we file out from the other end of the line, leaving me to bring up the rear. John's voice echoes through the room as we exit. "You will have to complete two tests: one physical and one mental. If you fail, you will be demoted to militia."

Demoted? How is that demoted? First of all, they haven't even gotten in yet, so they can't be demoted unless they were first a part of Taai. Second of all, the militia is just as important. Almost all of Bloot were members of the Diligent. We had inside men spreading the word to get ready. That is the only reason it was so easy, and it wasn't even *easy*. Without the militia, we wouldn't stand a chance against Bestellen. We still have five states and Metropolis to go. We are nowhere near finished.

When we enter the cafeteria, we are greeted with a large amount of applause. People cheer, whoop, and holler as we make our way through the crowds. Eric told me that coming home after fighting for what you believe in has always been considered a great feeling, but I never expected to be praised for it.

My eyes fall on Mavis, who stands with Janice and Mandy as they clap for us all. Eric follows me as I make my way over to my welcoming committee. Mandy rushes through the crowd and over to me before anyone else and gives me a quick squeeze. She chuckles over my shoulder, "I'm so proud of you!"

Janice follows and gives me a gentle hug and pat on the back. "Good job, Logan!"

I thank her and move over to Mavis. She pauses for a moment before leaning in and wrapping her arms around my neck. She gets on her toes to put her head over my shoulder, and we freeze. She whispers into my shoulder, "Thank you for coming back."

I mutter back to her, "I wasn't going to leave you."

The only way I can describe the feeling in my stomach I get when I'm around her is like I swallowed a million live butterflies, and they won't stop fluttering about. People back home used that expression all of the time, so I feel like using it is too cliché, but I can't help it. Though I get butterflies around her, I also feel warm and like I can talk to her about anything. At this very moment, I am hugging my best friend.

"And who is this?" Mandy scoots past Mavis and me over to Eric. She holds out her hand for a shake and smiles. "Are you one of Logan's elite teammates?"

I roll my eyes as Eric chuckles and takes Mandy's hand. "I guess you could say that. I'm Eric Barnes."

Mandy wiggles her eyebrows at him and doesn't let his hand go. This time, the chuckles Eric give are slightly more nervous as he pulls his hand away from Mandy's. He and I look around to see the rest of the Taai, finding seats at tables with people they know, when I realize something.

"Where's Sam?" I ask the group as they all take their seats.

Mavis shakes her head and folds her hands in her lap. "I don't know."

I look to the others, and they both shrug.

Eric and I take a seat across from the girls. "Nobody knows?" I ask.

Mavis shakes her head again. "No." She looks over to Janice, then back to me. "Can I tell you guys something?"

Everyone but Eric nods and says something along the lines of "Yes, of course."

She looks around the room, then back to me. Her eyes narrow in on mine as she takes a deep breath. "I am worried about Sam."

"What?" Mandy interjects. "Why?"

The commotion around us grows louder as someone in the kitchen drops a pan. It crashes, and a group across the room erupts with laughter.

"He . . .," Mavis continues hesitantly. "He has been running off a lot. And every time he comes back, he has pink in the whites of his eyes."

She turns to Janice, who has reached out for her hand. The empty trays in front of them make my stomach growl, but I shove the feeling of hunger aside as Janice smiles to Mavis, trying to ease her worries. "The pink in the whites of his eyes is just a side effect of his medicine, dear."

She shakes her head in disbelief. "How often is he supposed to take the medicine?"

"Well, it is different for everyone. The medicine he was supplied is for him to take whenever he needs." Janice releases Mavis's hand, picks up the trash off the table, and begins stacking the trays. "Just like with you. I don't think that you should turn to the medicine immediately until you have tried everything else, but if you feel like you need it, it is your right. I won't stop you."

Everyone at the table seems to agree, but Mavis doesn't seem any more comforted. She looks over to me, and we glance from Janice's pile of trays and trash back to each other.

After a few moments of silence, Mandy clears her throat. "So, Logan, Eric." She turns to Eric and winks. "How was the mission?"

I look to Eric, who has a goofy and nervous smile on his face. I answer Mandy, "It was a success."

"Less than eight hundred civilian deaths overall," Eric adds.

"That's great!" Mandy exclaims. Mavis looks down to the table, avoiding eye contact, just as we all realize we are talking about her state.

"So . . . um . . . Mavis," I ask her, "have you . . . um . . ." How are you supposed to ask someone if their dad is dead? "Have you seen your . . . um . . ."

"No." She shakes her head and continues to look away from me. "My dad is dead. And so is my uncle." Everyone at the table says that they are sorry and gives her their condolences. She fakes a chuckle and looks back up to us, waving a hand. "Thank you, but I'm fine."

"Fine?" Mandy asks. "Your dad—"

Janice elbows her in the ribs before she can finish her insensitive statement. Mandy never means to be rude, but she can be at points. Now is definitely not the time for it.

"Yes. I'm fine. I can handle it." Mavis looks over to Mandy. "One person I know made it out, and that's enough for me."

That's not true. Her smile, though as big as it usually is, shows a sort of pain. She may try to hide it, but she isn't okay. I don't expect her to be. She just lost her dad. The more I think about it, the more I feel like it's my fault. I'm in the Taai, and one of the Taai's responsibilities was getting the civilians to safety.

Eric nudges me in the arm as I pull my hands apart to keep from rubbing my fingernails. "Do you want to go get food?"

I nod, and we head up. As we go through the line, Eric hesitantly asks me if Bloot was Mavis's state. I tell him it was, and he goes quiet, not sure what to say.

When we get back to the table, the instrumental anthem comes on, and we all rise to do the pledge. Everyone faces the flag and remains silent as we listen to the music and remember all of the loved ones we have lost fighting for freedom.

Halfway through the pledge, Sam walks into the cafeteria. I can't help but notice what Mavis said is true. The corners of his eyes are tinted pink.

He comes over, sits in the seat besides Mavis, and plops his head down on the table.

Mavis takes notice and turns to me, mouthing "See?"

The pledge wraps up, and we sit back down. Sam keeps his head on the table and ignores us.

We all exchange glances, and I lean in. "Sam?" I ask. "Are you okay?"

He grunts and brings his head up. "Fine. I'm going to go get food."

"You better hurry." Eric swallows a chunk of food. "The first breakfast shift is almost up."

Sam turns his head and looks over to Eric. His eyes slowly begin to grow, showing how pink they really are. Eric's eyes grow at the same pace as Sam's the longer they look at each other.

Sam's face scrunches into a scowl as Eric averts his eyes and looks down to his tray. Everyone else at the table is looking back and forth between the two, trying to figure out what's going on.

Mandy finally speaks up after what feels like a lifetime of awkward silence. "Sam? What's wrong?"

Sam continues to stare at Eric as he shovels food into his mouth and avoids eye contact. "Do you want to explain, or should I?"

Eric looks back to Sam with a clenched jaw and wide eyes. The bell rings before he can answer, but nobody at our table moves. Everyone around us scurries away and tumbles through the traffic, causing it to be even louder.

Eric finally speaks up when he realizes no one is going to move. "What all do you remember?"

"I remember you. I remember your thug friends shoving me . . . throwing me." Sam continues to stare straight at Eric, somehow holding his gaze in such a way that Eric can't look away. "And I remember you just watching them call me a retty. I remember you watching them stab me with my own vial!"

"Hey!" Eric sets down his fork and leans into the table. "I stood up for you."

"Only after I was pinned against the wall and your meathead friend was strangling me!"

"After Uri stuck you in the leg and they left, I tried to make sure you were okay! I helped you out of the hallway and into the restroom, but you yelled at me and told me to go away!"

I look back to Eric, setting my fork down. "Eric," I utter, trying to make him realize he isn't helping anything by yelling.

Sam rises to his feet with the commotion in the background. "You stood, watching me get bullied and called a retty, and you did nothing to help."

His tone even more strict than usual, Eric rises to his feet and narrows his eyes back to Sam. "I have never once used that term, nor have I ever supported it or those who do."

Sam walks around the end of the table toward Eric, who is standing still, but not backing down. I rise to my feet and stand between the two. Sam stops inches away from my chest and glares at Eric through me. The girls across the table all look terrified. No, even worse, shocked . . .

At me.

They look at me like I'm the bad guy, doing an awful thing.

Janice rises to her feet. "Mr. Barnes, would you come with me please?"

He nods and breaks his staring contest with Sam. Janice and Eric head out of the room, but Sam continues to glare at him as he walks out. After Eric makes it out of sight, Sam shifts his focus to me.

Backing away from me, he fumes, "Whose side are you on?"

"I'm not picking sides," I say, scoffing. "I'm preventing a fight that won't end well for anyone."

Sam rolls his eyes at my answer and storms off into the crowd. I turn to the girls and meet their eyes as Mavis and Mandy stare at me from the other side of the table.

"Did you know?" Mavis asks me as she rises. "Did you know he did that? That your friend did that?"

I shake my head to her, trying to come up with an answer, but I am still confused on what had happened. What even is a "retty"?

She backs away and gets lost into the crowd, just as Sam did, leaving Mandy and me alone.

"You had no idea?" Mandy asks me, throwing her bag over her shoulder.

"I didn't."

She nods to me and sucks her teeth. Her head bobs as she walks off into another direction. I sit back down at the table and finish my food alone with nothing but my tray and Eric's.

Mavis

Back in Janice's classroom, the children around Sam and me stir. Logan hasn't come back, and I don't think he is going to come. Being a part of the Taai, I imagine he and Eric are going to be pretty busy for a while. The classroom grows louder as they realize Janice still isn't in the classroom yet. She is out in the hallway talking to Eric about . . . the situation . . .

I can't help but hope Eric gets into some sort of trouble for what he did.

I turn around in my seat and look to Sam, who has his arms crossed and his eyes fixated on his desk. I take a breath and look back over to Henry's empty seat. He was one of the only people in Bergland who actually made an effort to welcome us. I mean, most people tried to be kind, but they could never quite manage a welcome the same way Henry did. Just seeing his desk empty causes a gut-wrenching feeling.

He was too young to die.

Too kind.

I hate to think about it, but I have to wonder if he was ever bullied the same way Sam was. Was he ever pushed around, hit, and abused? I know there are kids in this class who picked on him. I could hear their comments whenever Henry answered a question. But did they ever actually take to physical abuse?

I shake off the thought of Henry being beaten and turn back to Sam, who is frozen in his seat. "Hey," I whisper to him.

He doesn't flinch.

"Are you okay?"

Sam doesn't move. He doesn't answer. It's like he isn't even here. In order to keep from causing any more anger, I turn back around.

Sam is upset. I can't blame him.

Janice enters the classroom with a content look on her face. As she closes the door behind her, I see Eric pass by, walking freely in the hallway.

"Okay, okay." Janice raises her voice to the class and waves her hands at them to sit down. "Get to your seats!"

Why does she look so smug? Why is Eric walking out instead of being escorted out by our police? I thought the Taai were supposed to protect and serve the people of Bergland, not stand by and watch people get bullied for their disabilities. Yeah, Eric may not have bullied him directly, but watching without doing anything is just as bad.

As Janice begins class, all I can do is dwell on this issue. I can't listen to her talk about political parties anymore. I want to know what she said to Eric. I want to know what kind of awful excuse he came up with to get himself out of trouble. I want to know if Logan defended a bully or if he really didn't know anything about it.

"Mavis," Janice calls out my name in the middle of her lecture, causing all of the heads in the class to look over. "What was I just talking about?"

My eyes meet with hers as a smirk rises on her face. She knows I wasn't listening, so why ask? Why call me out?

Janice continues teaching the class, and I watch her as if I am listening, but I can't seem to get my mind to focus. Why would she call me out like that? Why would she let Eric walk off like that?

Why does she say she has no tolerance for bullies but is acting like one herself?

CHAPTER TWENTY

Logan

McCullough, on the end of my row, lowers his wrists and stops filming as John's speech comes to an end.

My team, Delta, has been driving since John accepted two out of the three newcomers into the Taai. We drove all day and all night and are now less than an hour away from Bouw, our assignment. Nobody here expects this war to last much longer because of our foolproof plan.

Alpha, the largest and most skilled group of Taai, is going to Verwend. Verwend is the state of Bestellen that surrounds Metropolis. It is the state that manufactures all of the country's weapons. Beta is going to Hout, the lumber state. Gamma is going to Meer, the aquaculture state. And Zeta is going to Minje, my home state.

Each team is split into two divisions. The first division is to go and take out the major air defenses and weapons building. The second team, like ours, will go in after the video has aired and help pave the way for the Bergland army.

Some of the other teams have been driving since before we freed Bloot. We have to drive around the wall and make sure to stay a safe distance away until we are ready. Since some of the states are on the opposite side of the country and there is no way to cut through, it is taking a lot longer for other teams to get to their target location than it takes us to get to Bouw.

As the van shakes and wobbles its way through the woods, I watch John type something into his hologram and McCullough patch in the video feed. Eric and I sit beside each other in silence, not knowing what to say. In the day we have been here, we have gone over our plans multiple times, have run through dozens of scenarios, have eaten, and have slept. We haven't had a whole lot of time to actually chat, and now that we do, there's nothing to say.

Or there's nothing we're saying.

Eric finally speaks up after we finish filming John. He continues staring forward, just as I do. "I'm not a bad guy."

I stay silent, not knowing what to do or how to answer. From what little I've heard from Sam, Eric is a bad guy. Eric watched Sam get bullied and did nothing about it.

"The guys were messing with Sam in front of me, and I got them to stop. After Uri and the others left Sam on the floor, I helped him to the restroom."

I've heard this before. I don't know why he is going on about it.

"And after Sam told me to get out, I stayed outside of the bathroom to make sure he was going to get out okay."

I turn my head to Eric to see his face is as serious as could be. His brows are furrowed, his jaw clenched, and his eyes stare straight into mine.

"I waited over a half hour for him to get up and to come out. The second he came out of the restroom, I walked off so that he wouldn't feel like I didn't think he could handle himself."

"Really?" I ask, not fully convinced. From what I know about Eric, this sounds just like something he would do, but I don't know enough about him to believe his story over Sam's.

"Yes. Really." Eric looks back to the wall in front of him as we continue to drive. He rests his head on his seat. "After I left the restroom, I met back up with Uri and the others. I confronted them about what they did."

I scoff. "Oh yeah?"

"Yep." He turns back to me. "You don't believe me, do you?"

I suck my teeth and cock my head. "I can't say that I do."

Eric sits up straight and unbuckles his gear.

"What are you doing?" I ask him.

He looks to me as he slides off his vest and pulls up his shirt, revealing a battered and bruised abdomen. Black, purple, and red marks are scattered all over his chest and stomach. "This is what they did to me." He lowers his shirt and rolls up his sleeves to reveal more bruising. "I told them that what they did was wrong and brainless. I called Uri out and said that he only ever picks on people weaker than himself because he can never handle a real fight." He lowers his sleeve and begins putting back on his vest. John and the others had glanced over but have lost interest and gone back to their typing on their holograms. "I guess that's when he decided he was ready to fight someone more skilled than himself."

I watch him wince as he slides his armor back on over top of his injuries. "You and Uri fought?" I ask, still not sure what to think.

"At first, it was just us." He clips on his armor and leans back into his chair. "But like I said, he usually only takes on those who are less skilled than himself. After he threw the first punch and missed, I took him down. Not too long after the fight started, he called in his friends to help take me down."

I look over to John as he finishes typing something and attaching his video, then back to Eric. "Why didn't you tell someone?"

"Uri is dead now. It doesn't matter."

"What about the others? Are they Taai?"

Eric shakes his head. "Only military."

We pause for a moment. The only sound in the carrier is the sound of the twigs snapping underneath the tires as we drive.

"I'm sorry," I tell Eric.

"For what?"

"Not believing you."

He turns to look back at me. We both find ourselves giving a small appreciative nod.

"All right!" John grabs everyone's attention. "Look to the screens, boys." Everyone's eyes fall onto the picture that he projects onto the back doors of the carrier, a picture of Chancellor Lance Meir II.

John clears his throat and points to the screen. "This is the live broadcast showing on every screen in Bestellen."

Meir sits at his beautiful wooden desk from where he gives all of his speeches. His white facial hair continues to be groomed to sit right around his mouth and to be the same snow-white color as the hair on his head. He wears a black suit jacket, his signature purple vest, a black collared shirt underneath the vest, and a purple bow tie to tie his outfit together.

"I want to say, 'Good morning, Bestellen,'" he says with a soft, yet angered voice. "I want to congratulate you on your hard work and prosperity, but I am unable to do so. Word has gotten around the country of the incident that occurred in Bloot two days ago. Though you may have heard different, I am here to clarify and let you know what really happened. There was a revolt in Bloot, one that killed hundreds of citizens and even more of our soldiers who fight every day to keep the peace. Due to the loss of life, labor, and capital during this inhumane and selfish act of revolt, all Bestellen welfare programs will be paused to deter any further revolt or disrespect of this nation. Welfare programs including health care . . ." John and McCullough pull up their holograms and type one last thing in. As Meir lists the programs he is getting rid of, I could practically hear the revolts starting. "These programs will be reinstituted after all of the lost resources have been made up."

The video feed is interrupted as John's face glitches onto the screen. Everyone in the car cheers as his video begins addressing the entire nation of Bestellen.

"Good morning, Bestellen. What your chancellor has just told you is untrue. There was no revolt in Bloot, only a revolution." Everyone in the carrier is frozen with a mixture of emotions. We all watch as John's message streams through the country. "Chancellor Meir will never stop punishing you, the citizens of Bergland, for anything and everything that goes wrong. He blames you when he wastes resources on frivolous projects. He blames you when things don't go his way. And he will continue to blame and punish you for the rest of your lives unless you help us now. If you want freedom from his oppression, then you should fight with Bergland. Fight with my nation as we come in to free you from destitution. If you want freedom, get ready to fight with Bergland and fight for the freedom you have been deprived of all your lives. The Diligent will always come out on top, so fight for what you believe in. Fight with Bergland!"

The screen goes dark, and the whole car stays silent. All anyone in Bestellen sees right now is a black screen, just as we do.

Before John can say anything, a deafening blast hits our ears, and our carrier soars through the air.

CHAPTER TWENTY-ONE

Logan

Fuzzy.

It is too fuzzy.

They're dangling.

I'm dangling.

Blurry.

They're all blurry.

They're not moving. The only one who is moving is John.

As my surroundings come into focus, I realize the carrier has flipped onto its side. McCullough, Eric, and I are on the top end, dangling above John and two others.

I squint and look around the carrier, trying to get my vision back, and see Eric barely conscious. He pulls one of his hands off his head to reveal a large bloody gash and looks at it with a sense of horror. I watch as he tries to unbuckle his harness for a few moments before it occurs to me to unbuckle mine.

John and the two beneath us free themselves from their harnesses with ease and stand in an awkward position with their heads right beside me on both sides. John reaches over and helps me unbuckle while the other two help Eric down and check his head.

"I'm all right," Eric continues to insist, waving them off him. "I'm fine. Go check on Somar and Torez."

One of the two who helped Eric weaves through the disheveled carrier and makes it to the drivers as John helps me down. The moment my feet hit the floor, John grabs my head and turns it to him.

"What are you doing?" I ask him. Too weak to shake him off, I try to pull away but fail.

"Quit whining." John releases my head and pulls away, shifting his focus to McCullough, who hasn't moved from his harness. He places his fingers on McCullough's neck for a few moments before pulling away. John looks past me to Eric and the two others. "We lost McCullough."

The soldier who checked on the drivers returns to Eric's side with an angered look on his face. "Somar and Torez are gone too."

The moment he finishes his statement, I feel a gentle drop of blood travelling down my face. When I bring my hand up to my head, I find the source of the blood and the pain I hadn't yet noticed.

John sees me touch the wound on my temple as he wipes his nose with the back of his hand. "Forge. Don't mess with it." He comes over to me and grabs my arm, holding my sleeve onto the wound. "Hold it. Don't mess with it." He hesitates for a moment before pulling away.

We all stand on the side of the carrier and look around. McCullough continues to dangle, along with the people in the front. The number of arms hanging above us is unsettling, and so is the blood dripping from McCullough's head.

John bends over and opens the hatch beneath his seat to pull out his gun. He barks at us all as he loads his gun with tranks, "Ready up!" The small yellow glass casings that hold the tranquilizers look eerily similar to the medicine vials back at Bergland, causing an uneasy feeling in my stomach.

Everyone follows his lead and loads up their weapons as John uses his cuff to radio the other teams.

"This is Young. Delta's carrier is down. We lost three." John brings his wrist down and pulls out more ammunition to load up.

Another man's voice echoes through the carrier, radiating from John's cuff. "This is Horton. What happened?"

John clears his throat and wipes his nose with the back of his hand again, this time revealing a small amount of blood. "We came in too far. Somar and Torez should've stopped the carrier after they saw the first bomb planted. Is everything else going as planned?"

A silence fills the air as we wait for the man over the cuff to answer. I pull my hand and sleeve back to reveal that I have got the blood to stop dripping but have definitely ruined this shirt.

John pulls up a three-dimensional map on his watch. We see each team's marker floating above their location, along with our marker still far out in the woods. There are a large number of green markers covering a few of the states and spread out in such a numerous way that I am led to believe these represent Bergland's army.

Eric scoots past me and slides open one of the side windows, now on the ceiling.

"No planes," he tells us as he sticks his head out, along with a pistol, aimed and ready. "No other carriers."

John heads to the front of the van and picks up one of the bomb scanners that the two up front were supposed to be using. My eyes follow John to the front, then make their way past him through the shattered window and to the huge crater nearly twenty-five yards in front of us. Staring at me as he passes, John shuffles through the carrier back to the window above us. He sticks his head out and holds the nearly busted scanner to his face and spins around.

"Hornet's nests," John states as he crawls back down into the van. "They're everywhere." He looks to each of us with a look that I can only describe as disappointment. "We are extremely lucky that we didn't land on another one when the van tumbled."

Hornet's nests? Is that what they call the land mines? I can't ask without furthering John's assumption that I'm an idiot, along with possibly causing the rest of my team to assume the same.

John's cuff gives off a small amount of static as a voices call out, "This is Rodgers. Alpha is approaching Verwend."

A moment of silence passes before the rest of the teams tell us their status. "This is Corey. Gamma is in Hout."

"Chambers. Zeta is approaching Minje."

"Horton. Beta is in Meer."

John nods to us as he talks back to the cuff. "Young. Everything is going according to plan?"

"Horton. Everyone is in their assigned locations or on their way to it other than Delta. Hout, Meer, Bouw are all rebelling."

"What about Minje?" John asks.

Horton comes back on over the cuff. "Zeta didn't take down their security towers in time. The citizens are being held at gunpoint in the squares."

John pauses and looks back over to us all.

Before he can say anything, Horton's voice echoes back through the carrier. "Beta has Meer under control. I will send some of my guys over to Bouw to handle them until you all get there."

"Got it," John says into the cuff. "We'll be there soon." He turns to us all and shouts again, "Ready up!" Without any hesitation, John kicks the back doors of the carrier open and heads out with his gun ready and aimed. Eric and the two others zoom past me in the same stance as John, leaving me to follow. As we head through the woods, we don't have to worry about the hornet's nests because of their programming. One of the first things Sam, Mavis, and I learned when we came to Bergland was that the reason the rescue team couldn't drive too far into the woods was because of these mines that blow up when vehicles drive by or over them. Lucky for us, these same mines are programmed not to blow up when wildlife is near, just vehicles.

After we make it to the edge of Bouw, John commands everyone to activate their gloves and boots. I watch them as they all clench their fists and tap their feet with their knuckles. I do the same and listen to my gear whir to life. Neon blue lines run up my hands, seemingly outlining my bones, and lead to small blue circles on each of my fingertips.

We each place our hands on the concrete wall and begin climbing. Forcing my 180-pound body up this wall without any bars or support besides my own strength is much harder than I originally anticipated. But I manage to make it up the wall at the same pace as the rest of my team.

John makes it to the top first. He pauses on the side of the wall and pulls out his gun, mouthing cues to us. The moment he nods, we all hop over the side railing of the wall and land on the security guards' walkways. With our guns perched on our shoulders and our eyes looking through the sights, we find that every security guard has already been taken out with tranks. As we lower our guns, the bigger picture appears. The war waging beneath us is getting worse and worse the longer we wait here. The Stellen citizens and Bergland army are taking on Bestellen's militia. By no means is the militia winning this war, but they are doing a great job of taking as many lives as they can as they go down.

One particular person catches my eye from afar. I adjust my scope on my sight and look to the running woman. I watch the last few seconds of her life as a Stellen official shoots her repeatedly until she falls to the ground lifeless, killing an infant in her arms.

"Delta!" John shouts at us, stealing my attention from the lives I just watched be taken. "Go and take out your assignments. I'll finish mine and McCullough s." He sprints off without giving another order, leaving the four of us in a rushed panic mode.

Well, leaving *me* in a rushed panic mode.

Eric and I sprint off in the opposite direction as the other two members of Delta, and we don't stop until we see our assigned weapons station. The moment the building comes into sight, Eric begins climbing down that side of the wall, leaving me to follow him every step of the way.

Our feet hit the ground, and we sprint off to take cover behind an old building. I look down to my vest and count the clays. Four on my left and four on my right, each with their own activator.

With the sounds of gunfire, screaming, and so much more going on in the background, I look to Eric, who is resting his head on the wall of the building.

"Hey, Barnes." I nudge him with my elbow.

He looks back to me and shakes his head quickly, causing a few more drops of blood to fall.

"Are you okay?"

He nods and looks around the corner of the building. "Three officials are by the main entrance." Eric pulls out his pistol and clips in a pack of ammunition that looks nothing like the tranks. "Ready?"

I nod; and he turns around, firing the pistol once, twice, three times.

Eric speeds off, and I follow. We sprint past the three dead guards as we each pull off one clay from our vests. Eric throws his onto the top-right corner of the giant steel door protecting the weapons station, and I throw mine onto the bottom left. Our pace speeds up as we run back behind the building where we took shelter moments ago.

We prop ourselves back up against the side of the building as Eric pulls out his pistol and fires at the clay in the top-right corner. The whole front of the building flies off in hundreds of pieces. He and I only wait a moment before sprinting into the weapons station and planting the rest of the clays where we feel they will do the most damage. What's left of mine gets thrown and placed onto ammo containers and the building's support beams while Eric runs around and places his directly on the larger weapons and all communication devices.

I pull my last clay off my vest and look around the building. The only support beam I haven't hit yet is the one in the back left. I look to Eric, who seems to be done placing all of his, and realize just how slow I am.

"Forge, hurry up!" he barks at me just as John does to us.

I nod to him, about to take off running to the back to place the last clay, when the sound of gunfire rings through the air, and a strong sensation of stinging takes over the side of my thigh. I feel as if someone took a long metal rod that they had resting in the fire and is holding it on my skin.

Immediately, I dive to my right and meet Eric as he flips a large steel table onto its side. I scoot back and lean up against the table as Eric pops his head up from behind it and tries to shoot.

Glancing down to the source of my pain, I see that the bullet has ripped through the side of my thigh, leaving my flesh exposed. At first, it looks quite frightening; but after a moment, I realize that it is superficial enough that I will be fine.

Well, that I *would* be fine.

The deafening sound of gunfire continues to grow louder and stronger the longer we hide. The table we are using as a shield begins to give in. The metal is getting warmer, and I can feel it bending as it gives way to the bullets.

"Press the button!" I shout at Eric as he crouches back beside me.

"What?"

I toss the final clay as far to the back of the building as I can. "Activate the clays."

"What? No. There has to be another way."

A bullet flies right over top of the table, bouncing off the corner and hitting the ceiling above us.

"This is our assignment!" I shout to Eric. "We have to finish it!"

Eric looks to me as his eyes grow. He knows we have to. He knows this is our job and that if we don't do it, the consequences could be dire. Eric looks down to his cuff and pulls up a small holographic board with fourteen boxes. He clicks box 1, box 2, box 3.

He looks to me and takes a deep breath as one of the bullets makes it through the table.

Box 4, box 5, 6, 7, 8 . . . box 11.

The gunfire behind us increases as screams and shouts fill the room.

Twelve.

Thirteen.

Fourteen.

Eric moves his finger toward the small red button in the corner to activate the clays just as all gunfire stops. We wait a moment, assuming this is a trick, but the silence continues to grow.

Eric turns around and peeks over the table.

Nothing happens. I follow his lead and pull myself up off the ground. We rise to our feet and watch a man stand over four dead officials, holding a machine gun.

"Are you okay?" he asks us.

We remain silent, trying to catch our breaths as Eric closes the clay's screen.

The man looks us up and down. His eyes follow Eric's hand as he closes the hologram, and he nods to us and reloads his gun with an extra clip he kept on his hip. "Werner Rhodes."

"Rebel? Or Berglander?" I ask, trying to maintain my balance without putting any pressure on my leg.

"Rebel. From Bloot."

"Bloot?" Eric looks around the building to make sure all of the clays are still in place. "So you just came from Bergland?"

"Not exactly." Werner finishes reloading in a hurried manner. "I stayed behind when Bergland freed Bloot. I came to Bouw and spread the word." He takes a step over one of the official bodies and looks at our vests. "And you two are?"

Eric pauses for a moment and looks to me. He glances down at my left leg, which I am barely putting any pressure on, and turns back to Werner. "Special forces. We need you to get all civilians away from this building."

Werner pauses a moment, as if he has to think before trusting us. When he sees my leg, he nods to Eric and runs out of the building, shooting the gun. I can hear him yelling something as Eric takes my arm and puts it around his shoulders.

Eric grabs my wrist and my waist and practically picks me up from my side. "Come on."

"North gun tower is down. Repeat," John's voice blurts from our cuffs as a large explosion echoes through the town. "North gun tower is down."

Eric brings his cuff to his mouth and presses a button on the side of it with his chin. "Forge has been hit. It's not too bad, but he can't walk."

John's voice comes back up. "How close are you to killing the weapons station?"

Eric looks over our shoulder. "All set and ready. We have someone getting all of the civilians away."

We continue to limp another twenty-five feet before John answers, "Good. Get far enough away from the station and park yourselves behind a building. We will send a van for you when we can."

We quicken our pace and manage to make it behind an old termite-ridden bakery. Eric sets me down to sit on a pile of wet firewood as he pulls up the clays' activation screen.

The explosion echoes through the town, this one much larger and louder than the north gun tower. The ground shakes as Eric radios back to the rest of the team. "The weapons station is down. Repeat. Weapons station is down."

He wastes no time to turn from watching the debris from the weapons station fly over to me. He unclips the bottom strap holding his vest close to his body and straps it tight on my thigh above my wound.

Eric tightens it as tight as it will go and readjusts his vest. Now instead of one strap up top and one strap toward the bottom, he has one strap in the middle, and it causes his vest to be much looser than it is designed to be.

"Don't take this off." Eric points to the tourniquet. "Got it?"

I nod as muffled shouting voices boom over to our ears as five more officials run around the corner of the bakery and right into us. The officials, without their helmets on, allow us to see their surprised expressions, but only for a moment. They all raise their guns to us but are taken out almost immediately by Eric and me.

We shoot every official we see for the next few hours.

Bullet by bullet.

Life by life.

If I didn't have a slight case of OCD, these men could've been me. I could've been the one running around in the dark suits being shot at like target practice. I could've been the one who was forced to kill innocent men, women, and children alike.

No.

Even if I was assigned to the military and given these jobs, I never would've been like the official who shot down that woman as she ran with an infant in her arms.

I never would have been like the official who killed my mother.

The more I try to avoid thinking about my leg, the more it seems to throb. The beating and pulsating feeling grows stronger and stronger the longer I sit on these wet logs. Eric continues to stand by one corner of the building while I do my best to keep my leg up.

"Hey, are you okay?" I ask him, feeling the need to switch places with him. Not switch places painwise, but to give him a chance to sit. "I can come and watch for a while if you need."

Eric shakes his head. "I'm fine. You need to sit."

Before I can say anything, the cuffs call out, "This is Chambers. Minje is under heavy air strikes. The air hangers in Verwend will need to be taken out before Zeta can go any further."

"Rodgers. Alpha has had a little change in plans. Backup should be here any minute."

"Young," John's voice exclaims from the cuff, "Delta has one more defense tower to take out before we have Bouw."

A small explosion echoes over all of the gunfire and shouting. Our cuffs light up as the voice of one of the two other Delta team members comes on. "South defense tower is down. Repeat. South defense tower is down."

Eric and I look to each other as a feeling of relief floods over us.

"This is Young. Bouw is secure."

Another radio, with a similar sound as our cuffs, sounds off from in front of the bakery. "Last defense tower is down. Evacuate. Repeat . . ."

The number of footsteps coming from the side of the building leads me to pull myself up off the logs and go over to Eric, ready for a fight. We peek past the corner to see a dozen or more officials all crowded together, holding their weapons.

I bring my pistol up, ready to aim, but am stopped almost immediately when Eric grabs me and pulls me back behind the building. As my back hits the disheveled wooden paneling, Eric meets my eyes and holds his finger to his mouth. "Quiet."

We peek back around the corner and watch each official as they salute one another and pull the triggers on themselves.

Listening to the echoes of their gunshots, along with the thuds of their bodies as they each hit the ground, leaves me speechless.

Eric shakes his head and takes a seat on the pile of firewood.

"Why . . . why did they do that?" I stammer out.

Eric looks back up to me and slides his pistol back into its holster. "They're cowards."

Without another word, I hop back to my soggy seat.

We wait for what feels like a lifetime listening to people cheering, Bergland's militia vans rounding people up and taking them to safety, and the shouts of the few officials left who are fighting.

"Are you going to go and help?" I ask Eric. "You know, help them round people up?"

He shakes his head. "I will wait here until help comes to get you."

Our cuffs light up and call out, "This is Corey. Meer is secure."

After the cuff cuts off, Eric's breathing pattern catches my attention. Not only does it lack any sense of rhythm, but it is also more of a gasp for air. I take notice of how heavily he is breathing, how he hasn't opened his eyes since he sat down, and how he is holding his hand to his side.

"You were shot," I state as I see a small amount of blood come through his hand.

Eric looks to me and shakes his head. "I'm fine. It just grazed me."

I unclip the tourniquet off my leg and hand it back to him. "It grazed you because you weren't wearing this! Why didn't you tell me you were shot?"

Eric tears the strap out of my hand and forcibly puts it back on me. "It won't do me any good now." He looks back in my face and growls at me, "Keep this on!"

"Why didn't you tell me you were shot?" I half growl back at him.

"Because me whining wouldn't have helped anything! I'm fine. I can walk. You are in worse pain."

Unable to think of any response that will do any good, I remain quiet.

The large mixture of sounds around us quickly becomes drowned out by the overwhelming sound of jets flying over us. Their presence shakes the ground, forces both my head and my heart to pound, and drives all of the termites around us crazy.

"That must be the backup," Eric weakly chuckles.

Minutes later, we feel the ground shake again, this time like when we blew up the weapons station.

"This is Rodgers. Verwend's defenses have been taken down. Alpha is heading in."

Sam

The cold classroom becomes even colder as the air vents in the center of the room cut on and blow air right onto Mavis and me. The low hum is the only noise I hear besides the complete and utter boredom of this class as we listen to Janice babble on about history.

History!

How can we even be sure that this stuff is true? If everything they taught us in Bestellen was false, then the garbage that comes out of Janice's mouth can be too.

The rest of the students in the room ignore Janice's agenda and shout out questions about the war waging in Bestellen at this very moment. They ask her what's going on, where we are attacking, if we are winning, and so many other questions. I assume they are just trying to get her off topic because of how boring her class is. Anything to avoid learning, right?

Mavis and I listen to the rest of the students and Janice as we sit and simmer. Neither of us has spoken to Janice since she let Eric go without any sort of punishment.

"We have no tolerance for bullying in Bergland," Janice told me. "Anyone who messed with you can and will have serious punishments if I find out the names."

She wasn't even sure what had happened originally; and she was more prepared for punishment then than she is now that she knows I was attacked, thrown down, drugged, and left to die in a bathroom.

Janice was prepared to go and check the security cameras when she found out I was picked on, and now that she actually knows who it was, she isn't going to do anything! Just because he is in the "elite force."

Special treatment, anyone?

The anger inside of me has been brewing all day and all night ever since she let Eric go. If it wasn't for the vials to help keep me calm, I don't know what I would've done. I don't know how Mavis has been able to hold herself together this whole time. It is obvious that she became upset when she found out what happened. She became especially upset when she watched Logan defend Eric over me.

Logan.

Why did he have to do that? Just because they are both doing the same job doesn't mean he has to defend him! What about me? What about all we've been through? Even if you forget all of that, he still defended someone who helped attack me.

The bell rings overhead, marking the end of another day of history class. Half of the students who packed up their school supplies early zip out of the class while the other half linger behind to continue questioning Janice.

"You are an official!" the annoying girl who never raises her hand shouts at Janice. "You have to know something more!"

Janice shakes her head and waves them out of the room. "I am not allowed to disclose anything else about what's going on. Go to your next class."

Mavis and I stand side by side, waiting for the rest of the students to file out. I lay my hand on her shoulder to grab her attention, and she jerks her head back to me. The whites of her eyes have begun to turn pink, and her usually bright green irises have become a bluish green.

"Mavis," I mutter, not really knowing what to say.

She takes one big sniffle and wipes the tears from her cheeks. "I'm fine."

"What's wrong?" Just as the words escape my mouth, I remember the news she has just received.

Her friend, shipped off to war.

Her dad and uncle, killed in the process of rebellion.

From what I understand, she has no family left.

Mavis clenches her jaw and takes a breath. Another tear escapes her eye but doesn't make it too far before she wipes it with her sleeve.

I take the hint that she doesn't want to talk and pretend I don't notice the tears. "Can we stay behind and talk to Janice?"

She nods while trying to steady her breathing. I rub her shoulder for a moment and let my hand fall as I walk over to the front of the room.

Janice turns her attention from her hologram cuff to Mavis and me. She chuckles at us. "Well, I was wondering when you two were going to talk to me again."

In silence, I brush off her infuriating comment and sit in the student desk closest to her. After a moment, Mavis takes a seat back in her original desk, which lies a few desks behind Janice and me.

I clear my throat and fold my hands in my lap, trying to speak to Janice calmly. "Eric."

Janice closes her hologram and leans back in her chair. "What about Eric?"

"Why did you let him off with no punishment?" I ask without hesitation.

Janice pauses. Without ever breaking her eyes from me, she gives me a little side smile. "There are certain things that should probably remain confidential." She straightens up and leans toward me a bit, folding her arms on her desk. "Do you trust my rulings?"

"I used to!" I spout. "But then again, I used to believe you had a higher moral standard than this. I mean, letting someone who attacked me go just because he is part of the Taai?"

"Sam . . ." Janice tries to calm me, but I've already started.

"What if it had been Mavis? Would you have reported him then? Is it just a 'boys will be boys' thing? No, it isn't. It is a special treatment thing!"

Janice takes a deep breath and rises to her feet. She calmly walks over to the door and places her hand on the handle. "Will either of you get into trouble for being late to your shifts?"

Neither of us answers.

"Okay then," Janice says as she closes the door. She makes her way back over to her chair and takes a seat. "Sam, tell me what happened."

I pause. "What happened? What do you mean? What did Eric say?"

"Please, Sam, tell me your side of the story."

I take a deep breath and pop one of my knuckles.

"Calmly," she adds.

Though I am facing Janice, I can feel Mavis staring at me from behind. I haven't told anyone what happened. Only what I said in the dining hall is what is known by others, and that wasn't even the full story.

"What all do you want to know?" I ask Janice.

"What happened. What happened in your eyes."

I take another deep breath and finish popping my other nine knuckles. I calmly explain to the two that I stepped out of the orange room to go to the restroom when I was confronted by a bunch of thugs. The big one with a zigzag pattern shaved into the sides of his hair started it, and they all started shoving me around, calling me names.

Calling me "retty."

They told me that there was a reason Bestellen didn't want me, and it wasn't because I was special. Once they had pounded on me a good bit, the big dude took one of my vials and stuck me in the leg with it.

"And then what happened?" Janice asks me.

"What?" I scoff. "Why does that matter?"

"It matters. Just finish the story please. Tell me what happened up to you coming back to the orange room."

"Eric, who I didn't know at the time, stayed behind and took me to the restroom. He didn't want his victim just lying around," I growl.

"Did he stay in the restroom with you?"

"No."

She nods to me. "Why not?"

I pause. "Don't you twist this story! That attack was not my fault."

"No," she pleads. "Sam, this wasn't your fault. I am asking you these questions so that I can make sure Eric was telling the truth."

I pause again.

"Why didn't he stay in the bathroom with you?"

I look back to Mavis. Though she has stopped crying, her facial skin is blotchy, and her eyes are still slightly glazed over. She continues to stare at me until I finally answer Janice. "Because I told him to leave."

Janice nods. "Okay. Thank you, Sam."

"What did he say happened?" I ask her.

"Exactly what you said happened. Just a different point of view."

"What?" Mavis and I ask in harmony.

Janice pulls her chair forward to get closer to me, and she pats the seat behind me for Mavis to come. We wait awkwardly as Mavis approaches and takes a seat.

"Sam, I'm not going to treat you like a four-year-old and ask you if you remember Eric ever actually hitting you or if you remember him ever laughing with the other guys. I'm not going to ask you this because what you suffered should never have to be suffered by anybody, and I'm so sorry that happened."

"Then why didn't you do something about it?" I half shout.

"I tried to do something about it that day, but you wouldn't let me."

"Well, how about now? How about now that you know who did it!"

"Sam . . ." Janice sits up straight in her seat and meets my eyes. "The man who did all that to you is dead."

"What?" Mavis interjects. "Eric is dead?"

"No, I mean Uri Thomson. The one you described with the zigzag haircut."

"Yeah!" I fume. "I realize. He died when we had that bomb in the tunnel."

Janice nods. "Yes. The other boys in the group were all military and are all out fighting in Bestellen right now."

"Okay," I dismiss. "Well, why didn't you do something when they were here if you know what happened?"

"They were already loading up for their assignments when Eric told me their names. It was too late. I will speak to them when and if they get back."

When and if.

They may die out there never having received their punishment. I don't know how I feel about that statement. The men who almost killed me may die rather than receive a minimal punishment . . .

"What about Eric?" I ask. "Why didn't you punish him?"

Janice clears her throat. "Because he has already received his punishment for being involved with that group."

"How so?" I ask. "You just found out about this."

"Do you really want to know what happened, Sam? What actually happened?"

I nod with an annoyed look on my face. Why else would I ask her what happened?

"Okay," Janice answers. "That day, Eric was walking with Uri because they were both coming from the same place and heading to the same place. On the way, they ran into some of Uri's old roommates. One of the roommates decided to take a detour, so everyone followed, including Eric. That is when they ran into you."

I nod, waiting for the rest of the explanation.

"You know what all happened from there until the restroom, but the one thing you may not have noticed was that Eric, from behind the group, tried to get them to stop."

"What?" I shout. "He barely tried! And he only started after I almost blacked out!"

Janice nods her head and speaks to Mavis and me in a calm tone, hoping to somehow calm me with it. "After Eric left the restroom, he stayed in that hallway until you came out just to make sure you were okay."

"Big whoop!" I mock. "He stood around. Good for him."

"And after that came the punishment. Eric confronted Uri and his roommates right after you made it to class. He told them off." Janice clears her throat again and looks to Mavis and then back to me. "Uri and the others ended up beating Eric worse than they beat you."

The room fills with silence. An uncomfortable silence.

I rise to my feet and leave the room without another word.

I listen to the sound of my footsteps as I walk down the empty hallway. The sounds coming from the other classrooms are a mixture of joyful chatter and unenthusiastic teaching.

Confused.

That's all I am.

Confusion.

That's all that's in my mind.

I am still upset, but not as much. I am upset that I got bullied and beaten, but I am slightly happy that Eric did too.

Why would I be happy that Eric was beaten? He was the only person who defended me.

Why was I happy to hear that the roommates were shipped off to fight only to hope they live through it? Sure, they bullied me. Sure, they beat me. Sure, they beat up Eric, the only person who seemed to have a shred of morals. But why would I be happy that they may die?

Confusion.

That's all I feel.

CHAPTER TWENTY-TWO

Sam

The walls shake around us as another bomb drops.

I stand by my bunk, watching Mavis hold her knees to her chest on the bottom bed. She wraps her arms around herself and rocks, keeping her head in between her knees as she moves back and forth.

Everyone else piles in like we have been doing every other time we needed to come down here. This is the ninth set of bombings since we freed Bloot. It has been weeks since we sent our armies over there, and we only have four out of the six states taken over, not counting Metropolis.

When we captured Bloot so easily, many people felt a large boost of hope. When we captured Hout, Bouw, and Meer all in one day, the hope of Bergland grew even more. But now? Weeks later? Verwend and Minje are both in lockdown and are now pure military camps with thousands upon thousands of civilians being held captive, and Metropolis hasn't even been touched.

The deep roar of the planes overhead interrupts my thoughts. Another bomb falls and shakes the bunker. Mavis continues to hold herself under my top bunk as I continue to stand by the feet of the beds.

As I look around, my eyes fall upon two guys all huddled in between bunks a few yards away. One of the men catches my eye as I realize

I recognize his neck tattoo. With Mavis preoccupied with calming herself, I decide to head over.

"Hey!" Bram calls out the moment he notices me coming over. "Look who it is!"

"I'm surprised you remember me," I tell him, earning a confused look from Bram's friend.

"Well, how could I forget ol' Sammy boy?" He pats me on the back and smiles to the man standing across from him. "Marky, meet Sammy." Bram turns back to me and smiles again. "Sammy, meet Marky."

The other man rolls his eyes and shakes my hand. "I'm Markus."

"Sam." I nod to him and release his hand.

"Cool," Markus replies.

"Sammy here," Bram says as he pats me on the back again, "has got something that provides him with an unlimited amount of vials."

Markus excitedly chuckles, "Whoa! Really? That's so cool."

"What? How so?" I ask the two. They both shoot each other a funny look before a smirk rises upon their faces.

"How so?" Bram asks me. "What do you mean how so? You can take as many as you want without having to worry about running out!"

I shrug. "Yeah, I guess that's nice." But it would be nicer if I didn't have to take them at all.

"It is," Markus agrees, pouting. "I have to go and buy more if I want more than they give me per month."

Bram nods. "Except for down here. Down here is where we come to 'enjoy the bombs,' if you know what I mean." Bram snorts as he elbows Markus playfully.

"You know it," Markus chuckles back.

"What do you mean?" I ask them both, earning another look of confusion and amusement.

Bram scoffs at me as another bomb drops, shaking the room again. "What, are you new here, Sammy?"

I nod and chuckle back. "Yeah, actually."

"No way!" Markus's jaw drops. "When did you get here? You're from Bestellen?"

I nod again, feeling a little overwhelmed by their excitement.

"Are you from Bloot?" Markus continues.

"No!" Bram nudges Markus. "I met him before we freed Bloot."

"No you didn't," I tell Bram. "We met the day the people from Bloot came in."

"What? Really?" Bram looks down to the floor for a few moments as he thinks. I can almost hear his brain cramping from overexertion. He looks back up at me and nudges Markus in the arm again. "Yeah! I did! So you are from Bloot!"

"No. I'm from Bouw."

Markus's jaw drops once again while Bram looks at me with confusion. "But everyone from Bouw is still in Bestellen."

"I came here a few weeks ago."

"What?" Bram asks me. "How did you get—"

Markus slaps Bram's chest with the back of his hand. "Dude, he came here through the woods. When Bestellen threw him out."

Bram looks to me with an expression of awe. "Oh man, that makes total sense."

Markus rolls his eyes at Bram and looks back to me. "So you don't know anything about Bergland, do you?"

I shrug as another bomb drops. This one causes the lights to flicker and a few kids on another hall to scream. I quickly look back over to Mavis, who has not changed positions since I left, and shake off my own fear. "Well, I've been here for a few weeks, so I guess I know a little."

"Ah." Markus nods slowly with a smirk curling up on his face. "But you don't know the good stuff." He takes a few steps past me and points at one of the nurses at the end of the halls. This nurse appears to have the same clothing as the ones who originally came in and administered the medicine to Mavis when we spoke with Emily Hash.

"These nurses will give you vials for free if you ask for them and if you are on the list." Markus looks back to me and chuckles. "And with whatever you have that gets you unlimited amounts of vials, you are definitely on the list."

"Yeah." Bram takes a seat on his bottom bunk and looks back up to Markus and me. "Down here is one of the only places in Bergland where we can take the vials with no questions asked."

Markus climbs up and lies down on the bed above Bram. "They think we need it," he snorts.

"Well, don't you?" I take a seat on an empty bunk beside them just as another four bombs drop in a row. The floor shakes, a few pieces of ceiling crumble and rain down, and the lights flicker once again. I try to shake off the fear in my stomach and turn back to the boys.

"Yeah," Markus chuckles and points over his shoulder. "But it looks like your friend needs it more."

My eyes follow his gesture over to Mavis, who has her head in between her legs as she is frozen in fear on the bottom bunk. Immediately, I rise to my feet and make my way over to her. I listen to Bram and Markus chuckle about something as I walk off, but I don't pay enough attention to understand.

The moment I take a seat beside Mavis, her head pops up, and she looks at me with a few tears falling from her eyes.

"Hey." I place my hand on her back and see her relax a small amount. "Are you okay? Do you want a vial?"

"No," she sniffles as she places her head on her knees.

"Mavis." I scoot a little closer to her as the actions of Logan come to mind. The first time we met Mavis, she was having an anxiety attack. Logan hugged her, and she calmed down.

My arm wraps around her as she loosens up but doesn't move. I don't really know what to do when the person you are hugging won't hug you back.

She has always wanted to comfort me when I was anxious and panicked, and I want to do the same for her. Mavis is like my sister, and I absolutely hate seeing her scared.

I hate it.

She hates it.

I have to help her.

I unwrap my arm from around her and make my way down the hall to the nurse.

"Excuse me, sir," I say hesitantly, not really knowing how to approach. "May I please have a vial or two for my friend?"

The nurse looks at me with confusion. "What's your friend's name?"

"Mavis Wamsley."

The nurse pulls up his hologram and types something in. A picture of Mavis pops up, along with written information I can't read backward.

"Okay." The nurse rises to his feet and places his bag over his shoulder. "Where is she?"

I point back over to our bunks but stand in front of the man. "She is over there, but she would much rather me bring her her vial. She wouldn't want someone she doesn't know administering it to her."

The nurse narrows his eyes at me. "What's your name?"

"Mine? Um . . . Samuel Beckman."

The nurse pulls up another screen, this time with my picture and information. He nods as he reads and looks back to me. "You know, if you wanted the medicine, all you needed to do was ask."

I nod with a sense of relief. "Yes, sir, I know. But this really is for my friend."

He nods and pulls out a vial in each hand from his bag. "Will she be needing the full dose or a small one?"

I look to both vials. The size difference between the two is almost laughable. One is about as large as the full length of my thumb, while the other is the length from my wrist to the top of my middle finger.

"Could I please take both?" I ask the nurse. "Just in case?"

He shoots me a suspicious look but hands them both over. "If you need anything else, come ask me. Got it?"

I nod and walk back over to Mavis as another bomb drops. Other than her, nobody else in the bunker seems affected by the bombings. When I get back to our beds, I find Mavis sitting with her fingers in her ears and humming the Diligent's anthem.

"Hey," I say to her as I retake my seat from earlier. "Mavis."

Her shaky breath becomes even harder to steady as she looks up to me. Her crying has stopped, but she is still obviously having a hard time.

"Look." I hold out the two vials side by side. "I went and got you these. The big one—"

Before I can finish, Mavis begins scooting away and shaking her head. "No. No medicine."

"Mavis." I put my hand on her leg and hold out the vials again. "The big one is the full dose, so it should help you sleep if you want. But the small one will just help you relax if you want to stay awake."

She pauses and looks to the vials. Without saying anything, I put the large one back into my pocket and hand her the small dose.

Mavis takes it from my hand and stares at it for a bit, without injecting it or giving it back.

"Please take it," I ask her. "This way, you will still be awake, but you won't be suffering."

She sighs and takes another moment to contemplate. Mavis injects her thigh with the vial just as another bomb drops. I watch as her eyes express pure horror in one second and slowly move to relaxation in the next. Her pupils take their time and dilate as the medicine kicks in and calms her.

Mavis pulls her knees back up to her chest and rests her head on her kneecaps without another word. I assume she is doing what I do and taking her time to enjoy the relaxation that we don't ever seem to get without the medicine.

"So can I talk to you for a little bit?" I ask her.

She nods, never looking up.

"Thank you." The more I speak of things other than the mountain and the bombs, the more Mavis will feel better, right? "So I am not much of a flower person. I mean, I like flowers, but not as much as my mom. She happens to be obsessed with lilies. Those orange and yellow ones to be specific. I don't really know why, but she doesn't like the pink or purple ones."

Mavis's breathing slows as I continue. "I guess her love of lilies has rubbed off on me. Just the other night, I couldn't sleep. And for some reason, I couldn't stop thinking about the orange and yellow lilies and how much better they are than the pink and purple ones."

As I try to keep Mavis's mind off the bombs, the chatter in the rest of the bunker steadily comes into focus. Everyone else in the bunker seems to be having a good time or is catching up on paperwork that they would be doing if they were back in their offices.

No one else seems to need the medicine.

I climb back up onto the bunk above Mavis and lie back onto the protruding mattress spring and the flat pillow. The large vial in my pocket I just received from the nurse clinks against another vial I have had in my pocket for an emergency.

The nurse won't need the full-dose vial back; he has plenty in that bag. No one else really needs the medicine anyway.

I should probably keep it.

Mavis

I poke at my serving of mush with my fork as I listen to Mandy happily blab about something she heard earlier today from a friend.

I say "listen," But I mean "tune out."

After we freed Bloot and brought who we could back to Bergland, the announcements came back-to-back. "Meer has been successfully taken. They are now aiding us in the war . . . Bouw has been successfully taken. They are now aiding us in the war . . . Hout has been successfully taken. They are now aiding us in the war . . ."

We had four out of the six states captured within three days of this war. Everything was looking bright for the future. Everyone told me that this war would be over quickly, but everyone lied. It has been weeks since we have captured a state.

The last real announcement we heard came last week. General Wilson said that we moved all of the civilians back to Bloot, which had been secured, and that we would be dealing with Verwend and Minje after the announcement ended.

But guess what—we had been dealing with the two states for weeks, and no new news has come to the Bergland citizens. Janice knows what is going on, but I have only got to see her when she is teaching class, and she leaves right after to go and do "official" duties. I will admit, though, that she has done a great job of not leaking anything to her students who badger her with questions.

"Mavis?"

I look up from my food and to Mandy. "What?"

She narrows her eyes at me and gives an amused smile. "I figured you weren't listening."

"No, no." I shake my head and smile to her. "I was."

"Oh yeah? Then yes or no to the last question I asked you."

Mandy and I lock eyes for a moment.

"Okay, maybe I wasn't listening *intently*."

"Right." Mandy nods and looks back to her food, staring down at it. Her face freezes with a serious expression as her eyes focus on what's left in her tray. Both she and I stay quiet for a moment—she, out of focus, and me, out of confusion.

"You see this?" she asks me without looking away from her scraps. "This is what you were doing."

I roll my eyes as she breaks her gaze from her food and laughs at me.

"What were you thinking about anyway?" she snorts.

I shrug. "Nothing. I just got stuck staring."

She nods. "I do that all the time. Just the other day, I got stuck staring at someone's face as they were talking to someone else. Oh man, it was so funny. When he saw me star . . ."

My eyes fall on Sam as I begin to tune Mandy out once again. I watch him stand in the corner of the room, chatting to two other guys who seem a little older than we are. It is the same two guys for whom he left me this morning and went to talk with. I recognize them only because of the hammer tattoos on the neck one of the guys.

I have to wonder whether or not he left me for them because I didn't hug him back. When he put his arm around me, it was one of the most comforting, yet uncomfortable feelings I've had in a long time.

Though I think he already felt like he needed to stay with me, the reason I didn't hug him back is because I didn't want him to feel like my babysitter. The hug that he gave me was comforting. I just wish I could comfort him the same way.

Vulnerability is not something I deal with well, and I have begun to think Sam feels the same way. Why else would he not allow me to comfort him when he was upset? The only real way that I can explain the fact that we don't like being comforted is because the need to be comforted implies that we are vulnerable, weak even.

My brother felt the same way.

Back when Mom was with us, everything was great. No one was scared of coming home, and no one was scared of getting hurt.

Before Dad started seeing things, everything was great. Mom was with us, and no one was scared of him.

Before Dad's drinking got bad, everything was great. We could afford food, and Steven and I were together.

The group of girls that sit behind us roar with laughter, bringing me back to Mandy's story. "And that's how I met Jonah. You remember me introducing you to Jonah, right?"

I look back over to Mandy and shake my head. "No. I don't remember Jonah."

"Are you sure? I thought I introduced you two."

I nod. "I'm sure."

The shift change bell above us rings, and the entire cafeteria scatters. Mandy waves goodbye to me and scurries off through the crowd. I take a few bites of my untouched meal and take off as well. Sam, Logan, and I usually are with Janice between breakfast and the first class of the day; but since she is preoccupied, Sam and I are free to go wherever. Today, I decide to head to the track and let Sam be with his new friends.

I get into the large and open room with the oval-shaped course and see people sprinting in one lane, jogging in another, and walking in the last lane. I decide to join the walking lane and take a few laps as I wait on the never-approaching announcement of our victory in the war.

Our.

I don't know if I have the right to say "our" for either side. I was born a Stellen and have just recently become a Berglander. Bergland has the principles I agree with, but Bestellen is home. Everything I once knew is a lie, and everything I once thought to be home is now rubble.

Home.

I walk and think about Mom, Uncle Randy, and Steven. I think about how much they would have loved Bergland.

I walk and think about Derek and his mom. I think about how I have no clue whether either of them is alive at this very moment.

I walk and think about Logan and Eric. Logan took Eric's side of the fight even though I doubt Eric even told him that anything happened.

I walk and think about how this war was supposed to be over within a week. How come it has been taking so long? How come we haven't been told anything when there are obviously a million things they could have updated us on?

I walk and think.

Walk and think.

CHAPTER TWENTY-THREE

Logan

With my pistol holstered on one leg and a healing and throbbing wound on the other, I walk with Eric around the hospital of the injured we have been assigned to help protect. We notice that the bottom edges of the building have obvious damage from previous flooding. Neither of us is surprised. Almost every building in Meer has some sort of water damage in one way, shape, or form.

"I've always wanted to move here," Eric confides in me after almost a half hour of silence between us.

"What?"

"Yeah." He nods as we continue treading through what feels like swampland. "When we learned about all of the different states and about the careers each state offered, I always figured that I would have wanted to be a fisherman." He pauses to pull his boot out of a pile of muck. "Though I have yet to see any of the lakes around here."

I chuckle as we continue around the building. It amazes me how certain areas are filled with mud or drowned by rainwater, while other areas are as dry as can be, filled with sand and dried grass.

Though I missed being able to slosh around in ankle-deep rainwater when I was in Bergland, walking on dry land is much easier on my leg and back. With every step I take, the pain on my spine increases. The gunshot wound on my leg continues to throb, but it doesn't seem to hurt nearly as much as my lower back. The nurse who treated me told me the back pain was a product of overcompensation, but that it should get better once I start walking around like I used to.

I don't know if the nurse told me that because it was true or whether it was so that she could go work with the rest of the injured people. I understand either way, but it would be nice to know.

Though the pain can be blinding at times, I can handle it. There are so many other people who have been hurt worse than I have who need attention. Thousands upon thousands as a matter of fact. This hospital that Eric and I are guarding is only one of almost thirty within Meer alone.

All of the Stellens and Berglanders who have been hurt have been taken to one of these hospitals to be treated. Believe it or not, there are quite a few Stellens who have refused any help from Bergland because of how much they believe in Bestellen's way of life.

Most all of the Stellens who don't know anything about Bergland are together within their given state and having everything explained to them. I don't know how exactly, but I imagine that Emily Hash has a whole presentation lined up for each one of the groups that includes around the same points that Mavis, Sam, and I were shown.

After they have been prepped and had things explained to them, all of those who want to help with the revolution are being utilized in one way or another. Most are off fighting; but others are helping in hospitals, fixing up and securing buildings, and helping explain to others what is going on.

While everything in these states is being taken care of, Verwend is in shambles. As the state that trained all of Bestellen's military, produced all of their weapons, and protected its capital, it has taken the heaviest attacks and, at the same time, protected itself the best.

As almost every Verwend citizen fights against Bergland, the people of Minje have been viciously protected by its overwhelming official population. What we have heard is anyone who tries to rebel and fight with Bergland is shot by the nearest official, which is very difficult to avoid in Minje.

Through every twist and turn I made back when I lived there, I found one of the dark-suited men with his hand on his weapon. If that was the way Minje was before the war, I can't imagine how it is right now. There is no doubt in my mind that Gramps was killed in an attempt to revolt. He was always the type of man who would stand up and fight if he needed to, no matter the cost. I do believe the only reason he wouldn't have fought when John made the announcement to the states would be because he was already dead.

We were told that once we take over Minje, we should be able to move onto Verwend; and once we take over Verwend, Metropolis will surrender. They will have no choice in the matter. Metropolis is a glass-domed city inside of Verwend and has nowhere to go.

General Wilson has made it very clear to everyone. "If Meir and Metropolis do not surrender, they will be bombed. We will not invade and lose any more of our men and women."

As Eric and I round the corner of the hospital and make it back to the front of the building, a familiar face approaches.

"How is hospital patrol going?" Werner asks us.

Eric chuckles and raises one of his boots to show the muck dangling off it. "Decent if you enjoy having to pull your feet through mud."

He nods. "I see. How's the pain treating you?"

"I'm actually feeling great." Eric twists his body to show how well his side has healed.

"What about you, Forge?"

I shrug. "I can't complain."

"Have you been taking any of the medicine they set aside for you?" he asks us.

We shake our heads and answer in unison, "No."

Werner allows a gentle smile to curl up on his face. "Good for you. They aren't worth it."

It pains me to see someone so opposed to painkillers the same way people are opposed to alcohol. Werner confided in us a week or so ago that his dad died of an overdose when Werner was a child. After buying and dealing different sorts of medication for years, his dad bought a bad batch because of how desperate he was for a hookup. Little did he know that bad batch would cost him his life.

Over the few weeks of the war, Werner has been promoted from Bloot rebel to Sergeant Rhodes. He has been all over, following General Wilson's commands and doing whatever is needed of him. Today's job must have included something that requires a bulletproof vest and a full suit ready for war.

"What are your plans for today, Rhodes?" I ask, scanning over his suit.

"I just came from a meeting with Young right outside of Minje."

Eric and I exchange a glance. Eric asks him, "What's going on?"

Werner pauses a moment. He takes a step away from us and looks around.

"That good, huh?" I joke.

Werner nods us over, and we follow. We begin walking away from the hospital but still keep our eyes on it just in case we are needed.

"We have all but one of the officials' quarters secured in Minje," Werner tells us. "All of their bunkers too."

"What?" Eric half shouts. "How come we haven't heard anything about this?"

Werner whispers back to us, "Young launched a Taai attack last night, along with a lot of help from the citizens inside of Minje."

"How soon do you think—"

My question is interrupted by the sound of jets soaring over us. Their power and thundering vibrations send a horrible throbbing sensation back into my wound, as well as a hard feeling of sharp pressure in my back.

One jet, two jets, three jets all fly over our heads. The three of us can't help but lower into a slightly crouched position as they soar. Once they get far enough away, I turn back to Werner. "How soon do you think we will have the final officials' quarters?"

"They were sending in a team as they sent me back here."

A large smile of relief grows on my face as the idea of being able to see Gramps comes to mind. I quickly force it out and try to prevent myself from deceit.

Gramps is dead.

Gramps is dead.

If I convince myself of this, I will either be prepared for the news, or I will be pleasantly surprised.

Gramps is dead.

Eric, Werner, and I continue walking away from the hospital and are passed by a few of the first aid vans rushing over to the doors. Though seeing people needing urgent care is a sad sight to see, Eric and I have been seeing this all day. The hospital we were assigned to watch is the largest and most efficient hospital in Meer, meaning the ones who need the most care come here.

Eric and I can't help them any more than the mud can, so we continue to walk with Werner.

"I imagine that those jets were actually sent to take out some of Verwend's defenses," Werner tells us. "Which means we may already have Minje secured."

The three of us walk in silence for a moment as we realize this war is coming to an end. The silence we enjoy is short-lived and interrupted by another two jets.

The first one soars over us as quickly as the first three, but just as the second one follows, a long string of gunfire interrupts. I look to the source of the shots to find that a defense tower less than a mile from us is responsible.

"The tower's been hijacked!" Werner lifts his cuff to his face and begins barking codes into it. "Meer's defense tower 10 east has been hijacked. Repeat . . ."

The shots fired by the tower are drowned out as one of the wings blows off the jet. The three of us watch the aircraft as it spins out of control and plunges in our direction. We sprint away as another jet soars overhead, and the fiery vessel plummets, crashing into the hospital behind us.

Mavis

As I chop and Sam peels another one of Bergland's "superfoods," everyone continues to watch all the news coverage. All day long, on every possible screen, we watch as a reporter tells us about the war.

The last update she gave us was "Minje has been captured and secured. Almost all of its citizens rebelled when they had the chance. I guess holding them at gunpoint wasn't the best play, was it, Meir?" She went on to tell us that most of Verwend's officials and citizens who refuse to fight with Bergland have retreated back to Metropolis while all of the Bergland sympathizers are currently fighting with our army.

"Here." Sam takes the knife from my hand and switches places with me on our worktable. "Let's take turns."

I smirk at him and wipe all of the excess peel on the table into the trash pot. "Does your desire to switch have anything to do with the fact that you are much faster at peeling than I am at cutting?"

He chuckles, "What? No."

It does.

I glance at the large pile of the peeled fruits in between our stations and realize that they are piling up in the peeling area.

Chuckling, the two of us begin our new tasks, and I notice that Sam is much quicker than me at cutting too. Just about any time that he and I have a job to do that involves preparing fruits and vegetables, Sam always manages to do a better job than I, as well as complete it quicker too.

We continue with this task for hours and listen in to the news.

"This just in. We have secured the western portion of Verwend."

"This just in. We have secured *another* officials' quarters."

"This just in. We have secured the final defense tower."

"This just in. We have Verwend."

Everyone's attention shifts from what they are doing to the screen nearest to them. The clattering of dishes echoes through the room as everyone sets down their pots, pans, and utensils.

"Now the live coverage of General Wilson's final announcement."

The screen changes over to a live feed of the outside of Metropolis. Their usually perfect glass-dome surrounding is covered in soot and rubble and has many broken pieces that have fallen into the city. "Chancellor Lance Meir," General Wilson's voice echoes through the room as we watch the screen. "This is General Luke Wilson of Bergland. You have exactly thirty seconds to surrender by sounding your anthem in the last of Metropolis's working announcement speakers. If you do not within those thirty seconds, what is left of Metropolis, and everyone in it, will be destroyed. I will repeat this once more. This is General Luke Wilson . . ."

We listen in pure suspense as he repeats his claim and watch the outside of Metropolis. We watch the clouds and smoke behind and in front of the dome float overhead. We watch the fire in the distance from the previous bombings. We watch as the wind blows the few trees left in a swaying motion.

"Thirty. Twenty-nine. Twenty-eight. Twenty-seven . . ."

We listen to Wilson count down and wait for a surrender, but it never comes. When he reaches five seconds, we hear him bark the orders, "Prepare to fire!"

The last four seconds are pure silence. We then watch bomb after bomb, missile after missile, completely destroy the dome and everything inside of it.

Everyone in the kitchen cheers with joy, with the exception of Sam and me. We hear utensils clash together with pots and pans, we hear people crying with joy, and we hear people singing the Diligent's anthem.

Sam and I turn to each other. We stare for a moment before he leans in and wraps his arms around me. I return the hug, and we freeze in this position, not really sure how to feel. Everyone in the kitchen is happy and excited, but how are we supposed to feel? Our home was just destroyed in war, and everything we knew is now gone.

There is no going back.

"We won," Sam says to me, trying to steady his obviously shaken breath.

I pause, not wanting to put a damper on his happiness.

He pulls away and gives me a teary smile. "Maybe now I can go and see my mom again."

I nod. "Maybe."

I doubt anybody else in this kitchen is really considering anything but getting out of this mountain. They have been dreaming of this moment their whole lives. I doubt they are thinking of anyone and everyone they may have just lost.

To be continued in *The Broken Peace.*

Printed in the United States
By Bookmasters